ASHES TO Strength

Criminals Never Forget

STEINAR KRUSE

SCRIPTOR HOUSE

Scriptor House LLC

2810 N Church St Wilmington, Delaware, 19802

www.scriptorhouse.com

Phone: +1302-205-2043

Published by Scriptor House LLC

Paperback ISBN: 979-8-88692-272-1

eBook ISBN: 979-8-88692-273-8

I dedicate this book to my wife.

*In addition to being the love of my life,
she is my biggest supporter.*

Thank you, Olga.

Part I

Jasper, Alberta, Canada

"Mommy, I'm home."

TJ (Tehya Jane) was in good spirits and looking forward to telling her mother what she had been doing this afternoon. She had been down at the local schoolyard with some girls her age playing softball. They had played into the early evening, but she had been told by her mother to be back by 7 p.m. It was already 6.30. Her mother did not want her nine-year-old girl to be on the road any later than that. TJ was bicycling home now; her long black hear was trailing behind her. It was quite far, about two miles. She was very hungry and wondered what her mother had planned for dinner.

She hoped it was pizza, her favourite. It was not often that her mother allowed them to have pizza; she mostly cooked healthier meals, but maybe tonight would be the night for pizza.

Papa had bought a cabin up near Jasper several years ago, outside the centre of town at Patricia Lake. Mama really enjoyed being up there and took TJ and her brother AT (Albert Tokala) there whenever she got the chance. Papa was often too busy with work during the week, but he always followed on the weekends. The three of them were there alone now.

It was about 6.45 when TJ turned into the driveway towards the cabin. It was a beautiful cabin, close to the water, and with a full view of the beautiful and well-known Pyramid Mountain, which was visible on the horizon across the lake. The cabin was placed in the perfect spot, just high enough to remain dry all year long, even during the spring thaw.

TJ noticed the large dark car parked near the cabin and wondered why the car doors had been left open, but then she thought nothing more about it. She put the bicycle in the woodshed and ran into the house.

"Mommy, Mommy, I'm home!"

Something hard hit her on the head.

How long she had been unconscious she didn't know, but when she came to, there was a strange man standing over her.

He brutally pushed her head down onto the floor and held it there.

Another man was holding her mother down on the floor in the kitchen by the counter. He was naked from the waist down. TJ could see how her mother was struggling, trying to bite or kick him, but he was too strong for her.

The man holding TJ down ripped her clothes off, opened his pants, and lay down on top of her. She also tried to kick and fight back, but it was impossible. He forced his way into her. She screamed in pain as well as for help, but no matter what, she could not resist the man's strength. The following minutes seemed endless. Then darkness overcame her, and she knew no more.

Her mother continued to scream, but TJ couldn't hear or see her.

After some time, TJ regained consciousness, not knowing how long she had been out. She woke up to a tremendous noise, then another one and then a third one. As soon as she regained awareness, she looked over to the spot where her mother had been, but neither she nor the man was there any longer. Then the man came back, still naked, with a revolver in his hand.

"What the hell have you done!?" the man who had raped TJ asked his companion.

"She fucking tried to get away!" he said, pulling up his pants.

TJ was experiencing a great deal of pain throughout her body, but she tried her best to get up to find her mother. Then another blow to the head knocked her unconscious again.

The next time TJ came to, she was under the woodshed. She could hear people screaming and running everywhere.

The cabin was completely engulfed in flames.

She had no idea how she had come to be under the woodshed. However, she must have been down on her hands and knees. It couldn't have been more than 50 centimetres between the ground and the floor. The shed rested on four wooden posts, but in the middle, there was an extension of a smokestack. That was where TJ was hiding.

She didn't make a sound from her hiding place; she muffled her face in her sweater so no one could hear her breathing. She thought she heard voices calling, "Is there anyone in the cabin?"

She heard sirens and saw several cars coming down the road, first a police car, then a fire truck, and then an ambulance.

The police ordered people to get out of the way, and the firemen began to put out the fire. The cabin was completely engulfed in flames, so there was not much that they could do. They could only wet down the area and prevent any outbuildings from catching fire.

As the flames spread to the woodshed, one of the firemen immediately began extinguishing it. What was that? Two eyes seemed to shine out from behind the flames. Was it an animal? He looked again. No, it was a person. He pretended not to see it, then gave a discreet signal to the police officer Joan Arnolds, who signalled to her colleague, and they began to circle around to the back of the woodshed towards TJ's hiding place.

Joan used her flashlight. She jumped at the sight of the half-naked girl curled up as far underneath the shed as she possibly could get. Joan saw she was scared to death and probably in shock.

Joan tried to speak to the girl while her colleagues called out to the paramedics, "Over here!"

The paramedics were getting out of the ambulance. A man and a woman ran over to where the police were. The policeman spoke quickly to them. Joan was still trying to calm TJ. "Hi. Don't be afraid. It's over now. We are here to help you." TJ only tried to crawl further under. Joan turned and spoke to Jennifer, the female paramedic. "I think it's best if you do this."

Jennifer knew at once what she meant when she saw the frightened eyes of the half-naked girl. It was not necessary to put any more pressure on her right now. They got down and began to slowly creep nearer to TJ.

Joan said to the girl, "What's your name? My name is Joan. I am a police officer. I work for Department 3342 of the Royal Canadian Mounted Police.

"This is Jennifer; she works for the Jasper Rescue Squad." Joan had read Jennifer's name badge.

"You don't have to be afraid any longer. We're here to help you."

TJ didn't answer. Joan said, "We know that you're afraid. You have experienced a terrible thing, but it is over now,"

Joan was listening. Did she try to say something? No, she couldn't hear anything.

"Come, we shall help you."

TJ still didn't try to come out. She just looked at them. Joan crept nearer and held out a blanket for her.

"Here, put this blanket around you. You'll feel better then."

TJ still did not move.

"Is there anyone here besides you?" She just looked right through them.

Joan tried again.

"We are here to help you. We know you have been through some real bad stuff."

Joan finally reached TJ. She took the blanket and wrapped it around her. Now Joan could hear TJ mumble something. Straining to hear, she thought the girl said, "Mommy, Albert."

Joan hugged TJ and said, "Come. We can't stay under here. Let's all crawl back out again."

Tears ran down TJ's face. Again, she said, "Mommy, Albert."

They finally got her out from under the woodshed and put her on a stretcher right away. Her whole body was shaking uncontrollably. She kept crying, "Where is mommy? Where is Albert?"

Jennifer and the other paramedics carried the stretcher over to the ambulance, with Joan following behind.

Joan said, "I know this is difficult, but can you tell us if anybody else is here?"

Joan tried carefully to get any information that could help them. TJ was still crying, but she answered, "Mommy and Albert. Then I came home."

"OK, that's enough. Now you must rest. I just have to go do something for a second, but I'll be right back. Jennifer will stay right here with you."

She squeezed TJ's hand for a moment before she went out.

When she came back, she had a man with her.

Joan took TJ's hand again. "Here I am again, and I have this man with me. He is my boss, and his name is Robert Blake. He is a lieutenant. Now he was wondering if he could talk with you a little. Do you think you can answer him?"

Robert spoke: "How do you feel?"

TJ looked back at him with tear-filled eyes and asked, "Where are Mommy and Albert?"

"Were they in the cabin?" he asked carefully. TJ nodded.

"Were there others?" he asked.

TJ closed her eyes and began crying again as she called, "Mommy, Mommy!"

Lt. Robert Blake looked at Joan and said, "I think we've got enough information for tonight. Let's take the rest later."

Two hours later the cabin were reduced to a large glowing ash heap. The only thing left standing from what was once a cabin was the chimney, but even that had been badly damaged.

There was a strong smell of burned tar in the air, mixed with another, unknown smell. The firefighters were still moving around the site, monitoring the last of the burn. The police cordoned off the area.

CHAPTER 1

Kongsberg, Norway

13 August 2005, 1 p.m.

"From dust have you come, and to dust you shall return," recited the priest, as he sprinkled a handful of earth over the coffin. "And peace be with you."

The funeral of Nils Henrik Ellefsrud twas over.

Nils Henrik Ellefsrud had been a well-known person in Kongsberg, but his funeral was a private one. That was his last wish. He'd written it down himself shortly before he died.

His personal friend and attorney Conrad Heen had received a letter four weeks earlier. And as soon as he heard of Nils Henrik's death, he took the letter and gave it to Henrik. Nils Henrik had specifically written that after his death, the letter should be given to his oldest son, Henrik. He'd also specified that only his nearest family, the housekeeper, and Conrad should attend the funeral.

No death announcement was to be made in the paper until after his funeral, and no flowers should be on the casket. He also wished to be cremated, so there would be no burial. He wanted his ashes to be spread out over the river by the cabin down there. He'd built this little cabin more than twenty years ago, and he loved that place more than anything else. That was where he went when he needed to be alone. He could spend hours, even days, down there all by himself. This was where he'd been on the last day of his life.

It was the eighth of August. Nils Henrik had left a note on the table at the house saying that he had gone down to his cabin. It had been quite a while since he had been there. His illness had prevented it. The last time he had been there was six weeks earlier. Henrik had driven him down there, and the visit was only for a few hours. He had asked Henrik to leave him there alone, and after a short discussion, Henrik had allowed it. The son understood his father's situation.

Nils Henrik also wrote in his letter that after his funeral there could be a memorial service if they wanted; it was completely up to them. Now they were gathered together at Nils Henrik's house, where they all sat and thought about Nils Henrik Ellefsrud. Who was he, really?

What was it they didn't know about him? Why would he never speak about his time over there in the USA and Canada? What had he done there?

He had been involved in many different things after he had come back to Norway, but he'd never had any regular employment. However, he'd always had money. Where did it come from?

There were so many questions, but not many answers.

His lawyer, Conrad, was also there. Conrad was getting ready to return to Oslo, but Henrik had especially asked him to come to the house, as he was Nils Henrik's closest friend and pretty much a member of the family.

Nils Henrik had first met Conrad on one of his trips down to Kiel. It was the only form of vacation he allowed himself. They'd meet in one of the bars on board the ship and become very good friends. Henrik even thought Conrad was Nils Henrik's only friend. At least he was the only one his father had ever spoken about.

Conrad visited Henrik's father at home often. They hunted and fished together regularly. Conrad lived in Oslo and used to be a partner in the law firm of Rushfeldt, Herlofsen, and Heen, but just before he met Nils Henrik, he had left the firm. There had been one case he had lost at court, one that he couldn't forget, in which the accused was sentenced to a long prison term. Conrad was shocked and appalled by the harsh sentence, which caused him to leave the firm. He wished to pursue the case further and appeal it, and he believed that by leaving he could devote more time to the case. Up until that time, Conrad had developed a strong reputation and was highly respected in the legal community.

Instead, he started his own small legal firm to primarily deal with business and property inheritance cases. That was how he'd come to work for Nils Henrik.

It was decided that everyone would meet back at Nils Henrik's house Saturday, 16 August, at eleven o'clock. They would then walk down to the cabin and spread Nils Henrik's ashes out over the river. Afterwards, they would go back to the house to have lunch, and Conrad would read the will.

8 August, 10 a.m., at the cabin

"Keep the change. You earned it." Nils Henrik's voice was very weak. He paid the taxi driver for the trip from the house to the cabin.

It was not a long drive, and normally it only took around ten minutes to walk the distance, but Nils Henrik was in no condition to make this walk now.

"Can you help me over to that table?" Nils Henrik pointed to a table and bench at the side of the cabin. That was all he was able to say. *Fucking emphysema,* he thought. His mind was still clear, but the pain in his chest was just about unbearable.

"Of course," said the taxi driver.

Tina, his dog, long-time partner, and friend, a mix between Dalmatian and something else, no one knew what, was already there and sat quietly waiting for him.

The driver brought around the walker from the trunk and helped Nils Henrik behind it. Then he lifted out the oxygen tank and loaded it into the basket attached to the walker. He supported Nils Henrik while he moved from the walker to the bench. The bench had been tipped over by the wind, but the driver set it up straight before helping Nils Henrik onto it.

"Thank you for the help," Nils Henrik said, again very weak. He shook the driver's hand. The taxi driver went back to his car and drove away.

Nils Henrik was sitting listening to the silence. He had done that many, many times before, so it was nothing special today. But it felt quieter today than the other times.

He started to think about himself, thinking about how strong he used to be. Now he was only a fraction of what he used to be. He could do nothing. And this was bothering him. He had become totally dependent on others. Never mind the hair loss, the chance of hair colour, and whatever else. He had been looking in the mirror. He had just grown into an old, sick person.

The water gently rippled; the air was soft, warm, and humid. He looked up and wondered, *Will it begin to rain?* He looked down at Tina, who had lain down next to his feet.

"You are my best friend," he said to her.

Tina wagged her tail just as if she understood him.

Nils Henrik sat and gazed out over the river. He began to think back over the life he had lived, his time in the USA and Canada, and his childhood. He remembered how he had to help out at home, but he was always finding time to pursue his own interests.

He learned to ski early, and then to ski jump. That was not so unusual when someone lived in Kongsberg, a place from which many of the biggest names in ski jumping came at that time. There was a ski jump made up at practically every hill around. In the summer they made ramps out over the water where the jumps were translated over to a dive into the lake.

Then it was soccer, track and field, and handball. It was a different and time a really busy life, but then again it was also very educational.

The first thoughts Nils Henrik got were of that day, the day his whole life was changed forever. It was 15 August 1965, 9.35 p.m. He'd never forgotten it, or the words of Lt. James Dunn; "There has been an explosion and fire out there. Two persons are missing, and one girl was found."

There was not a day when Nils Henrik didn't remember those words. Everything that was said after that was gone. He also could not remember how he had come to be at Jasper hospital that night.

It started to rain lightly, so he wanted to move inside. He placed the walker so that he could use it to lift himself up and to stand, which took a considerable effort. It left him breathless. Afterwards he had to stay still for a while, so he could recover his breath. It was so difficult for him to breathe now that it took many minutes for him to move the twelve feet to the door of the cabin. Tina followed him. She had stayed and watched over him the whole time. Now she ran over and opened the door for him. Nils Henrik had specially trained her to do that.

He started to think about the hospital, how helpless he had felt sitting there by her bed that night, at the same time not knowing what had happened with Sisiska (Bird) or Albert.

He had been completely worn out. And what about OJ? What had happened to him?

Now his thoughts went to New York, Ellis Island, how he had been processed through immigration, and other things that happened to him during the two years in New York. It seemed so long ago now. He started to think about the conversation he had overheard at the construction site that afternoon when he was in the men's room.

Did that have some connection with all that later happened to him there in Canada? The collapse of the building at Jackson Heights, the explosion and fire at the cabin. He had thought of all this before, and so had the police, but there were no known connections in the case. Nevertheless, Nils Henrik was completely sure that there was a connection somewhere as yet unfound.

At 11.30 a.m., the rain stopped, but Nils Henrik was still sitting inside. It would have taken too much strength for him to get back out again, so he just stayed where he was.

His thoughts began to wander again. The oxygen bottle was in its basket.

Tina was still lying there looking at him. He wondered what would happen to her. He was hoping Henrik would take care of her.

Damn the cigarettes. If he never had begun smoking that time in New York. But that was in the early days when everybody smoked and before all the warnings. Everybody smoked back then. People's social lives involved cigarettes, both in New York and up in the Yukon. Now he was paying the high price for all those years smoking.

Who was Nils Henrik Ellefsrud?

He was born on 22 September 1929 on the Ellefsrud farm outside Notodden in Telemark, Norway. He was the first boy in a family of seven siblings: three boys and four girls. The oldest was Reidun, then came Ellen, Nils Henrik, Rolf, Ragnhild, and Erik. The last was Marie.

Mama and Papa were Borghild Tomine and Oscar Hoffmann respectively. They both had come to Notodden from Skien, Borghild as a seamstress and Oscar working on the railroad. They married on 1 May 1919, and Reidun came into the world in December of the same year. That was probably the reason for the wedding taking place in such a timely manner.

After spending the first twelve years in Notodden, the family moved to Kongsberg. Oscar Hoffmann got a job working for the mining company, and they moved into a house owned by the company.

However, Oscar had a strong wish to have his own small farm that he could operate in addition to his job. It would take some time for him to realize this dream.

After eight years in the company house, they were finally able to purchase a farm of about fifty acres, half in forest and the rest in fields. It was an idyllic place located along the shoreline down towards the river that floated through the valley. They bought it for eighty-five dollars, which was a lot of money during those times. In order to be able to purchase it, they needed Borghild's uncle Ernst to lend them thirty-five of the eighty-five dollars they needed. Borghild stayed at home with the children but took in sewing jobs to earn a little extra money. The three last children were born in Kongsberg.

Nils Henrik grew up like any other child, but it was recognized early on that he was a bright kid with a strong interest in books and language. He was already well on the way to being able to read and write when he began at school. By the time he was ten years old, he was able to read English, not fluently but well enough to be able to understand a great deal of it. In addition to these talents, he was able to work very proficiently with his hands, as were all boys born during those times.

It was soon clear that he was an adventure lover, and he read all books he could find about America and Canada. He had a special interest in the Yukon gold rush at the end of the 1800s.

The history of how the Indians "Skoogum Jim" and "Dawson Charlie"—the latter later known as Tagish Charlie—together with Seattleite George Carmack found gold in Rabbit Creek, right outside Dawson City in the Yukon Territories. These books became Nils Henrik's biggest interest. He read them over and over again and dreamed about them almost every night. He knew all the stories in detail and began to be very restless; it was the beginning of his wanderlust, which focused on him going to those places one day.

The Yukon gold rush began one afternoon in the middle of July in 1896. When the camp of the three, Skoogum Jim, Dawson Charlie, and George Carmack, was visited by Robert Henderson, a seasoned prospector. He told George Carmack about some good finds he had made up at Gold Bottom Creek in the Klondike River Valley. There was an unwritten law between prospectors that they shared their knowledge and findings with each other. Henderson wasn't any different.

George Carmack asked him if there was a possibility for him to stake a claim around there. The Canadian authorities permitted at that time, as they do today, that there could only be one claim per person. Henderson answered in a loud voice, loud enough for Skoogum Jim and Dawson Charlie to hear: "Yes, you can, but not him or your brother-in-law there."

George Carmack's wife was an Indian squaw, the sister of Skoogum Jim. George didn't answer the statement, but he did notice it. A few days later, early in August of the same year, George Carmack, Dawson Charlie, and Skoogum Jim took their boat up Rabbit Creek, a tributary of the Klondike River. Rabbit Creek and Gold Bottom Creek were both tributaries of the Klondike River, but they were separated from each other by a ridge, not particularly high, but high enough that no one could see from one side to the other.

As soon as they got there, they took a trip over the ridge to visit the camp of Robert Henderson. Again, he treated them with rudeness and ill-will. This time he had tobacco to sell, which he denied to Skoogum Jim and Dawson Charlie. Only George was allowed to buy it. George Carmack was later to say that this small action had cost Robert Henderson a fortune.

George Carmack and his two friends went back to Rabbit Creek and began to wash through some interesting pans which tailings showed the promise of more gold to come. They began to look for the area where the bedrock lay easily accessible as the stream washed away more soil. They soon found the first real proof that there was gold in this spot when they washed out a gold nugget as big as a ten-cent piece. As they loosened all the rock in the area, they found more and more gold, in a thick vein sandwiched between the rocks. The date was 16 August 1896.

George Carmack, Skoogum Jim, and Dawson Charlie staked their claims to that spot the very next day. Then they changed the name of Rabbit Creek to Bonanza Creek and went down to Dawson City to register their claims.

The world didn't know what had happened in the Yukon until July 1897, when the SS *Explorer* docked in San Francisco, with gold worth half a million dollars on board, and the SS *Portland* docked in Seattle, with gold worth more than a million. Six months later more than one hundred thousand people from all over the world were on their way to the Yukon Territory.

Nils Henrik also read the story of Jefferson Randolph "Soapy" Smith, of how he and his gang of more than three hundred men operated and how they controlled and tyrannized Dyea and Skagway. He read about the duel on Juneau Wharf on 8 July 1898 between Soapy Smith and Frank Reid, which resulted in the end of the lawlessness in Skagway.

Now Nils Henrik sat at his cabin and thought back over all the stories he had read from that period in time. He wondered how his life would have been different if he never had read about any of those men. Then he thought no more about it.

Patricia Lake, Alberta, Canada 15 August 1965

"What the hell was that?" Brian looked at Ivan when he spoke.

"It sounded like a gunshot," Ivan replied.

Before they were finished talking, two more shots broke the evening. They both got up and went out on the balcony.

"Where did it come from?" Brian asked.

It wasn't so unusual to hear a rifle shot out there, especially during the hunting season, but at this point the season hadn't started yet.

Had the shot come from the Ellefsrud cabin? Brian and Ivan looked down towards the cabin for a while, but nothing looked unusual.

It was only Ellefsrud's wife and the twins staying there. Brian had observed them earlier that morning.

The two men went inside again to keep on listening to the hockey game, the Toronto Maple Leafs versus the Royal Canadians. The hockey season had not officially started yet, but every year at this time the finalists who played in the Stanley Cup the last season always played a charity game close to the beginning of the new season.

Suddenly Brian said, "Did you recognize the car parked outside the Ellefsrud cabin?"

Ivan looked over at Brian. "No. I can't say I've ever seen a car like that around here either."

Brian got up without saying anything more and went out the door. Suddenly, the sky was filled with a big bright flash of light, and an enormous explosion followed.

"Call the police," Brian shouted out, as he ran down the stairs from the balcony. The Ellefsrud cabin was engulfed in flames. Brian notice that the strange car was now gone. But when he looked up the hill on the other side, he saw it driving up the road. The car was travelling at an extremely high speed. Whoever was in the car was in a big hurry. Ivan ran back in and called the police. Then he ran down to the cabin. It felt like an eternity before they finally heard sirens in the distance. Then they saw the cars, first the police, a unit from Jasper mounted police unit. Shortly after, the Jasper firefighters, Unit 34, came down the road to the cabin. The firemen's feet were on the ground before the two trucks had even come to a complete stop. Moments later the first fire hose was rolled out and they started dousing the flames.

The cabin was not to be saved. It was already too far gone before the firefighters even arrived, so all they could do was to keep the fire under control and prevent it from spreading to other buildings, particularly to the two closest buildings in the yard, a woodshed and a garage.

The ambulance from Jasper Rescue came last.

The police quickly located Ivan among the crowd. Ivan had identified himself when he called in the fire.

Lt. Robert Blake asked for him as soon as he arrived.

"You called this in, right?" Lt. Blake asked before presenting himself. "Yes."

Lt. Blake continued, "OK, what can you tell me about what happened here?"

Lt. Blake was facing the flames when speaking to Ivan. Brian joined them.

"Can either of you two tell me if there was anyone in the cabin?" Lt. Blake looked at both of them now. The only thing they could say was that they had observed the wife and the two kids earlier that morning. Lt. Blake thanked them, gave them his business card, and asked them to contact him if they remembered anything else later.

None of the other neighbours could give the police any more information besides what Brian and Ivan had told them. However, one married couple from further up on the road could confirm that the car was a green station wagon. They were not completely sure, but they believed there were two people in the car.

Lt. Blake turned around to look for the captain of the firefighters, whom he found over by the woodshed. He walked over to him.

"Hi. I am Lieutenant Robert Blake. I've spoken with a few witnesses. They don't know if there was anyone else in the cabin when the fire started. But we have the girl, and we know what she was whispering when she was crying. We also have neighbours who observed the family here earlier in the day, but nobody knows if they were here this evening. The same person who told us this said there were three shots fired, and he saw a green station wagon fleeing from the scene at high speed."

The fire captain said, "OK, we will handle this as there were people in the cabin and proceed accordingly." He turned and gave the orders.

Royal Canadian Mounted Police

#3342, Jasper, Alberta, Canada

The station chief, Lt. Robert Blake, had gotten ready to go home and was already out the door when the alarm went off. Officer Joan had answered the call when Ivan had called in, and immediately transferred the call to the ambulance and fire department.

Lt. Blake and his people were instantly on the way. The RCMP headquarters was about 8 kilometres from the location of the cabin, with a driving time of normally about fifteen minutes. It felt to the officers that the ride took much longer.

From the moment the call came in, Lt. Blake had a feeling that there was much more to this than just a fire. He had a nasty feeling and didn't know why. He wondered about it but had no answer for it. It was just a feeling.

Two hours later there was nothing left of the cabin. There was just a heap of red glowing ashes with only the chimney standing. There was the distinctive odour of burnt tar. The woodshed and garage had been caught up by the fire as well, but thankfully after the little girl was found. She was now on her way to the hospital in Jasper. Officer Joan had gone with her in the ambulance.

It was going to be a long night.

Range Road No. 73, Drayton Valley

The time was 9.35 p.m. when the car drove up to the house.

Nils Henrik noticed the car as soon as it pulled into the driveway. He was sitting outside on the balcony with his thoughts. He had just poured himself a whisky, a Canadian Club, which he mixed with ginger ale. Even though the drive from the road down to the farmhouse was about 1.4 kilometres, he could see the car from the point where it entered the road and down to where the road went behind the little hill over by the summer barn. He especially noticed the speed at which it was travelling.

It had been more than six weeks since the building collapse, and he had yet to hear anything from OJ. Nils Henrik had been very busy down in Jackson Heights after the collapse. Now he felt tired. He was known to be a person in good shape. Yes, he was a strong man, and he was only thirty-six years old. Well, there had been a lot to deal with lately, police, bankers, insurance agents, and so on. There were so many questions that needed clearing up about the case. The police were investigating together with the insurance representatives. They were trying to prove that the explosion was not an accident. There were many sure signs pointing to that conclusion.

Then there was the disappearance of OJ. From two days before the collapse, no one had seen or heard from him. Nils Henrik had been to his house on Hope Road three times hoping to find him. The police had searched OJ's house, but they'd found nothing.

There was no sign of the architect Jimmy Hudson or the engineer John Robinson either, the two who were responsible for the project. Now Nils Henrik sat and looked at the car that came up the driveway so quickly. As it came closer to the front porch, he saw that it was a police car. The car stopped right next to the steps. Two men got out, one policeman wearying an Alberta police uniform and one man in a suit. They came quickly up the steps and knocked on the door. Nils Henrik came in off the balcony and went to the front door to answer. "Nils Henrik Ellefsrud?" asked the man in civilian clothes.

"Yes," Nils Henrik answered.

"My name is Lieutenant James Dunn, and this is Officer Danyshyn. Can we come in?"

"Yes, of course." Nils Henrik imagined that they were there in connection with the collapse. He offered them something to drink, but they declined.

Lt. James Dunn spoke, "Do you own a cabin up on Patricia Lake?" "Yes." He was beginning to feel uncomfortable now.

"We are here to bring you bad news."

Nils Henrik felt ice-cold, and very frightened.

"There has been an explosion and fire out there," Lt. Dunn spoke again. He looked into Nils Henrik's eyes as he said it. "It appears that two people are missing. One girl has been found. She looks to be in good condition, but she is in shock. She has been sent to the hospital there. There is a suspicion of sexual abuse. Could this be you daughter?

"We don't have very many details as of yet, but it appears that the fire was intentional, some kind of a hit-and-run action. We are very sorry to have to bring you this news, and we feel for you."

Nils Henrik stood and held tightly on to the railing of the stairway going up to the second floor. He couldn't believe what he had just heard.

"Is there anything we can do?" asked Lt. Dunn.

"We have been assigned to drive you up there to whichever place you would like to go." Lt. Dunn had to repeat the question, as Nils Henrik, instead of paying attention to the lieutenant's words, was thinking about the threat he had found in his mailbox.

"What exactly happened?" he asked.

"It's too early to say, but this much we know: there was an explosion which resulted in a fire. A car was observed leaving the scene at high speed. That's all we know as of yet," Lt. Dunn answered.

"Where is TJ now?" Nils Henrik asked. "Who?" Lt. Dunn replied.

"TJ, the girl, my daughter," said Nils Henrik.

"She is being taken care of by the police and is in the hospital in

Jasper," Lt Dunn answered.

Nils Henrik went pale. After thanking Lt. Dunn and Officer Danyshyn, he said, "I don't need you to go with me. I'll drive myself."

Sometime after midnight, Nils Henrik turned off the Trans-Canadian Highway No. 22 and onto Pyramid Lake Road. The drive had taken him about three and a half hours. He couldn't remember much of it, but he had decided to swing by the cabin on the way to Jasper hospital. He wanted to see the cabin. And hopefully there would be more news of his wife.

The scene that greeted him there was enormously upsetting. The glowing heap of ashes was all that was left of what was once a comfortable place for his family to enjoy. The firefighters were still working on putting out the fire.

The police had cordoned off the area and assigned a guard to keep anyone from coming in. Nils Henrik was therefore stopped at the bottom of the hill. However, once he explained who he was, he was quickly let through.

One of the policemen on the scene saw that this man was let through and assumed it was Mr Ellefsrud. He immediately approached him. "Mister Ellefsrud, I assume?" He put out his hand by way of introducing himself.

"Yes," Nils Henrik answered. He put out his hand as well. "Lieutenant Robert Blake here. Is this place yours?" "Yes."

"Can you tell us who would have been here at the cabin this afternoon?"

"My wife and my two children, nine-year-old twins, a boy and a girl." "OK," Lt. Blake answered. "Let's go over here and sit down." He pointed to the bench outside the garage.

"Can you describe the girl?" Blake asked. Nils Henrik answered him as best as he could.

OK. A girl fitting the description of your daughter has been transported to the hospital down in Jasper. The whereabouts of your wife and son are unknown at this time." Lt. Black continued, "We are afraid that criminal activities have definitely taken place here against your family, and that the fire was intentionally set." As he spoke, he looked closely at Nils Henrik, who looked back right through him as if he weren't there.

"We have found gasoline cans that we believe were used to start the fire. We also have the statements of your neighbours Brian and Ivan, which describe a dark green station wagon fleeing the scene. Do you know anyone with such a car, or have seen a car like that out here before?

"I have the understanding that you know Brian quite well. He told us that he heard three gunshots from somewhere nearby. He is not sure, but he thinks they came from your cabin. They were listening to the hockey game when they heard the shots. They went out on the balcony, and that was when they saw the car. Brian said he had never seen this car there before. It was too dark to see the make or model. Then, before he knew anything else, came a blinding flash of light lighting up the sky, followed by an explosion. The whole cabin was immediately engulfed in flames. Then they observed the green station wagon going at a high rate of speed leaving the scene on the road at the other side of the hill. Another couple also saw the car escaping.

They say there was possibly two people in the car. That's all the information we have for the moment. Your daughter, as I said earlier, is at the hospital. We found her hiding under the woodshed. She has had a very terrible experience. She keeps calling for Mommy and Albert continuously.

"There isn't anything else we can do here tonight. I can drive you to the hospital, because I need to go there anyways to speak to Officer Arnolds. I have to consolidate all the information we have gathered so far, and then we can do a further investigation in the morning."

Nils Henrik sat still, as if he were made of stone.

"Mister Ellefsrud, we will come back here again tomorrow morning. There is nothing else we can do here tonight. Your daughter is at the hospital. She needs you," Lt. Blake said as he bent over and helped Nils Henrik up and over to his car.

They arrived at Jasper hospital at 3.30 a.m. They were immediately sent up to the room where TJ was. Officer Arnold was sitting on a chair next to the bed. He was reading. TJ was asleep, having been given a strong dose of a sedative. Joan shook hands with Nils Henrik. It was not necessary to say anything. They both knew all that had happened.

"How did it go with her?" Lt. Blake asked.

"She was examined, and there is no doubt that she was brutally raped. She has not said anything else. She only asks about her mother and Albert, crying uncontrollably," Joan answered him.

"OK, you can go home now if you want to. Mister Ellefsrud is here now."

"No, I'll stay here. I promised her that I wouldn't leave her. I need to be here when she wakes up," Joan answered.

"OK," Lt. Blake answered, "but try to get a little sleep. Tomorrow is going to be a long day as well."

Nils Henrik did not participate in the conversation. He was just sitting very still, holding TJ's hand in his.

CHAPTER 2

Norway Departure, 1946

The day Nils Henrik Ellefsrud turned seventeen was the day he felt himself ready to fulfil his wanderlust. This, of course, was not good news for his mother and father, but both of them knew that he had reached an age where they could no longer suppress his dreams.

He began to investigate different possibilities of how to get to the United States as quickly and inexpensively as possible. He had saved up $275, which was going to have to support him until he could arrive in the USA and find work. However, it was still more than six months before he finally packed his most precious things in a suitcase and said goodbye to his mother. That was exactly one year to the day that the war had ended in Norway, 8 May 1945. Today, 8 May 1946. Oscar, his father, followed him to the train station. At 2 p.m. Nils Henrik was at last on his way to America.

The first stop on his journey was Oslo. He was going to sleep over on the sofa of his mother's sister, Aunt Sophie. She had moved to Oslo many years before. She lived alone in a tiny apartment up in Blindern, a subdivision. This was near to her workplace, Ulleval Hospital. Nils Henrik was not sure exactly what her job entailed, but he was grateful for a place to stay while he plotted his strategy of finding transport to America.

He ended up signing up as a crew member on board the SS *Stavanger-fjord*. She was set out to make her first trip across the Atlantic Ocean now that the German occupation of Norway had been lifted. The departure was set for 31 May 1946 at 10 a.m. Nils Henrik was to receive eighty cents a day, with a bunk and meals included. It wasn't much, but it enabled him to make the trip without using any of his own money.

On the dot ten o'clock, the ship's whistle blasted one time. That was the signal for last call for all passengers and crew to board the ship. The docks were crammed with people all dressed in their best clothes.

They were there to wish their family or friends a safe voyage. It was a big event when ships were setting out on their voyages to America. The officer on the pier was shouting through a megaphone, "All aboard, all aboard! First-class passengers, please embark on the forward gangway. Second and third class, use gangways one and two at midships. All ship personnel, kindly go to the rear gangway immediately."

As soon as everyone was on board and the gangways were taken away, the Vålerenga brass band started to play the Norwegian national anthem. They had been playing for a while already, but they were now finishing up with that, as was always the case. All the men in the crowd took off their hats, and all ship's officers and crew stopped doing what they were doing and straightened themselves up. When the last note was being played, the second officer on the bridge found the button and pressed it three times to give three short blasts of the ship's whistle. The ropes were loosened, and the longshoremen threw them down off the docks. The tugboat started to pull, and as soon as the *Stavangerfjord* was clear of the docks and had turned around, the captain gave the order: "Start engines!" An enormous smoke cloud came out of the smokestack. The boilers had started, and the steam engine was started. The SS *Stavangerfjord* was on her way.

Nils Henrik had boarded the ship three days earlier. He was very excited but also afraid. Now he was starting on a journey which he had no idea how it would end.

The ship was carrying 650 passengers and 280 crew members, and this meant that there were hundreds of pounds of potatoes that had to be loaded for the voyage. And since this was the first voyage the ship was taking after being restored and repaired after the occupation, it required complete provisioning from scratch. There was nothing on board from previous voyages.

The SS *Stavangerfjord* had been seized by the German Navy, der Deutsche Kriegsmarine, and was used from 1940 to 1945 as living quarters for their soldiers. She was built in Birkenhead, England, in 1917. And during her earlier days, she was often called "the Queen of the Atlantic Ocean". She was constructed with one mast and two smokestacks and weighed 12,977 gross tons. When she was first launched, she could accommodate 88 first-class passengers, 318 second-class passengers, and 820 third-class passengers, and carry a crew of 300. Now after having been refurbished, her capacity was 122 first-class, 222 second-class, and 335 tourist-class passengers.

Her tonnage was upped to 13,156 gross tons. Her machinery included quadruple expansion engines with 8 cylinders for 1,567 horsepower; 8 single boilers; and two propellers, all of which gave her a maximum speed of 16 knots—not at all bad for those times.

Nils Henrik had sneaked out to the crew deck to see the departure, but now he was back in the galley. He had what seemed like several tons of potatoes to peel. He had been quartered in a twelve-man cabin, with his bunk somewhere in the middle. There were four sets of bunks with three beds in each. He had to be up at 6 a.m. and had a twelve-hour workday.

He had gotten acquainted with two of the guys in his cabin, Rolf and Arne. Rolf had been to sea before, and he had also sailed on the Trans-Atlantic convoys during the war. He was a messman for the crew mess hall. Arne was like Nils Henrik, a rookie. They worked together in the galley.

The Skagerrak Ocean, the ocean between Norway and Denmark, couldn't have been any better. The ocean was just like a dining room floor.

When Nils Henrik and Arne finished working the first day at sea, they got a cup of coffee and sat down in the corner of the mess hall. They waited for Rolf, who would finish around 9 p.m.

They wanted to go out on the poop deck and enjoy the mild evening. There were a lot of people who'd had the same idea. It was already crowded out there on the deck by the time the three men made it up. People were spread out in small groups; one guy was playing a guitar. "That's Jan Wilhelm; he's an able-bodied seaman. I think he's from Arendal, but I'm not sure. They say he was a crew member on board here several times before the war," Rolf said. "I also heard that he sailed out from Liverpool during the war. But I never met him. If you have any questions, I am sure he can help you."

Nils Henrik and Arne nodded as an acknowledgement. They found themselves a place on the starboard side and sat down.

Nils Henrik woke up to a huge crash and a tremendous shaking the next morning. He rolled over in his bunk. Everything around him was vibrating and in constant movement. The SS *Stavangerfjord* had crossed in to the North Sea and was in the process of entering the Atlantic Ocean. What had started out as a mild and beautiful two-day journey had now turned into a nasty storm. The weather report called for high winds and rough seas, which were already being felt. These conditions would be continuous for the next twenty hours.

The *Stavangerfjord* had just caught a wave broadside; that was the crash that had awakened Nils Henrik. First, he was scared, having come from the countryside, but then he pulled open the curtain of his bunk and looked out. Everything was swaying with the movement of the ship. He looked at the clock and saw that it was only twenty minutes until he had to be up. He hopped out of the bunk and went to his locker. But before he knew what happened, and without warning, everything that was in his stomach came up. He tried his best to throw up in the washbasin, without much success. The colour in his face changed from normal to a greenish hue. He was dizzy, and everything around him seemed to be floating and moving. He held fast to his locker, but another big wave chose just that moment to broadside the ship and he and his locker fell over. He could hear things tumbling around out in the corridor and a door slamming.

There was a terrible smell in the cabin. He wondered where this awful weather had come from. It had been so nice last night.

Nils Henrik tried to stand up, but the whole deck came up to meet him. He fell down again. Rolf came in and said, "You should try to get back to bed.

"I guess now we'll see what you are made of," he said, smiling. He continued,

"How do you feel? Here are some dry crackers. They will help you. They will remove the bad taste from your mouth and help you to feel better. Also, don't drink any kind of fluids, including water, as that will make it worse."

Nils Henrik tried to hear what he was saying, but he was feeling so ill that he almost didn't know who he was. He tried his best to focus his eyes on some point on the wall.

Rolf said, "I'll tell the first steward that you are sick. Just take it easy for now." Then he left.

Nils Henrik slowly crawled back to his bunk. He closed his eyes but opened them again quickly. It felt better if he could fasten his gaze on a fixed point on the wall. He tried to hold on and keep himself from falling out of the bunk.

The fact that Nils Henrik had a cabin all the way up towards the front of the ship did not help. In this area, the deck could move as much as 5 to 6 metres from the highest to the lowest in rough seas.

Nils Henrik stayed in his bed for the rest of the day. He must have fallen asleep shortly after he'd returned to his bunk.

When he woke up again it was 3.37 p.m. He still was sick, but not quite as bad as earlier. He pulled the drapes again and looked out to the cabin. There was no one there. A couple of chairs had fallen over, and pretty much everything else that was loose was now on the floor. The cabin smelled very strongly of vomit. He looked around a little more, but there was nothing more to see. He could hear the sound of snoring, indicating that there were others lying in their bunks.

He wondered if Arne was sick as well.

He lay still for a while and listened to all the sounds that came from around the ship. There were creaks and voices in the hall. He also thought he could hear the water outside the ship.

He thought about his job. Had they found somebody else to do it? He thought about all the other crew members and wondered how many of them were sick.

What about the passengers? Should he try to get up? This was only a thought. He felt completely wrecked. Suddenly he remembered the dry crackers Rolf had brought to him earlier when he was feeling his worst. Now he found them and took one out of the wrapper. He looked at it but had no wish to eat it.

New York, USA

On the radio, CBS began its morning news with the broadcaster announcing, "This day, June 11, is a big day for New York, "The *Queen of the Atlantic* is being announced back in the city for the first time after war in Europe. Estimated time of arrival is 11 a.m. We all welcome her back. She passed Breezy Point at 7.30 a.m. and is now entering the Lower Bay. We will keep you posted."

New York City was dressed up in its best. It was a beautiful sunny day. On the way in, the SS *Stavangerfjord* passed by Coney Island, Gravesend Bay, and the Verrazano Narrows. After that she came through the Upper Bay before entering the Hudson River. She was met with an escort of small boats. When she passed between Staten Island and New Jersey, the tugboats came out and shot off their water cannons. New York welcomed the *Queen of the Atlantic* back.

It was an impressive sight, the Statue of Liberty, the Manhattan skyscrapers. It was fantastic.

Finally, she came in to her new place and made her acquaintance with Dock 46, which would become her regular docking place when she visited New York. It was a wonderfully friendly greeting to receive after six years of absence. The dock was jammed with people, many of them looking forward to greeting their family or friends who had been detained and unable to come back home during the long years of the war.

Nils Henrik had gotten permission from the steward to go up on deck to witness the entry into New York. He was very glad to know that his period of work was over, but he had gained some valuable experience and insight into how things functioned while on board. He also considered that this might be his only experience working on a ship, and he was glad to have had it. The steward would have liked him to remain working on board as crew and offered him a permanent job where he could move up in over time, but Nils Henrik had politely declined the offer. He had bigger and better plans for the future.

The transport for immigrants which would take them to Ellis Island (the federal immigration station for anyone who wished to enter the United States at that time) didn't arrive until 6 p.m. It was a barge pulled by a tugboat down the Hudson River and into the harbour at Ellis Island. The immigrants, 279 in total, were for the most part third-class passengers. Those among the crew who were also immigrants were moved over from the personnel list to the passenger list as third-class passengers. This was done for technical reasons.

There were eight men from the crew who wished to immigrate. Nils Henrik was one of them.

First- and second-class passengers went through the immigration process on board the ship and were able to go directly into New York. They were seldom immigrants.

Ellis Island was located in the Upper Bay all the way in, near the coast of New Jersey, in the shadow of the Statue of Liberty. Ever since 1890, when President Benjamin Harrison officially granted the island to the federal government, it had been used as and referred to as "the Gateway to the New World". During its time as an immigration station, more than twelve million immigrants passed through its doors. Most of these were people from England, Ireland, Germany, and Scandinavia. The first immigrant was processed on 2 January 1892. Her name was Annie Moore, a fifteen-year-old Irish girl who had come through with her two brothers. Sixty-two years later, the last one to come through was a Norwegian seaman, Arne Petersen. Ellis Island's immigration station was then officially closed in November of 1954.

The trip over to Ellis Island took a little over an hour. On the way they received a label card which certified which ship they had arrived on. Nils Henrik received his with "SS *Stavangerfjord*" marked on it.

Once they arrived, they were placed in long lines. The first thing they needed to do was to undergo a medical check, for which every person was required to remove his or her clothes. The men were examined by a male doctor and the women by a female doctor. All of them were checked for infectious diseases and mental deficiencies.

Then came the criminal background check, where they were each asked twenty-nine questions, the same twenty-nine they had been asked before leaving Norway.

After four hours, Nils Henrik was through immigration and was an official immigrant of the United States.

Finally, he thought. *I am finally here.*

He walked down the marked corridors towards the official arrival hall of Ellis Island. The time was approaching midnight. He wondered if Kjartan had come through yet. They had decided to stick together and enter New York City together.

The hall was full of people. Nils Henrik looked around but didn't see him anywhere. He had met Kjartan six days after the SS *Stavangerfjord* left Bergen. Kjartan, an able-bodied seaman, had decided to get off the ship in New York. He wanted to try his luck on dry land. Nils Henrik found himself a bench and sat down to wait for his friend. "Hi" said a voice, and then there he was. "I see that they decided to let you in too," he continued without waiting for an answer. "Here's the deal. We can take a ferry in to the city tonight, or we can stay here until the morning. If we go in tonight, we might possibly find a bed to sleep in, and if we stay here we will have to share a hard bench with eight or ten other people. What do you think?"

"Let's go in to New York," Nils Henrik answered, "and we'll take it from there."

"OK, let's go then." They got on the line to board the ferry which would take them into the city.

CHAPTER 3

Kongsberg, Norway

16 August 2005

Henrik woke up early. He had not slept well ever since the funeral. He awoke often and wondered what was in his father's will. There was so much he didn't know about his father, Nils Henrik Ellefsrud. He had been a good father. He had also been good and kind to Henrik's mother, but there were facts concerning his father that he knew nothing about, things that he would never talk to his children about. He thought that maybe today he would finally get some answers.

He went to the refrigerator and looked for some breakfast. It was 7.15 a.m.

Usually he had a light breakfast, cereal and yogurt, maybe with a little fruit, some orange juice, and a cup of coffee, but on Saturdays he always made himself bacon and eggs. There was no reason why it should be any different today.

He was well into his breakfast when Reidun, the oldest daughter of Aase, Henrik's only sister, came downstairs. She was eight years old. She was blonde-haired and blue-eyed—the typical Scandinavian girl. "Hi. Do you want some breakfast?"

"Yes, please," she answered.

Reidun and her younger sister, Nina, had stayed with Henrik after the funeral. It was a few more days until school started, and Aase had given permission for them to stay. They liked to stay at Grandpa's house, where Henrik also lived. They always came home a bit spoiled afterwards.

Aase had gone home immediately after the memorial service, but she would be coming back today with the train. It would arrive at Kongsberg Station at 9 a.m. Henrik had promised to pick her up. She lived in Asker, where she had moved after she married Per nine years earlier. She was only twenty at the time, and Per had just started up his own electrician business.

After six years, the business failed and Per committed suicide. This left Aase alone with a stack of bills and all the inherent problems. She had to sell the house and the vacation cabin to pay the creditors, which just added to the problems and difficulties for her and the children. Later she was able to buy back the house with a loan from her parents.

At the present time, Aase worked from home. She had taken a few accounting jobs with a couple of large well-known firms in the area not far from her house. She was able to handle these accounts from home, which was her wish while the children were young.

She was a student when she met Per, studying to get her CPA, but she left school when she became pregnant with Reidun. Now after Pers's death she was alone again. She took up where she'd left off before and finished her degree by way of correspondence course.

Roald, Nils Henrik's youngest son, was also coming to the house at 10 a.m. He would come together with his wife Lisa and their son, Erik. They only lived a few kilometres away. Roald was a carpenter and had his own construction company. Erik was seven years old and had just finished his first year in school. He would turn eight in October. As far as Lisa went, Henrik was not really sure what it was that she did. He seemed to have heard that it had to do with the stock market. Both girls were served eggs and bacon.

They were very happy to have this for breakfast, as it was never on the menu at home in Asker.

"Don't tell your mother about this now. Remember, you're not allowed to have eggs and bacon at home." He just smiled at them. He knew for a fact that this would be the first thing they would tell their mother once she arrived. He enjoyed spoiling them when they came to visit. Henrik didn't have any children of his own. He had never married either. Even he didn't know why, as he had many opportunities.

After the girls cleaned up the breakfast dishes, they went upstairs and got ready to go to the station and meet their mother.

Now everyone was at Nils Henrik's house. The only person missing was Conrad. He had said that he would be coming by car directly down to the cabin.

Henrik had gotten the urn with the ashes sent over from the funeral home the day before. Now it was standing on a table in the living room. Henrik was to take it to the cabin. Nothing was said during the walk down to the cabin, which took ten minutes. Now everyone was seated inside the cabin waiting for Conrad. Henrik, Roald, Lisa, Erik, Aase, Reidun, Nina, and the housekeeper, Ruth.

Then the sound of a motorcycle, a Harley-Davidson Special Edition, was heard.

Henrik thought to himself that Conrad must have taken the good weather into consideration and therefore switched his mode of transportation.

As soon as Conrad arrived, everyone came out and moved over to the deck at the edge of the water, where Nils Henrik had put some tables and chairs. He used to sit there often by himself listening to the birds and the passing water. There was also a bench a little farther out towards the water.

Both these places had been his haven on earth. It was so strange not seeing him at either place today.

Henrik opened the urn exactly at eleven o'clock and said, "Papa, now you are home." He turned the urn upside down so the ashes could fall out of it. The wind took the ashes and blew them farther out over the river. Nothing more was said. There was complete silence except for the singing of birds in the trees nearby, just as Nils Henrik had wished. All these birds were his friends. He had sat down there many times with them before. Everyone quietly watched the ashes slowly disappear.

The clock in the living room chimed loudly one time. Henrik had always hated that clock—it used to wake him up at night, sometimes even just by the loud ticking—but the clock meant a lot to his father. It had belonged to his grandma. His father was the one there took care of it and wound it every seven days. Henrik thought that perhaps they should have stopped this clock when Nils Henrik died, but it was decided to stop the clock in his office instead, as the symbol for the end of a life.

Ruth, Nils Henrik's housekeeper for many years, came into the living room to let everyone know that the luncheon was served.

The menu included crawfish soup with white wine to start. The main course was filet mignon of moose with potato and a mash of root vegetables. The wine was a 1984 Merlot. For dessert, crêpes Suzettes with vanilla ice cream and cherry sauce. It was a meal after Nils

Henrik's taste. The crawfish and moose were from Nils Henrik's freezer, things he had fished and hunted together with Conrad. That was for more than a year ago. It was almost as if he himself was sitting down with them.

Nils Henrik had the whole thing planed, from the funeral, to the spreading of the ashes, to the luncheon. And the last event was the reading of the will.

It was 3 p.m., 16 August, in the office of the deceased, Nils Henrik Ellefsrud.

Present were the following: Henrik Ellefsrud, Roald Ellefsrud, Aase Ellefsrud (she had reassumed her maiden name after the death of her husband), Ruth Moen, and the reader of the will, Conrad Heen, lawyer and friend of the deceased. These were the people Nils Henrik wished to have present at the reading of the last will and testament. Conrad read from the paper he had in front of him. He sat behind Nils Henrik's desk. The others sat on chairs that had been brought into the office from the living room. They were facing him.

There was electricity and anticipation in the air. Everyone was in suspense. No one knew what was going to happen next.

Conrad addressed Henrik: "Will you please inspect the envelope and the signature on this envelope?" Henrik did as he was asked. He took the envelope and read the signature on it.

He was in the process of handing it back to Conrad when he said, "Your signature is not here?"

"No, that is correct. I have not really been involved in this at all. Your father only gave me this envelope along with this letter expressing his decisions about the funeral and all that we have done today. Now you have to write down your name and sign it." He handed Henrik a pen. Again, Henrik took the envelope from him and did what Conrad had asked. Then he handed it back to Conrad, sliding it across the desk.

Conrad said, "As you all now have been witnessed, Henrik Ellefsrud has witnessed the signature of attorney Rolf Schroder and Reidun Hiis. Rolf Schroder was your father's lawyer until he died. Reidun Hiis was his secretary.

Is there anyone else who would like to see the envelope before we proceed?" Conrad looked around the room. "All right, let's move on."

He turned the envelope over, opened it, and started to read. "Now you are all sitting in my office, and you will now hear my last wish. "Henrik, I wish you to oversee and take control of what is about to be revealed to you all.

"Conrad, I wish and hope that you also will participate and that you will help Henrik in any way you can with this. I know that I have never before asked you about this, and I'm sorry for it, but I hope you will accept the challenge that is coming your way.

"Further, Aase and Roald, I wish both of you to be governing members together with them in Canada.

"You will all take a share of the responsibility that is being given to you now.

"The wishes written here in this will indicate how I wish to distribute what I have built up and own. You will soon understand what I am getting at.

"In this letter you will only find some numbers. These are the combination to a safe that only I have known of before now. The safe is located behind the bookshelf to the left of the desk."

Everybody looked over at the bookshelf and at each other. "Lift up the second shelf to the left and it will be easy to move the bookshelf out and to the side. You shall use the code: 43 (three times to the right), 35 (four times to the left), 25 (two times to the right), and 10 (once to the left). The key is hidden in the small case on the same bookshelf." Henrik and Roald got up and went over to the bookshelf. They lifted up the second shelf and slid it to the side. The safe came into view. It was built into the wall right in the centre. They found the key right where Nils Henrik had written it should be.

It was a completely normal-looking safe of German fabrication. How long it had been there no one knew. The bookshelf had been there as long as they could remember. The safe, well, no one had known of it. Neither had Conrad. He remembered that Nils Henrik on several occasions had asked him if he could hold some important papers for short periods of time. Why would Nils Henrik have asked him to do that if he had his own safe?

Conrad read further: "Henrik, what I now ask you to do could be very difficult, but I am sure you will succeed if you all work together. I know the best families can turn against each other in situations like this. I hope you will all remain friends.

"Now you may open the safe."

Henrik asked Conrad to read out the code to him.

"OK, ready? Forty-three, right four times." He looked up. Henrik zeroed out the dial before he began. He found 43 and turned the dial to the right, and then he found the last number, 10, turning the dial left.

Conrad looked up again. The key was turned. *Click.* The safe was open.

The safe had two shelves and a little drawer at the top. It was not very large safe. What was inside took up almost all the space it had.

Henrik took out the contents of the safe and gave them to Conrad, who sorted the items into a more organized pile.

Then he picked up one of the envelopes and read out loud what was written on it: "Open this first." He used a letter opener from the desk of Nils Henrik to open it. He took out the contents and started to read: "Sorry, Conrad. I had to do it this way. You will understand better when you have read my final notes and the will, which you have witnessed my signature on. Yes, you had it in your safe, but you didn't know it was my will at that time. You may remember I showed you some papers regarding Canada and I asked you to witness my signature."

Conrad suddenly felt very uneasy. He looked up at everyone and said, "I didn't know anything about this."

He continued reading: "Conrad, now you must open the big envelope." Conrad found it and picked it up. Before he opened it, he read, "My last will and testament, Nils Henrik Ellefsrud." It was signed by Nils Henrik and witnessed by two persons unknown to Conrad.

"When you now read my last wishes, and go through my papers and other possessions, you will find out many things about me that you never knew before. Much of it I am proud of, but some of it I am not. I can only hope that you will rejoice with me in the positive and forgive me for the negative." He mixed up his English and Norwegian a little, a common thing to someone who has lived in both places for extended periods of time.

Conrad continued to read: "Now, take out the three envelopes with the names Reidun, Nina, and Nils Erik." Conrad picked them up and kept reading. "Conrad, inside these envelopes is a bank book. Each of these indicates an account bearing someone's name and containing sixty-five thousand dollars." The accounts were to be inaccessible to each beneficiary until each one either began college studies or built a house. If they chose not to study or build a house, they could have access to the money when they reached thirty years of age.

The next envelope was addressed to Ruth. Conrad looked through the envelopes again and opened hers. He quoted Nils Henrik and said, "You have been an excellent housekeeper all the years that you have been with us, and I especially wish to thank you for all the extra hard work you did during the time while Ellen was ill, and later with my illness. I cannot thank you enough for that."

Tears ran down Ruth's face when she heard this. Conrad kept on reading: "Inside here in your envelope you will find the deed to the little house you live in down the road. That means that it belongs to you now. I also give you a bank account with sixty-five thousand dollars. As you know, I am no longer in need of your help, but Henrik might like to have you continue to work for him. That has to be his decision."

The next envelope was marked with Conrad's name. He opened it up and read out loud again: "In addition to everything I have stipulated and that shall go to you, I also enclose the deed to the cabin in Hemsedal. I remember how much you enjoyed the place and what fun we two had there. Please think of me sometimes when you stay there and drink an occasional Canadian Club whisky in my name."

There were three more envelopes left, one for Henrik, one for Roald, and one for Aase. Conrad read Roald's first: "Roald, you are the youngest. I will be forever thankful for you and for all that you did for your mother while she was sick. You have also been a very good son, and I have always been proud of you. You may not have thought so, but it is true. Enclosed here are two bank statements, one containing one hundred and twenty thousand dollars, and another to cover the outstanding balance of the mortgage of the house you and Lisa live in. I have checked with your bank to see how much that is, and they allowed me to know the number. Please don't be angry at them for giving me that information. It is your choice whether to pay off the mortgage or not."

Conrad found the next envelope, which was marked with Aase's name. "Aase, you have always been the girl of my heart. There were many reasons for that, some of which you do not know yet. Your mother and I were also very proud of you, and we felt very badly for you when Per passed away. We both knew how proud you were, so we held ourselves a little in the background during that time. Maybe we shouldn't have done that, and we should have been more aware and sympathetic when you had to sell the house and your cabin, but that is hindsight. We hope you can forgive us.

"Enclosed you will also find a bank statement for an account in your name containing one hundred and twenty thousand dollars. In addition, you will find the deed to the cabin which you had to sell. Those were the last words your mother said before she died, that she wished we had bought that place for you."

Conrad now picked up the last envelope and handed it over to Henrik. "To you, Henrik, will I say that you have been the most important thing that ever happened to me in my life and my greatest motivation for change for the better. A new door opened up for me when you came into the world, and I began to believe that I could live my life again without being afraid. My nightmares began to disappear almost the moment your mother showed you to me for the first time.

"As Conrad has already read, it is my wish that you take over the leadership of the Ellefsrud family. I realize that this is a great responsibility. You will come to understand more about this very soon.

"I have studied you over time without involving you in any of this, but I believe that you have the makings of a strong leader, and I wish you good luck with it.

"Enclosed you will find the same amount of money as I have left for Roald and Aase, one hundred and twenty thousand dollars. Also, I give you the deeds to both the house and the cabin down by the river. There is a small clause attached to this; if either Roald or Aase wishes it, I would like you to grant them each a piece of land from the parcel where the cabin is located.

I have made a few notes of favourable locations for two more cabins on the site, and I wish you to subdivide them and put the lots in their names.

"Then I have one more wish that I hope you will do for me. I would like for you to continue to employ Ruth as your housekeeper if she so wishes. You can pay her salary out of your inheritance. If you don't want to employ her, your inheritance shall pay her a salary for the seven years she has left to work before she retires. It would not be easy for her to get another job at her age."

Conrad looked at Henrik before continuing.

"You will find a key taped to this letter. This key is to a safe deposit box at the Norwegian Credit Union in the town centre of Kongsberg. I want you to go together with Conrad and fetch the contents of the box. There you will both find the beginning of the answers you will be looking for, but only the beginning. If it was possible for me to give you all the answers in this letter, I would have, but that would be impossible. I only hope that in the fullness of time you will find the answers for me.

"Henrik, it is you who are in charge now. I wish you only the best of luck in the future, and of course I thank you for all you have done for me and your mother."

Conrad looked up. "That's everything that Nils Henrik has written down here in his last will and testament. There are still several envelopes here, but they are unmarked. Please go through them, Henrik. Since they are not named in the will, they will become your responsibility."

Henrik got up and retrieved the remaining envelopes.

"If anyone has anything they wish to add, they need to speak up right now."

Conrad looked around at everyone. "All right then, this meeting is now officially ended." He took out a document and wrote while speaking clearly:

"The time is 4.37 p.m. and we are now finished reading the official last wishes of the deceased Nils Henrik Ellefsrud."

He specified that each person must sign the document, starting with Henrik, who then passed it around to the others. He thanked everyone for coming and wished them farewell.

"I don't know exactly what I am feeling right now, but I think a drink would be good." The others nodded.

"Let's go into the living room." Ruth quickly resumed her duties as house-keeper. She also felt the need for a drink and treated herself to a glass of sherry.

20 August 2005

The safe deposit **box**

Henrik and Conrad arranged to meet again on the following Wednesday, 20 August. They decided to meet at the railway station café, where the train from Oslo was due to arrive at 9 a.m. Today the train was five minutes early arriving at Kongsberg, so Henrik was not there yet. Because of this, Conrad went into the café alone. He found a table before ordering a thermos of coffee and two cups. He knew that he wouldn't have long to wait before Henrik would join him.

Henrik did arrive just a few minutes later. Conrad poured him a cup of coffee as soon as he got there.

The Norwegian Credit Union was located at the end of the main street just a few blocks from the train station. It took them only five minutes to walk down to it. They were both in suspense. They walked into the bank and over to a window that was open for business and explained what their errand entailed. They would need to go down to the vault where the safe deposit boxes were located.

The teller took a good look at them before saying, "Come with me." She came out from behind the counter where she was working and led them to an office in the corner. "Please sit down and wait here," she said. "Randi will be right with you." Then she went back to her station.

"Hi, my name is Randi. What can I do for you?" Henrik explained to her again what they were there for.

"OK, do you have some identification and a death certificate?" she asked.

"Yes." Henrik gave her the death certificate along with his own driver's licence.

Conrad gave her his driver's licence as well.

She examined the identification cards closely before returning them to the two men. Then she opened one of the drawers of her desk and began searching for something. Apparently, she was unable to find what she was looking for.

"In cases like these," she said, "I must attest that I have seen the death certificate, and there are some papers that you will be required to sign. It looks like I don't have them here. I have to go and get them.

I'll be right back." She was back in about five minutes.

"OK, which one of you was Henrik Ellefsrud again?" she asked. "I am," Henrik answered.

"Can you please fill out these papers?" she said, handing him the forms.

Henrik took the papers and read over them quickly before he began to fill them out. Then he signed them and gave them to Conrad, who also signed them. Randi took the papers back, quickly checked out their signatures, and then set the papers aside.

"Shall the box be closed out?" she asked.

That was something they hadn't thought about. They looked at each other and quickly decided to keep it, at least for the moment. It would be a good idea to keep the box in case there was anything in the box that needed to be kept in a safe location like a bank.

"No, I think we will keep it for the moment," Henrik answered "OK, what name shall it be under?" Randi spoke again.

"You can put it under Henrik Ellefsrud," Henrik answered. She put his name on the form. "Address?"

"The same as my father's."

She wrote again.

"Do you have the key?" she asked, pulling a big ring of keys from the top drawer in her desk. Henrik held the key up. "OK, let's go downstairs."

The stress in Henrik's body and the butterflies in his stomach became even more active. Ever since Saturday his thoughts had been going around and around about the safe deposit box and what it could possibly contain. He wished so much that it would finally explain what had happened to his father in the USA and Canada. Why would he never talk about any of it?

However, there was a general understanding that he had done well and that he had some money. But that was about all.

Box no. 0063 was located approximately in the centre of the right wall of the safe. Seen from the outside, it was one of the largest boxes, about 400 millimetres wide and 300 millimetres high. How long it was they would not be able to see until it was opened. Randi went over to the front panel of the box and put in her key. Then she turned around to look at Henrik to get him to put in his key. They turned the keys at the same time, and the door was opened. She began to pull out the box. It seemed to be quite heavy, so Conrad came through and gave her a hand.

The box was about 700 millimetres long. They carried it over to the largest alcove and set it down on the table. Randi said, "When you are finished, just push the button there." She pointed towards a button on the other wall. "I'll then come back, and we can put it back and lock it up again." Then she left.

Conrad opened the fastener on the box. A pile of envelopes came into sight. They were all marked with letters and numbers, and some also had writing, but the one on top was marked clearly "Open this first." Under that envelope were several other envelopes, packets, and boxes, some large and some small, of different sizes and weights. But one package stood out from the others because of its large size.

Conrad looked at Henrik. "I think we might want to take this with us. It will take some time to go through it all," he said.

"I agree, but where shall we go? If we take it home, we'll have Roald coming over immediately," Henrik answered.

"You have a point. Maybe we should book into a hotel and get a couple of rooms," Conrad said.

"That sounds like a good idea," Henrik answered.

"Let's put everything into your backpack. I can take the rest under my arm," Conrad said.

Henrik had brought along the backpack that he usually used when hiking in the mountains. He threw it on the desk and started loading it with the contents of the box. Conrad took the largest of the envelopes under his arm. Henrik laced up the box, and they replaced the empty box on the shelf and rang the bell. Randi came immediately and locked the box again. She gave the key back to Henrik.

Henrik and Conrad each took a room in the Quality Grand Hotel downtown Kongsberg. Henrik took a normal-sized room, and Conrad requested a larger room where they could spread everything out and get to work. They quickly came to the conclusion that it was going be a long day, and probably a long night, before they would be able to get through everything Nils Henrik had left them in the safe deposit box. They took the elevator up to room S008, Conrad's room. Henrik threw the sack on the bed. Conrad put all the envelopes on the desk in the corner. The room was quite large, with a sofa and chairs as well as a double bed. There was also a coffee maker and a minibar, but Conrad ordered room service. He asked for two thermoses filled with coffee, eight bottles of soda, four Pepsis, and four 7 Ups. He also ordered food: two club sandwiches, salads, French fries, and ketchup.

He asked them to wait until about 2 p.m. before sending up most of the order, but he asked for the sodas and coffee to be delivered immediately.

Henrik went to his own room, no. 434, threw down his jacket, and took the opportunity to use the bathroom. Fifteen minutes later he was back in Conrad's room. Conrad was already holding the envelope that read "Open this first." Henrik looked over at him. "What is it in that envelope?" he asked, as he spilled out the contents of the backpack onto the bed.

Conrad didn't answer the question; instead he asked, "How do we do this? If one of us goes through the envelope, the other go through the packets and boxes?"

"OK," answered Henrik.

"What will you take?" Conrad asked, looking at Henrik while he asked.

"You can read," said Henrik. "I'll take the others. You are more used to massive amounts of paperwork than I am."

"OK," said Conrad. He began to sort the envelopes in front of him on the desk. Again he found the envelope marked "Open this first."

He held it up and turned it around a few times in his hands before he opened it. He began to read out loud: "Henrik and Conrad, the time has come to tell you both the whole story of Nils Henrik Ellefsrud. There is much I wished to tell you both, especially you, Henrik, before I died, but I was unable to do so. I was afraid. I was afraid that something would happen to you and/ or all of you like it did to me. "Ellen, your mother, Henrik, knew everything since the beginning, but we agreed to keep it from you all. Whether this was right or wrong I will never know, but it was wholly my decision, and I hope that none of you will blame us for it.

"You will soon find out that you are rich now. How rich even I don't know." Henrik asked, "What does he mean?"

"I have no idea, but you are all rich; that's all I know. Let me get busy reading this."

Henrik began to sort out the pile of things that had come out of the backpack. He said, "OK, I'll begin with this pile on the bed."

There were five heavy packages, which he placed on top of the pillows together with a big package. All of the other small packages he let lay where they had fallen out of the sack. He asked himself where he should begin. He picked out some small boxes. The first had jewellery in it, a brooch and some earrings. They looked like silver with blue-green stones. At first glance they looked like they might be some cheap costume jewellery bought somewhere like a fair or carnival under a tent, like in the old days. He put them back in the box and put them aside. He picked up the next box and shook it a little before he opened it. He found some more jewellery, again looking like silver with the same blue-green stones as the first pieces, but they were not earrings; they looked more like a brooches. In this box he found a necklace and a bracelet with an interesting design that he remembered seeing on a picture of a Native American woman.

Henrik also laid this aside in its box. The next box he chose was longer—not especially big, but bigger than the first two boxes. He began to unwrap it and inside found several small and delicate tools, some made of bone and others made from stone, or what looked like stone.

Conrad looked over at Henrik and asked, "What are those?" Henrik said, "I can't exactly place them, but they bring to my mind some articles that I have read in connection with Native American Indians."

He set them aside as well and began opening one of the packages which was part of a set of five that he had placed on the pillow. They were all quite heavy, and they made up only a very small part of what was in the safe deposit box. He wondered to himself how his father had been able to lift all of these things in and out of the safe. He laid aside those thoughts and concentrated on the package in his hand, rolling the wrapping paper off. "What the hell!" he said. Conrad quickly looked over at him.

"Look at this, Conrad. Is it a gold bar?!" He held it up for Conrad to see. "Are the other packages gold bars too as well?!" Henrik asked. Without waiting for Conrad to answer, he began to unwrap the other four packages, one after the other, and sure enough, there were gold bars in all of them, five in total. He could hardly believe it.

"How much are these worth, Conrad?" Henrik asked.

"I have no idea, but it should be easy enough to find out," he answered. He took out his cellular phone and looked for a number before dialling it. "Hello, this is Conrad here. It's been a long time since the last time we talked. I need some information. I remember that you were always very interested in gold and silver prices on the world market and that you did some investment in gold. Now I have a case in which the current gold price has come up. Can you tell me what the price of gold is today?"

Conrad waited. The person on the other end of the line said, "When I checked yesterday, it was US$587 per troy ounce."

"OK, can you tell me how many grams there are in a troy ounce?" Again, he waited for the reply. He jotted down some numbers. "OK, 31 grams. So how many troy ounces does a gold bar weigh?"

Now there was a dead silence at the other end of the telephone, before the question came.

Conrad repeated, "What am I working with? I'm sorry, but I can't reveal any information about this case, as you know. But it is a very interesting case. I will tell you all about it at a later date, after it is concluded.

"OK, one gold bar weighs 400 troy ounces, you say, or something like 12,400 grams?

"You say that is transport weight, but the bars can be smaller? It is known that some miners used smaller moulds when they melted down the gold they found, and those moulds were made by the gold miners themselves," Conrad said.

"Thank you very much. You have been a great help.

"Yes, let's get together and have a beer sometime soon. I'll call you up and we'll keep in touch. And thanks again."

Conrad hung up.

"How much do you think these gold bars weigh?" Conrad asked Henrik.

"I have no idea, but we can surely find out," answered Henrik. He took one of the gold bars and rolled it back into the paper it was wrapped in.

Then he folded up the other four papers and put the bars all together into the backpack before he headed for the door.

"Where are you going?" asked Conrad.

"Down to the reception desk. I want to weigh this bar," said Henrik.

Then he left the room.

"Can I help you?" asked the receptionist.

"Yes, I hope that you can," said Henrik. "Is it possible that you have a scale I can borrow? I am going to send something in the mail, and I need to how much it weighs."

"I think we should be able to do that," said the receptionist. "We have a scale in the back room."

"Great. Can you go get it?" said Conrad.

"No, sorry. You will have to come in. It is placed fastened down on top of a shelf. Just follow me through here." She pointed to a door around the corner. Henrik followed her through, and sure enough, there stood a scale. "Help yourself," she said. Henrik checked the calibration and found it to be correct. He found the package and laid it on the scale. He read 4,250 grams. The next thing he weighed was one of the papers, 150 grams. At last he weighed all four papers together: 600 grams.

Henrik thanked the receptionist and went back up to the room. He calculated quickly in his head while going back up in the elevator. Each gold bar would weigh, 4,250 grams, minus 150 grams for the paper, which equalled 4,100 grams. If they were all the same, which he assumed they were, then all together it would be 4,100 grams times 5, equals 20,500 grams, or 45,195 pounds.

Once Henrik arrived, Conrad asked, "How much does it weigh?" "Four-point-one kilograms," Henrik answered.

"OK, that makes it 20.5 kilograms, 45.195 pounds, altogether, if all the bars weigh the same, which we will base it on," Conrad answered. Henrik could see that Conrad was figuring furiously in his head. "That makes 661.29 troy ounces, and if we multiply that by US$587, we have a net worth of US$388,177.23."

They both looked at the gold bars thoughtfully.

"Have you come to any conclusion?" asked Conrad.

"Not really," Henrik answered. "Didn't your friend mention the transport weight of gold bars, saying that the bars could be different if the prospectors melted the gold themselves?"

Conrad kept on reading.

"Henrik, your father is mentioning two letters that he wanted us to mail as they are. There are two envelopes already addressed. Can you please find them for me?"

Henrik stretched out and took a little pile of envelopes that looked just like any normal mailing envelopes. He looked at them and read the markings on them, then separated two of them from the pile. One was addressed to a Lt. Robert Blake, Range Road 73, Drayton Valley, Alberta, H1D 4S5, Canada. The other one was addressed to TJ, Box 3088, Drayton Valley, Alberta, H1D 4A2, Canada.

Henrik gave them to Conrad, who looked at them and put them on the desk. There was a knock on the door. Henrik quickly threw his jacket over the gold bars before he opened the door. It was the food Conrad had ordered earlier.

Both men concentrated on the food. Henrik suddenly said, "How on earth did my father get those gold bars? Is the answer to that here in this room, Conrad?"

Conrad didn't answer. He just looked at him. Henrik's telephone rang. "Yes?"

It was Roald's voice. "It's me. What can you tell me?" Henrik could hear the emotion in Roald's voice immediately.

"Hi, Roald. Well, for the moment, not much, but there are a lot of interesting things."

"Oh yes? Like what?"

"Roald, you have to give us more time. We are in possession of everything that was in the safe deposit box as of now, but it's going to take some time. We will try to be finished by tonight, but it might take us some of tomorrow morning as well."

"All right, but you must surely be able to tell us something by now. And by the way, where are you? I tried to call you at home, but you weren't there."

"I'm not going to tell you where we are right now, but we took all the contents of the safe deposit box to a neutral place, somewhere where we thought we could be in peace while we go through the contents. I can tell you so far that Papa has left behind a riddle. He also has let us know that we are very rich."

"What do you mean by very rich?"

"Well, during his time in the USA and Canada, he did very well for himself—extremely well. But, Roald, let us get back to unravelling the riddle.

I promise that I will call you as soon as we find out something more concrete. It might not be until tomorrow, OK?" "All right."

"Can you please call Aase for me and let her know what's going on?" Henrik asked.

"Yes, but please call me as soon as you can. Will you promise me that?"

"Yes, I will." Henrik hung up the phone.

Conrad and Henrik resumed their investigation of the contents of the safe deposit box. Conrad read, and Henrik went through all the loose boxes and packages. There were four packages left. He picked up the one closest to him. It contained silver and gold coins, about fifty or sixty of them. What they were worth, it was impossible to say.

The next package contained jewellery again, mainly gold jewellery. There were also two rings. They could have been engagement or wedding rings. They were both engraved with "To my love".

The next package was the largest; Henrik had looked at it several times, but he had disciplined himself to leave it until last.

Conrad had read through most of the first envelope, and so far he had not discovered anything other than what they'd already been told: that they were very rich. He had not yet been able to determine how rich. He wondered for the hundredth time what Nils Henrik had really meant.

Conrad continued to read:

I wrote earlier that I was a rich man but that I didn't know how rich I am. That is the truth, with certain modifications. Yes, it is true that I do not know my true worth. When I came back to Norway, I made the decision to keep a low profile. There were several reasons for that.

Henrik wasn't used to drinking alcohol in the middle of the week, but it had been a pretty special day.

"OK, sounds like a good idea," he answered.

They asked the receptionist where they could find a bar.

"There is one at the corner here," the receptionist said. "You can go through the restaurant, which, I apologize, is closed for renovations. We can, however supply room service. Otherwise, there are a couple of restaurants right across the street from the bar."

Conrad and Henrik thanked her for the information and went through the restaurant and into the bar.

Conrad and Henrik became guest numbers 3 and 4 in the bar. The two others were a young couple in their twenties who didn't even notice them; they were too caught up in each other.

Conrad and Henrik went over to a table in the opposite corner. The bartender had seen them come in and was already waiting to take their order. "Famous Grouse with ice, please, and a glass of club soda on the side, also with ice."

The bartender turned and looked at Henrik.

"Gin tonic, please. And do you have any peanuts?"

The bartender was already on his way to get the drinks when Henrik asked for peanuts, but he must have heard him, because there was a small dish of peanuts on the tray when he returned with their drinks. Henrik lifted his glass. "Toast, Conrad," he said. "What kind of intrigue are we sitting in the middle of, and why did my father have that revolver?"

Conrad answered, "I knew Nils Henrik for almost ten years, but in all that time he never talked about his business or what he had done in the United

States and Canada. He had spoken a little bit about his time in Canada, just talking about how fascinating the country was and how much he loved it, but he had never gone any further into what he had done or experienced there. But now that we are speaking about it, I remember one time when he may have wanted to tell me about it but he just couldn't. I didn't think anything particularly about it at the time, but now that we have come this far, I'm beginning to see why."

"What about the part he wrote that he was a very rich man?" asked Henrik. "We always knew that he had some money, but we never imagined that it was a fortune. He absolutely never showed us that." Conrad just looked at Henrik and let him continue. "What do you think about getting yourself involved in this? Do you think it would be worth it?"

Conrad emptied his glass and signalled the bartender. He asked Henrik if he would like another drink as well, and he said yes, so he signalled the bartender again and pointed to Henrik's glass.

"Well, I don't know any more than you do, Henrik, but one thing I do know for sure is that Nils Henrik would not have written all this down unless it was true. I definitely know that about your father. That being said, whether or not I decide to explore this further with you is another matter. I do have the time to do it, so, I am thinking strongly in favour of it. And I think it will be extremely interesting.

"Now we need to go through the rest of the stuff. However, I will be looking very closely to make sure there isn't any illegal activity. If that is discovered, I will not be able to go further. If not, I am all in." "Thank you, Conrad," said Henrik.

They both finished their drinks and readied themselves to leave.

Henrik left a nice tip for the bartender.

"Chinese, sushi, or pizza?" Conrad asked. "Whatever you want. It's all the same to me."

"OK, then it will be sushi," said Conrad. They walked into a restaurant called Nippon.

Henrik was too fired up to go to sleep immediately, so he decided to call Roald, even though it was quite late. He was quite sure that Roald would still be up and waiting for his call. He went over to the minibar, took out a bottle of red wine, and found a glass before opening it. He took both the glass and the bottle with him over to the easy chair and sat down. He started to think about what he would say to Roald while he picked up his phone and pulled up his contacts list. He punched in Roald's home number and waited to get through. It rang for quite some time before Roald answered, but finally he heard Roald's voice on the other end.

"Hi, this is Henrik. Is it a bad time to talk?"

"No, I was just down in the cellar for a moment, so I didn't hear the telephone. So, come on, talk to me. In fact, if you wait just a minute, I can get Aase on the line. I just need to call her and then hook her up. I have spoken with her several times already this evening, and she is just as excited as I am to hear what's going on."

"OK, do what you have to do. I'll wait," Henrik said.

"Hi, Aase, this is Roald. Would you like to be in on a conference call with Henrik? I have him on the line. He will tell us what he has found out so far."

"Yes, of course. Connect me."

"OK, Henrik, we're here." It was Roald again.

Then Henrik began to tell them what he and Conrad had found out so far. Roald and Aase listened quietly until he mentioned the gold bars, then the silence was broken. Both began talking at the same time, but they were silenced when Henrik said the value of these gold bars could be as much as US$388,177. That of course would vary depending on the price of gold at any given time, but the fact was that the gold bars in total weight were 20.5 kilos, 45.195 lb.

The next thing to unleash the conversation was, of course, the revolver. They wondered why their father had it.

Then when Henrik ended the conversation with the statement that their father had said they were rich, but that he didn't know how rich, Aase said, "Papa, what the hell were you involved in?"

Roald didn't say anything; he was completely silent.

Then he said, "Henrik, call me tomorrow after you have gone through the rest. I need to think of this overnight and alone. Aase, good night." He hung up.

Henrik and Aase continued to talk for a few more minutes, then Henrik said that he was tired and needed to get to bed. Tomorrow would be another day.

Conrad had ordered a 6.30 wake-up call, as he wanted to swim some laps in the pool before breakfast. Ever since he had left his law firm, he had forced himself to make time for one hour of exercise every day. The results of this wise decision were a loss of 28 kilos of weight. He had never been in such good shape since he was a youngster. It wasn't always easy to find the time, but he had made a bargain with himself that no matter what, he would continue with it.

At 8.27 Conrad entered the room where the hotel was serving breakfast. Henrik was already there. He had found a table a little distance from the other guests and sat with the newspaper and a cup of coffee in front of him.

"Good morning," said Conrad. He sat down.

"Good morning," said Henrik, as he looked up from his newspaper. "Have you eaten yet?" asked Conrad.

"No, I was waiting for you."

"OK, let's find something to eat then."

"I almost didn't sleep at all last night," Henrik said. He continued: "I called Roald and Aase last night after we parted. They were as amazed as we were at what we have found so far."

On the way back to the rooms, Conrad went to the reception desk in order to mail the two letters that were addressed to Canada.

Back in Conrad's room, the two of them took up where they had left off the night before. Conrad began to read the résumé of Hans Arne Moen. Moen had also begun in the police department, but he didn't have nearly as much experience in other departments as Ole G. Olsen had. What he had been involved in were murder cases, with a high success rate solving these cases. Conrad didn't know anything about him personally, but his name had come up fairly regularly in the news media. He thought that he would check both of them out a little more thoroughly later, but his gut feeling told him that it would probably end up being Ole G. Olsen.

Henrik had opened the last box. Again, it was jewellery. He put it back and started to organize all the boxes by putting them together. There were only three large envelopes, all marked photographs, left on the bed now. One envelope was marked Canada, and one was marked USA. The third one didn't say anything specific. He opened the envelope marked USA and dumped all the pictures out over the bed. It was a large number of black-and-white photos, many of them of people, but some of landscapes and buildings. Henrik recognized New York City in several of them, but there were also plenty more of country-like settings that could have been taken anywhere, most likely New Jersey or Long Island. Some of the photos had a date and a place written on the back. One of the pictures with a date on it caught Henrik's attention. It was a toilet at Knudsen's building site, Bronx, New York.

The envelope marked Canada was next. And as he'd done with the first envelope containing pictures, he spread the contents across the bed. Most of these photos were also in black and white, but there were also a few in colour. He looked through them all, turning each one over to look on the back to check for anything written on them.

Again, there were pictures from many different places, and a number of them had a date written on the back as well. This time he organized the ones with notes on the back in a separate pile. He started to look at the photo showing Nils Henrik standing in front of a sign that read "Winnipeg", the largest city in the province of Manitoba in central Canada. In the picture he was well-dressed in pants, a nice sweater, and a jacket. He was smiling and pointing to the sign. The date on the back was 16 October 1951, and the title was "Arrival into Canada".

There were more pictures from Winnipeg, and most of them had Nils Henrik in them. There were two other people appearing in some of the photos, OJ and Bob. OJ was also in some of the pictures from the USA. Bob was not seen in any of the other photos.

The next photo that really captured Henrik's interest was dated 22 October 1951. The image was of Nils Henrik in front of the CN Train Company's terminal with his suitcases. On the back of this picture he had written, "On the way west". After that there followed some pictures from their trip to

Canada, one from the bar on the train, and one with Nils Henrik and OJ standing talking to a pretty woman.

The next picture with handwriting showed Edmonton, Alberta, and marked, "An important building". Most likely it was the capital building of the province—a big white building. However, no name was written on it to let Henrik know where it really was.

Henrik didn't find any other pictures of interest.

Conrad had finished both reports that Nils Henrik had written about the two investigators. He had made several telephone calls in order to fill in the blanks on both of them and was now ready to confront Henrik with his first choice of a candidate to help them investigate this case. It was Ole G. Olsen. He had sensed it from the very first minute he had read Nils Henrik's wishes that they should have professional help to find the answers.

"I have gone through the reports and résumés for both candidates. I have also spoken with several of my earlier contacts who know both of these investigators. My conclusion is that we call Mister Olsen first."

"All right then, if that is what you think would be best, then that's what we'll do," Henrik answered. "Will you call him, or should I do it?"

"I'll do it," Conrad answered. He was looking at the last envelope when he answered. He continued, "If you don't mind, Henrik, I'll take this last envelope home with me and go through it there. It's forty- eight pages and the writing is very small, so it's going to take some time."

"Of course, no problem. But please let me know if you find out anything important from it," said Henrik.

"OK."

"Let's gather together everything we have here. You take home all the things you have unpacked, Henrik, and I'll take all the envelopes with me. I'm sure that Roald and Aase want to see everything we found here. After that you better take the gold bars and the revolver back to the safe deposit box."

Henrik agreed and started to put all of the boxes and the gold bars into the backpack again, together with the revolver and ammunition. Conrad packed all the papers he had gone through into a box that he had gotten from the reception desk and tied it up with a rope.

CHAPTER 4

Norway

8 August 2005, 11.45 a.m., at the cabin

Nils Henrik's thoughts wandered back to the hospital and to TJ's

bed that night. It was so unbelievable that his whole world had been turned upside down that night. He sat and cried while thinking about what had happened.

He looked at TJ. She was lying there peacefully sleeping because they had given her a strong sedative. He thought about what she had gone through that evening. She was only nine years old, just a small child. What was going to happen to her now?

He remembered that he must have slept a little, because when he awoke he heard TJ cry out, "Mommy."

She had just awakened but was probably still in shock. Tears were running from her eyes. He got up, went over to the bed, and took her in his arms. He tried to comfort her to the best of his ability. It wasn't easy. She was still asking for her mother.

Joan was sitting sleeping in a chair on the other side of the bed. She woke up almost the same time as Nils Henrik. She smiled at TJ and asked her how she was. TJ just looked at her and didn't say anything. "Do you remember me from yesterday?" Joan took the girl's other hand. TJ nodded to her shyly. "Well, now you just need to relax and take it easy. Everything bad is over now." Joan tried to be as positive as it was possible for her to be. TJ didn't answer her but continued to ask about her mother.

Lt. Robert Blake, arrived back at the hospital around 10 a.m. He greeted Nils Henrik and nodded to Joan. Then he turned to TJ and asked, "How are you?" TJ didn't answer; she just looked at him.

Joan said, "It's OK, TJ. This is my boss. He is here to help you just like I am."

Lt. Blake smiled at TJ again and said, "It's going to be all right." Then he turned to Nils Henrik and asked, "Can we go somewhere where we can talk?"

"Of course," Nils Henrik answered.

"You come too," Blake said to Joan.

Joan turned to TJ and said, "We'll be right back, OK? We'll only be a moment, so don't be afraid."

Once out in the hallway, they found an empty waiting room and went in. There Lt. Blake started to inform them of what the investigators had learned so far. They had found evidence that the explosion which started the fire had been deliberately set. Therefore, they believed that both Nils Henrik's wife and Albert, TJ's twin brother, most likely were in the cabin when it was set on fire. They had built this evidence partly on what TJ had told them when they found her. They really didn't have any other clues to go on but her testimony. The search for the remains was already under way, and Lt. Blake asked whether TJ was able to communicate any further details as of yet. She was the only witness who could shed any light on what had happened, and so her description of it was of the greatest importance. For that reason, he asked if it would be possible to question her. Nils Henrik answered that if it was all right with TJ's doctor, it was all right with him that she be questioned further.

The doctor was not sure whether TJ would be able to withstand any questions but was willing to let Lt. Blake try, provided that he would be both careful and gentle. Her condition was still not very good.

Lt. Blake decided to wait. He didn't wish to set TJ up for more trauma than she had already gone through.

Instead he agreed to let Joan use the trust she had established and try to ask some important questions after a while. He went to his car and drove away.

Joan went back to TJ's room. She was lying in her bed with her eyes closed, but she was awake.

"Here we are again," said Joan. TJ opened her eyes. Joan asked the girl some questions while she was looking at her father.

"We heard that you were out playing softball yesterday afternoon. Is that true?"

TJ nodded.

"And then you bicycled home? What time do you think it was when you got home? Just nod when I say the correct time. Six in the evening?" No answer. "Seven? Seven thirty?" When Joan said seven thirty, TJ nodded.

"Did you see anything unusual when you came home, like maybe a strange car or anything like that?" Again, TJ nodded.

"Could you describe the car?"

TJ shook her head, no.

"Do you remember anything else? Was there anyone outside the cabin?"

Again no.

"Did you go inside? And was there anyone else in there?" Again, TJ nodded.

In this way Joan was able to get some answers from TJ. The girl either nodded or shook her head. These were the only answers she was as yet able to give.

When the questions began to turn towards her mother and brother, she began to shake and tried to hide herself under the blankets. Joan realized at once that she shouldn't ask her any more questions now. Instead she said, "You are a very grown-up girl, and you have been a big help so far. Now you have to relax and try to think some good thoughts while we try to do our job, trying to find your mama and Albert." While she said this, Joan bent down and gave TJ a hug and smiled at her.

"Now I am going away for a little while. Your papa will stay here with you. I'll come back later this afternoon." TJ nodded her answer. Joan looked at Nils Henrik. "I'll be back this evening."

"OK."

Now he sat here at the cabin thinking about it again, as he had done more times than he could count. He thought about that evening and the next few days, and there was not one word that had been said or one tear that had fallen that he did not remember. It was the worst night he had ever had in his life. He had tried to get through to TJ, but she didn't really respond. Why? She used to be so close to him.

His thoughts went back to the cabin fire and the subsequent investigation. It was there that he had met Lt. Robert Blake. He was a few years younger than Nils Henrik, maybe seven or eight. He was not a very big man, but it was easy to see that he kept himself in good shape. This showed that he had good self-discipline.

When Lt. Blake and Officer Arnold came back to the hospital, it was past 4 p.m. They came directly up to TJ's room. Joan gave TJ another hug as soon as she came in. Nils Henrik felt relieved. Even though he had tried to comfort his daughter, TJ had just kept on crying.

Joan turned to Nils Henrik and asked him if they could have another word in private. They went back to the same waiting room they had used earlier that morning.

Lt. Blake explained to him in detail what they thought had happened the night before. However, there were still many pieces of the puzzle that were not yet in place.

Nils Henrik had asked him about his wife and Albert, enquiring whether they knew anything else about what might have happened to them, but the police had nothing more to add.

Lt. Blake had asked Nils Henrik if he knew anyone who hated him enough to do something like this to his family. Nils Henrik

remembered the threat that John had given him, but he didn't mention it. He wasn't sure how much Lt. Blake knew about the collapse in Edmonton, or if he knew that Nils Henrik himself was the prime suspect in that case. He just shook his head and said no.

Lt. Blake contented himself with this answer, but he made Nils Henrik promise to let him know if anyone came to his mind later. They were about to leave the waiting room when Nils Henrik said, "There are a few things I have to do first, but after that I will come out to the scene of the fire, if that is OK."

Lt. Blake said, "Yes, absolutely. There might be things we can talk about while we are out there too."

The conversation was over, and they said goodbye to each other again. Nils Henrik went back to TJ's room to check on her. She was asleep again.

He used the opportunity to go to the nurses' station and ask if there was a telephone he could use. The nurses pointed to a telephone booth. He went over to it and walked inside. He dialled the number.

That was a very difficult telephone call to make. He could still remember it word for word.

The party on the other end picked up the phone.

Nils Henrik heard it and said, "Hi, this is me, Nils."

"Oh, hello," was the answer. "How are you, and also where are you?" "I am not very good," he answered.

"Oh, why is that?"

He began to tell everything that had happened on the previous night and that morning.

The person at the other end listened quietly to the whole thing. When Nils Henrik was finished, the other person asked, "And now what?"

Nils Henrik said, "Well, I don't really know, but I certainly could use some help from you."

"OK, what can I do?"

"Would you be able to come to Jasper hospital and stay with TJ for a while? There are a few things I need to do," he answered. "Of course. I can be there in two to two and a half hours."

"That would be good," said Nils Henrik. "We can talk some more when you get here."

"OK, see you soon," the other party answered.

They hung up.

Nils Henrik's thoughts went to the person he had talked to on the telephone that evening.

The voice belonged to TJ's grandfather Curley Fox, a Yuma Indian, and the son of a chief. It was said that he was a direct relative of the famous Crowfoot Siksika, the chief of the Blackfoot tribe, otherwise called "the First Nation Peoples" in Alberta. It was he who had signed the important treaty with the Canadian government at the end of the 1800s. But Curley Fox himself denied the relationship when asked about it.

Curley Fox, the father of Nils Henrik's wife, was a full-blooded Blackfoot Indian. He was often called Jimmy.

Nils Henrik and his wife were not married in the eyes of Canadian law, but they had gone through the spiritual ritual the First Nations used as a wedding ceremony and were therefore married in their own eyes.

He thought about how they had met each other. It was the last year they were up in the Yukon Territory. He had met her because of her younger brother. Nils Henrik and OJ were down in Dawson City to get supplies when they stumbled over an Indian who was lying dead drunk in the street. They stopped and tried to help him up and out of the street. Then before they knew it, a woman came up to them and introduced herself as his sister; she said that she would take care of him.

Nils Henrik saw her again the next day. She was sitting on a packing crate in a side street crying. He had gone over and spoken to her. He asked if there was anything that he could do for her. She had just looked at him for a few moments and then shook her head. He had introduced himself to her before asking her, "What is your name?" She looked at him for a long time before she answered. "Why do you want to know?"

He answered, "Because I like to know the names of my friends." She said, "Are you sure that you want to be friends with me? You are white, and I am an Indian."

"Yes," he had answered.

So, she said very hesitantly, "My name is Sisiska." "Why are you sitting here and crying?"

She looked at him again. He could see that she was trying to say something but couldn't say it.

Nils Henrik asked, "Is it your brother?" She nodded. "Is there anything I can do for either of you?"

"Thank you anyway, but no," she answered. Then she ran away.

They had just settled their bill after eating dinner at Judith's Diner and were now going through the exit door. They were heading for the Armpit Bar. Maybe Sluice Box Harry was there. Of course, he would be there; he was always there. All over sudden, there she was again, standing just in front of them. Nils Henrik had told OJ about meeting her earlier in the day, but he didn't say anything to him about how much he cared for her. Now she was standing there right in front of him again. She just stood there and looked at Nils Henrik. OJ kept walking towards the bar.

"Can I help you?" Nils Henrik asked. "Maybe," she said very quietly.

He waited for her to tell him what she wanted. He could see she was trying, but she didn't manage to say anything.

"You have to tell me what it is that I can help you with. Do you need money?"

She had answered no to that before she began to tell him about her brother. She said that he had come to Dawson City to try to find a job but had fallen in with bad company. Now she was asking Nils Henrik if he would help her brother find a job. She knew that they were miners and thought that it would be good for her brother to get out of Dawson.

Nils Henrik asked her what her brother's name was. "Silver Fox," she answered. "But everyone calls him Jim."

He asked her for some time to think about it. They agreed to meet again in the morning. She nodded quickly and disappeared again.

Jimmy Curley Fox arrived at the Jasper hospital about 7.10 p.m. He had his wife Peta (Golden Eagle) with him. They went directly up to TJ's room. TJ was very glad to see them. Her grandmother went right over to the girl and gave her a big hug.

Jimmy went over to Nils Henrik, and they went out in the corridor. He asked what had happened, and Nils Henrik tried his best to explain it all. Jimmy listened quietly until Nils Henrik was done telling the terrible story. Then he said to him, "Go, my son. We will stay here and take care of TJ. You need to go and find out who is behind this."

Nils Henrik took a taxi out to the site of the burned cabin. He had driven to the hospital with Lt. Blake the night before, so his car was still parked out there. The police had cordoned off the whole area, so he was stopped when he tried to go through the police line. Lt. Blake saw it and went over to tell the constable that he was allowed in.

Once Nils Henrik entered the area, he asked Lt. Blake if he had found out anything more.

"Well, as you can see, we are still conducting the investigation. We have found something more, but nothing that can give us the answers we wish."

"What about my wife and my son?"

"Nothing so far. We are still going through the ruins now." Nils Henrik asked, "Can I help?"

"No," the lieutenant answered. "These people here are professionals and know exactly what they are looking for and what they have to do to find it."

"I know," Nils Henrik said.

"But what you can do to help is to tell us when the cabin was built and how the various rooms were placed."

Nils Henrik made a floor plan for him. The first floor was made up of the living room and dining room, which were connected to the kitchen; the master suite with a walk-in closet and a bathroom; and the entrance with a pantry. The second floor had two bedrooms plus a family room. There was no basement.

He drew up the floor plan, including the garage and woodshed. There was a gravel driveway wide enough for cars to approach right up to the cabin.

Forty metres further, down towards the lake, there was a dock with a small boathouse on the inner end.

Nils Henrik felt so unbelievably tired and sad that he could no longer hold back his tears.

He must have fallen asleep for a little while.

"Mister Ellefsrud, Mister Ellefsrud, are you awake?" Joan had come over to the bench.

"Yes," he answered.

"Will you please come with me?" Joan asked.

Nils Henrik followed her over to Lt. Blake, who was walking towards them.

"Mister Ellefsrud," he said, "we have just discovered a corpse. It appears to be an adult woman, but it is difficult to tell for sure because of it being very badly burned.

"Do you have any idea what kind of clothes your wife would have been wearing yesterday?"

"No. She dressed like any other woman. Usually out here at the cabin she wore jeans. She only wore her Indian clothes when she was going out to visit at the reservation."

"The reservation?" Lt. Blake asked.

Nils Henrik explained that his wife was a member of the First Nations, saying that she was a Sisiska and the daughter of Curley Fox. "I know who that is," said Lt. Blake. "Can you tell me about any distinguishing clothing or jewellery she might have been wearing?" He answered, "She always wore an amulet around her neck, a carving of a hand with the palm engraved with a picture. The picture was a symbol of the relationship between the sun and the moon. It was carved out of bone."

Lt. Blake had looked at Joan before he spoke again. He looked at Nils Henrik and asked, "Is this the one?"

Then he held up an amulet in his hand. The amulet was just like the one Nils Henrik had just described.

That was too much for Nils Henrik. He could no longer feel the legs beneath him.

It was the amulet that belonged to Sisiska which Lt. Blake had held out. Joan held on to Nils Henrik as she helped him up off the ground. He started to scream out loud and began crying again. She let him cry without saying anything.

He asked if he could see his wife.

"I think you better not right now. It's not a very pretty sight." "I want to see her right now," he said.

Lt. Blake looked over to Joan before he answered.

"OK, we have to go over to that van over there, which is the coroner's van. The remains are there."

Lt. Blake personally opened up the back door and pulled out the stretcher for Nils Henrik.

Nils Henrik's thoughts went back to the moment after they had found

Sisiska. So many things had happened in his life since that time. He believed that the day before when he got the news of the fire and saw what condition TJ was in was the worst day of his life, but he was wrong. This day was much worse. It was the most terrible and macabre sight he had ever seen. The only thing he could recognize about his wife was the moccasin she had on one of her feet. His senses were so traumatized that he had to be sent to the hospital in order to be sedated. They wanted to admit him, but during the time he had been there, he had calmed down sufficiently, so they just gave him a prescription and let him go.

He remembered the next thing he did. He made a trip to the liquor store, where he had bought three bottles of whisky. Then he found a cheap motel and hid himself where he thought nobody could find him.

It was Jimmy, Curley Fox, who found Nils Henrik. He knew that something was wrong when he didn't return to the hospital and to TJ. He had contacted the police, who told him that Nils Henrik had been taken to the hospital for observation. They added that he had gone into a shock shortly after being told about Sisiska and moments later identifying her body.

After that nobody had any information about Nils Henrik. His car was still out at the crime scene, so Jimmy began a systematic check of all the hotels and motels in the vicinity of the hospital. He finally found his son-in-law at the Red Roof Inn. He was a complete mess.

Jimmy brought Nils Henrik some food, but he wouldn't eat it. It was then that Jimmy showed his inner strength, as he changed from a friend and father-in-law to the truly important chief that he was. He used Nils Henrik's Indian name which he had received during his wedding ceremony to Sisiska.

"White Eagle, you have a responsibility. Come with me." He said it in English because Nils Henrik had not yet fully learned the language of the tribe.

Jimmy's authoritarian speech enabled Nils Henrik to pull himself together. He woke up and realized that the world was still turning and would go on. Jimmy chose not to tell his son-in-law that they had found a second corpse, and that this one was the body of a child. It was impossible to identify, but obviously since Albert was the only other person missing, and since the boy was presumed to have been with Sisiska at the time, they had a strong suspicion that it was him. No other corpses were found in the burned cabin.

Canada

27 August 2005

The mirror was completely covered with steam, so she couldn't see anything in it. She used a hand towel to wipe it off. She stood looking at her reflection and examining herself critically.

She was still in good shape in spite of her forty-nine years. She looked at her breasts. They were still firm, but maybe not quite as firm as they used to be. They weren't too big or too small either, though there was a period of time when she thought they were too small, but that was a long time ago. She had lately become totally satisfied with them and had let it rest there.

She wondered if she should do a bikini shave. She looked at her body again in the mirror and concentrated on her pubic hair. She had a lot of it but had always kept it well-trimmed. She made the decision: not today. She was still presentable in that department, and she had no plans of showing herself naked to anyone, so it was not that important.

As a matter of fact, she never showed herself naked to anyone. Suddenly she felt terribly lonely. She hadn't heard anything from Asha (Hope) for a few days either. It had been almost a week since they had spoken on the telephone. Even though Asha was now a fully grown woman, they still communicated with each other regularly during the course of a week. This week had been a little different.

Asha had telephoned and said that she would be going on an excursion for about two weeks with some friends. They were planning to go up to Glacier Creek Indian Reservation and there was no cellular phone service up there.

She began to dry herself. As she did this, she began to feel a bit warm. She began thinking about sex. She had never been able to get over the terrible experience that had happened to her as a child, and therefore she never really had any sex life with anyone but herself.

The first time she really experienced what sex was when she was down in Mexico. She was thirty-seven years old at the time and had taken a few days off to go to Acapulco. In the afternoon during the siesta time, she had taken a long walk along the beach. The sky had turned blood red as the sun descended below the horizon. It was truly a beautiful sunset that gave her a wonderful feeling of contentment. She took off her shoes and went into the water. It felt so warm and relaxing. As she walked back to her hotel, she began to think a little about what she would do later in the evening.

She passed a young couple who were wholly absorbed with each other, lying in the warm sand. She smiled and was just about to say to herself that she envied them when a voice broke into her thoughts. "*Buenas tardes.* May I walk together with you?"

She jumped at the sound of this voice because she had believed herself to be alone. She looked at the man who had spoken to her, and answered, "I can't very well forbid you to walk with me, since the beach is a public place."

The man put out his hand and said, "Neal. Neal Bond." TJ smiled. "Are you sure you don't mean James Bond?"

"If that is what you would like my name to be, then that's what it is," he answered.

She took his hand and said, "TJ."

He hesitated at her name for a moment but then let it go.

"Beautiful evening," he said.

TJ nodded but didn't answer him. "Have you been here long?" he asked.

"I have been here for four days, and this is the first time that I have seen you here. I usually walk along this beach every afternoon and early evening."

"I arrived late last night," she said. "Well then that's why," he said. "I'm from Atlanta," said Neal.

Again, TJ didn't answer him. She tried to seem as uninterested as possible in him, but in reality, she thought that he really was quite a handsome man. He was tall with a finely tuned body. Maybe she should have let him know that she was interested in him. This thought had barely entered her mind when he asked her if she would like to join him for a drink. He pointed to the cantina they were just passing. She may have answered a little too quickly. "Yes, please."

They came in off the beach and sat at a table. Neal ordered two Coronas. The server arrived with them right away. He also gave them some nachos and salsa to go with the beer.

Neal lifted his bottle in a toast, as he was not given a glass. TJ did the same. Besides Neal and TJ, there were two other couples enjoying the cantina.

They were talking about all kinds of things, until a mariachi band came in and began to play.

"Do you like mariachi?"

TJ said, "I don't know. I don't know what it is."

"What it is, is Mexico's own unique music," said Neal. He waved the band leader over to their table and began to speak to Spanish. The band began playing "Bésame Mucho".

Neal spoke fluent Spanish. He ordered two more Coronas and two tequilas to go with them.

TJ said that she was not at all sure about drinking any tequila. He assured her that it was no problem, she didn't have to drink it, but she was tempted to take a small sip. They sat there in silence for a while. She had a wonderful feeling in her whole body, and before she was aware of it, she found herself in Neal's hotel room. She felt like she was glowing and was not sure whether it was the tequila or just her own nervousness. She also felt a strange feeling in her body which she was unused to and didn't know how to explain.

After they had entered the room, he turned her around and kissed her. She felt that the whole room was turning. She was weak in the knees and just let her feelings go wild, not thinking too much about the situation. She had no idea how it all happened, only that this was the first time she was completely enjoying everything that was happening to her and living in the moment.

They made love the whole night, and when the next morning came, she had no regrets or doubts.

The next two days would prove to be the most intense time of her life. She and Neal didn't leave each other's side. They ate together, slept together, and made love together. It was a time in her life that had really made an impact on her. She knew that it was going to end there in Mexico.

That was almost seventeen years ago now, TJ remembered. Every time she thought of that interlude, she became warm. This time was no different. She went naked over to her bed and lay down on it.

TJ had received the letter from Nils Henrik today. She was very surprised since she had only received two letters per year from him over the last six or seven years. One would come at Christmas, and the other on her birthday, 28 May. She had received a letter this year as well, but this one was written by hand. In that particular letter he had not written anything more than a birthday wish. The handwriting was very shaky and uncertain, and he had apologized, simply saying that the reason was that he was getting old. She felt sad about that, but when she mentioned it to Robert, she was told that Nils Henrik had had a bout of influenza and therefore was not in his usual form since he was still recovering.

Today she opened the letter and she read:

My Dear TJ,

This is the last letter you will receive from me. When you receive it, I am no longer. I have been sick for some time now, and I feel guilty for not telling you about it before. But I did not want you and Asha to be sad or to mourn for me. There was absolutely nothing either of you could have done anyway. I have caused enough problems for you both over the years. I wish things could have been different.

I have endured great pain inside of me ever since the day it happened, and not a day has gone by that I did not think about you or both of you. August 15 and 16, 1965, still stand as the worst days of my life.

The happenings of June 1971 did not make anything any better, but now I am at rest finally. You must know that I wish both you and Asha all the best for the future. Robert will be contacting you very soon. He will explain and clarify what will happen to you both in the future.

I hope that you can find it in your heart to forgive me.

Good night, my dear. I love you both very much.

CHAPTER 5

New York

11 June 1946

The first three hotels they stopped at didn't have any vacancies, but at the fourth, Berit's Boarding House, they found a place. It was on 12th Street and Broadway and was run by Berit and her husband, Peter Holm. They had to ring the bell several times since it was about 2 a.m. and the boarding house was closed for the night. There was a note on the door, "Kindly ring the bell." Later, Berit had told them that they were hoping for some new immigrants to come and stay that night, since the *Stavangerfjord* was arriving for the first time since the war.

Berit was from Rauland, in Telemark, and Peter was from Flekkefjord, both in Norway. They had immigrated to the United States back in 1925, and it appeared that they had done well for themselves. Either that or they had just been lucky. They had not always been so. When they first came to New York, it was only a few years until the Great Depression happened, and they, along with almost everyone else, had fallen on hard times. Luckily after a few more years, the times got better and they were able to make a go of it.

They had met each other while they were both so poor that they had to make use of a soup kitchen on 42nd Street and Fifth Avenue in Brooklyn just to survive. They had found a place to stay in a flophouse occupied by homeless immigrants, with Peter in one place and Berit in another. Both of their beginnings were equally dismal. Peter had been lucky one day to get a job in a factory, but it was only for a single day. Afterwards it might take days or even weeks before he would be able to work again. At that moment when they met, he didn't have more than a few pennies in his pocket, but he had decided to try to buy a loaf of bread. He hadn't had any bread for three weeks. On the street outside the bakery, his eye was caught by the sight of a young woman crying.

"What are you crying for?" he asked.

"I am hungry, but I don't have any money to buy food," she answered.

Peter felt sorry for her and said, "Here, you can have some bread from me." He showed her the loaf he had just bought.

That was in the fall of 1930. They got married later that same year. Now they owned a boarding house together. They had three children who had just started school but who helped with the work when they had time off. Besides working in the boarding house, Peter had a job as a carpenter.

Berit's Boarding House was often the first place that new immigrants stopped at or stayed in, particularly Scandinavians. Peter liked to take charge of the new arrivals as they came through. He often gave them help and advice about where to find a job. There were several firms in the area that sent him messages when they were in need of workers.

This day was no different. He sat down together with the three new hopefuls and told them who was looking for people to hire and where those companies were located. Nils Henrik and Kjartan would head up to Queens, so they received information about whom to contact when they got there. Arne was going out to Long Island, so Peter gave him some addresses of people out there who might be able to help him.

When Nils Henrik and Kjartan said goodbye to each other at the subway station in Queens, they promised to keep in touch. Now Nils Henrik started to look to make his way to his mother's sister's place. He had asked several passers-by for directions, but there were not many people who would answer his enquiries. He was sent in the wrong direction several times. By the time he finally found the address, 89-09 133rd Street, Richmond Hill, he found that it was a typical subdivision housing project, five stories high. All housing was built at this height according to a regulation stating that buildings higher than five stories needed to have an elevator installed.

It was almost 5.30 p.m. Nils Henrik was completely worn out. He had not travelled particularly light either; his backpack was heavy, and he carried a medium-sized suitcase as well.

It was his mother's sister Arnhild herself who opened the door to Nils Henrik's knock. She lit up like the sun when she saw him. "Nils Henrik, you're all grown up! When did you arrive?"

"Yesterday afternoon, but it took us the whole evening to come through immigration. Then it was so late that we took a room at Berit's Boarding House."

"Oh yes, I know them. Well, you must be very hungry then. Come in and sit down."

"I have a little space to fill," he said. He smiled and patted his stomach while he walked in after her.

"In one hour, Frank will be home and we will have dinner," she said. "Meanwhile, here's an apple to tide you over," she said, as she passed him a fruit bowl. "Take two if you like."

Nils Henrik gave his thanks. She said to him, "You must tell me how your trip was and also how everybody is back home. But you can do that later. Your mother wrote me to let me know you were coming. She asked if you could stay here until you found a job and got established. Did you receive my answer?"

"No," said Nils Henrik. "We had not yet gotten a letter before I left, and that was over a month ago."

"Well, the answer is yes, you can stay as long as you need to. The space might be a little tight, but we will make do. Go ahead into the living room and relax for an hour until dinner is ready, OK? I'll be in the kitchen if you need anything," she said. Then she left the room.

Nils Henrik awoke to someone calling his name. He had no sooner sat down in a comfortable chair than he had fallen asleep. The apple he'd had in his hand was lying on the floor. "Time to eat." It was his aunt Arnhild again. She stood in the doorway and called him.

"If you like, you can use the bathroom out in the hallway to freshen up before dinner," she said.

"Yes, I would like that," said Nils Henrik. "Don't take too long. We're waiting for you." Nils Henrik hurried out into the hallway.

When he came into the dining room, everyone was seated at the table waiting for him.

Arnhild got up from her place and went to stand next to him to make the introductions.

"This is Nils Henrik Ellefsrud, Borghild's son. He has just arrived from Norway and will stay here with us for the time being." She looked at him and said, "He is my family."

She continued the introductions. "The man sitting at the end of the table is my husband, Frank." Then she pointed towards the youngsters. "This is Egil. He is eight years old and going to junior high. This is Reidun and Johanna. They are twins, which you might be able to see, and they are going to be twelve years old soon."

Nils Henrik went around and the table and shook hands with everyone. Then he sat shown down in the empty seat at the table.

Nils Henrik's aunt Arnhild was considerably younger than his mother.

She had immigrated to America in the summer of 1932. Her aunt on her father's side had been home to Norway that summer and had taken Arnhild back to America with her. Arnhild's first job had been as a serving girl for the family of Fredrick William Vanderbilt in their mansion on the Hudson River. It was through her aunt's housekeeper that she was able to secure that job.

The Vanderbilt family was one of the richest families in the country, and maybe even the world, at that point in time, but when the Great Depression came, they suffered huge losses. The patriarch of the family, Cornelius Vanderbilt, had made his fortune first in shipping and then in railroads. When he died in 1877, his estate was worth more than one hundred million dollars, which was an astronomical sum of money at that time.

It was while Arnhild was working for the Vanderbilts that she met Frank. They married a short two months later. Frank had worked as a handyman for the family, but he was now employed by a building contractor by the name of Roar Knudsen.

Roar Knudsen was an immigrant from Norway who had done very well for himself in the building trades.

The conversation around the table that first night focused mainly on how things were going back in the fatherland after the end of the war. The conversation was mostly done in Norwegian, but occasionally it turned back to English, especially when one of the younger ones was speaking. The children were very interested in hearing about their grandparents back in Norway, since they had never met them.

After dinner, and once the children had gone off to bed, Arnhild, Frank, and Nils Henrik sat and talked some more. The conversation slowly shifted to Nils Henrik and his plan to find a job. He told them that Peter Holm had given him some names of businesses that needed workers. Then he took out the list and showed it to Frank.

"I know both of these places, and they are good places to work, but if you want to, you could come with me in the morning and I will introduce you to Roar Knudsen. Let's see what he has to say first. I have heard that he is also looking for workers."

"OK," said Nils Henrik. "What time in the morning will we be going?"

"We have to leave here by 7.15."

"I'll be up in time to go with you. But now I need to get some sleep. It's been two long and eventful days, and I'm longing to get to bed." "Everything is ready for you. You will share a room with Egil. He has the top bunk. You can have the lower one."

Nils Henrik thanked them again, and said, "I'll try my best to get a place of my own as soon as possible."

"No need to worry about that right now," said Arnhild. "You are welcome to stay here for as long as you need or want to."

"I agree. Everything will work out just fine," said Frank. Arnhild showed him the way to Egil's room.

Nils Henrik woke up at 5 a.m. He just couldn't sleep any longer even though he had spent a restless night. So many thoughts and ideas were running through his mind that he had to get up and go into the living room. He sat down by the window and gazed out at the view of 133rd Street, Richmond Hill, in Queens. If he looked up, over and behind the building in front, then he could see the skyscrapers of Manhattan. They were all lit up. It was pretty, but different from what he was used to at home. Still, even that couldn't stop the flow of thoughts from racing through his head.

Arnhild got up around 6 a.m. "Did you sleep well?" she asked. "Well, not really. I have too many thoughts in my head."

"I understand," she said. "Would you like some breakfast?" "Yes, please."

Frank came in and poured himself a cup of coffee right away. He needed a little more time than Arnhild to wake up. The coffee was very welcome to help him. Arnhild put out some bread, cheese, and cold cuts on the table and started making a lunch packet for Frank. "Would you like me to pack you a lunch too, Nils Henrik?"

"Yes," said Frank. "Make him a lunch in case he gets a job and needs to start right away."

"Do you have any work clothes?" he asked Nils Henrik. "No."

"OK, then you can borrow some from me. They will be a little large for you, but they should do the job."

He left the kitchen and came back with work pants, a shirt, and a light jacket. "Here, try these on."

Nils Henrik went back to Egil's room and put on the clothes. They weren't too bad of a fit. He went back to the kitchen. "They look all right," said Arnhild.

"Yes, they do, so if you are ready, let's get going," said Frank.

The construction site where Frank was currently working was in Harlem, and they had to take the subway to get there. It wasn't a long trip; in ten minutes they had arrived. They went in through the gate and directly over to a trailer where the time clock was located.

Everyone who wanted to come onto the site had to pass through this way before entering their respective workplaces. Frank went over to a shelf on the wall, took out a card, and slid it into a machine that Nils Henrik had never seen before. The machine made a stamping noise. Then Frank took out the card and put it on another shelf. He knew that Nils Henrik didn't know what he had just done, so he explained that the card was a time card and the machine was run by a clock which punched the correct time onto the card. That way it measured exactly when each employee arrived at and left the workplace, to make the payroll more accurate.

Then Frank took him over to introduce him to Roar Knudsen. He had his office in another trailer further in to the construction site. Frank knocked on the door.

"Come in." Frank grasped the door handle and opened the door. "Good morning," he said.

"Good morning, Frank. How can I help you?" Roar Knudsen answered.

"Not me, but maybe you can help him." He pointed to Nils Henrik. "He has just arrived from Norway and is looking for work." "What's his name?"

"His name is Nils Henrik Ellefsrud, and he is the son of my wife's older sister."

Roar Knudsen came over to Nils Henrik and shook hands. "How old are you?"

"I'll be eighteen on the twenty-second of September," Nils Henrik answered.

Roar Knudsen kept on talking. "Well, we all were eighteen once. Well, what kind of experience do you have?"

"I have to be honest: I don't know how to do much. But whatever I set my hand to usually turns out all right. Unfortunately, there were very few opportunities for anyone to find work during the war," Nils Henrik answered.

"Well, I am sure that is true," said Roar.

"But I do have this," said Nils Henrik, who reached into his pocket and took out the reference he had gotten from the steward on the SS *Stavanger-fjord*. He had been given it right before he landed in New York.

Roar read it and said, "This is a good reference," looking over at Frank.

"I need people in the floor-laying department. Do you think you would want to work in that?" he asked Nils Henrik.

"Yes, of course," he said.

"You will be paid seventy-five cents per hour. The workday is 8 a.m. to 6 p.m. six days a week, with a half-hour lunch break each day. Can you do that?"

"Yes, I can."

Roar put forward his hand. The two men shook on it. "When can you begin?"

"How about right now?" answered Nils Henrik.

"All right, why not?" said Roar. He went over to his desk, which was piled up with papers, and started to look for what Nils Henrik thought could be a small ledger/address book. Then he picked up the telephone and dialled a number.

"Hi, John, I have a new guy here for you. I'll send him over with José, OK?"

He hung up the phone.

"Well," said Frank, "I'd better get to work." He shook hands with Nils Henrik, thanked Roar, and left.

Roar got up and took Nils Henrik out of the trailer. When he was out in the parking lot, he whistled loudly. A car pulled up. "Can you take this boy over to John?"

"Sure, boss," the chauffer answered.

Roar turned to Nils Henrik and put out his hand once more. They shook. He said, "Welcome aboard." And then he went back in to his desk.

Roar Knudsen was the sole owner of Knudsen's Construction Inc. He was born in the United States of a Norwegian mother and a Danish father from whom his last name came. He had been in the building business all his adult life, first working for several different companies before he started his own company in mid-1930. Coming from Scandinavian parents, he had the characteristic Caucasian look, blond hair—or it used to be—blue eyes, and a rather husky physique. Of course, now at the age of fifty-one, his body had started to slow, but he was still a strong individual.

Even though he did employ workers from everywhere, his was one of the companies at which young immigrants could easily find work when entering the promised land.

John was waiting for Nils Henrik outside a large building which was in the process of being finished. The building's façade was clean and new, with freshly painted window and door frames.

"Hello," he said. "Are you Nils Henrik?" "Yes I am."

"I'm John, your foreman. What can you tell me about yourself? Have you ever done flooring?"

"No."

"OK, I'll put you up with someone you can work and communicate with. His name is Harry Hansen, and he has a lot of experience in this department. I would like you to please pay close attention to what he teaches you. Then it won't be long until you get the hang of it. Harry is a very good teacher."

They entered the building and went up two floors. John called Harry. "Yes!" came an answer from one of the rooms nearby.

"I have a new man for you." Everything was quiet for a moment, and then a head looked out from door number five. He just looked at John and Nils Henrik.

"This is Nils Henrik Ellefsrud. Can you take charge of him for me?" Harry still didn't answer. He just stood and looked at the two of them. Harry had been with Roar since he'd started his company; however, he was going to return home to Norway the next summer.

"Are you related to Oscar Hoffman Ellefsrud?" Harry asked, at last answering John.

Nils Henrik was startled. Then he answered, "Yes, that's my father." "How is he?" Harry asked.

"He's fine. He works for a mining company in Kongsberg now." "We moved to a small farm up near the river, a little north of Kongsberg." Nils Henrik didn't know what else to say for a moment. "How do you know him?" he added.

"We went to school together," Harry answered.

"School? You mean the school in Skien?" Nils Henrik asked. "Yes. We went there together back during that time, but then my father went to America. Three years later we followed him, my mother, my sister, and I. We've been here ever since," Harry answered.

"It certainly is a small world," Nils Henrik said. "Did you come over alone?" Harry asked.

"Yes, I did."

"Well, then the first thing I would like to do is welcome you. Then I will see to it that we make a good floor layer out of you."

That evening at the dinner table, Nils Henrik had a lot of positive things to tell his aunt and uncle. He felt that he was off to a very good start with his immigration to America. All the things that he had done so far in his young life were nothing special, and he had not been particularly ambitious to learn a trade, partly because of the occupation and war. Now, however, he was determined to learn everything he could and move ahead in life. This would be quite easy for him, as he was very observant and had a gift of learning languages easily. English came to him very quickly.

He made some new friends in a very short time, and it wasn't long before he was able to move out of his aunt and uncle's house and into his own apartment with a colleague from work, OJ. This took him only two months to accomplish.

He was, of course, very grateful to his aunt and uncle for the start that they had given him, but the time was ripe for him to move on. It also didn't take long for Roar Knudsen to give him a raise, and now he was already making $1 per hour, which was a very good salary.

After he had been with Roar Knudsen for about one and a half years, Nils Henrik became painfully aware of criminal activities going on inside Roar's company.

Nils Henrik had been at work all morning, and now he was taking a break to use the bathroom. While he was there, he heard two men whispering together. He didn't know where the voices were coming from at first, but then he realized that he could hear them talking through a water pipe, which transported the voices like a telephone line. The pipe came from a room above and next door to him. There was a hand-wash station there. Despite the fact that the men were speaking very quietly, Nils Henrik had no problem hearing what they said. The ones who were up there did not knew that Nils Henrik could hear their conversation. At first, he tried not to listen, but the voices came through loud enough that he couldn't help but hear everything they were talking about.

He learned fast and without a doubt that he was a witness to a conspiracy, an attempt to sabotage and gain control of Roar Knudsen's construction company.

As soon as he realized that, he hurried out of the bathroom and quickly went to the main building. He hid himself around the corner and waited for the two men to come out of the building so he could identify them. He pretended to be busy moving some materials so he would remain anonymous. It wasn't long before two men came out and down the steps. He knew one of them, the foreman of block 4B, but he had never seen the other man before. Block 4B was in the final stages of being finished.

Nils Henrik was uncertain about what he should do with the information he had received. He thought about it for almost two days before he went to Frank. He knew the place where Frank usually sat and had his lunch. He went over there to see him.

"Frank, I have something I need to talk to you about." "OK," said Frank.

"Let's go and sit over there," Nils Henrik, pointing towards a place about 30 metres away. They both sat down on a pallet before Frank asked, "OK, what is it you need to talk about?"

Then Nils Henrik told Frank what he had heard, but he didn't give him any names. He wanted to sit on that information until he heard how Frank would react to the news. Frank sat very quietly. Nils Henrik asked him, "What shall I do?" He could see that his uncle was deep in thought.

"Nils, this is very dangerous information. You have to be extremely careful with it. Don't tell anyone. But you must inform Roar of it." "How do I do that?"

"I don't know any more than you do, but tomorrow I'll go and talk to him. I'll ask him to have a meeting with you. Then I will suggest having this meeting outside of this area. I think it would be too dangerous to meet here. I'll contact you as soon as I have set up the meeting with him. The message that I will give you is that Aunt Arnhild wants you to come over for dinner on the day he will meet you. Then we take it from there. I'll let you know more after I have spoken to him."

Nils Henrik agreed.

Two days later at 7 p.m., Frank and Nils Henrik walked in to Joe's Restaurant on 97th Street and Amsterdam Avenue. It was far enough away from both Frank's and Nils Henrik's apartments that it would not arouse any suspicion. They were quite confident that nobody they knew would go there and notice them. They had taken the subway to the restaurant together.

Roar was going to meet them in about half an hour.

They sat down in the bar and ordered a beer. When Roar suddenly turned up, they all played a little charade as if the meeting were unexpected. Roar took Frank by the shoulder and said, "What are you two doing here?"

"Yeah, well, we decided to have a boys' night out and have some drinks and dinner. It's a pretty good place to eat. Have you had dinner already?" Frank asked.

"No, not yet."

"Do you mind joining us?" Frank asked. "Not at all!" The play continued.

"Shall we get a table then?" Frank spoke again. "Sure, why not?"

Frank spoke to the bartender and asked for a table a little bit away from everybody else. He held a dollar bill between his fingers as he asked. The bartender said he would try. Then he took the dollar and went over to the head waiter.

The three men sat for a while and talked about everything under the sun until a young pretty girl came over to them. "Your table is ready. Will you follow me?" As she said that, she picked up their beers, put them on her tray, and took them along to the table which had been set up for them.

"Thank you." It was Roar who spoke now.

They sat down and continued with their beers. They received menus and began to read them.

"Have you ever eaten here before?" Frank asked Roar. "Yes, a couple of times. The food is pretty good." "Can you recommend anything?"

"Well, before you go any further, dinner is on me, so don't look at any of the prices. And as to what I recommend," he said, looking at Nils Henrik, "have you ever had a really good steak before? I'm sure you've had beef, but I'm talking about an excellent beefsteak. They have the best here. Or if you want something else, try their liver and bacon, which is also very good."

"I'm going to try that beefsteak you recommended," said Nils Henrik.

Frank chose the same.

During the meal there was not much in the way of conversation. What was said took place mainly between Roar and Nils Henrik. Roar had heard that Harry Hanson and Nils Henrik's father had gone to school together back in Norway and thought also that the world was a smaller place than it seemed.

After they had pretty much finished the meal, the conversation steered its way to what Nils Henrik had heard. They spoke Norwegian while discussing this. Nils Henrik was very nervous, but he knew that the information had to be given to Roar so he could act on it.

Roar began by saying, "I understand that it is likely very unpleasant for you to have to give this information to me, but as you know, there are some situations in life when you must do things that you don't want to do. I promise you that no matter what happens, I will never let anyone know who gave the information to me. What takes place here in this restaurant is between only the three of us and will never go any further."

Roar nodded at Nils Henrik, and the latter nodded back. "So, what is it that you have heard?"

At that moment the waitress came back with their dessert and coffee and put it down on the table. As soon as she was out of earshot,

Nils Henrik began to talk of what he had heard while he was in the bathroom.

"I went to the bathroom about 9.15 a.m., and while I was in there I heard voices. At first, I had no idea where they were coming from, but after a while I realized that the voices were travelling through the pipe from upstairs. The first voice asked, 'Is everything ready?' The second voice answered, 'Yes, we will do it just as planned and like you said we should. The action will start at 10.30 Friday morning on the eleventh of September. I have put everything together that I need to start the fire. We will have all the heavy machinery placed in front of the entrance, so the fire trucks will not be able to get in. By that time the building will have its certificate of occupancy and therefore should be empty of any workers. We already have agreed that nobody will get hurt or killed.'

"'Yes, that's correct,' the first voice said. 'It will be your responsibility to see that the building is empty. Can you absolutely guarantee that it will take place exactly as you now say?'"

"'Yes,' replied the second voice.

"'OK then, proceed with your plans,' came the first voice. "'What about my money and guarantees?'

"The first voice answered, 'I'll come back here with half of the money, twenty-five thousand dollars, on the ninth, two days before. You will get the rest after it is done.'

"'OK, but what happens afterward?' the second voice asked. "'You don't need to worry about that,' the first voice replied.

"'OK, but I want it in writing that I will be promoted and will receive the position of construction leader in any future projects you will receive after you take control of this firm. And the agreement is also that I will receive 5 per cent of the stock in the company.'

"'Yes, you'll get that too when I come back on the ninth,' the first voice said."

Nils Henrik continued, "That was the last thing I heard. I hurried as fast as I could over to the other building and made myself busy. That way I could see whom these to voices belonged to without them knowing what I'd heard."

"Who was it?"

"I only know who one of them was. It was, Roberto, the foreman of block 4B. I don't know his last name."

Roar sat completely still for a few moments while he continued to look at Nils Henrik. Then he said, "Roberto Gonzales.

"Nils Henrik, I can never thank you enough for this information. This is very serious. I can't say for sure who is behind it, but it seems like it's the Mafia. Neither of you should give this another thought. It's my turn to take over. Please promise me to be extremely careful and never, ever speak about it to anyone. Promise me that right now." He looked at both and they nodded their agreement.

They sat in complete silence around the table.

Then Roar said, "I better get out of here. As soon as I pay the bill, I'm going to go. You two wait awhile before you leave." He nodded at them both, and neither said anything at all. They fully understood the gravity of the situation.

Roar received and paid the bill, thanked the two men once again, and reminded them how dangerous it would be for them if they discussed the matter with anybody else. And he added that the best thing would be for them to forget it completely.

Frank and Nils Henrik waited for about fifteen minutes before they left the restaurant. They walked directly to the subway station. They didn't speak at all on the trip home. They just said goodnight to each other back at the station before they each headed home.

Oslo, Norway
8 September 2005

Conrad's office—meeting with the investigator

Henrik and Conrad sat and waited for Private Investigator Ole G. Olsen. After they had gone through all the items and papers in the safe deposit box and discussed it thoroughly with Aase and Roald, Conrad had called Ole G. Olsen's office and spoken to his secretary. He was informed that Mr Olsen currently was in Spain and that he no longer took many new cases. Conrad explained that he understood but said he would greatly appreciate it if the secretary would pass the message along to him anyway, adding that he would wait up to one week to hear from Olsen. She answered that she would try her best.

Five days later

"Yes," answered the voice on the telephone. "Hello, is this Ole G. Olsen?"

"Yes."

"This is Conrad Heen. I'm calling on behalf of a client. We were wondering if you were available and if you could take on an assignment for us?"

"Well, I have pretty much retired now."

"We had heard that, but we also heard that occasionally you take on certain special assignments?" "Yes, that's true."

"I believe that I have a very special and extremely interesting case." "And what is that?"

"It's pretty difficult to explain over the phone. Would it be possible to meet with you? Either here in Norway, or I can come down to Spain if necessary."

"Can I have a little more to go on first?"

"Yes," said Conrad. He gave Olsen a brief, rough description of what they had become involved in.

"OK, it's possible I could take an assignment like that. We can meet in Norway. I'll be back in Oslo in one week. My daughter is getting married. We can arrange a meeting while I'm home. Please get back to my secretary and set something up. She organizes everything for me."

"I'll do that," said Conrad. There was a click on the other end of the telephone. Ole G. Olsen had hung up.

Ole G. Olsen was fifty-four years old and had been married for eighteen years. But like so many other marriages among police officers, his marriage had ended in a divorce. He had two children, one girl named Rebecca, who was twenty-four years old, and one boy named Jens Ove, who was eighteen years old. Rebecca was about to be married to José Pérez, who lived in Mallorca. Jens Ove lived together with his mother in Oslo. After the divorce, Ole G. Olsen had gotten himself a small studio apartment in a suburb called Hasle. His office was located down the street from there, at St Bernard's Place. Ole G. Olsen found his interest in being a police officer while he was in the military. He had served in the military police, and during his service he was involved in several investigations. The first was an auto theft at the camp where he was stationed. The next one was more serious; one soldier had shot another soldier. It seemed at first to be an accidental shooting, and the police had satisfied themselves with that decision. Ole G. Olsen, on the other hand, had the feeling that this conclusion was too easy. There were factors that he was not comfortable with, so he began his own investigation. The result of this was that the case was reopened and the soldier who had fired the shot was found guilty of murder.

After Olsen left the military, he went to the police academy. He was chosen on the first round of applicants and began his education within the same year. His first police service was like that of everybody else who had just graduated from the academy, walking a beat on the street. It didn't take very long for him to begin to be involved in detective work. By the time he was thirty-three years old, he was promoted to the special investigations division, and then in another five years he was moved to the white-collar crime division. Once there he concentrated mainly on foreign investigations. After that he became head of department for London and Lebanon.

In 1988 he left the police force and began his private investigating business. It didn't take long for him to make a name for himself in that capacity. He had investigated several cases where people were wrongfully convicted, but after he'd become involved, they were found not guilty and freed.

Ole G. Olsen entered the office of Conrad Heen exactly at a quarter to ten. They politely greeted each other, first Conrad and then Henrik.

Conrad offered him a chair in front of his desk.

"Please be seated. Would you like coffee?" Conrad asked. "Yes, please."

"Henrik, would you like a refill?" "Yes, I would."

Conrad poured both a cup before he poured one for himself. He sat down again. Then he began to speak. "First, I would like to thank you for agreeing to give us the opportunity to go over this case with you. We have prepared a little résumé about it for you. After you read the résumé, and if you still are interested, we will let you have all the material we have in our possession."

"Sounds good to me," Ole G. Olsen answered. Conrad continued, "What do you know about me?"

"Not much, but I have made some enquiries. I learnt that you were a very distinguished trial lawyer until you left the law firm of

Rushfeldt, Herlofsen, and Heen. It has been said that you left because of the Stovner case."

"Yes, that is correct. We can talk about it at another time."

"Other than that, I don't know very much about you. As for Henrik here, I only know that he is from Kongsberg and that he is single." "Well, this case involves Henrik's father, Nils Henrik Ellefsrud, who passed away on August 8. Nils Henrik was a client of mine, as well as my very best friend, and it was he who recommended that we use a private investigator to help us find the answers to this case."

Ole G. Olsen nodded and said, "I see. So, what does the case involve?"

"It is a case, or more correctly cases, that took place in Canada. They go far back in time, possibly as long ago as the nineteen sixties, and right up to today," said Conrad.

Ole G. Olsen just looked at Conrad and Henrik. Conrad continued, "It seems to be lots of money involved, but in which way we do not know. There are also many mysteries which we as yet know absolutely nothing about."

"So that's why you need to hire me as your private investigator?" "Yes," Conrad answered. "It was also Nils Henrik's last wish that you would take the job. The materials that you see here are only a small part of what we have in our possession. The rest is over in Canada.

But he wanted a Norwegian detective. He didn't specify why. If you take the case, we will pay all your expenses and one thousand US dollars per day. The investigation may take a long time. When you think you have found the answer we are looking for and we are satisfied, we will pay a bonus of two hundred fifty thousand US dollars. The bonus can be adjusted if we are completely satisfied with the results, but it can never be reduced.

"If it happens that you wish to close the investigation before you are finished, you will be paid for your time already served plus expenses right up until the last day. In that case there would be no bonus."

Ole G. Olsen looked at Conrad. "That is a pretty big chunk of change, and extremely tempting, but of course I need to look into the case further before I say yes or no about taking this case."

"We are in total agreement with that," said Conrad. "We have the rest of the papers here for you to take with you, so you can get a clear picture of what the case involves."

Henrik had been listening to the conversation with no comments as of yet, but now he stood up and poured himself another cup of coffee before asking if anyone else would like some. Conrad said yes, but Ole G. Olsen said, "No, thank you."

Olsen asked, "How much time will you both give me to go through all this and give you an answer?"

Conrad looked at Henrik and said, "We were hoping for an answer as soon as possible. Shall we say one week—or do you think you need more time than that?"

"No, one week should be enough," Ole G. Olsen answered. "But that means I will take a step back now and start to go through the material you have given me. If I have any questions or need a better understanding of anything, I'll call you."

Conrad agreed. Ole G. Olsen shook hands with both men and then made his way to the door. Right before he got there, he turned around to them and said, "From now on you can call me Goggen." Then he left.

CHAPTER 6

New York to Dawson City, Canada

Exactly eight months after they left New York City, they arrived in Dawson City. There was still a lot of snow up on the hills, but that didn't matter. Nils Henrik had finally made it all the way to the Yukon Territory. His dream was finally about to become a reality.

It was the note in the mail that was the main reason for breaking up and moving, but after more than two years in New York, Nils Henrik felt that the time to move on had come anyway. It was on a Friday night that he opened the mailbox and the letter appeared.

Dear Nils Henrik,

I am writing this to you because I am concerned, concerned for your well-being. It has come to my attention that there are people looking for you. I don't understand how these people have found you, but I suggest you pursue your dream sooner rather than later.

I have deposited $10,000 into your bank account as a gesture of ap-preciation for what you did. Please take care, and again thank you.

Roar

On the next Monday, Nils Henrik went to work as usual, but only to pack up his stuff and to say goodbye. He stopped by Roar's office and shook his hand. Nothing was said, but Roar couldn't stop himself: he grabbed Nils Henrik and gave him a big hug. Then Nils Henrik returned to his apartment.

The journey up north was laid out in detail. What he now needed to do was to convince OJ.

Everyone knew about his wish to get out to the Yukon Territory. And it was never far from his thoughts: the Yukon, Dawson City, and gold mining. He had done a good job of filling his friend OJ's head with the stories and legends he had learned, and OJ—his full name was Ole Johnny Larson—had finally agreed to go along with him out into the wilderness. But now that the day had come earlier than first planned, he needed to pursue him a little again.

Nils Henrik didn't say anything to OJ about the letter from Roar. The conductor blew the whistle and the locomotive began to move. They could feel it in the car in which they sat. Nils Henrik and OJ smiled excitedly at each other because they were finally on their way. The dream was about to become a reality. The Yukon Territory and Dawson City. The time was only 8 a.m.

The first leg of the trip was from New York to Winnipeg, Canada. The train passed through Pennsylvania; Cleveland, Ohio; Chicago, Illinois; Milwaukee, Wisconsin; and Minneapolis–Saint Paul, Minnesota. There they had to change trains. The US railway didn't service Canada, so they needed to change to a train from CN Railways, the Canadian national railway system, which would take them to Winnipeg. The time showed 9.45 p.m. on 3 September.

They had been travelling for seventy hours already. Nils Henrik had to go through the Canadian immigration when they crossed over the Canadian border. This was because he was travelling with a Norwegian passport. OJ only had to show his US identification papers.

They left the train and began to look for a boarding house where they could spend the night. Then in the morning they would take a good look around for somewhere more permanent to stay. Their plan was to stay here in Winnipeg and find a job for the winter, before setting their course for Yukon in the spring.

It was too early, or more correctly too late, to go up to the Yukon at this time of year. Winter was knocking at the door, and the activities in the area came almost to a standstill during the winter. Finding a way to travel there at this time of year was also almost impossible. They stored their baggage at the station for the time being and planned to come back the next day for it after finding a more permanent place to stay in Winnipeg.

That night they were able to find a cheap room to stay just a few blocks from the railroad station. However, they regretted their choice just a few minutes later. Shortly after entering the room, they saw a large rat, which made them decide that next time they would have to spend a little more money.

"More coffee?" Anna the waitress asked them.

Nils Henrik and OJ had already left the cheap boarding house and were having breakfast. They had not slept very much at all, so by 5 a.m. they gave up, gathered their things, and left. It felt good sitting in Eli's Breakfast and Diner now, and to be out of that awful boarding house. They both said yes. She was back with the coffee pot in record time.

Then she asked, "Are you new in town?"

"Yes, we came in late last night from New York." "Are you staying long?"

"Well, we are planning to stay here for four or five months. We're on the way to the Yukon Territory and Dawson City. We thought we would stay here until the winter is over. Nothing is going on up there now."

"No, that's true," said Anna. "Have you decided what you would like to eat?"

"Yes, I'll take a lumberjack special," said OJ. "I'll have the same," said Nils Henrik.

Anna didn't write anything down but just went over to the kitchen with the order. Then she came back with two glasses of water.

"Do you know if there is any work to be found around here?" asked Nils Henrik.

Anna thought for a moment and then said, "What kind of work are you looking for?"

"Pretty much anything," he said. "We just want work to tide us over until we begin our trip to the Yukon Territory in the spring."

"Well, I can't promise anything, but I know a married couple who own a restaurant and bar over in Bird's Hill. The last time I talked with her, she was looking for some help, but that was almost a week ago. I can call her up around 8 a.m. It's too early to call her before then."

Nils Henrik and OJ nodded and agreed.

A small bell rang, and Anna went over to the kitchen. Then she came back with their breakfasts.

Nils Henrik and OJ took their time at Eli's Breakfast and Diner, as Anna invited them to wait until she had called her friend in Bird's Hill. They didn't really have anything else to do, so they were happy to wait. If it turned out they were able to get jobs this fast, they would be very satisfied. Anna came over every so often and refilled their coffee cups. After the breakfast rush was over, she came back to them with her own coffee cup.

"It's my break, so if you don't mind I'll sit down with you for a few minutes. It has slowed down, so Judith can handle it alone."

During her break, Anna often left the table and returned. At one point when she came back, she said, "I just got off the telephone with my friend Laurie, and yes, they are still looking for help, but only one person. She said that you can both come over and talk to her, and then she will see. She mentioned that she might know someone else who needs help."

About an hour later the two men said farewell to Anna and made sure she knew how grateful they were for her help.

Laurie's Restaurant was quite a bit larger than Eli's Diner, and it had a bar in one corner. They had just seated their first lunch guests when Nils Henrik and OJ arrived. Laurie recognized them the minute theycame in as the young men whom Anna had described for the available job, so she greeted them right away. "Hi. I'm Laurie, and that is my husband, Rudolph." She pointed to the man behind the cash register. "You can say hallo to him later.

"I hear that you both are looking for a job."

"Yes, that's true, but not permanently. We're on our way up to the Yukon Territory in the spring."

"Yes, I heard," said Laurie.

"Well, what we are looking for is someone who can help my husband work in the bar over the next three or four months. Have either of you worked at a bar before?"

Nils Henrik shook his head. "What about you?" she asked OJ.

"Yes, I worked for a while in a bar in Manhattan when I waseighteen."

"What did you do there?"

"I mostly did clean-up, but whenever they got really busy, they would allow me to serve at the tables. It was usually the others who took care of the orders. I just ran the drinks."

"Well, here you would have to take orders and serve drinks. Are you interested in taking the job? It pays fifteen cents per hour plus your tips, usually 15 per cent. If you provide very good service, it can even be more. How much this adds up to depends on how many guests we have. Some of our bartenders make as much as twenty or even thirty Canadian dollars in one night."

"Yes, I am very interested," OJ answered.

"OK, then you've got the job, with a trial period of two weeks to see if it works out."

Laurie then looked at Nils Henrik. She said, "I'm sorry I only have one full-time job, but I do have a part-time job, mostly on Saturday nights. You can have that job if you want it."

Nils Henrik could read it in Laurie's face that she really was sorry not to be able to offer him more.

She continued, "I did notice when I was filling my car the other day that there was a Help Wanted sign at the gas station. If you want me to, I can put in a good word for you—if you think you are interested." "Yes, of course I am," said Nils Henrik.

"OK, then sit down for a minute. I'll be right back."

It took more than twenty minutes before she came back, because the restaurant had begun to fill up.

"I talked with Olsen and he said that the job is to be an assistant in the gas station. The pay is forty-five cents per hour, and you might get tips there as well, but not much." She looked over at OJ before continuing to speak to Nils Henrik. "Mister Olsen said that if you are interested, he would like you to come over right away so he can talk to you directly. You can put your baggage in the room over there." She pointed to a door on the other side of the restaurant.

Mr Olsen was a man in his early forties with a lot of grey sprinkled through his otherwise black hair. He was surely not happy about it, but there was nothing much he could do. His name was Richard, but he insisted on being called Dick. He became very enthusiastic when he heard that Nils Henrik was a recent immigrant from Norway. He himself was second-generation Norwegian.

Nils Henrik and OJ had been in Winnipeg less than twenty-four hours and both of them had already found work. They were greatly satisfied with the day's results. They had found a place to live as well. It just so happened that Dick Olsen had a room to rent upstairs from the gas station, and he was glad to let them rent it. It was a rather spacious room with two beds, one on each side of the room, and a table, some chairs, and a small sofa in the middle. The bathroom was outside in the hallway, but there was a small kitchenette with a stove in the corner. They decided to rent it right away, the rent being only $15 per month.

***

After ten days of waiting, the message came through that the road was open and the first convoy to Dawson City would be on its way the next morning at eight o'clock.

During their time in Winnipeg, Nils Henrik and OJ had planned their trip north in detail. The first part, to Calgary, was going to be with the Canadian railroad company. From Calgary they would need to take a bus. But from White Horse, the southernmost town in the Yukon Territory, and up to Dawson City, they weren't sure what kind of transportation they would end up with.

There were already a lot of people at the station when Nils Henrik and OJ arrived at 6.15 a.m. The station was filled with freight of all kinds which needed to be loaded onto trucks, and also some onto the busses as well. There were three busses that would travel along in the convoy.

"You two can have a seat in bus C," said the traffic assistant who was in charge of the activities of the crowd gathered around the busses. Nils Henrik and OJ went directly over to the bus and found a double seat three rows back from the front. They believed that a seat nearer to the front would be the best to travel in for such a long ride. They wouldn't get through until sometime the next day. Their baggage was stowed safely in the baggage compartment at the back of the bus. They'd almost forgotten to take out the food and drink that they would need to have with them on the trip, but they were reminded about it by the baggage master.

The convoy was not loaded and ready until almost 10.30. After a long winter there was a lot of freight that was needed up in the Yukon. Besides the three busses, there were eight trucks and four escort vehicles.

The trip was long and boring, and OJ complained a lot on the way. "How did I ever let you talk me into this?" he said, shaking his head. "Quit your complaining," said a smiling Nils Henrik. "Think about all the wonderful experiences you are going to have."

OJ continued to shake his head, but it didn't stick too deep. He became very enthusiastic every time he saw animals along the way. The animals were attracted by a newly ploughed road and came out of the forest to graze along the sides of the road where it was easier to find grass. It was also easier for them to move around on the road than it was in the deep snow. Mostly what they saw was moose, deer, and elk, but there was also the occasional wolf and bear. They even saw a mother bear with two cubs. The cubs were very young and ran right out into the road. The mother was right behind them. This brought the entire convoy to a stop. Nobody got out of any of the vehicles. The people in the escort car become very aware; a mother bear with small cubs is very dangerous. Bears give birth to their cubs at the end of their hibernation period, sometimes three weeks or a month before they reawaken.

Nils Henrik had seen similar animals at home in Norway, but it was an entirely new experience for OJ, who had lived his whole life in New York City.

Almost three years after leaving Norway, Nils Henrik had arrived at his destination: Dawson City. The last stretch of the trip had taken twenty-nine hours. A large group of people had gathered at the stopping place, as they had just spent a long boring winter and this was some excitement for them. It was the fifteenth of April 1949.

Oslo, Norway
8 September 2005

Goggen went straight back to his office. But when passing the deli at the corner, he realized that he was hungry, so he stopped by and ordered a tuna fish sandwich to take back to the office with him. The deli was particularly known for their tuna sandwiches. Back at his office, he heated up some water to make a cup of tea. He tried not to drink too much coffee over the course of the day.

His secretary was off for a few days and had gone back to her hometown to attend her grandmother's funeral. She had died the Wednesday before, at ninety-two years old. The water heated up very quickly. Goggen made the tea, took it to the desk, took out the envelope that Conrad had given him, opened it, and began to read.

Nils Henrik Ellefsrud, dated October 10, 2004

The collapse of project no. 34 in Calgary was my first unsuccessful project during my time in the United States and Canada. It was June 19, 1965. Until then everything had only gone one way for me, and that way was up. Now suddenly that had come to an end. Two years earlier I started a corporation. It was with OJ, me, Jimmy Hudson, and John Robinson. I didn't know the last two until then. And it was OJ who had brought them to me and introduced them. Jimmy Hudson was an architect.

John Robinson was a contractor. They were a few years older than OJ and I. Both had families, and they were both Americans. The company was going to do real estate, buying and selling of existing buildings, but also building new ones.

The business did well for the first two years and we began to make a name for ourselves in the industry. We had just won the bid to build four new buildings up on Jackson Heights in Edmonton. We believed that that project would bring us a good profit, and also that it would be our ticket to bigger and better building projects in the future.

It did not go as planned.

During the construction of building no. 2 came the catastrophe. The building was about 80 per cent finished when it suddenly and without any warning collapsed. Nine people were killed, seven workers and two passers-by. I was declared as missing in the collapse, but I was almost one hundred miles away attending to another deal at that time. My partners were fully aware of this, but they reported me missing anyway. It wasn't until much later that I found out why. My partners also managed to imply to the police that I had deliberately caused the collapse. At that time news didn't travel with the lightning speed that it does today. An unbelievable eight days had passed before I heard about it. My partners used that time to empty the company's bank accounts and also mortgage the already con-structed building before they disappeared. OJ had been missing for two days before the collapse. They also managed to produce evidence for the police that it was me who was behind all of this, and they documented it. They testified that I had accessed the building site and had placed explo-sive devices. Nothing could have been further from the truth.

The only connection that I had to these projects was as an investor. The whole thing was run by OJ, Jimmy, and John. It hurt me very deeply to think that OJ would have played a part in the deception. However, I have always tried to tell myself he didn't, and I based that on the fact that I never saw or heard from him again after that happened. He just disap-peared into thin air and left no trace. I have tried very hard for all these years to find out what happened to him, with no results. I blame myself for not spending enough time trying to find him, but so many things happened that took up my time in an even more important way.

I sent many letters to his family in New York. He had given me an address down there a long time ago, but I never got an answer. His disap-pearance has been a hard burden for me to bear.

We had been together for more than ten years, and for that entire time he had been nothing but honest to me and dependable. I met him when I was working for Roar Knudsen in Manhattan, soon after I arrived in New York. His real name was Ole Johnny Larson, but he always used the name

OJ. He was the son of a

Swedish couple who had immigrated to the USA from Malmo almost thirty years before I did.

OJ and I both worked laying flooring. We were often called floor layers. We became friends very quickly. He often heard about my dream to go north to the Yukon and try my luck as a gold miner. When the time came for me to start my journey north, he agreed to join me, but only after a lot of deliberation. We became very close friends. There wasn't much that one of us did that the other didn't also do.

It's easy to understand that I was in big trouble after the collapse, first because of the false evidence given by the other two partners, but also because OJ had disappeared. I worked very hard to clear my name of those charges. I was well on the way towards doing that when I received the first threat from John, one of the partners in our business. He was the construction manager. He just informed me that if I implicated either him or Jimmy in any of the charges or even tried to contact them in any way, no matter how I chose to do it, something terrible would happen to me or to those nearest to my heart. At first, I didn't take the threat as seriously as I probably should have. Looking back after the unthinkable happened to my family, I hold myself responsible for that, as I will do forever. It made me more afraid than I have ever been in my life. It happened two days short of two months after the building collapse, and I couldn't help but think that it was John who was responsible for it.

Goggen paused in his reading and looked at the clock. It was getting late. His stomach was also giving him signs that it was going to need to be filled soon, so he stacked up the papers, put them in an envelope, and then put it into a drawer in his desk. He got his jacket, put it on, and went out the door.

After the divorce he mostly went out to eat, he wasn't one who enjoyed working in the kitchen. His dislike of cooking wasn't so bad that he would die of starvation if all the restaurants suddenly closed, but still his cooking experience was rather limited. As he walked down the street, he thought over what he had learned so far in the Nils Henrik Ellefsrud story. As he passed Pizza Hut, he suddenly asked himself if he wanted pizza for dinner tonight, and the answer he gave himself was "Why not?" So, he turned around and went in.

Goggen was in his office early the next morning. His secretary was still away, so he quickly scanned the pile of mail he had picked up from the mailbox on his way up. Then he opened the drawer and took out the envelope with the papers Conrad had given to him. He had thought a lot about what he had read so far but still hadn't come to a decision as to whether the case was for him or not. He took out the papers again and took up where he had left off the evening before.

TJ was operated on several times. I was with her as often as I could be, but it was her grandfather and grandmother who stayed with her the whole time. It was an extremely traumatic experience that she had gone through. She was only a young girl of nine years when it happened. I felt so helpless, but I was obligated to continue my work in clearing my name after the building collapse in Edmonton. I was not comfortable about leaving her alone for even one minute, I knew that she was in good hands with her grandparents, and I communicated with them daily.

Naturally TJ later developed psychiatric trauma after her experience, and she became very aggressive.

Once she was discharged from the hospital, she went to her grandparents' house and we registered her in a school in their neighbourhood. After three months went by, things seemed to be going better. Jimmy informed me that they were beginning to see the happy, lively girl they had known before.

Then he was called into the school one afternoon. He was just letting out the cows after milking them when Peta ran out into the barnyard and told him that he had a message to come to the school immediately.

He was shown directly up to the principal's office. When he entered, there was TJ.

"What happened?" he asked her.

The principal looked at TJ before he answered. "She attacked one of the girls in her class and knocked her down on the floor. Then she tied her up to her desk."

Jimmy looked at TJ. "Why did you do that?"

She didn't answer him or look at him. It was just as if he wasn't there.

The principal said, "I'm sorry, but it is going to be necessary to punish her for that."

"I see," said Jimmy.

"We are going to have to suspend her from school for one week. We can't allow something like that to happen without a reaction. She also threatened the teacher who came in and tried to stop her. She had a baseball bat in her hand."

"I see," answered Jimmy. He looked at TJ again. Now she was looking down at the floor.

Jimmy got up and went over to TJ. He took her by the arm and they went out of the room. Over his shoulder, Jimmy nodded his farewell to the principal.

Once they were out in the car, Jimmy asked her again, "Why did you do it?"

She wouldn't answer him. On the entire ride home, she was completely silent and only looked out of the window. When they arrived home, she went directly to her room and didn't come out of it, not even at dinner time. Then her grandmother Peta went up to her room and saw that her eyes were very red. She had obviously been crying for a long time.

"What is it that's the matter?" asked Peta.

"I don't want to go to that school anymore," TJ answered. She started to cry again,

"What happened? Why don't you want to go back to school?" her grandmother asked.

"They called me an Indian whore," answered TJ. "Who?"

"Everybody in the class," TJ answered. "Why did they do that?"

"They know about the fire in the cabin," she answered.

When we signed TJ up at this school, we'd decided not to bring up what had happened to her. We thought the school was far enough away from Patricia Lake that no one would have heard about the tragedy and try to use it against her. Indians were not treated especially well in Canada at that time, especially those Indians who married white people. I made a special trip up to the reservation to speak with TJ, but she wouldn't talk to me at all.

It was as if I didn't even exist for her any longer. I then went to the school and had a meeting with the principal, and this time I told him everything, including the trauma of what TJ had been through, both physically and mentally. He listened to me with interest, but he disagreed and felt that Indians were not treated particularly badly at his school. However, he did promise to keep his eyes open to see if anything like that happened again.

The situation did not get any better. TJ was regularly involved in confrontations and then sent home. In the end it became impossible for her grandparents to have TJ live with them any longer. We therefore had to find a new home for her. She absolutely wouldn't have anything to do with me, no matter how hard I tried. It was like she blamed me for all the terrible things that had happened to her.

We found a new home for her out in Hinton. There was a married couple whom Jimmy knew well and who had some other children around TJ's age. We thought that it would be good for her to be with other children, and it did go well for a while. Then after about three months, the same thing began to happen there. She became aggressive again and behaved so badly that it was no longer possible for her to continue at this new school. We had to move her again to a new home and school.

It went on this way until she turned fourteen and the situation became so difficult that she was placed in a psychiatric hospital.

The first time I met Lt. Robert Blake, it was in connection with the crime committed at my cabin. We had a lot of contact pertaining to that case, and a friendship developed between us.

He had contributed much to me in the way of help, both with the cabin fire and with the building collapse down in Edmonton. He went out of his way in his effort to find a connection between the two events. He became more and more sure that that was the case even though they were not able to find any concrete evidence tying these two crimes together. However, there were strong indications that they were related.

I continued to receive threats that if I pursued the investigation, something would happen to TJ, the only person I had left in my family. The threats always came in the form of a letter, posted from different places. At any rate, I had no power to stop the investigation; it was in the hands of the police now.

After six months, the case against me regarding the building collapse came up for trial. When it was over, I had been cleared from any responsibility, but our company was ordered to pay 2.8 million Canadian dollars to the families of the people who'd been killed. That was a huge amount of money, and the company had absolute no way of coming up with it, especially in the situation in which it now found itself. I had to sell everything that the company owned, but it was still not enough. There was still over CAN$950,000 to be paid out, so I needed to file for bankruptcy. I managed to pay the people later with money from my own pocket, as much as I had personally. The rest I paid with a loan from the Bank of Alberta.

Lt. Robert Blake was very involved in helping me with this process of paying out the money. It was not necessary for me to pay out this money because the company was a corporation, but

I felt a terrible responsibility for those people who had lost their loved ones.

The investigation of the collapse was taken up again after I was found not guilty. But now the police decided to link the cabin fire to the collapse of the building in Edmonton. That was a result of Lt. Robert Blake's work. There wasn't any new evidence, but there were strong suspicions. The setback was that the investigation would be conducted by the Edmonton police, not by Lt. Blake. Chief Detective Lt. McKenzie was put in charge of it. So there the case was, as it still is today, unresolved and gathering dust.

I tried my best to investigate it myself, but it became almost impossible for me at that point—all the threats and so on. However, I never gave up completely. And Lt. Blake assisted me as much as he could. The problem was that he was still on the police force and therefore had boundaries and ethics to uphold as to how much he could do, so it was mostly out of his hands, although he did stretch himself as far as he possibly could for me. After I left and went back to Norway, he became—and still is— my long arm in Canada.

It has always been very frustrating to him and to me that we have no way to prove the connection between the two crimes.

After the car accident on September 6, 1972, I decided to go back to Norway for a while. But I intended to return to Canada at some point as soon as things died down a bit. You all know now I never did return. Instead I went back for four weeks two times a year using my Norwegian passport, on which my name is spelled "Ellefsrud". In Canada I changed my name to be spelled "Ellfsrud", which is easier for Canadians to pronounce.

I always feared for the safety of TJ and her daughter. I have never forgiven myself for the pain and fear that she went through at such a young age and for my part in causing it to happen. I also never gave up trying to find the guilty parties, but this became more and more difficult as time went on. This is the reason why

I have specified in my will that you all should use a qualified investigator to help you through it and maybe finally find the answers that I never found.

Now I will go to my grave never knowing who committed these terrible crimes, but please be aware that at some level I will be looking over your shoulder. I think that it is very understandable that I wish for those who committed such terrible crimes more than forty years ago to be brought to justice. It offends me deeply to think that they might be out there somewhere living in luxury on what they stole from us.

I have always thought very much about OJ and what could have happened to him. As I mentioned earlier, he disappeared two days before the building collapse. You will find a lot of information that Robert and I have compiled regarding OJ and the various investigations that we have conducted regarding him over the past forty years. Robert will help you to the best of his ability with anything you might need when you get to Canada.

It was almost noon, and time for lunch. Goggen suddenly thought of calling Conrad and seeing if they could have lunch together.

Conrad walked in the door of the Theatre Café just a few minutes before 1 p.m. After Goggen had called and arranged the lunch meeting, he had made a few telephone calls and cancelled his afternoon meetings. Then he'd grabbed his jacket and went out the door. His office wasn't very far away from the restaurant, so he'd decided to walk. It would only take him fifteen minutes or so, and it was a nice day. They had agreed to meet at 1 p.m. Goggen was already there when Conrad arrived. He had taken a table by the window. Conrad greeted him, and they shook hands. "Have you been waiting very long?"

"No, I just got here."

Conrad sat down on the other side of the table. It had been quite a long time since he had been here last. He used to come here often when he was with the law firm of Rushfeldt, Herlofsen, and Heen, but since leaving the firm, his style usually leaned towards a bagged lunch at his desk.

The waitress came over and asked if they would like anything to drink. She laid two menus down on the table in front of them. Ole G.

Olsen ordered a cup of coffee and a pint of beer, since he had decided to take the afternoon off. Conrad ordered coffee and a glass of water since he was going back to the office after lunch.

Goggen ordered two open-face sandwiches, one with shrimp and one with roast beef, and Conrad decided to have two smoked salmon sandwiches. The waitress wrote down their orders and left.

Goggen said, "I have read through most of the papers that you gave me. This case is going to be a huge amount of work."

"A case that is stretched out over the last forty years couldn't possibly be anything but a huge amount of work," answered Conrad.

"What makes you all believe that we will possibly be able to solve even part of this case?" Goggen asked.

"To be totally honest, we don't know. We know very little about this case ourselves, and we have discussed the time factor at length. The way that Nils Henrik wrote about this implies that the answer lies right in front of our noses. However, we certainly haven't gotten that impression at all as of yet."

Goggen studied Conrad for a few moments before he continued. "Who was this Nils Henrik, and who are the people he mentions in Canada, for example TJ?"

"Well, I only knew him for about eleven years," Conrad answered. "The people that he refers to in Canada he never named or referred to in all the time that I knew him. They came as a complete surprise to me, to us. That does not mean that he wasn't closely connected to them in the past. The fact is that Nils Henrik Ellefsrud was a very fine man and a good friend to me. He just had a lot of secrets that no one had any idea about, not even his own close friends and family." Goggen said, "This case interests me, but I don't see how I can guarantee anything."

"We understand that. Nobody can guarantee anything, but a final result would be well worth it," Conrad answered.

The waitress came with their order, set it down in front of them, and wished them a pleasant meal.

"What I have seen so far has gotten my interest, but I will need to see the rest of the materials," Goggen continued.

"I understand," said Conrad. "But for that to happen we have to travel to Canada. We have already planned to leave as soon as possible; we were only waiting for an answer from you. If it was negative, we were ready to go on and contact another investigator."

"I understand," said Goggen. "All right then, there's no need to dwell on it any further. I will make a deal with you. I will agree to take the case, go along with you to Canada, and go through all the materials that have compiled so far. If I think there is a possibility that I can get us further along with the rest of the information that you give me, I will continue. But if I conclude that the case is too old and I can't get anywhere with it, I will speak with you and voluntarily withdraw from it. Then I will only bill you for the time already spent."

"That will work for us. Does that mean that we have a deal?" Conrad looked at Goggen when he asked the question.

Goggen put forward his hand, and Conrad answered with his. They shook on it and the deal was done.

After that was over, the atmosphere became considerably more relaxed and the two men thoroughly enjoyed the lunch.

"Now that we have made an agreement, how long do you think it will take you to be ready to leave for Canada?" asked Conrad.

"I can be ready by tomorrow. I don't have anything else to deal with at the moment. But what I would like to do first is to go up to Kongsberg, get an idea of how Nils Henrik Ellefsrud lived, and go through the rest of the material that you have there. It shouldn't take very much time."

"OK," said Conrad. "When will you take the trip to Kongsberg?" "Tomorrow, if that isn't too early. You don't have to go with me, as I'm sure that Henrik can show me what I want to see and answer any questions I might come up with."

"Sounds good to me. I'll call Henrik and let him know that you plan to come up tomorrow. I will begin the travel plans for Canada," Conrad answered. Then he tried to pay the lunch bill, but Goggen insisted on paying it instead.

"Don't worry; you will be paying it later. It will be the first item submitted on my expense account." Goggen smiled when he said that. Conrad smiled back. They shook hands and left the restaurant.

CHAPTER 7

Alberta, Canada

12 September 2005

The telephone rang. "Robert Blake here."

"This is Conrad Heen. I am calling you from Norway." "OK" came from the other end of the phone.

"I was a good friend of Nils Henrik Ellefsrud," said Conrad. "Oh yes, I have waited for you to call. I was sad to hear that he passed. He was a good man."

"Yes," said Conrad. "He was a very nice man."

"I received his last letter a few days ago, and he mentioned that you might want to come over here for a while." "That's right," said Conrad.

"He also mentioned that you were going to look into his cases here.

It makes me very happy to hear that. Nils was extremely involved in this, and there was nothing he wanted more than to find the answer to everything. He wanted the responsible people to pay their dues for it. When will you be here? Nils and I have collected a large amount of material regarding this. I have it all in my possession."

"We are making the necessary arrangements right now and hope to be over there within two to three weeks."

"OK then, just let me know when you are coming, and I will arrange for someone to pick you up at the airport. You should fly into Edmonton International Airport."

"Thank you. I will get back to you with the details as soon as we know them. We are looking forward to meeting you." "Same here."

Conrad hung up.

Robert Blake was a lieutenant in the Royal Canadian Mounted Police, popularly called "the Red Jackets". He had now reached the age of seventy-one, but he still remained a very active person. For the last thirty-five years he had run his own security service, Blake's Security.

He had started his company with a modest start-up sum of around one hundred thousand Canadian dollars, but as the years went by, his company had grown quite significantly, and now they took on more than $150 million worth of business every year.

Security was a branch of business which had grown by leaps and bounds, particularly after 11 September 2001. And Robert used to say as a joke that Osama bin Laden had done a huge favour to the world's economy, that he was responsible for the creation of more jobs than anyone else, especially in the security branch. Ironically enough,

Robert's statement wasn't very far from the truth. In recent years the company had also expanded their activities to include bounty hunting of parole violators and other missing people. His sons George and Mark had taken over many of the responsibilities of the security side of the business, while Robert himself ran the parole and bail bondsmen part of it.

After high school Robert attended the Royal Canadian Mounted Police Academy. He had wanted to be a policeman since he was a little boy and had never faltered or doubted that this was what he was meant to be doing to this very day. It didn't take long for Robert to be noticed. He had a unique talent for quickly absorbing what was said and remembering it almost infallibly; he was a natural leader to the other students in the academy; and it was even rumoured that he had a photographic memory.

He never forgot his first assignment and the first arrest he made. It was an American who had run away to Canada because he was being drafted to the US military. It was during the Vietnam War, and the man was only one of many thousands who made that decision. For the most part the Canadians accepted the draft dodgers and left them in peace, but this person had begun to be a nuisance to the locals and farmers on the outskirts of Edmonton. He had fled up into the Rocky Mountains on the border between British Columbia and Alberta. He was wanted for armed robbery, violence, and attempted rape. There were two older women who had been forced to stop their car on a remote road while on their way home. There was a tree blocking the road. He stole their car after first robbing them and then tying them to the tree that was blocking the road. Of course, it was he who had placed the tree there in order to block the road and make them stop.

He was quickly identified by the police as an American named Glenn McDonald.

Before this incident, McDonald had tried to rape a fifteen-year-old girl who was on her way home from school. The only reason that the rape had not taken place was a lucky well-placed kick that the girl was able to administer to him and thereby render him helpless.

Robert was called in to the office of the region chief and asked if he would like to take the assignment. Robert had said yes immediately.

During the briefing Robert was informed by the region chief of who Glenn McDonald was and what he had done and attempted to do. They were not sure exactly where he was right then, but it was somewhere around Maligne Lake.

Robert readied himself for two weeks out in the woods. That was standard procedure unless otherwise instructed. The plan was enacted early next morning. At 8 a.m. he led the horses out of their stable.

He had loaded up two horses that were specially trained to be out in foul weather. So a rainstorm like the one they had now, which was forecasted to last all day, was no problem for them. He would ride one of them, and the other would be used as a packhorse. His dog Petra, a Pyrenees mastiff, was of course also to join him. She always accompanied him.

The first night, he stayed in a cabin which was the property of the police, cabin no. 3328. He was happy when he finally saw the cabin. It had been a wet day. The rain hadn't stopped all day. He was glad the cabin had a shelter where he could place the horses.

He waited to contact headquarters and give his nightly report until he had fed the horses and eaten a quick meal. Then he turned in. Petra ate the same as him. Now she was lying at the bottom of the bed with him.

The weather had lightened up a little since the night before, but there was still rain in the air. Robert did the same chores as the night before, feeding and watering the horses, and then he ate some beef jerky and gave a little to Petra. He was anxious to get as early a start as possible to reach the area where Glenn McDonald had been seen last, up at Maligne Lake's north end. Some fishermen were paddling their canoes and doing some fishing when they passed a cabin there belonging to one of their friends and noticed that someone was staying there. Since it was neither the friend nor anyone else they knew they saw there, they called the owner and asked if he had rented it to anyone. The answer was no, so the police had been contacted.

The description of the man they had seen going in and out of the cabin matched the description of Glenn McDonald.

Robert Blake arrived on the south side of Maligne Lane a little before 2 p.m. He began to move up to the north end as quickly as possible, without being seen from anywhere on the lake. When he was quite near, about 200 metres from the cabin, he secured the horses behind a little hill where they would be safe and remain undetected. He then studied the cabin. It was quiet, so he decided to leave it for today.

Tomorrow, if there wasn't anyone to be seen down there, he would go down and have a look. He had already put the horses in a secure place. Now he needed to find a place to bury the food container. He didn't want to be disturbed during the night by an unwanted guest, like a bear.

Things were looking the same the next day, quiet. Robert was now hiding in the back of the cabin. After he woke up and examined the area, he started to move towards the cabin. The only way to get to the cabin was to go across the water or ride up on a horse. Robert didn't see any boat down there, and he didn't think Glenn McDonald would use a horse. He therefore decided to take a closer look. He moved carefully around the cabin with a plan to enter through the back. Now he was there looking through the window.

The cabin was empty, but there were plenty of signs indicating that someone had been there quite recently. Who that was he couldn't know, but it was very likely that it was Glenn McDonald. If so, perhaps he was temporarily away from the cabin and could come back at any time. Robert moved quickly away and back into the woods, where Petra had been told to wait for him. She would have given him a signal if anyone had approached the cabin while he was there.

As soon as he was back in his camp, he took out his radio and called the headquarters to give his report, but he was unable to say who had used the cabin, if it was Glenn McDonald or someone else.

On the third day, something finally happened. Robert suddenly spotted a boat coming up on the other side of the lake. He was sitting in the sun in a little sheltered spot when he suddenly saw the boat.

The time was 3.03 p.m. He quickly went back to his camping spot and fetched Petra.

As soon as he took cover, he started studying the boat. Had he been spotted? He looked again carefully. No, there wasn't any sign of that. The boat came to rest on the little beach in front of the cabin. The report on Glenn McDonald had not included his being armed, but the briefing Robert had received before leaving headquarters indicated that he should assume he was. Virtually everyone who stayed out in this remote area had some kind of weapon for their own protection or for hunting.

Robert carefully studied the man through his binoculars. It was surely Glenn McDonald. The question now was, who was the woman he had with him in the boat? There was nothing about her in the report. Robert continued to study both of them very carefully, Glenn first. He was about 180 centimetres tall with an average-size body.

His age, according to what Robert had read, was twenty-two years. The woman was more difficult to judge. She could have been any age between fifteen and thirty years old. She had dark hair and was dressed in typical backwoods/hiking clothes. As they came up onto the beach, Glenn jumped out and dragged the boat up on the beach. Then the woman handed him some bags and jumped out after him.

The headquarters would now send out two men for backup. Robert was instructed to stay where he was and do nothing but observe and wait for them to arrive. They would come down from Jasper by car and then travel up the lake by boat. They didn't have any personnel any closer to the vicinity, and they would not possibly be able to arrive any sooner than the next afternoon. They would contact him the moment they were in the area.

Robert had just finished taking care of the horses and was making himself and Petra something to eat on a small spirit stove when suddenly a shot rang out. Then came another, and then the third. In the instant it happened, he grabbed his pistol and had it at the ready position. The shots had come as a complete surprise to him. He quickly went to his observation site which he had set up earlier. Dusk was beginning to fall as he quickly swept the cabin area with his binoculars. He spotted the American out near the woodpile, leaning against it. He was only dressed in shorts and a sleeveless undershirt, but what was truly alarming to Robert was what he was holding in his hands. In one hand was a liquor bottle and in the other was what looked remarkably like a sawed-off shotgun. As dusk was falling quickly, Robert was not completely sure what he was seeing.

It was very evident that McDonald was not sober. He was looking around wildly. Robert quickly swept the area again, and there near the corner of the cabin was what looked like a pile of clothes on the ground. He kept the binoculars focused on them. Suddenly he thought he saw a movement. Yes, there, it moved again, he was absolutely sure of it. McDonald had not yet noticed the movement, or at least it didn't appear so. He was standing looking down the hill and still drinking.

Had he shot the woman? Since she had moved, she was obviously still alive. Robert knew he needed to get closer to the cabin. He took his Winchester, a .44-calibre Model 1892, and began to move down from his observation spot towards the cabin. Petra accompanied him. They went slowly and quietly so as not to be noticed. Darkness had almost fallen now, which was a help to them in remaining unnoticed.

Glenn McDonald was still standing at the woodpile.

Robert gave a signal to Petra to lie down and wait. They were about sixty metres from the cabin. He was still moving in, but on the other side from where McDonald was. He could now see the woman, who was lying on the ground. His night vision was quite good now, and the light coming from the cabin window was a help for him to get a better understanding of what was going on.

Robert got a very special feeling; he was not exactly afraid, but he was deeply unhappy with the situation. This was his first experience of this kind. He had never shot a living person before. Of course, he was trained to do it, but training was just not the same.

Suddenly McDonald went over to the woman. He was mumbling something to himself which Robert was not able to hear. He stood over her and spilled some of the contents of the bottle over her, then laughed and threw the bottle away. Now he lifted the shotgun and aimed it at the woman. It was a sawed-off pump-action type of shotgun. Robert signalled Petra with an almost silent whistle, and she replied immediately with a bark. McDonald whirled around and shot blindly into the woods in Petra's direction. She kept completely still until Robert quietly whistled again. She barked a second time, this time from another location. McDonald again fired aimlessly into the woods. Robert had lifted his Winchester and had McDonald in his sights. The latter was still looking wildly into the woods and at the cabin, but then he turned back to the woman on the ground and took aim at her. A shot in the shoulder is very damaging and painful, but Robert didn't have a choice.

Nor did he have one second to spare if he was going to save the woman's life. He pulled the trigger.

McDonald spun around, dropped the gun, and fell down on the ground. He lay there writhing in pain. His right arm was paralyzed, but he tried to pick up the shotgun with his other hand. Petra came at him with her teeth bared, and he gave up and lay completely still. Robert was still holding his rifle at the ready as he moved rapidly towards them. He immediately began to check and see if McDonald had any other weapons. Then he handcuffed McDonald's left hand to his right leg. Petra guarded him while Robert made his search. He went to the woman and checked her for injuries. She had a lot of blood on her right arm and shoulder, and some more on the right side of her head. He checked her for a pulse. She had one, but it was very weak. If she was going to have any chance of surviving, he needed to get her to a doctor as soon as possible. He carried her into the cabin and laid her down on the bed. There was not much he could do for her except to stop the bleeding. He needed to go and get the medical kit he had brought with him. But first he teared up some bed sheets and made a hard compress, which he applied to the wound to stop the bleeding.

McDonald was still lying on the ground moaning and cursing. He promised Robert that he would take revenge on him. The bullet had broken his arm. Robert quickly examined him and determined that he would not die from his wound, so he went on to fetch the medical kit. Petra continued to stand guard over McDonald.

The next day, just after 2 p.m., the ambulance and rescue personnel finally got through to the cabin. They had to come by boat from the end of Ranch Road. The woman didn't make it through the night despite Robert's efforts to save her. She died of the wounds that Glenn McDonald had inflicted on her.

His condition was somewhat better, but he was loudly complaining of extreme pain. Robert had given him some painkillers from the medical kit, but they had not helped very much. He had complained and moaned uninterruptedly and threatened Robert the whole night long.

Norway

8 August 2005, at the cabin

At 12 midnight, Nils Henrik started to think about his relationship with TJ. It was never the same again after the cabin fire and what happened there. She became more and more difficult and aggressive, and there didn't seem to be anything he could do about it. He and her grandparents thought at first that it would pass after some time, and she did settle down for a little while after changing schools and neighbourhoods, but in the long run she just became worse and worse. After three or four months in a new place, the same problems would start happening again. She could not get along at all with the other students. Then there would be fights; she would start to hit or punch people again. By the time she reached fourteen years of age, there was absolutely nothing else to do but put her into a psychiatric hospital. This was extremely difficult for Nils Henrik to do. It was also devastating to her grandparents. They had tried so hard, but in the end, they just had to throw in the towel. So, she was committed to Alberta Psychiatric Hospital in Edmonton.

Nils Henrik visited her as often as he could, but there was never a change. Each time she saw him through the glass, she would close her eyes and say absolutely nothing. He was so affected by this that he started to drink too much. He did this foolishly thinking that he could stop the pain, but it just depressed him more. He began to think about his reasons for living and whether those were enough.

In the end what kept him going was the hope that he would find out who was responsible for all this pain.

He got to thinking about all the things that happened around him and his current situation and wondering how much he was responsible for what had happened. What had he done in his life that was so terrible that it could have caused those things to occur? His wife, Sisiska, was gone; his son Albert, was also gone; and his daughter, TJ, was in a terrible mental condition and wanted absolutely nothing to do with him. And last but not least, OJ had completely disappeared. Nils Henrik was so terribly alone.

TJ's condition was looking as though it would be permanent. She never spoke to her father again, but finally she began to communicate a little with her grandfather. They didn't really form a relationship, but she was able to let him know about a certain nurse whom she didn't like and had aggressive feelings about. Also, TJ was unable to cope with strangers. Jimmy, her grandpa, had asked the doctors and other personnel about this, and they were unable to explain why these things were happening. They had also noticed her aggressive feelings, and she was being treated with medications to combat them. She kept almost completely to herself, even while in the company of others.

TJ had been a really good student at school before all this happened, and she always came home with the best grades and was in every way a happy and well-adjusted child. She was always helpful, and one of her favourite things was helping her mother do the cooking. Her relationship with her twin brother, Albert, was also very good; they were almost inseparable. Even though Nils Henrik was very busy with his businesses, he was very involved in his children's lives. They both loved to be outside, and since Nils Henrik had been raised in Norway, where everyone spent a lot of time outside in nature, and because the children's mother was a First Nations woman, a full-blooded Native American of the Blackfoot tribe, they both had a lot they could teach their children about the natural world.

One evening Nils Henrik visited TJ and it appeared that she wanted to talk to him. She seemed to be different on that day, but she was not able to express herself. However, this gave him hope. He went back the very next day and the day after. Unfortunately, nothing came of it.

This was how things continued to be for almost a year, all the way up to the twenty-eighth of May, her birthday. The telephone rang at 4 a.m. The call was from the mental hospital. They told Nils Henrik to get there as soon as possible, so he threw on some clothes and raced for the door. As soon as he got in the car, he realized that he had left his car keys in his other pants pocket. He ran back to the house to get them, when suddenly there was a gunshot sound and a bullet buried itself in the frame of the door he was about to enter. He threw himself down on the floor inside the house and waited. It was very quiet.

He waited a few minutes, but nothing else happened. He got up and waited some more before moving over to the window. It was quiet out there.

Nils Henrik had bought the house seven years earlier when everything was going well. He had just come back from the Yukon Territory, and they had done well this season. It was a ranch 448 acres in size in the Drayton Valley, about 145 kilometres from Edmonton. It consisted of one house, two barns, a woodshed, and a smokehouse. It was a spacious house with two stories.

He concentrated, looking at the corner of the driveway. Still there was nothing to see. He quickly dropped to the floor again when a window shattered. He didn't know which one it was. Then he heard the unmistakable sound of car tyres spinning and a car quickly disappearing into the distance.

As soon as he heard that, he got up and raced over to the telephone to call Robert Blake. He wasn't aware of how many times the telephone rang on the other end before he heard the familiar voice answer, but it felt like an eternity.

"This is Nils Henrik." "OK."

"Somebody just shot at me," answered Nils Henrik. "Where?"

"Here at my house." "Are you all right?"

"Yes, but I am on my way to the hospital. They called me and asked me to come immediately. Something very important must have happened out there. I ran out to the car, but then remembered that

I had left my car key in my other pants pocket. When I reached the front steps, a shot just missed me. I threw myself down on the floor inside the door and lay still and waited, but there was just that one shot. Then I heard a car driving away at a high speed. How long afterwards I'm not sure, but a window was also broken, I don't know how."

"OK, I'll be over as quickly as I can." "But I have to go to the hospital."

"That's fine but take a taxi in case someone has tampered with your car."

"OK," said Nils Henrik.

"I'll take a look around your house before you get back from the hospital."

"Thank you," said Nils Henrik, before hanging up.

When Nils Henrik arrived at the hospital he was even more afraid than he'd been when the shot rang out. Blue lights were flashing over the whole parking lot in front of the hospital. He counted five police cars and an ambulance. He rushed into the lobby, where he was met by one of the hospital's nurses. She hurried over to him and asked him to come at once. The name Rebecca was on her name tag. They went quickly into an office with a sign on the door that read "Director". She turned to him and asked him to please sit down.

He sat down on a chair over by the wall. She looked at him closely. "Thank you for coming so soon. Something very sad has happened here tonight," she began.

Nils Henrik waited in suspense.

"One of our doctors has been murdered, and one of our nurses has been badly injured."

Nils Henrik sat totally still, hardly daring to breathe.

She continued, "It looks like it was TJ who killed the doctor and seriously wounded the nurse," she continued.

At first, Nils Henrik sat still, as though in shock, and then the tears began to run down his face.

"I'm so sorry to have to tell you this," said Rebecca.

Nils Henrik buried his face in his hands. He was unable even to get his thoughts together. Everything was just spinning, the explosion and fire, the building collapse, the deaths of his wife and son, the disappearance of his best friend OJ, and now this.

That was the last thing Nils Henrik remembered. Everything ran together, and he went into shock.

Robert noticed Nils Henrik stirring and said, "He is waking up. I'll need to speak with him for a moment, if you wouldn't mind giving us some privacy." The nurse who was in the room looked at him and went outside.

"How do you feel?" Robert was sitting on a chair that he had dragged over to the bedside.

"Where am I?" asked Nils Henrik. "You are in the hospital where TJ is." "What happened?"

"You had an acute attack of … well, I can't exactly remember the name of it, but you fell into some kind of a trance immediately after you heard what happened and found out that TJ was the one who did it. You need to try not to think about it right now."

Nils Henrik just looked at Robert.

"How do you think that is possible for me to do? I've lost every one of them, my wife and Albert, TJ, and maybe OJ too, all the people nearest to me."

"I know how you must be feeling, but you must not blame yourself for it."

Nils Henrik closed his eyes. The tears started falling again. Robert took his hand and said, "I know it's difficult, but it's still the truth. You have to convince yourself that you're not responsible for any of this."

He looked at Nils Henrik. Neither of them spoke. A deep silence filled in the room. Then Nils Henrik broke the silence. "Have you been out to my ranch?"

"Yes, I have, but we aren't going to discuss it here right now. We'll talk about it after you get out of here."

A nurse entered the room to check on Nils Henrik.

"Get my clothes and we'll get out of here right now," Nils Henrik said. "You are not going anywhere," the nurse replied, having heard what he'd said. "The doctor says you have to stay until at least tomorrow.

You just regained consciousness after eight hours. You probably don't remember, but you became quite difficult, so we needed to calm you down. You have been given some strong sedatives."

Robert had just been listening. "That is OK. I promise to come and get you tomorrow morning," he said to Nils Henrik.

"What about TJ? Where is she, and what have they done with her?" Nils Henrik asked.

"She's still here in the hospital, but they have put her in isolation. They also put a policeman outside her door."

"Can I talk to her?" Nils Henrik's voice was shaking when he said this.

"I'll do what I can to get them to let you see her. Normally they don't let anyone in to see someone in isolation," Robert answered.

Nils Henrik nodded. He and Robert shook hands and embraced each other, and Robert left.

Nils Henrik and Robert Blake had developed a good relationship which then grew into a strong and unbreakable friendship. It was no secret that this friendship was going to be of great help to Nils

Henrik during the difficult times he was about to go through. Robert had come and picked him up and driven him home on more than one occasion when Nils Henrik had drunk too much. He had tried to talk to him about the fact that alcohol was not the answer to his problems, which would only make things much worse, but still it hadn't really helped. What Nils Henrik needed most in the world was comfort, but comfort could absolutely not be found in a bottle. Deep down inside Nils Henrik realized this too, but it was not clear enough to him as of yet.

The next morning Robert came straight to Nils Henrik's room. "Good morning. I see that you are up. How do you feel today?" "I certainly could feel better."

"I'm sure that's true. They are going to sign you out in a few minutes, and I have used all my influence to get you permission to go in and see TJ."

"Thank you, Robert. I don't know what I would have done without you. How is she?"

"It's difficult to say. We'll know more when we see if she reacts at all to seeing you again. She is under sedation."

Nils Henrik had already dressed himself, hoping he would be released. He had not slept very much. The doctor came in around 8.20 and asked him how he felt and looked him over one more time.

"You feel better today than you did yesterday, I assume?" "You could say that," Nils Henrik answered.

"Well, you have received a strong shock, and you are not quite over it yet. I'm going to prescribe some tranquillizers and some sleeping pills for you to take with you. You can use them both, but you cannot drink any alcohol while you are using them. Do you understand that?" He looked over at Robert when he said this. "Are you his friend?"

"Lt. Robert Blake, Police Inspector," Robert said, reaching over to shake hands with the doctor. "And yes, I am also his friend," he added.

"Good. He needs all the friends and support he can get right now, so I am really glad that you are with him."

"I'll do my utmost to help him," Robert answered.

"That is good," said the doctor. "Good luck to you both," he said.

Then he left the room.

It was not more than five minutes before the nurse named Patricia came in. "It looks like you are ready?" She looked at Nils Henrik. "Here are the pills that Doctor Hill prescribed for you. There is also a prescription in case you need more of them." She smiled at him.

Nils Henrik thanked her for the prescription and also for all the help that she had given him. He started to shake her hand, but then he hugged her instead, which she allowed him to do. She said, "Now

I hope that the meeting with TJ will go well. You both need that to happen."

Robert thanked her too.

Out in the lobby they were met by Joan, the policewoman. Robert had asked her to come and be there with them when they met with TJ. It was Joan who had found TJ under the woodshed after the cabin had burned down. Robert thought that she could be of some kind of positive help and that she might be able to get through to TJ better than they could. Joan had asked Robert more than once how the girl she had found was getting along. She had agreed to sit in on the meeting even though it meant a three-hour drive. After the cabin fire she had been transferred further north and had also been promoted to lieutenant. She was now the senior officer of the Royal Canadian Mounted Police Department 4342 up in Grande Cache.

She came in together with a man dressed in white, obviously a doctor, and a uniformed policeman. She greeted Nils Henrik politely and then introduced the man as Dr Miller. The policeman just nodded to them. Joan took over the meeting, asking Nils Henrik how he was feeling.

He answered that he was OK.

"This is a very sad situation," she said. "Has Robert explained to you why I am here?"

"Yes, he did."

"Good. We believe that my presence will help to get TJ to open up a little bit. From what I have heard, she has locked herself up inside.

Doctor Miller has explained the situation to me. I would like to find a place to sit down and discuss more about the situation. I understand from Robert that you have not had many answers about what has happened, aside from the fact that TJ has allegedly killed Doctor Irvine Jr. and injured Nurse Mary."

She looked closely at Nils Henrik, who answered that he was OK. She then looked at Robert, and he nodded.

"OK, let's sit over there." She pointed to a grouping of chairs and a sofa over in one corner of the room. They all went over and sat down.

Joan began: "When Robert asked if I would take the opportunity to come down here to meet TJ again, I got in contact with the local police and familiarized myself with the case and with what exactly happened. I was then told that one of the doctors here, a Doctor

Irvine Jr., and a nurse by the name of Mary were stabbed with a large screwdriver, and that Doctor Irvine Jr. was killed. Then I was told that TJ was responsible for these crimes. Doctor Irvine Jr. was overcome in his office, and Nurse Mary was found outside in his waiting room. It looked as though she was stabbed first. Doctor Irvine Jr. and Nurse Mary were on duty that evening. They were usually on shift together. TJ was not his regular patient. It was only when he did his night shifts or when he filled in for her regular doctor that they came in contact with each other. Also, how she was able to get the screwdriver is a mystery.

"Anyway, with that screwdriver she stabbed Doctor Irvine Jr. fifteen times and Nurse Mary four times."

Joan paused and looked at Nils Henrik. He just sat there staring straight ahead. She tried to meet his gaze but was unable to get through.

"Are you OK?" she asked. He answered stiffly that he was.

She took one better look at him before she continued.

"At least four of the stab wounds received by Doctor Irvine Jr. were deadly, as was one of the wounds received by Nurse Mary, but amazingly she is still alive. TJ was found sitting next to Doctor Irvine Jr. with the screwdriver still in her hand, covered with blood."

Nils Henrik was no longer able to hold back his tears.

Robert tried his best to comfort his friend, but he couldn't find the words to say.

Nils Henrik wiped away his tears and made an attempt to pull himself together.

"I'll be OK now," he said.

They sat there for a little while in silence before Joan continued. "How shall we do it? How do you want us to proceed and to question her?" She addressed this question to Dr Miller.

He said to Nils Henrik, "Well, what kind of relationship did you have with her? And did she acknowledge you as her father lately?"

"I truly wish I could answer yes to that question, but I have to in all honesty answer no." He still had tears in his eyes when he said this. "I lost my connection to her after the explosion and fire. It seemed as though she blamed me for what happened and anything else afterwards that happened to her."

"That is not unusual," answered Dr Miller. "How was your relationship with her before the fire?"

"It was very good," said Nils Henrik. "What about you?" he asked Joan.

"I cannot admit to having any relationship with her before the fire.

I didn't know her at all, but I was the one who found her under the woodshed and took care of her afterwards. It was I who went with her to the hospital and stayed with her while she was being treated.

"It was also me who tried to explain to her what had happened, and she opened up to me a little on that occasion. I had three other opportunities to see her afterwards. She was always cooperative with and glad to see me. The last time was two years ago."

"Well, that's better than nothing."

"And you?" Dr Miller looked towards Robert. "What is your relationship with her?"

"Absolutely nothing. I only met her during my investigation of the cabin fire, and once more after that."

"OK, then I suggest you, Joan, go in to see TJ first," Dr Miller said. "Then we take it from there." This decision was accepted by them all. They got up and moved towards the closed area.

The room that TJ was in was separated from the rest of the hospital. It was firmly locked down, and those who were in there were not allowed to mix with the other patients. It was strictly for dangerous patients. TJ was now considered one of those.

Joan walked over to the room that was assigned to TJ and showed her badge to the policeman who was guarding the door. He looked at the badge and opened the door for her. TJ was sitting on her bed with her legs folded underneath her. She was pale, and Joan could read in her face that she was very afraid. Even in the terrible situation she was in, she was still a very beautiful girl. She had the dusky colouring of a Native American, blended with the best of the Northern European features. She looked blankly across the room as Joan came in. Joan moved carefully. She picked up the only chair in the room and moved it over to TJ's bed. She took a good look at the girl before speaking. "Hi," she said. "Can you remember me?"

No reaction whatever from TJ.

"It's Joan again. We met up a few years ago at Patricia Lake." She waited before continuing. "That was down by your cabin."

Complete stillness.

"I have come here to help you once more."

Still no reaction whatsoever.

"Is there anything that you want to tell me?" TJ's gaze was completely blank and empty.

"I was hoping that you would give me a starting point so I can help you. I know that you have been through a terrible and gruesome thing, and I know that you have been very strong. I don't know if I could have been as strong as you if I had been faced with what you have been experienced."

Stillness.

"I want you to know that there are many people out there who want to help you. I am only one of them." Now TJ had tears in her eyes.

"Can I sit up here next to you?" She pointed to a space on the bed. TJ nodded, and Joan moved herself over onto the bed. Joan let TJ become used to the idea that someone was sitting right on the bed with her. Joan allowed her to cry. Then she put her hand over TJ's and asked, "Can you tell me what happened?"

No answer.

"Can you tell me anything, anything at all, that will allow me to help you?"

Still TJ gave no sign of answering, so Joan changed her direction a little.

"I have your father here. He's sitting right outside this room. I wish you would let him come in."

She waited for a few moments.

"He is very sorry, and it is so very difficult for him right now. You are the only one he has left, and he loves you very much, now more than ever."

Joan had her arm around TJ now and was holding her close.

"Shall we let him come in?"

TJ didn't answer. Joan stood up from the bed and went over to the door. She gave a sign to the policeman on guard to let Nils Henrik in. The latter rushed over to the door and was immediately let in.

"TJ, here is your father."

She wouldn't look at him at first. Her gaze went back to that first cold, empty stare that she had when Joan first came in.

"He wants very much to help you. He would sacrifice everything he has for you. But it is up to you to let him and us help you. You must talk to us and tell us what happened. You are the only person your father has left in the whole world. He loves you very much."

TJ's gaze remained the same. They all sat in silence together for a while.

"Well, TJ, we have to leave now, but we will come back tomorrow. Maybe you can use the time until then to think about what you will tell us which will help us to help you. You can do it. I know you can." Joan looked intently into TJ's eyes. She believed that she could see a small response deep within them.

Joan and Nils Henrik got up and moved towards the door. The policeman opened the door. Nils Henrik went out first.

"Same bad man," said TJ.

Joan turned quickly around and looked towards the bed.

"What did you say?" she asked. "Bad man. Bad man," TJ said. Joan went back to the bed.

"Bad man, bad man," TJ said again.

"Talk to me," said Joan. She looked at TJ again, but nothing more was said. TJ closed down again. Joan went to the door and left.

When Joan and Nils Henrik came out, they tried to analyse what had happened and what TJ had said.

What could that have meant? Was what she'd said related to the happenings after the cabin fire or here at the hospital?

Joan was thinking while the others spoke quietly together.

Then she said, "It seems to me that she wanted to talk but was unable to do so. I also felt that she was much closer to talking to me when we were alone in the room. How many medications do you have her on?" "Several, but not so many that she wouldn't know who you are or who she was with. And today we only gave her a tranquillizer." Doctor Miller was reading from TJ's chart, which was hanging on the wall. "Thank you for your help," said Joan. She put out her hand to shake

Dr Miller's. "You have been a very great help. We're leaving now, but we'll be back very soon."

Nils Henrik and Robert also thanked the doctor before they went out. They quickly found Robert's car. All three of them got in, Robert behind the wheel, Joan on the passenger side, and Nils Henrik in the back seat.

Robert drove away from the hospital.

"What did you get out of that?" he asked Joan.

She thought a little while before she answered him.

"Well, it's like I said in there. I feel that I can get through to her. We had some kind of contact—vague, but nevertheless a contact." "What possible reason could there be for her taking up a screwdriver and killing that doctor with it?" Robert continued.

"That I cannot say. There can be many reasons for that. Let's just hope that she'll open up and give her own explanation for it, but it may take some time," Joan replied.

"What do we do in the meantime?" asked Nils Henrik. "TJ has been in that hospital more than a year now and they haven't been able to do anything for her. I cannot believe that my little girl is some kind of monster. There simply has to be more behind this."

"There's nothing else we can do but wait," said Joan. "I'll go and visit TJ again tomorrow. I think it's better if I go alone this time. I will be around for the rest of the week. When Robert called me and asked me to come down here, I decided to take some vacation time and visit my sister who lives around here."

"I am so thankful to you for doing this for me and TJ," said Nils Henrik.

"You are welcome. I feel so badly about you and TJ and all the terrible things that happened to you. She has been in my thoughts since that first day when I found her under the woodshed. What she has gone through is probably the worst thing a young girl can suffer. I feel as strongly about it today as I did back then. If there's any way I can help her, I want to do it. So, don't think any more about it.

"Anyway, you and Robert have something else you need to concentrate on. Robert told me about the shooting episode at your house."

After they got back to the house, Nils Henrik asked Robert to tell him what he had found out from his investigation the day before. He showed Nils Henrik where the bullet that had been fired had hit near the doorway. It had hit one of the poles that held up the overhang. After he had found the bullet hole, he was able to deduce approximately where the shot had been fired from. Now he asked Nils Henrik exactly where he was when the shot was fired.

He had just grasped the door handle. Robert thought to himself that the shot had hit more than two metres away from Nils Henrik.

Robert took another close and intense look at the bullet hole, and then he looked over at where the shot had come from, and then over at the door.

"I believe that the shooter fired at you to scare you," said Robert. "What do you mean?" asked Nils Henrik.

"If he had really meant to shoot you, he would have shot directly at you or in front of you."

Nils Henrik studied the pole with the bullet hole and the door. Then they went inside. As soon as they were in, Nils Henrik went directly over to the cabinet where he had his bar. He opened it and took out a bottle of Seagram's 7. He asked Robert if he would like to have a drink.

"No thank you, and you'd better not have one either. You have had a severe shock and are not yet recovered. And remember what the doctor told you: no alcohol to be taken with the drugs you have been given."

Robert looked at Nils Henrik. "Alcohol doesn't help anything, and it usually makes things much worse. Now, I want you to come up and stay at my house for a while. We can keep each other company during this difficult time. You can bring Princess along. She can temporarily move in to Petra's old doghouse."

Nils Henrik looked over at Robert. "Thank you very much for the offer, but I think I'll stay here."

"Why? It will do you good to come away from here for a little while. There are too many memories here. Come on over; at least try it. I don't live very far from here, and remember you were just shot at. Do you think that whoever did that would try to pull a stunt as crazy as shooting at the house of a policeman? What do you say?"

Robert fixed Nils Henrik with his most innocent gaze. He had gotten the idea as soon as he noticed his friend going directly for the whisky bottle when he got home. He knew that if he could get him to come home with him, he could keep an eye on his alcohol intake. Plus, he would have someone to talk to when needed. Nils Henrik certainly didn't need to be all alone in that big house with his sad thoughts.

Robert, as well as Joan, had come to very much like the adventurous Norwegian and his daughter. Robert wished so much to be able to help him solve the mystery of the terrible and traumatic things that had happened to them.

He said, "It will also make it so much easier for us to conduct the investigation we are entering into. We can share information and ideas even at the breakfast table."

Nils Henrik sat on his chair in the corner. He didn't say anything, but it did look like he was thinking.

"OK, we can give it a try for two weeks," he answered.

Yes, thought Robert. *Now I have a possibility.*

CHAPTER 8

Dinner was over. Most of the patients sat in the main gathering room. TJ sat all alone. She didn't believe that she had one single thing in common with the others who were in there. But she was in there anyway. Mary the nurse came over to her and said, "Hi, TJ. You have to come with me over to the doctor again tonight, OK?"

TJ didn't say anything.

"You know what will happen if you don't come with me, don't you?"

She looked at TJ, but her gaze was completely closed.

"See if you can get yourself together. I'll come over again in a little while, OK?"

TJ still didn't say anything, but she got up and went over to her room. She shared room with Madeleine, who was out in the main room with the others.

TJ went in and took a shower. About twenty minutes later, Nurse

Mary came to pick her up.

"That's better. You look so pretty now. Come on, let's go over to the doctor now," she said. They started to walk down the hallway in the back of the main building. This hallway was more discreet than the main hallway. Nurse Mary was leading, with TJ following her.

When they reached the doctor's waiting room, Mary told TJ to sit down and wait. Then she went alone into the doctor's office. Five minutes later she came out with some pills and a glass of water. "Now take these," said Mary, "and everything will be much better." She held the pills and the glass of water up to TJ and smiled at her. TJ took them both without saying anything. Then she flung the glass and the pills across the room.

Mary became very angry.

"Pick them up at once! We can't keep the doctor waiting unnecessarily!"

TJ had been told earlier that she was required to wait fifteen minutes from the time she took the pills until the doctor could see her. She got down on her hands and knees and started searching for the pills. One was yellow and two were white. Mary watched closely what TJ was doing, and then for just a split second she looked away. TJ, grabbing the screwdriver from under her skirt, where she had fastened it with tape, jumped up and lifted it above Mary's head with one quick movement. As Mary turned around, TJ let it come down again with every bit of strength she had. It was a terrible blow. The screwdriver entered far into Mary's shoulder, right up to the handle, seven inches. Before Mary could even reach out, TJ had wrenched it out of her shoulder and brought it down again, this time into her back.

Mary tried to scream, but it came out as just a little croaking sound. TJ wrenched the screwdriver out again and stabbed Mary in the back a third and fourth time.

Mary lay lifeless on the floor under the desk. Blood began to stain her white uniform and run out onto the floor. Everything was completely quiet. TJ wiped the blood off the screwdriver and returned it to her home-made tape holster under her skirt. She looked in the mirror and didn't see any blood on herself. She double-checked: no blood.

She waited ten minutes, ten minutes that felt like ten hours. Then she knocked on the doctor's door exactly as usual.

"Oh, you look so pretty today," said Dr Irvine Jr. as he came towards her. He put his two hands out in front of him and beckoned her to come forward. He pulled her into his arms and kissed her ravenously. She let him do it.

"You are so beautiful," he said, "and tonight we are going to have a very full night."

He looked at her and smiled. He knew that afterwards she wouldn't remember anything that happened, since he had doubled the regular dosage of the pills.

"You know what? I asked Mary to join us tonight."

He looked at TJ. "I'm sure that you will like it a lot. Mary has said to me many times that she would love to have a threesome with us. She likes girls very much."

He was absolutely sure that anything he said or did to TJ this evening would not be remembered tomorrow morning. Well, of course she would be a little swollen and sore, but that was about all that she would feel.

"Come over here and sit down," he said lovingly. "Mary will be here in a minute." He sat down on the sofa in his office and patted the empty spot next to him.

TJ had been committed to the psychiatric hospital about three months when Nurse Mary came to fetch her for the first time. Mary had come to her with a dose of pills and said that the doctor recommended that she take them in order to be able to sleep better. TJ had had a lot of problems sleeping lately. The cabin fire had come back more and more into her dreams.

After she took the pills, she couldn't remember anything. She would wake up the next morning with a bad taste in her mouth and the smell of something she couldn't quite place in her nose. Whatever it was, it was terrible. There was also a soreness far back in her throat. She didn't know how it had happened, but she did realize after a short time that it always came after she took the pills that Mary had given her. She went over to the sink in her room and washed out her mouth. "Is your mouth sore?" her roommate Madeleine had asked.

After two weeks, Nurse Mary came to get TJ again. This time she told TJ to come with her at once. When they were in the doctor's waiting room with the door closed, she took out the same pills as last time.

"The doctor wants you to take these tonight again." She placed them on the desk in front of TJ.

"No, I don't want to take them. I don't need them," said TJ, crying. "Yes, you do. Doctor's orders," Mary replied.

"No, I'm not doing it."

"Well, that means that you're going into isolation," she said, and pointed to a straitjacket hanging on the wall.

TJ gave up and took the pills. She woke up the next morning with the same sickening smell in her nose and taste in her mouth. She was also very groggy. She went over to the sink and rinsed her mouth.

Madeleine, her roommate, asked, "Did you give a blow job to Doctor Irvine Jr. again?"

TJ just looked at her and had no idea what she was talking about. She was only fifteen years old. Madeleine was about twenty.

"Doctor Irvine Jr. likes young girls," said Madeleine. Then she went out through the door.

It was five weeks before Nurse Mary came to get TJ again, and again she was told to follow her to the doctor's office. TJ refused, but Mary asked two of the male nurses to come over. They put her into a straitjacket. Mary then forced the pills down her throat.

When she awoke after this third episode, not only was her mouth and throat sore, but also she was swollen and sore in her female parts and her underwear was flecked with blood. Madeleine took one look at her and asked, "So now he fucked you too?"

TJ and Madeleine shared a room, but that was the only thing they shared. They rarely talked to each other because TJ thought Madeleine was an extremist. Now, however, her curiosity was aroused, and she only had Madeleine to explain things to her. "What is it that you are talking about?" she asked.

Madeleine looked at TJ for a long time before she answered.

"Now it is you who is hot. Earlier it was me."

TJ slowly began to understand. She had never met Dr Irvine Jr. She couldn't remember anything at all. She did remember that she blacked out when Nurse Mary gave her the pills. She had no idea what the pills were for.

"It begins when he rapes you and fucks you in your mouth," said Madeleine. "After a few times he goes further. I don't know for sure, but I think one of the girls that he had used that way for a while killed herself after she found out that she was pregnant."

Madeleine got up and went out of the room.

TJ stayed behind. It was lunchtime, but she wasn't hungry.

After that, TJ was fetched by Nurse Mary regularly. It was always the same procedure. Mary came and got her and forced her to take the pills, and if she refused, she was threatened with being put into isolation. One time she spit them out, which got her three weeks in isolation. What was the real reason for using isolation at all? She didn't have the slightest idea.

Now she was sitting in Dr Irvine Jr.'s office on the sofa again.

Ever since the day she had spoken with Madeleine and found out what was going on, she had been planning this. She had lost count of how many times she had been brought here.

The behaviour of her roommate Madeleine changed after this. She began to see the desperation building in TJ's eyes. One morning after TJ had been brought back from the doctor's office, she began to tell what had happened to her and of all the times she had been taken there. She then taught TJ a technique of how to hide the pills in her mouth so they could not be seen when Mary checked to make sure she had swallowed them. The next three times TJ used this same technique, but she couldn't do it as well as Madeleine had. Out of three pills, she did manage to hide one of them. The other two went down. Now she knew who Dr Irvine Jr. was and what he did with her. The problem was that she was still so doped up that she was unable to protest.

The last time that Mary came to get TJ, it was unusually late in the evening. Most of the other patients had already gone to bed. Suddenly Mary was standing next to her bed in the room. She tried to be as quiet as possible, but TJ sensed that Madeleine was awake. She winked at TJ as the latter was forced to follow Mary out of the room. TJ had given up trying to protest. Mary would just call the male nurses to come and force her. So now she was sitting in the waiting room again and Mary had just brought the pills and the glass of water. "Be a good girl now and take these, and everything will be so much better."

TJ bent over and picked up the pills with her left hand. She then dumped them over into her right hand and put them into her mouth. Then she picked up the water glass and drank.

"That was a good girl. Now open your mouth and let me see if you really took them." She came over and looked into TJ's mouth. "OK then, we have fifteen minutes before we go in to visit Doctor Irvine Jr."

Mary looked up at the clock on the wall while she sat down behind the desk. She began to look at some papers.

"Can I go to the bathroom?" asked TJ.

"Yes, you can, but leave the door open," said Mary.

There was a bathroom right off the waiting room.

TJ went in and lifted up her nightgown before she turned around and sat on the toilet seat.

Mary was watching. When she was finished, she took some paper from the toilet roll and wiped herself. She got up from the toilet and threw in the pills before immediately flushing it. She had made it; she had managed to hide the pills.

"Come on, the doctor is waiting for you," Mary said from behind the desk.

She got up in order to escort TJ in to Dr Irvine Jr.

TJ was afraid, but there was nothing she could do to stop what was going to happen. She knew that without any doubt. Dr Irvine came out from behind his desk and leaned her backwards over the edge of it.

"Look who we have here. It's my little friend," he said.

He waved Mary out of the door.

"My little private dove, what can you do for me today?" he asked. "Why don't you come over here and sit down on your knee?"

He began to open his pants. She sat down in front of him. His fingers worked frantically until his pants were opened fully. He pulled them quickly down over his hips, pulling down his underpants at the same time. His cock stood straight up. He was very ready.

"Take it in your mouth," he commanded, but TJ wouldn't move. "Take it in your mouth, damn you."

He grabbed hold of her head and forced it down, guiding his penis into her mouth. He stopped when it reached the back of her throat so he wouldn't suffocate her. She was so afraid that she would give herself away and he would find out that she hadn't taken the pills. He couldn't help himself and started moving in and out of her mouth, holding her head still so she couldn't move. She felt again that same sickening choking sensation that she had awakened with so many times. He stopped, knelt down, turned TJ around, pulled her underwear down, pushed her down onto the floor, and entered her from the behind. He was completely wild and out of control.

TJ cried quietly, grating her teeth and trying to bear it, until she felt a gush of warm liquid enter her body. Then he pumped in and out a few more times and drew himself out of her.

He got up, pulled up his pants, and buttoned them up. TJ was still lying on her stomach on the floor and silently crying. Dr Irvine Jr. didn't notice it at all. He went behind the desk, sat down, picked up the telephone, and dialled a number.

Now TJ was again sitting on the sofa beside Dr Irvine Jr. in his office without any drugs in her bloodstream.

"Shall we begin without Mary?" he asked, beginning to fondle TJ's small breasts. She retaliated with an intentionally clumsy move that made his glasses fall off. TJ reached for the screwdriver. Damn it, he'd managed to catch the glasses in mid-air without them falling on the floor. She sat up straight again. Had he noticed anything? No, it didn't appear so.

She got her break when the telephone rang. He cursed before crossing the room and walking over to the desk to answer it.

"Irvine here," he said. That was all the opportunity TJ needed. She quickly retrieved the screwdriver from under her skirt and quietly approached the desk, where he was standing with his back to her. Again, she used all the strength she possessed and all the weight of her body to plunge the screwdriver deep into his back. Dr Irvine Jr. stiffened, dropped the telephone, and fell on the floor. She stabbed him again and again, counting the stabs—fifteen of them, for the fifteen times that he had raped her. Madeleine had told her that that was how many times they had come to get her.

She fell down to the floor and just lay there. She was unconscious for a short while. The screwdriver fell out of her hand and down on the floor. There was blood everywhere.

The person on the telephone was calling, "Doctor Irvine! Doctor Irvine!"

Dawson City, Yukon Territory

Nils Henrik and OJ went directly to the claims office, where all gold had to be delivered. Nobody was allowed to bring their own gold with them to sell anywhere else. This was because the Canadian government regulated that 14 per cent of all gold mined belonged to them. After that was paid, the rest was owned free and clear by the claim owner/gold miner.

Nils Henrik set the bag of gold on the counter under the sign that said "Gold here." A middle-aged man looked up from the papers he was working on. When he saw the size of the bag of gold Nils Henrik had set down at the window, he got up and came over to the counter at once. OJ was standing at Nils Henrik's side.

"Can I help you?"

"Yes, I would like to deliver this."

The man looked at the bag.

He said "OK" and reached for the ledger book before continuing. "Can you please be so kind as to write both your names and claim numbers here?" He pointed to an empty line in the book.

"Of course." Nils Henrik turned the book around, took the fountain pen which stood on the counter, and wrote down their names and claim: Nils Henrik Ellefsrud and Ole Johnny Larsen, Claim no. 6. He turned the book around again and pushed it back over the counter to the clerk, who had just brought forward the scale. He picked up the gold bag and started to pour the gold on to the scale as both Nils Henrik and OJ watched carefully. After the weighing was finished, the total amount was ready. The clerk wrote down the result, made some calculations, and wrote in the book again. Then he made more calculations and wrote more numbers in the book.

"OK," he said. He turned the book around and pushed it over the counter to them again while he spoke: "Here is your total amount." He pointed to the amount that was underlined twice. CAN$14,767.77. Nils Henrik and OJ looked at each other. They both had trouble keeping a straight face. They were in ecstasy.

"Sign on the line here," he said, and handed them a book with a double sheet of paper and a piece of carbon paper in between. "You both have to sign here as well." They both did.

The man took the book back, ripped out the second page, and gave it to them. There it was again for all to see: gold price per troy ounce, $116.42; total ounces, 146.59, minus 14 per cent, for a total of $14,676.77.

The money was put into an account which they opened while they were in the claims office. The Canadian government was helpful with this because there were a lot of foreigners with foreign addresses who had problems opening an account in the various banks in town. Nils Henrik and OJ were two of them.

"What do you say?" Nils Henrik asked OJ. "I think that we deserve a drink or five now."

He looked at his friend, who said, "I'm all for that." And they headed for the Armpit, one of the local bars.

There were only a few people there, nobody they knew. They went over to the bar and sat down. Judith, the bartender, came over to them to take their orders. She didn't recognize them at first.

"Hi, Judith," said OJ. She looked more carefully at them and then smiled.

"OJ and Nils Henrik. I didn't recognize you with all that long hair and those beards. How did it go? Did you find anything? I heard that you got a hold of Claim no. 6. Erik Engqvist did well with that claim before he disappeared."

"Well, we can't complain. We did find some gold, and we'll keep on trying."

Judith looked at them again. "OK. What will you have?" "Give me a beer," Nils Henrik answered.

"Me too," OJ said, following Nils's lead.

Judith took two glasses down from the shelf and filled them at the tap. "How long will you two be in town?" she asked.

"We think we will go back on Sunday morning. We just came in to town to get supplies."

"Don't you both need a place to sleep until then?" "Is the room that you rent out available?"

"It sure is."

"Then we'll take it."

"I charge five dollars a night," said Judith. "It's not cheap, but I'll throw in breakfast for that price."

OJ looked at her speculatively.

"I get it," she said, and set down the two full beer glasses in front of them. "Four dollars then."

After a while the bar began to fill up. And by the time the clock in the corner struck 6 p.m., the crowd numbered about twenty-five men and two women. The men were for the most part gold miners, but they paid primarily with paper money. A couple of the eldest and most experienced paid with gold. It wasn't quite legal, but nobody did anything about it. The Canadian government got their share of it no matter how the gold was delivered. Nils Henrik and OJ went over to Judith's house when the Armpit closed.

Breakfast at Judith's consisted of bacon, eggs, and pancakes with a lot of maple syrup. They sat and talked a little with her before they went out to make the necessary purchases of supplies that they had come to Dawson City for. These were mainly of canned foods, dried meat, flour, and potatoes. They also needed coffee. Finally, they bought six bottles of Canadian Club whisky. They had gotten used to taking a little drink of whisky each night before they turned in. After all their purchases were made, they arranged with Claus, a prospector there was very happy to have gotten away from prospecting and who now made his living taking people up and down to Dawson City, come pick them up and take them back to the claim the next morning.

They didn't go to the Armpit that evening. Instead they went to the Horseshoe Saloon. This was a place that served food in addition to being a bar. They found themselves a table by the window and sat down.

"Do you like to gamble, OJ?" Nils Henrik asked. He was looking over at a nearby table where five guys were playing poker.

"No, not really," OJ answered. "I tried it a couple of times down in New York but never had any success at it, and I really don't have any wish to try it again.

"But I say I don't like gambling. What can be more like gambling than what we are doing right now?" he added.

Nils Henrik smiled. "You right, but so far we have won."

"Well, so far we sure have," said OJ. "But I'm still wondering how you managed to lure me up here to get involved with this, though I can't say I mind it that much."

The waiter came back to them with the two beers they'd ordered when they'd sat down.

"Are you two just passing through?" he asked. "No, we're prospecting up near Bonanza Creek." "Oh, OK. Is it going well?"

"So far, we haven't gotten rich, but we haven't starved to death either," OJ answered.

The waiter continued, "I tried prospecting too, but I had to quit. We were attacked by two bears, and then I fell and broke my leg. I'm still not healed up, but I hope by next year it will be healed and I can go back and try again."

He went back to the kitchen to get their steaks, which they'd ordered at the same time.

The steaks were just delicious; they both enjoyed them. Out at camp the food was the same thing every day, canned food from different cans. Nils Henrik had never been a good cook, but he had improved some. OJ wasn't much better, but together they managed. So, a proper meal was welcome every time they were down for supplies.

Suddenly Nils Henrik took his last piece of steak and threw it outside through the open window.

"What are you doing?" OJ asked, looking at him strangely.

Nils Henrik just looked back at him and pointed out the window. There was a dog out there. It threw itself on the piece of meat like it hadn't had anything to eat for at least a year. What kind of dog it was, was hard to say, but there must have been some German shepherd in it. Nothing else was said about the dog. After paying for their food, the two men went straight back to Judith's place.

Judith had three rooms that she rented out. All the rooms had four beds, and that weekend she had rented out two of them, one to Nils Henrik and OJ and one to three other men whom Nils Henrik and OJ didn't know. However, they did come to know each other later that night.

That was when they all were awakened by a terrible racket about two in the morning. The front door opened with a crash. It was Judith.

It was quite obvious that not only had she sold a lot of drinks that evening. She had also taken in more than her fair share of them herself. Now she was home and she was not alone. She had male company with her. Nils Henrik and OJ went out into the hallway. Two of the men from the other room were already out there, and the third was perhaps still sleeping. First the noise was from downstairs in the kitchen, but after a while it moved up to Judith's room. There the sounds turned into other, more familiar noises. One of the men from the other room commented, "It doesn't sound like they're making a baby; it sounds more like they're killing one."

After the action was over, everything became quiet again, but now it took them a long time to fall asleep. Before Nils Henrik finally went back to dreamland, he heard OJ comment, "There goes our breakfast." He remembered laughing inside before he drifted off.

Claus was already at his place when they came over at 7 a.m. He asked them if they would like some coffee, and both of them gratefully accepted. As OJ had stated, Judith hadn't gotten their breakfast ready.

They went over to the country store to pick up their supplies. On the way over, Nils Henrik caught a glimpse of the dog from last night, but he didn't think more about it, because they had become busy with the supplies.

The supplies were loaded up on the back of Claus's truck, and now they were on their way out to their claim again. An hour later they came to the end of the road. From there they needed to carry the supplies the rest of the way, eight long kilometres. At 7 p.m. they were finally back at their camp. They still had the tedious job of unpacking the supplies and putting them away, packing all the food into containers and burying them so that the bears wouldn't get to it. Then they could finally go to bed.

Nils Henrik woke up to a heavy rain pelting the roof of the tent. It was not unusual for it to rain out here, but it was much more intense and heavier than usual. He looked over at OJ, who was still sleeping. He put on his raincoat and went outside to piss. It was already light outside even though it was only 5 a.m. On his way back to the tent, he thought he saw something over on the other side of the tent. What the hell was it? He went closer and said, "Oh shit!' It was the dog from Dawson City. *How the hell did it get here?* he wondered. The dog greeted Nils Henrik by lying down and putting its head onto its front paws. Then it just looked pitifully at him.

"What are you doing here?" Nils Henrik asked, and put the back of his hand forward so that the dog could smell him. The dog didn't move; it just lay there looking at him. It was soaking wet and cold. "What's your name?" Nils Henrik asked. He really didn't know why he asked, since he didn't expect an answer. The dog kept following Nils Henrik with his eyes. It probably was wondering just what Nils Henrik was going to do to it.

"Are you hungry?" Nils Henrik asked, as he looked around for something to give the creature. His eyes went to a can of stew that had been there since they'd first come up. Neither he nor OJ liked that stew, but they hadn't thrown it out because they thought one day they might need it. He opened the can and put the contents into a bowl. He sat it down in front of the dog, which looked up at Nils Henrik with a grateful look that seemed to say "Thank you."

The dog went back and lay down in the same place it was before. The dog had just adopted them. Nils Henrik saw that it was a female.

After their first season in the Yukon Territory, Nils Henrik and OJ travelled back to Edmonton. They closed up their camp for the winter on the sixteenth of September. It had already become so cold that the water that they needed for washing out the gold was starting to freeze. They decided to go south for the winter and to return early in the spring. They took down the tent, took apart their washing troughs, and put everything away in a safe, dry place. What remained of their food was left buried deep in the ground and covered with rocks so that the bears couldn't possibly get to it. Then they started south.

They each had their backpacks, Princess too. OJ had taken some of the sailcloth that they used to collect rainwater and fashioned a nice pack that would fit neatly over her back. They needed to go all the way down to Erik's place.

Erik was a loner who had settled himself into a camp at Jim's Pond.

He made his living primarily by guiding and transporting miners back and forth to Dawson City. When he first started, he used a horse and wagon, but now he had an old truck. Now and then it would happen that he would try to pan a little gold, but he didn't stick with it enough for anything to come of it.

"Hi, Erik. Can you take us down to Dawson?" said OJ.

Erik just stood there and stared at him. OJ could see that he was sucking on the last tooth he had left in his mouth. He looked both OJ and Nils Henrik up and down for a few moments before shifting his gaze to Princess.

"Have you two got a new family member?" he asked.

"Yeah, she just suddenly turned up. Her name is Princess," OJ answered.

Erik looked at her again. Then he said, "She's very fine. Do you want to sell her?"

OJ took a look at Nils Henrik before answering. "No, I think we'll keep her for a little longer."

"Just a question. Are you laying up for the winter?" Erik asked.

"Yes. The water has already begun to freeze, so there's nothing left to do. We're going down to Edmonton," OJ continued.

"Yes, I'll take you down to Dawson City, but you have to wait a little. I'm waiting for a Mister Robert W. Duff. He came in last week and ordered me to be ready today. He should be here any minute."

Nils Henrik and OJ resigned themselves to waiting. They each found themselves a place out in the sun on the grassy area near Erik's woodshed.

Mr Robert W. Duff arrived around 1.30. Erik came over to get them at once.

"Mister Duff is here now. We can go."

Neither Nils Henrik nor OJ knew who Mr Duff was. He was obviously not a gold miner, which they could see. He had come up to meet with one of the miners to form a business deal. He was in the real estate business. OJ sat in the back of the truck together with Princess. Nils Henrik sat in the truck cabin with Erik and Mr Duff, who was very interested in life out here in the wilderness. He asked Nils Henrik questions about how it was to go and try to find gold.

Nils Henrik himself was interested in what Mr Robert W. Duff did for a living, and since they were sitting next to each other, there was a lively conversation going on the whole way down to Dawson City.

Just before they parted ways after their arrival, they planned to meet for dinner. Nils Henrik had chosen the Horseshoe Saloon to meet, and Mr Duff thought that was a fine idea.

Nils Henrik and OJ went for the last time this year to the local gold delivery point, where they were required to bring in the gold they had mined. The total amount for the season, after the Canadian government had taken its share, was $97,655. This had very much exceeded their expectations. They deposited the money in the same account that they had opened earlier.

They shook hands with each other in self-congratulation before leaving the office. As soon as they came back out, Princess jumped up and followed them down the street. The Armpit was pretty crowded this afternoon. It looked like they weren't the only miners who had already closed down for the season. The noise level was high, and right in the middle of the room sat

Sluice Box Harry. He was in very good spirits. As soon as he laid eyes on Nils Henrik and OJ, he jumped up and waved them over.

"How did it go?" he asked. "Did you get rich?"

Nils Henrik could smell the strong odour of Harry from all the way across the room. He thought to himself that maybe he and OJ should have gone to the bathhouse instead of the bar. He was sure he didn't smell much better himself.

He answered Harry's question: "We did OK, at least we have kept our heads above water, but that's about all."

"Well, then you have done well. Everybody who says something like that has found more gold than they will admit." Then before Nils Henrik and OJ had a chance to answer him, they each had a drink in their hands which had come out of the bottle of Canadian Club whisky that Sluice Box Harry had in front of him.

It took them quite a while to tear themselves away from that gang, but when the clock struck four, they finally get out the door. Nils Henrik had already spoken with Judith about renting the room again, but this time the price was five dollars. He had neglected to mention the fact that they had Princess with them, but they would find a way to smuggle her up to the room. That dog had come to mean a lot to them. The next stop was the bathhouse. Nils Henrik was really looking forward to a bath and a shave. They didn't want to let Princess into the bathhouse, so Nils Henrik spoke gently to her and asked her to wait outside.

One pan of gold, Picture

Robert W. Duff was already waiting for them when they arrived at the Horseshoe Saloon. He had gotten a table in the corner. He waved them over as soon as he saw them come in the door. He said he almost didn't recognize them now that they were clean and shaven with new clothes on. They both just smiled.

"You both look great. Can I buy you a drink?" Mr Duff asked. "No," Nils Henrik answered, "we will buy you a drink. This is our evening. We have been to the claims office this afternoon and found out that we have done even better than expected this season. Therefore, it's time to celebrate."

It was an unwritten law among the gold miners never to speak about how much they had made during the course of the season. The man who worked in the claims office was also under a strict law of secrecy. The Royal Canadian Mounted Police enforced laws like these, and so did the other miners. If somebody told how much they or others made in gold, they might find themselves receiving a late-night unwelcome visit.

"Well OK then," said Robert Duff. "I'll take a pint of beer first. I'm thirsty."

Nils Henrik and OJ each ordered whisky.

Nils Henrik quickly began to question Robert Duff about the real estate business. It was an area that he was not very familiar with. He had listened to what Robert had to say on the way down to Dawson City, and now he was very curious about it. Bob willingly shared his knowledge and told them that if they wanted to invest in real estate, they should not hesitate to call him, as he would help them in any way he could. He had taken this trip up here to visit one of his best clients.

There were some properties going into foreclosure and he was going to buy them on behalf of this client.

"What is foreclosure?" Nils Henrik asked.

"That is when the owner of a house or a piece of land cannot pay the bank loan he has on the property. The bank then takes possession of the property.

Then the bank sells it for the amount remaining on the loan, which means that if a property costs twenty thousand dollars and the buyer has already paid seven thousand dollars of it, the bank will unload it for thirteen thousand dollars after a foreclosure, even if it is worth more. The loser in these cases is the owner who can't pay." Nils Henrik looked at Mr Duff. "Let me get this straight. The owner loses everything he or she puts into the loan?"

"That's correct," Mr Duff answered.

"But why doesn't the bank sell the property for the full price?" Nils

Henrik asked.

"The banks aren't allowed to do that. If they do, they have to pay back the money to the owner who lost it. The banks are not in the market of selling houses; they are just interested in getting back the loan."

Nils Henrik continued, "If I were the person who bought the house, then in reality I would be getting the seven thousand dollars' profit on the market value of the house."

"Yes, that is correct," Mr Duff answered. "Wow, does this happen often?"

"Yes, very often. It does go up and down a little along with the economy in general."

Nils Henrik had just gotten something to think about. He wanted to learn more about it, but for now he would just keep it to himself.

Nils Henrik and OJ had to wait until Friday, 23 September, before they could get down to White Horse.

Robert W. Duff had taken the bus down two days earlier, but since Nils Henrik insisted on taking Princess with them, he and OJ had to wait until they could hitch a ride on a truck. Now they were sitting together in the truck with Scott McCarter, the truck driver. Princess was back in the cargo area of the truck. There was a possibility that Scott might be going all the way to Edmonton, but he wouldn't know for sure until they got into White Horse. If he was going further, they would be able to continue on with him.

In White Horse, Scott drove directly to the goods terminal, which lay all the way down towards the mouth of the Yukon River. It was placed there because much of the goods traffic was distributed via the river. Nils Henrik and OJ went along with him.

"Will you find out now whether you'll go further or not?" asked OJ as they neared the terminal.

"Yes, I'll find out almost at once," said Scott. "Why don't you two get a bite to eat over there at Maggie's Diner? I'll come over there as soon as I find out. I could use something to eat myself."

"Sounds like a good plan," said OJ.

Scott swung the truck into the terminal entrance. Nils Henrik and OJ went over to Maggie's and walked in. Princess waited for them outside.

"You came down from Dawson, I think," said a voice right behind him.

Nils Henrik jumped. He hadn't seen or heard her coming over. "Yes, we did. How did you know that?" he answered.

"Well, we have our ways," she answered, and smiled. "It's profitable for us to know these things," she said, smiling even wider.

Nils Henrik and OJ didn't answer, but they both smiled back at her. "Can I get you anything from the bar while you decide what you want to eat?"

"Yes," said OJ. "I'll take a Moosehead beer." "And you?" she asked Nils Henrik.

"I'll begin with a CC and 7 Up."

She wrote down their order and said she would be right back.

"Wait just a minute," said Nils Henrik. "Is it possible to get a bowl of water for our dog waiting outside? I would also appreciate it if you have any leftovers or something you might be throwing away that we could give to her. I'll be glad to pay for it."

"Of course, she can have some water, and I'll go look for something to feed her," she said. Then she went into the kitchen.

After about forty-five minutes Scott came into the restaurant, went straight over to Maggie, gave her a big hug, and then gave her his food order before coming over to Nils Henrik and OJ's table.

"This is your lucky day. I am going on to Edmonton, tomorrow morning at eight o'clock. I hope that's not too early for you?" he asked with a smile.

"That will be just fine," OJ answered. Then he looked at Nils Henrik. "We need to find a place to sleep then."

"Maggie has a room in the back that she rents out. Why don't we ask her if it's available? I'm going to be sleeping in the honeymoon suite," Scott said with a big smile.

The room was available for $2.50 per night. The extra fifty cents was because of Princess. Nils Henrik and OJ thought that was just fine, so they took the room.

Nils Henrik, OJ, and Scott stayed in the restaurant talking for a while. Then Maggie came and joined them. It was then that Nils Henrik realized Maggie was Scott's wife.

It had been a quiet night at the restaurant, so Maggie closed early. It looked like a heavy rainstorm was coming.

They went to their room after setting up a time for breakfast. Scott said that the truck would be ready to leave around 8 a.m. Scott had met a friend at the freight terminal, one who used to be a driver, and he agreed to load the freight for a few dollars. He had lost all he had in his divorce, which had happened because of his dependence on alcohol. Scott hoped that the money would be put to better use than buying another bottle, but deep down he knew it wouldn't.

The rain that had passed through during the night had been quite heavy, but Nils Henrik and OJ managed to get through to the loading terminal without getting too muddy.

The men were still loading the truck when they got there, and Scott was already there. "We're almost finished loading," he said. "Just throw your bags up on the top. I'm just going to run over and kiss Maggie goodbye, and then we'll be on our way."

Scott came back with an old blanket and laid it in the back of the truck. That was for Princess.

Scott put the truck into first gear and said, "Edmonton, here we come!"

He was planning to make the trip in four days, and he had already arranged for a place to sleep the first two nights. The second two they would take as they came, but Scott was quite sure that it would be OK. He had made this trip many times, so he knew the route and all the good places to stop.

The first two days of travel went according to plan. OJ gave up trying to count how many black bears he saw after he'd reached thirty-five on the first day. Then there were the moose, which were extremely big. Again, Nils Henrik had seen a lot of moose back home in Kongsberg, but they were much bigger out here.

The men started out each day early in the morning and drove until about 9 p.m., which is when they stopped for the night. That's how the third day started as well, but this day turned out not at all like the others. It was about

11 a.m. when they passed Valleyview and started on the stretch down to White Court. The first small town was Little Smokey, a group of four houses and a gas station. Scott knew the area and the owner of the station. He always filled up here when he passed through, and that was his intention today as well. He told Nils Henrik and OJ to go and stretch their legs while he filled the tank, saying that afterwards they would have something to eat.

The first thing Scott noticed was that Joe was not at the station. He had become very good friends with Joe and his wife over the past few years. Besides the station, they had added a little restaurant in the back corner. Scott had planned to eat there.

Today it wasn't Joe who came out. It was someone who was a complete stranger to Scott. "Where's Joe?" Scott asked. "He's not here anymore."

"What happened to him? Is he OK?" Scott asked. No answer.

"Did he sell out?"

"Yeah, new owner," said the man who had come out. He answered without looking at Scott.

"So where is Joe now then? Did he leave?"

"Yeah."

"Do you know where?" "No."

Scott thought he could hear a little bit of an American accent when the man spoke.

OJ and Nils Henrik did what Scott had suggested, taken a walk around the place. Princess had jumped out of the back and followed them.

"Nothing much happens here." OJ was looking around himself when saying it.

Nils Henrik smiled. "It sure isn't Manhattan," he answered.

They walked back to the gas station, which was placed a little distance from the houses. They couldn't see Scott anywhere, so they went inside to look for him. They were hungry and were looking forward to something to eat.

The next thing that Nils Henrik knew was waking up with an enormous pain in his head. He was groggy and confused, but then he became aware. He noticed that they all were sitting on chairs with their hands and legs tied up. In front of them stood a man with a revolver in his belt. Another man sat at a table. Nils Henrik couldn't see if he had a weapon. OJ had not regained consciousness yet, but Nils Henrik could see that Scott was awake.

Nils Henrik looked at the table and saw that their money and wallets were there.

"Is that all the money you have?" It was the man at the table who spoke.

Neither Nils Henrik nor Scott answered him. He looked at them again.

"I know there's more. Where is it?"

He looked closely at them, one by one. Still no answer.

OJ began to come to. The man at the table looked over at his partner and nodded. He went towards OJ, taking out a knife. He went around behind OJ and put the knife against his throat.

"You have one minute to tell me where the rest of the money is hidden," the man at the table said.

"We don't have any other money," Scott answered.

"One minute," the man said again.

"But we really don't have any more," Scott again.

OJ was not yet fully awake, but he was regaining consciousness fast. "Thirty seconds," said the man at the table. The knife was pressed harder against OJ's throat.

She came without warning, flying across the room, and buried her teeth deep in the shoulder of the man holding the knife. The knife which the man had been holding at OJ's throat went sailing through the air and hit the wall. Princess held tightly on to him, and he fell onto the floor under her weight.

The man at the table was equally surprised. He stood up. Princess turned to him with her teeth bared. The man stopped all his movement. Princess backed up to a point where she could see both of the men, and then growled menacingly.

The man on the floor had gotten over the shock of Princess's attack. His arm was hanging down, completely useless. He slowly moved forward, keeping his eyes on Princess the whole time. Then he got up and ran quickly out the door. The other man followed after him.

Princess chased them. The man with the revolver used his undamaged hand to shoot at her—one, two, and three shots.

Five minutes later Princess came back through door unharmed.

Scott started to work at untying the rope around his wrists. It was tied very tight, and he couldn't get it loose no matter how hard he tried. The others had the same problem. Plus, they were placed too far away from each other to be able to help one another.

It was OJ who got the idea. He got Princess to drag his chair over closer to Scott's so he could use his hands to help Scott untie his ropes and then Nils Henrik's.

Joe and his wife were bound and gagged in the other room. She was still unconscious, but Joe was awake. His shirt had a big bloodstain on it. Scott pulled off Joe's shirt. He had a deep wound, probably a stab wound. His arm was useless. They found some clean cloths and bandaged up his arm as best they could. Joe's wife still hadn't come to. They were both placed in the back of the car. Scott drove nonstop to White Court.

CHAPTER 9

26 September 1972, at the ranch

"You take my car and drive with TJ. You both have a lot to talk about. My car will allow you all to stay in the front. Joan and I can take your car." It was Robert who suggested this. Nils Henrik and TJ had started to have conversations together again, and she had started to miss her father more and more.

After TJ was released from the psychiatric hospital, Joan invited her to stay with her. TJ felt safe with her, but she had begun to really miss her father.

Nils Henrik visited her as often as possible. She opened up more and more to him. She felt proud each time she could show him her little girl. She had baptized her Asha (meaning "hope"), which was the name that her grandmother had asked her to use, hoping that TJ would look to the future now. Both her grandmother and grandfather visited her often, and that helped greatly towards her regaining her self-esteem. She started to believe in herself again.

Today was a very special day. TJ would get back home to the ranch for the first time since the cabin fire. She was in suspense, but happy. She had dreamed about this day for a long time.

Nils Henrik and TJ got into Robert's car. They placed the baby on a special child seat between them.

"Are you going to stop by at Jimmy and Peta's?" Robert asked Nils Henrik.

"Yes, but just for a few minutes."

"OK, we'll see you out at the ranch then." He got into Nils Henrik's car along with Joan, and they drove out. They had a drive of about three hours in front of them.

All of a sudden there was strong flash of light, a loud bang, then another bang, and one more.

Joan looked over at Robert, who was slumped over the wheel. The car was still moving forward. Another flash and a bang. She felt something rip into the right side of her chest. She felt an enormous pain as she was thrown out of the car, landing on the side of the road. She looked around quickly to see where the car was. It was lying nearby with its wheels up in the air. There were flames shooting out from the engine. She could see Robert still behind the wheel. Despite the pain, she got herself over to the car as the flames began to grow. She noticed he was bleeding profusely from a head wound. He was unconscious. She had to get him out; the car could explode any moment. The steering wheel was bent at an odd angle and had trapped his body behind it. She tried to move him, but it was not possible. What should she do? She needed to get him out. She had to get to the other side. From there she could grab his legs and hopefully be able to drag him out that way. She crawled in to the car, undid his seat belt, and found his legs, first the right one and then the left. She got her arms around them and started to pull.

She never was able to explain how she managed to get Robert Blake out of the wreck. Everything went black around her, and she collapsed on the ground next to him. She could hear the flames crackling in the distance, but she was unable to see them.

Then she heard a voice: "Over here! There's two persons here. Hurry!"

She thought she knew the voice. Yes, it was Jimmy's. He was with the special unit of the mounted police force. His real name was Jimenez Franklin.

He saw immediately that Joan was alive and turned his attention to Robert. He bent down and felt for a pulse. There was one. It was weak, but he knew that would be the case.

"They're both alive!" he called. Suddenly there were people everywhere.

"Shouldn't Joan and Robert be here by now?" TJ looked at the clock at the dashboard. It showed 9.15.

"Yes, they should," Nils Henrik answered. "Where are they?" TJ asked.

"Well, you know that they both work for the police. Something could have happened, and they could have been called in to take care of it," Nils Henrik said.

"I guess they will be here soon or at least call us," he continued.

TJ got out of the car. She looked up at the house and thought, *It's been more than eight years since I have been here.* She took a look around. It didn't look much different from before. Maybe it was not quite as well-kept as when her mother was alive.

"Take the baby and let's go in," said Nils Henrik. He opened the car door for her. She leaned in and got the baby out of her seat.

"I kept your room exactly as it was. I did the same with Albert's room. Do you want to see it?"

"Not yet. I just want to sit here for a little while first." She sat down with the baby in her lap.

"It feels so strange to be here again. So many years, almost half of my life," she said. She had tears in her eyes now.

"Do you want something to eat?" Nils Henrik asked gently. He knew that he must be both careful and gentle. Even though TJ was beginning to find her way back to herself, she was still very sensitive. "Yes, please," she answered.

"What would you like to eat?"

"Can we have pizza?" she asked. She had very fond memories of the family eating pizza together. It wasn't often that their mother would let them have it, so those times were special.

"We can get a pizza, but I will have to order it from Domino's, so it might take some time."

"I can wait. I want Asha to sit together with us while we eat. Do you mind?"

"Of course not, if that's what you want. We should sit all together. We are the family now."

It was a late night for them—almost one in the morning before they finally went to bed. Nils Henrik had set up a child's crib in TJ's room. Her tears began to flow once again when she went to bed.

Nils Henrik was much too worked up to go to bed himself. Finally, he had been able to take his daughter home again. He went over to the bar and fixed himself a CC and 7 Up. He sat down in his chair, a chair he had sat and cried in many times before. His tears began to flow again, but they were tears of joy today.

After they'd found out that TJ was pregnant, things started to change.

After Dr Irvine Jr. was murdered, TJ was placed in isolation. She was a dangerous person now, and she sat in isolation for five months.

During this time, she didn't say a word to anyone. Nils Henrik visited her regularly, but all she did was sit there silently. The only person she said anything to was Joan.

One day when Joan visited her, she noticed that the girl looked a little strange around her waist. This prompted Joan to ask the hospital staff about her menstrual cycle, which, she discovered, nobody knew anything about.

This made Joan began put two and two together: the stabbing of Dr Irvine Jr. and now a possible pregnancy. She didn't say anything to the staff, but the very next day she called Robert and let him know her suspicions.

"Interesting," said Robert.

"How do we proceed with this?" she asked.

There was silence on the phone. Robert was thinking. Joan could sense his intensity. When he spoke again, he said, "Let's keep this between ourselves for the moment. Don't even say anything to Nils Henrik. Give me two days and then we'll talk again." Then he hung up the phone without waiting for Joan's answer.

Robert sat and thought of this for quite a while before he picked up the phone again and dialled a number. It rang at the other end. When his call was answered, he said, "Peter McKay please."

"May I ask who's calling?" the other party said. "Lieutenant Blake."

"OK just one moment."

"Good morning, my old friend. I know it's been a long time, but we've both been busy, so don't blame yourself for that."

"So, what is it that you need?" Peter McKay laughed off his ownremark.

"Well, first I was wondering if you have time to have lunch with me today," Robert asked.

"Actually, I don't. Is it important?"

"Yes, I think so, and if it is what I think it is, you'll be able to use it in your re-election campaign," Robert explained.

"I hear you," said Peter.

"Well, let's have lunch first. I do not want to talk about this over the telephone."

"OK, I'll cancel a couple of appointments and see you at the Blue Barge at one o'clock. Will that work for you? I know it's kind of a long drive," Peter said.

"No problem, I'll be there." Robert hung up and looked at his watch. If he was going to make it out to Lakeside, he would have to leave almost at once.

Peter McKay had not yet arrived when Robert entered the Blue Barge restaurant. Robert was five minutes late, but that didn't mean anything since Peter was almost always running behind schedule. The dining room was already full, but Robert asked the head waiter anyway if there was a table, possibly a little out of the way and undisturbed. The waiter answered that he wasn't sure, so Robert took out his police badge and explained that he was on police business and it was a working lunch.

"OK, we have a table available on the second floor. It's not usually used; it's only the owner of the restaurant who eats up there. He's not here today, so it is available." He looked up to make sure that it was not being used by anyone. "You can go ahead up."

"OK. Can you bring up Mister McKay when he arrives?" "Sure. Would you like to have a drink while you are waiting?" "Yes. Please bring me a beer and a cup of coffee."

"OK," said the head waiter. "I'll send that up with Rose. She'll be your waitress."

Peter finally arrived at 1.45. He apologized, saying that something had come up at the last minute and he wasn't able to get away.

"That's OK," said Robert.

"Can I get you anything to drink before lunch?" "I'll take a beer too."

Robert gave the drink order to Rose, who had just shown Peter McKay upstairs. The two men received menus and began to read them.

"Have you eaten here before, Peter?" "Yes, but it was quite a while ago."

"What do you recommend?"

"That's a difficult question. What do you feel like eating today, fish or meat?"

"How's the fish?" "Very good."

"It's not often that I order fish when I eat out. Restaurants serve so much fried fish. I prefer fish when it's broiled or baked. I learned how to prepare it from a good friend of mine, a Norwegian. He's also the reason I asked you to meet with me today."

"First, to answer your question, the trout is baked, so that should be something you would like. Next is, who is this man?"

They ordered their lunches.

"Well, the man's name is Nils Henrik Ellefsrud. I'm quite sure that you have heard of him."

"Not offhand, but please continue."

"I'll get back to him, but this man has a daughter, a beautiful young girl who has had nothing but problems for the last eight years. Now she is sitting in isolation in the mental hospital, Edmonton Psychiatric. Can you remember a few months ago when a Doctor Irvine Jr. was killed by one of the patients?"

"Yes, I can."

"Well, that was her, and it is me who is handling her case. After that episode she was declared to be criminally insane by another psychiatric doctor and put in isolation. The only two people who have been allowed in to see her are Joan, one of my colleagues, and her father. Normally no one is allowed into the isolation area, but since we are trying to find out some kind of a reason why she would have attacked both the doctor and the nurse, they allowed them. I can't remember the nurse's name. She was stabbed four times, but she survived. I think she is still on sick leave. However, since all this happened inside of the psychiatric hospital and between a patient and the personnel, it has been, and still is, very difficult to conduct an investigation. But now some new development has just come to light which might help us find out what really happened."

Peter sat and listened without saying anything.

Robert continued, "In order to conduct a more formal and detailed investigation, I am going to need your help."

"Why is that?"

"Because it is a hospital for psychiatric patients. I don't have permission to come and go as I please."

"OK, but how can I help you with that?"

"You can go to the health department or the minister of health and get me special permission granted to conduct a more detailed investigation."

"So, it's been that difficult?"

"Yes, it has," Robert answered. He continued, "My colleague Joan visited her yesterday, and she believes that the girl is pregnant. How that could have happened is a question in itself. She is in a psychiatric hospital for women only and has been there for almost two years.

How could she possibly be pregnant? There are only three doctors and a couple of male nurses in there. She has not been outside the hospital once since she was committed. On top of that, she has been in isolation for five months."

Peter looked at Robert for a long time before he spoke again.

"Are you saying what I think you're saying, that the doctor—what was his name again?"

"Irvine Jr.," Robert answered.

"Are you saying he might have abused her, and that this abuse might have led to the aggression which ended up with her knifing him?"

"I don't know, but I sure would like to find out. And by the way, it wasn't a knife, it was a screwdriver."

Peter sat and thought for a while before he answered.

"Robert, I can't promise anything for sure, but I'm willing to initiate an investigation. Can you arrange for me to meet this Norwegian? I would prefer to hear the whole story from the beginning from him. In the meantime, I'll pull some strings."

"Thank you, Peter, and yes I will arrange for you to meet Nils Henrik Ellefsrud," Robert answered.

Peter picked up his beer glass and emptied it. "I've got to get back."

He pointed to the table.

Robert said, "Don't even think about it." He knew Peter had asked about the bill.

"I'll pay for the lunch. It's the least I can do."

"OK," said Peter. He got up to leave. "I have a few loose ends to tie up this afternoon, but you will be hearing from me soon, in not more than two days, OK?"

"Of course. And thank you again. You won't regret it."

Peter smiled, turned around, and left.

Robert stayed a little longer thinking. He still felt guilty that the criminals who burned the cabin had never been caught. But after some time, the trail had gone cold and the central police had allowed the cases—all of them, the cabin fire, the building collapse, and the disappearance of OJ—to collect nothing but dust.

Joan and Robert Blake sat in Robert's office. They were waiting for a judge's order to allow them to speak with the doctors, nurses, and patients at the psychiatric hospital. This would enable them to hopefully find out what happened on that evening almost five months ago. Peter had come through for Robert and had gotten back to him the next day. The minister of health had taken a personal interest in the case and circumvented the rules of the hospital. This required a special order from a judge to make it happen, but the judge had been away for two days. Now they were waiting for his order to arrive. The plan was already in place.

The police lieutenant brought them the order immediately after receiving it. Robert opened it and read the contents. Robert looked up at the lieutenant. "Please, get everyone in to the conference room." "The receptionist too?"

"No, he can stay there. We meet in ten minutes."

Robert looked at Joan, who was still sitting with him in his office. "Finally, we might be able to get something good done for that family," he said. Then they went out.

"Hello, everybody. First, I would like to introduce Lieutenant Joan Arnold. She is the head of Department 4342. She is here to assist us in this operation. The reason that she is involved is because she has participated in this case since day one. You will eventually learn all about that. I know that some of you remember her from when she worked in this department as my assistant.

"So, on to this operation. Can you remember about five months ago when a doctor at Edmonton Psychiatric Hospital was stabbed by one of his patients?" Robert looked around the room. "Well, that is what this operation is related to. In my hand here, I hold a judge's order giving me the authority to do a proper technical investigation of that crime, something that was not done earlier.

She was a committed psychiatric patient and the hospital didn't want the police around the other patients. The case was pretty self- explanatory, they said, so it was closed.

"Now some new elements have come to light which require the case to be reopened and investigated.

"There was also a nurse who was stabbed, but she survived.

"We will now do a full investigation of this case, and we will start this evening. If any of you have other plans, you need to cancel them now. You are hereby ordered to be a part of this operation."

Robert looked around at everyone again.

"Is there anybody who needs to give a message to anyone saying that they won't be home until, well, who knows when?" A hand went up. "OK, give the message to Hans in reception. He will make the call for you and let them know that you have been ordered out on a special investigation. Anybody else?"

A woman's hand went up. "Same for you. The rest of you take five minutes. After then we will brief you on what we will be doing and to whom. You will work together in groups of two.

"There is nobody at the hospital who knows we are coming, or that we have this judge's order, and we want to keep it this way. We don't want any important evidence to disappear. We shall go through and lay out any material that could possibly be relevant to this case. This goes especially for anything Doctor Irvine Jr. was in possession of, as well as his assistant, Nurse Mary. It was she who was stabbed that night by the same patient. We must not forget anyone who is in isolation. Just because they are in there now does not mean they were isolated the night that Doctor Irvine Jr. was killed.

"What we are looking for is to find out how a female patient could get pregnant without having any interaction with any men. TJ was committed to a department for females only and with only female personnel. The only men that these women and girls have had contact with were a few male guards and three doctors, Doctor Irvine Jr., Doctor Miller, and Doctor James.

"We have to go through all their reports, evaluations, and medication logs. We also have to go through the pharmacy at the hospital and check their records and reports. We have to check out what medications were ordered and prescribed and to which patients they were given."

Robert stopped and looked around. "Do any of you have any questions?"

"All right then, you will all be given a list of what you have been assigned to do. As soon as you get your lists, please proceed to the van that is waiting outside. Erik here will give you your assignments." Robert and Joan went out of the room.

Precisely at 5.45 p.m. the ten police officers went into the reception area of Edmonton Psychiatric Hospital. They all knew exactly what their assignment was and whom they would be working with.

Lt. Robert Blake introduced himself to the receptionist and asked her to get the person in charge of Department B of the west wing.

"Just one moment," she said. She picked up the telephone and dialled a number. When her call was answered, she said, "Can you come to the reception desk at once? There are some police officers here who would like to talk to you." The receptionist listened silently to something being said. "No, you have to come right away," she explained to the other party on the phone, sounding a little nervous. "That's perfectly all right, we know the way," Robert said, as he and the others headed towards B wing.

"Open up immediately," he said to the guard at the door, showing his police badge.

"No, I cannot," answered the guard.

"If you don't open the door right now, we'll have to break it down," said Robert. He was beginning to be irritated. The guard tried to stop them. Robert waved to Erik, who was still near the reception desk. He went behind the desk, gently shoved the receptionist out of the way, and pushed a button marked "Door" which immediately released the door. Some of the hospital personnel were standing in the corridor looking at them. It was possible that they had some warning from the reception desk that something big was about to happen.

"My name is Lieutenant Robert Blake. We have come here this evening to do a house inspection. I ask therefore that you give us your full cooperation."

"You can't do this." The voice came from someone Robert couldn't see.

"Who is it that is speaking?" he asked. "Head Nurse Rebecca Daly."

"As a matter of fact, we can. I have a judge's order allowing us to inspect whatever we deem necessary."

Rebecca Daly took the paper from Robert and read it before she gave it back to him.

"We will have all reports, evaluations, and personnel files laid out for us to read. I want all paperwork dating back to January of 1971 and through to today. Please do not hide anything from us, because we will find it. If anyone tries to hide anything, they will be held in contempt.

"We will also have a list of who shared rooms together and lists with dates of anyone who was put in isolation during that same period." Robert waited for a moment before asking, "Is that understood?"

All personnel stood completely still.

"I will also speak to each patient one-on-one."

"No," said Rebecca, "you can't. You aren't qualified."

"You might be right," said Robert, "but I will be the judge of that. If I require a qualified person to help me conduct any interviews, I will be sure to have one assist me."

He gestured to the sergeant and said, "Let's get to work."

"While we are waiting for the patient interviews to begin, we two can have a little talk," he said to Rebecca Daly. "Is there a place we can use to speak in private?"

She reached out her hand and pointed to a door across the hall.

"OK then, we'll go in here."

Once they were in the room with the door shut, Rebecca asked, "What is this about?"

"It is about an uninvestigated case that happened here five months ago. I can't remember seeing you here then. Were you?"

"No, I was in Department F then. I was moved to this position when Nurse Mary was stabbed."

"Well, that is the very case that we are now investigating. We never were able to see any material, personnel, or patients at that time. I am sure you know why."

"No, I do not, but what changed to make you so interested in it now, and to get a judge's order?" she asked.

"Well, now it looks like the person involved in this is pregnant."

How could that be possible? This is a woman's hospital and all the personnel here are women, other than three doctors and a few guards that you use in the special departments. So, how could that possibly happen?"

Rebecca shrugged her shoulders. "That is something I cannot answer." She sat very upright and looked tense. "I have never met the person you are referring to. She was moved over to a lockdown department the same evening that the incident happened."

"Yes, we know that." It was Joan who spoke now. She continued, "She is now being tested by a police doctor from Calgary, who also brought with him a gynaecologist."

Rebecca didn't answer on this piece of news.

"Are you sure there's nothing else you can tell us?" "Like what?"

"Anything that you found to be suspicious or curious here in this department?"

"No, nothing that I can remember."

"If anything should come to you, please let us know. Now can you please show us where the personnel lockers are? We want to check the locker of Nurse Mary. Do you have the key?"

"No. We all have our own private combination locks." "That's OK. We have a bolt cutter with us."

"Bingo!" one of the sergeants said, as he was going through the employee lockers.

"What is it?" asked Joan.

"Just come over here," he answered.

He was in the process of going through the lowest shelf of Nurse Mary's locker. In the very back was a small flat folder which he had opened up for inspection. There were some handwritten notes there. He started to read them. Now he handed them to Joan for her to read.

Patient TJ brought in to Dr. Irvine Jr. at 7 p.m., May 21. Medication: 500 mg Rohypnol, 500 mg Valium.

June 11, 7 p.m., patient TJ brought to Dr. Irvine Jr. Same medications.

Fourteen times it was notated at different times in the evening.

The fifteenth entry was not fully filled out, but it was notated that Nurse Mary upped the dosage of Rohypnol to 1,000 milligrams. The investigators also found two bottles of pills, one with Rohypnol and one with Valium.

Joan turned to the sergeant and said, "Find Lieutenant Blake and bring him here."

He turned at once and went up the steps, the locker room being in the basement.

Joan kept on reading. The next page read as follows: "Patient Madeleine brought to Dr Irvine Jr." It was much the same written about her. Madeleine had been taken to Dr Irvine Jr. eight times. Robert came down the stairs to the locker room and Joan showed him what they had found. She pointed out that Madeleine was the roommate of TJ. He then read the names of other patients that were written down the same way.

"Continue here. I'm going to find Madeleine and question her." He was already halfway up the stairs when he was saying this.

"Which one is Madeleine?" Robert asked one of the nurses who was watching the policemen going through all the drawers and cabinets.

"She's over there sitting at the piano. The one with the dark curly hair."

"Where is her chart?"

She went over to the nurses' station and started to look through the charts. As soon as she found it, she handed it over to Robert. He read through it quickly before he asked, "So, she was roommates with TJ?" "Yes, they shared the same room for about nine months."

"Can you get her over here for me?"

She didn't answer but went over to the main salon and fetched her right away. Madeleine willingly followed the nurse back to Robert. "Please bring her in here." He pointed to the room he had been using for interviews.

"Thank you. You can wait outside now," he said to the nurse who had just brought him Madeleine.

He turned his attention to Madeleine. "Do you know who I am?"

She shook her head.

"My name is Robert. I am a policeman."

She was watching him closely. She nodded.

"I need to ask you some questions, if you don't mind." He waited for a moment before continuing. "You were roommates with TJ, weren't you?"

"Yes."

"What can you tell me about her?"

"Not very much. She kept mostly to herself."

"Was there anything special that might have happened with her?" "Yes. She was taken by Nurse Mary every other Wednesday at 7 p.m., but the last three times it was later."

"Where was she taken by Nurse Mary?" "Doctor Irvine Jr.'s office."

"Did she tell you that?"

"No, but she didn't need to, because before she came, it was me who was taken to Doctor Irvine Jr. He liked to get blow jobs."

"What do you mean?"

"I mean that he liked to have me give him a blow job."

Robert had to concentrate very hard so as not to react visibly to such a disgusting piece of news.

"Did he do anything else?"

"Yes. The last three times before TJ came here, he took off my clothes and forced his cock into me. He thought that I was doped up too much to notice, but the four last times I didn't swallow the pills Nurse Mary gave me. I used a technique of hiding them under my tongue that I learned to do whenever they gave me pills that they said I needed." "What are you here in this hospital for?"

Madeleine then told Robert the reason for her having been placed into the psychiatric hospital.

The telephone rang, Nils Henrik looked at the clock before he picked up the handset. It was 5.09 a.m.

"Yes, Ellefsrud here."

He thought he had heard the voice on the other end before.

"This is the police."

Nils Henrik was sure that this was the same person who had met with him at the ranch that terrible night that he would never forget. "We have gotten a report that a car belonging to you has been involved in an accident out at Bragg Creek. Do you know anything about it?"

"No," Nils Henrik answered.

"Do you know the people who could have been in your car tonight? It was a man and a woman."

"Yes, it was my good friends Lieutenant Robert Blake and Lieutenant Joan Arnold.

"What happened to them?"

"Difficult to say. They were both taken to intensive care." "What happened?" Nils Henrik asked again.

"It is not exactly clear what happened. The accident is under investigation, so I can't go into it right now."

"Which hospital are they in?" Nils Henrik continued. "Drayton Valley."

"OK. Thank you for the message."

Nils Henrik didn't manage to go back to sleep. He thought about the call he had just received. Besides being worried for Robert and Joan, he thought about his daughter and granddaughter who were sleeping upstairs. How would TJ take this news?

"Hi, Papa."

It had been so very long since he had heard her say this.

"Good morning, my little girl." He tried to smile through his seriousness. He continued, "TJ, I got a telephone message early this morning. There has been a car accident up near Bragg Creek. It was my car, and Robert and Joan were in it. I don't know much of anything else about it except that they were taken to Drayton Valley Hospital. I need to go over there. I have already called Marie, Nils Henrik's housekeeper. She has a little place for herself at the house, but today she stayed with her daughter. I let her know that you two were here. She'll be here in an hour. Let her know if there is anything you need. I'll be back as soon as I can, OK?"

"How badly did Joan get hurt?" TJ asked worriedly.

"I can't say, but I believe that they are not in any danger of dying, OK?"

"Call me as soon as you find out anything."

Nils Henrik turned in to the hospital's parking lot. He was worried about Robert and Joan. He had tried his best to be positive and calm when speaking to TJ about the accident. He thought that was the best way to handle it until he learned how bad it really was.

He walked up to the receptionist and said, "Where can I find Lieutenant Robert Blake."

She looked through a pile of papers before she answered him.

"And what is your name?" "Nils Henrik Ellefsrud." "One moment."

She picked up her telephone and dialled a number.

"Mister Ellefsrud is here for Mister Blake."

She hung up the telephone.

"He is up on the fourth floor in room number 4H. Go that way and you'll find the elevator."

Nils Henrik thanked her and went in the direction where she had pointed. He was met by a plain-clothes policeman. Nils Henrik knew he had seen him somewhere before. "Mister Ellefsrud, do you remember me?" "Yes."

"Lieutenant McKenzie here." He put his hand forward and they shook.

"We met once before, but that was quite a long time ago. Shall we go over there and sit down for a minute?" He pointed to a sofa and a couple of easy chairs in the corner. Nils Henrik politely followed him over to them.

"How are Robert and Joan?" He was too impatient to wait until they were seated, but Lt. McKenzie seated himself before he answered. "So far it is difficult to say, but it doesn't look like his life is in danger."

"And what about Joan?" "The same there."

McKenzie asked, "How much have they already told you?" "Not much. I got a call around five this morning where I was informed that they had been in a car accident."

"Why did they call you?" McKenzie asked. "Because they were driving my car at the time."

"Why were they driving your car?" McKenzie continued.

"Because I was taking my daughter and her baby home to my ranch. And since my car is a van with only two seats, it would have been a little tight to manoeuvre the baby's car seat into it. Robert offered to let me use his car to make it easier for us. His car had more space for that. He knew that we were going home together and that it had been a long time since we'd spent time together at home."

"I had heard that. Joan is awake, so we'll go in to talk to her first. Before we do, I just want to let you know that it wasn't an ordinary car accident."

"What do you mean?" Nils Henrik got worried again. "The accident was the direct result of a shooting." Nils Henrik was struck dumb by this news.

"Yes, they were shot in the car while they were driving along. So far, we have been able to locate five empty cartridges, and therefore we believe that five shots were fired, but possibly there were more. Three of the shots hit Robert; one hit Joan. We're not sure about the fifth yet. The shot that hit Joan went through her shoulder. She lost a lot of blood but is otherwise all right.

"Robert is still on the operating table. How badly he has been hurt is yet to be determined, but he is expected to survive. A complete investigation has already been started, and in connection with that I will have to ask you some questions, but we can do that later. First let's go in and see Joan."

Speculation was high about why this shooting had happened. Was there any connection to the previous crimes committed against Nils Henrik Ellefsrud and his family? No one other than TJ and Nils Henrik knew that Robert and Joan were using Nils Henrik's car. It was also possible that Nils Henrik would have driven that way when he went home. In fact, it was he who'd told Robert about the shortcut.

Lt. McKenzie and Nils Henrik had just left Joan's room. She had been in good spirits but was worried for Robert. Now they sat down in the same place where they had sat down before they'd gone in to see her. "As I mentioned earlier, there are some questions that I must ask you," said McKenzie.

Nils Henrik just nodded.

"I know that you have a lot of thoughts and worries, but you understand." "Yes, I do."

"You told me earlier why you switched cars. Did you drive directly home?" "Yes."

"What time did you arrive there?"

"No, wait. We did stop to say hello to TJ's grandparents out at Wabamun Lake. We got home just before 10 p.m."

"Can anyone confirm that?"

"I don't know. Maybe Marie or Jimmy, my housekeeper and gardener, heard us come in. I also have a camera that records what goes on at night. It sends a message in to Marie and Jimmy."

"Do you have any enemies?"

"I surely must have some, but who they are I don't have any idea. If I knew that, everything would be so much easier."

"What do you mean by that?"

"Just a farce," Nils Henrik replied. He didn't want McKenzie to know.

Finally the doctor came out to see Robert's family a little after noon. Nils Henrik was sitting with them. Lt. McKenzie had left to go back to the investigation. The doctor went over to Robert's wife first, then to his mother-in-law, and then to Nils Henrik.

"First I want to tell you that the operation was a success. We were able to remove all of the bullets and the fragments."

He looked at all of them carefully before continuing.

"But I am sorry to say that one of the bullets hit his spine. That means that several discs on his spinal cord are damaged beyond repair." "What does that mean?" his wife, Lori, asked.

"Unfortunately, it means that he will never be able to walk again." Nils Henrik held Lori tightly while she cried. He didn't know what he should say or do. The situation was impossible.

The doctor stood there silently for a moment. "I'm so sorry," he finally said. "If there's anything you need from me, I'll be nearby. I need to go in to see him again, and as soon as he is awake you can go in and talk with him."

He went back in to Robert's room.

Oslo

8 September

Conrad, Henrik, and Goggen had agreed to meet in the departure hall of Gardermoen airport in Oslo at 6.30 a.m. Their plane was not scheduled to leave until 9.15, but it was an international flight and therefore passengers were required to be there at least two hours before departure. They were flying KLM via Amsterdam to Montreal. After that they would take Air Canada to Edmonton.

Henrik was nervous and in suspense.

The trip over the Atlantic went as planned, and they actually arrived in Montreal twenty minutes early. But then the immigration in

Montreal took a very long time. What reason there was for this was anybody's guess, probably just a lot of people going through. At least they didn't have any trouble making their connecting flight; the only problem was that it was cancelled. Now they were booked on a flight that was leaving two hours later. There was nothing they could do about it, so Conrad went over to the Air Canada desk and asked to place a call to Robert Blake and let him know about the delay.

Now they finally landed in Edmonton.

Conrad looked out the window of the plane. He looked at his watch and realized that it was 4.05 a.m. back in Norway. He hadn't set his watch to the correct time yet. Edmonton was nine hours behind

Norway, and therefore the time was only 7.05 in the evening. All in all, it had been a very long day.

A voice came on to the plane's public-address system. "Welcome to Edmonton, capital of the Canadian prairies. We will be taxiing over to our gate, which is number 24. Please remain seated until the plane comes to a complete stop and the 'fasten seat belt' sign is turned off. We at Air Canada thank you for flying with us today and hope to see you again in the near future."

The voice then changed and repeated the same message in French. They had arrived. Henrik had butterflies in his stomach; he was very excited. They walked along the stream of people getting off the airplane and heading over to the baggage claim.

There in the middle of a large crowd of people was someone holding up a sign saying "Mr Ellefsrud".

Conrad saw him first and gave him a wave. He came over through the crowd, and they shook hands and introduced themselves. Mark Blake had come to meet them.

"My father is right over there," he said, pointing to man in the distance sitting in a wheelchair.

"Yes, unfortunately he has a little trouble getting around. Can I help you with your suitcases?"

"No, we'll manage just fine," said Goggen, who then went directly over to Robert Blake. They all introduced themselves to him and shook hands again.

"Well, how was your trip?" asked Robert.

"Sorry you had to wait so long in Montreal, but that's very typical. I know that it's been a long trip for you all, so we will drive right back to the ranch. Are you hungry? I know that airplane food is nothing to write home about. I'll call Lori and ask her to fix us up something for when we get there, OK? It will take about an hour to get back, depending on traffic. There shouldn't be much on a Saturday evening."

Henrik awoke when the car stopped.

"OK, everybody, here we are."

He had fallen asleep before the car left the airport parking lot.

"I would like to officially welcome you to Nils Henrik's ranch. He bought it in 1958, but I won't give you any more details about it this evening. We can wait until tomorrow.

"Now we will give you all something to eat, and then I know that you would like to kick back and relax. You'll all stay in the main house.

That is also where Nils Henrik lived when he was here. Mark will take your suitcases over there, but dinner is at my house. So, let's go in."

Robert Blake's house was somewhat smaller than the main house on the property. It was well-furnished, and everything was on one floor: kitchen, dining room, a nice living room with an attached bar, and a spacious bedroom and bathroom. Robert's office was across from the main foyer, and there was a guest bathroom nearby. The house was built specifically for someone in a wheelchair. There was a second floor that had some guest rooms and baths.

"Can I get any of you a drink while we wait for dinner? Lori said it will be about fifteen minutes."

Everybody had a Molson brown ale.

Lori came in, introduced herself, and said that the food was ready.

Norway

8 August 2005, 1.45, at the cabin

Nils Henrik had thought through his whole life, and the time had

come. He looked at the red wine bottle to see how much was left. He had brought one of his favourite bottles, a 1992 Amarone, with him to the cabin today. It was still half full. He didn't want any more; he didn't want any more of anything. Tina was lying loyally right at his feet. He tried to bend down and pet her one last time and thought to himself that he hoped Henrik would take good care of her when he was gone. He looked at the bottle of pills in front of him. Now he looked forward to nothing more than the long permanent sleep that was ahead of him.

Part II

CHAPTER 10

Drayton Valley

9 September 2005

Canada showed itself at its best when they woke up on their first day there. It was a glorious fall morning. The sun was shining, and the temperature was very much like back home in Norway this time of year. They all went to bed as soon as they had eaten last night. Even though fighting jet lag, they woke up rather early. It seemed that by

7.00 all of them were up. Henrik had awakened a few times during the night, but he had just turned over and gone back to sleep again. Now they were all sitting in the kitchen at what Robert Blake called the main house of the ranch, the house of Nils Henrik Ellefsrud.

"Shall we make some coffee?" Goggen asked. "Sounds good," Conrad answered.

Henrik was looking out the window at the ranch.

"Conrad, did my father ever tell you about any of this?"

"No, he never talked about his time over here at all. Whenever the subject came up, he would change it right away."

Henrik was still looking out the window.

Goggen had found a coffee container in a cabinet near the coffee maker and had just finished making a pot. "Coffee?" Goggen held the pot in his hand. "Yes, thank you."

"How about you, Conrad?" "Yes, thank you."

Then he poured out three cups.

"I'm going to go out and look around," Henrik said, as he remained at the window. "Does anybody want to come with me?"

"I have to have a little more coffee and a little more time before I can function and fully wake up," Goggen replied. "Same with me," Conrad answered.

"OK. But I will." And then he went over to the door with his jacket in his hand. He took his coffee with him.

There were five additional buildings on the property besides the main house and Robert's house. Two of them looked like small houses or cabins, two were barns, and the last building was rather small and could be used for just about anything. There was also a three-car garage. All of these were situated on a small rise. Down below the main house was a pond with a little house floating on it. The little house had some ducks on a platform on its side.

Farther down was a nice stand of trees and an open field which looked to be very large. Henrik followed the hill and walked around to the other side. The field continued on that side.

"Good morning."

Henrik jumped. He hadn't seen that Robert was sitting outside on his balcony in the sun. He also had a cup of coffee in his hand.

"Good morning," Henrik answered. "I didn't see you there. I was so busy looking around," he continued.

"I saw that. What do you think? Do you like it? Nils Henrik loved this place. But he didn't or, more correctly spoken, couldn't live here. He made sure to say that every time he visited. There were too many unsolved incidents, and that gave him concern. That was the reason he left in January of 1972 to go back to Norway for a while. His plan was to return some day, but it was something that he never did," Robert said.

"So, Nils Henrik never spoke about this in Norway?" he continued. "No, that was something he never said a word about. I understand that our mother knew everything, but she never said one word about it to us either."

"Well, 70 per cent of it belongs to you guys now. The house I live in belongs to me. Nils Henrik built it for me. The rest he retained for himself. It's not a very large ranch by Canadian standards, only 448 acres, but we usually profit about a million and a half dollars per year from it. As you can see, I can't do very much, but I have been left in charge of running the entire thing by Nils Henrik. And that I have done. I have hired someone to do most of my legwork. His name is

Ivan, and he lives in the little house next door to you. You will get to meet him sometime today.

"But the ranch is not what makes us the most money. When Nils Henrik bought this ranch, he bought it as a foreclosure."

"What is a foreclosure?" Henrik asked.

"It means that the bank has taken over the property because whoever owned it couldn't pay their mortgage. Then the bank puts it up for sale, but they cannot ask market price for it. They have to sell it for the outstanding amount of the loan that is left," Robert explained.

"It was a friend of Nils Henrik who'd tipped him off about it, a Robert

W. Duff from California. Nils Henrik had met him up in Dawson City earlier. When Duff saw that this property was to go in to foreclosure, he tipped off Nils Henrik about it.

"But what was so special about this deal was that when Nils Henrik bought the ranch, he was able to buy it without any restrictions. Most properties that are sold have a clause that says you can own and farm the land but have no right to any future mineral rights that might come to light later.

"So then, what I am saying is that the usual clause was not present in this case. Not only that, someone from Chevron found oil up here, and most of it lies beneath this ranch. One hundred and twenty-four acres down at the south end lie over some very rich oil reserves. There are five pump jacks down there which are pumping out oil twenty-four hours per day. That brings us eight million dollars per year."

Henrik was almost unable to grasp what Robert was saying. "So, you see, your father didn't have any economic problems."

"Now I understand why he never took a job while we were growing up. He didn't need to."

"I am going to tell you another thing about your father. After the building collapse in Jackson Heights in 1965, he promised that no one would profit financially from that and that he would take responsibility for all who were hurt by it. They would be paid all the damages that they were entitled to. That accident affected him deeply. He started a business that would convert the income from the oil. He owned 55 per cent of it, and I have 25 per cent. The families of the victims get the other 20 per cent. He didn't need to do any of that, but it was his decision, and that's how it is. Again, it is me who runs and oversees this. That counts for the previous owner of the ranch as well. Nils Henrik couldn't just sit there knowing they'd lost everything, so when the oil was found he decided to give something back to them.

You should be very proud of your father." Robert Blake looked at Henrik.

"Later today I will drive you all around the whole ranch. I'll explain everything to you again, but right now Lori has breakfast ready. If you would go get the others, you can all come over and eat. How about ten minutes?" He smiled at Henrik and rolled himself towards his door.

"Well No. 5", it said on the sign. "Opened July 8, 1977."

Robert Blake sat on the platform where the controls for the pump were placed and explained how the machinery worked. There was a pump jack which went up and down. It was certainly not a noiseless operation. Robert explained that the pump jack needed to be lubricated every day. Other than the lubrication, it pretty well ran itself. There was usually a small structure over the pump, but the walls were taken away during the summer months to prevent overheating. They would be replaced before winter set in.

The tour was very interesting. They had been out more than three hours, and now they were standing on the north end of the property looking at the acre which was used for farming. It was mostly corn that was planted there, but they also ran a small meat production with about fifty heads. They were not able to plough anywhere near the pumps, but the animals could graze there and the grass was fine. Then there were some pigs and chickens, but they were only for personal use. The farm was pretty much self-sufficient.

"Well, folks, that was the tour around your property. Is there anyone who has any questions? I'm sure you do. We will have plenty of time to answer them all later. Meanwhile let's see if Lori has found something good for dinner. You have heard that the farm is self-sufficient, but now we need to show you." Robert smiled when he said this.

The trip back to the house took about twenty-five minutes. Henrik didn't say one single word during the whole tour, and now he just sat and looked out over the landscape. Goggen and Conrad didn't say very much either. They needed to digest all that they had seen.

Once they had reached the house again, Robert said, "Shall we say dinner around 7.30? That will give you some time to relax a little first.

You must be worn out—jet lag and so on. You also must have a lot to talk about. We can continue during the evening for as long as you wish, but I know it can take a couple of days to get over such a big- time change."

"That sounds like a plan," Conrad answered. "We'll see you at 7.30."

Once back in the house, Conrad asked, "What is the next surprise going to be?"

Then Goggen asked, "Didn't either of you know anything about any of this?"

"No!" both Conrad and Henrik answered at the same time.

"That's unbelievable. I guess now we just have to wait until the next surprise is sprung on us. I'm sure that will come tonight.

The time was exactly 7.30 when the three went up the steps of Robert's house. There was a ramp for his wheelchair, but it went in another direction. They knocked on the door. Lori, Robert's housekeeper, answered it almost immediately. "Come in, come in," she said. "The others are waiting for you." She had a little smile on her face.

"The others?" Henrik said.

"Yes," she said. Henrik didn't have time to ask whom she was talking about before they were standing in the living room. There were four people waiting for them, including Robert and his son Mark from yesterday. The other two they hadn't seen before, but they assumed one of them must be Mark's brother, as he looked just like him. Then there was a tall, beautiful woman about forty-five or fifty years old. "Oh, here you are. Come on in. Did you all get a little rest?" Robert asked.

All three said yes.

"Good." He continued, "As you see, there are two new faces you haven't meet yet here tonight. Yesterday you met my son Mark. This one is my other son, Mike."

All three shook hands with him before Robert continued. "But there is one other person I would like to introduce you to." He looked at the woman sitting next to him. "This is TJ, or Tehya Jane." All three shook hands with her too.

"They will be having dinner with us tonight. I hope none of you mind?" He looked at Henrik when he said this. "Of course not," Henrik answered.

Robert then looked at Conrad and Goggen. They answered the same. "That's good, because these people mean a great deal to me and they are going to be a big part of what we will be discussing tonight. But before that, what would you like to drink? Lori, can you please give them what they want?" Lori came over at once and asked what they would like. Henrik wanted a gin and tonic, Conrad asked for a Scotch with ice, and Goggen requested the same as Conrad.

"I see you don't follow in your father's footsteps," Robert said, looking at Henrik. "His favourite drink was Canadian Club with 7 Up. I can't remember him ever drinking anything else." Robert smiled.

"Today you have seen the property here. I understand that it was a complete surprise to you. I have also told you that it is I who runs the ranch and the oil operation. That is not all that I do. In addition, I—we—run a security firm which encompasses a private detective service and a bail bonds firm. I started that business after I was injured and lost my ability to walk, with the help of Nils Henrik. My two sons have now begun to take over more and more of the business for me, but I am still involved. The business is owned fifty-fifty by me and Nils Henrik. When we began, it was with a relatively small operation bringing in about two hundred thousand dollars' worth of business. Last year we brought in fifteen million dollars in business. "You see, Henrik, you are really rich now. Here is a rough description of the company's finances, along with information on Nils Henrik's private accounts here in Canada." He gave Henrik an envelope. "Please feel free to open it whenever you wish. But I have something else to tell you. Now that I have learned that Nils Henrik kept his life here in Canada from you, it will probably be a sure price as well." Robert looked at TJ when he spoke. "This is not news to you, TJ, but it is to you, Henrik. TJ is your half-sister." The room went completely silent. Conrad and Goggen looked at Henrik. Lori stood in the doorway. Henrik felt completely numb. Luckily, he had already set down his glass. Now he grasped it again and took a big gulp, then another one. He still couldn't speak.

He looked over at TJ and she looked back at him. She got up, walked over to him, and then put out her hand. "I'm sorry that you had to find out about me like this, but Papa told me he wouldn't tell anyone in Norway about me. He was afraid, he said, afraid that the same thing that happened to us could happen to you over there. I know that your mother knew about me, and we met a couple of times and spoke, but it wasn't easy. Her English was not very good."

She sat down next to Henrik, who was still in shock. Lori asked him, "Would you like another drink?" Robert nodded silently to her, and she went over to the bar and made him another gin and tonic. "Anybody else?"

It took about fifteen minutes before Henrik got up off the sofa and turned towards TJ. "Please stand up," he said to her in a quiet voice. She looked at him a little uncertainly, but she got up like he'd asked. He took both of her hands in his and gave her a hug. Tears began to flow. He didn't say anything else; he just held on to her tightly.

It was almost nine o'clock before Lori finally asked them to sit down for dinner. The conversation had become lively. Henrik had definitely gotten over the worst of his shock. Now he and TJ sat side by side during the meal. They had a lot to talk about.

The jet lag was still there, so shortly after dinner Henrik, Goggen, and Conrad all excused themselves and returned to the house. TJ followed them. She had her own room there.

Henrik needed to call Roald and Aase. He decided that he would try to catch them at home before they went to work.

The moment the men got back to the main house, Conrad turned to Henrik and said, "Well, what a day!"

Henrik agreed. "Shall we take a look at the finances?" Conrad held up the envelope that had been given to Henrik earlier.

"Oh, I had completely forgotten it," said Henrik.

"I saw that, so I took it. Do you want to open it, or shall I?" Conrad asked.

"Go ahead, you open it," Henrik answered.

Conrad opened the envelope and took out the contents. He looked at them, and then he read out loud: "RN Holdings, Nils Henrik Ellefsrud." His voice stilled.

Monday morning

They had used the whole of Sunday to familiarize themselves with Nils Henrik's holdings and his friends in Canada. They had already been greatly shocked, first when Robert told Henrik who TJ was, and then by the story of Robert and how he became crippled. Then came their surprise when Conrad opened the envelope that showed the details of Nils Henrik's business interests. His account at Alberta National Bank contained 94,345,565 Canadian dollars.

That was not counting what the businesses were worth. Henrik used much of the night to try to explain all this to Roald and Aase. Now he was waiting in suspense for whatever would come the next morning. Were there more surprises?

There was a table with coffee and bottled water in the conference room of Robert's office. There was also a pile of newspapers and newspaper clippings. It was obvious that they were not today's news. Henrik, Conrad, and Goggen had taken their places at the end of the table. Robert sat at the other end. "Good morning again. Yesterday was a day with lots of surprises for all of you, maybe mostly you, Henrik. Today you will learn a lot more about this man.

"I understand that Nils Henrik asked you in his last will to look into and, if you found it feasible, start an investigation of the happenings that occurred here in Canada and changed his life forever. Nils Henrik Ellefsrud went back to Norway because he didn't want anyone else to be hurt or killed. He was afraid, not so much for himself, but for TJ and her daughter. He hoped that when he disappeared, things would settle down. His plan was to return to Canada. He wanted TJ and her daughter to follow him to Norway, but TJ didn't want to. I was therefore asked to be her guardian until he came back. I agreed to that.

"He also wanted me to move to the ranch. At first, I didn't, but then he promised to build a house for me that would be totally accessible for me and my wheelchair if I would agree. It was a very good offer, but I didn't want him to spend that much money on me. It wasn't him who shot me.

"Nils Henrik wouldn't accept my refusal, and the day I came out of the hospital after my rehabilitation, the house was almost ready. I couldn't say no any longer, so I moved in. At that time there were no special facilities in houses or apartments for wheelchair users. We have lived here ever since. Nils Henrik returned to Norway only three weeks after I moved in there."

Then Robert changed the subject abruptly.

"In front of each of you are some newspapers and newspaper clippings. All these are of articles related to Nils Henrik Ellefsrud and all that happened to him. I think it is important for you to read them all. You can take them back to the house if you want to. There are a lot of other materials as well, but I don't have them here. Scott and Mark will get those things for you tomorrow and bring them over to you at the house.

"Nils Henrik didn't want to keep those materials at the ranch for two reasons. He was afraid that someone would come and take them or destroy them, and he was also afraid for us who lived there. Nils

Henrik never gave up on these cases. Even after the police closed the investigations, he still kept trying to the best of his ability. I assisted him as best as I could, but at that time it was obviously not easy for me to do much of anything. I was still officially a police officer and the cases were investigated by the Edmonton Police Department.

They had taken over all unsolved cases that Nils Henrik had been involved in. The person in charge of these investigations was Lieutenant McKenzie, who is now Captain McKenzie and the chief of police in Edmonton. I am not proud of how these cases were handled, but my hands were tied.

"That has plagued me for many years, but Nils Henrik wouldn't let me investigate any further. He made me promise not to after I was shot.

"He said that the time would come when we could take it up again, adding that it was too dangerous at that present time. I know that there was nothing more he wanted in this world than to find the criminals who committed those terrible crimes. Now he is not here any longer, but I'm sure that he is looking down at us from wherever he is, wishing us well.

"The materials that will be delivered to you need to be gone through undisturbed. I am sure a lot of questions will come up. Write them down. I believe that the best way to handle them is to answer them all in sequence when everything is read. Does that make sense?" Goggen looked at Henrik and Conrad before he answered, "Yes." "The next thing we need to deal with is transportation. I have arranged renting two cars for you all to use. They should arrive here later today.

"Then there is the last question: food. Shall I ask Lori to cook for you?"

"No, we can take care of that ourselves," Henrik answered. "OK then, we'll leave it at that."

Goggen had already gotten up and begun to compile all the newspapers and clippings into a pile. He thanked Robert for everything and headed for the door. Henrik and Conrad followed him out.

Around 2 p.m., six cardboard boxes of more than medium size were delivered to the main house.

"Here is some reading material that should last you for a few days at least," Mark said, smiling. "Enjoy it."

The main occupation of the next several days was the reading of the materials. Conrad and Goggen were very professional in handling these things. They tried to put everything in chronological order and to impose some order upon the huge amount of papers, but that was not always possible. There were more than a few things that were placed incorrectly when they'd received them. Henrik took care of reading the newspapers and the clippings. He also put himself in charge of food shopping and preparation. He had become a little familiar with the areas around the ranch by now. There was not much else that he could do.

After six days, Conrad and Goggen had managed to go through all the boxes. They had read every document and put them all into relative order. Now they wanted to sit down with Robert and go through the cases one at a time. They had not asked him anything in the last six days. Henrik had been over to see him a few times, but that was all. Henrik had kept TJ company a few times as well, and they had gone out to eat a couple of times. He had also met TJ's daughter, Asha, who was a beautiful woman of thirty-four years.

Conrad and Goggen had worked exclusively on the information that was delivered to the house in the boxes. Now all three of them went over to Robert's house.

They knocked on the door around 7.15 p.m. Lori answered their knock and welcomed them in. She said, "Robert is in his office, but I'll get him to come out here. He's in that office so much that he really needs a break. How are all of you? We haven't seen you since Monday."

"We had a lot to go through," Conrad said, "but now it looks like we have a better overview of the whole thing." She went over to Robert's office, and in just a few moments he rolled himself into the salon. "How are things going? Have you gotten a little more insight into the cases?"

"Yes, it's going well, and we are finished going through all the material you gave us. Now we are hoping that we can get you to spend some time with us going over it all. Maybe tomorrow morning?"

"Of course. Come over as early tomorrow as you wish." "Then we'll come after breakfast," Conrad said.

They got back up and were ready to leave, but then Robert said, "Why don't you stay for a little while and have a drink?" He didn't wait for them to answer before looking towards Lori. Then he continued, "And have you had anything to eat?"

"No, not yet."

"Shall we order some Chinese takeout? There's a good Chinese restaurant out in Drayton Valley, and they deliver. We can get dinner here in about forty-five minutes."

They all agreed. Lori went and fixed their drinks.

Now they were sitting around Robert's conference table again. It was 9.15 a.m.

Goggen said to Robert, "As we told you last night, we are finished going through all of the materials you and Nils Henrik have collected, and now we have put them in order. It is obvious that you guys have been very diligent about keeping track of it all, and we thank you for that. Enough said about it. We have written down a large number of questions. Now the big question is, how do we proceed with this? I think it would be best if you begin, Robert, and we will interrupt as you go along."

Goggen looked at Robert.

"OK, shall we begin with the first thing that happened?" Robert asked.

"That would be the building collapse in Jackson Heights. Yes, a good place to start," Goggen answered.

"The building collapse in Jackson Heights was the first downturn that Nils Henrik experienced here in Canada. Before that, everything he did here went well, including his businesses.

"I was not directly involved in that investigation. It fell under the jurisdiction of the police district of Edmonton."

"We read that," Goggen answered, before continuing. "Is there anything else you can add to what we already know? Anything not included in the court documents? Anything that wasn't answered?" "No."

"Nils Henrik involved himself heavily in that investigation, understandably, but what could he accomplish alone? However, he didn't stop just because of that. In fact, it was the reason why he wasn't out at the cabin with his family that day."

"We read that too, and we will come to that. We also read from the papers that two of the partners came under suspicion in that case. How did that happen?" Goggen asked.

"There were a lot of clues that pointed in their direction. They both disappeared, nobody knows where. But they didn't disappear until after they had taken out one-point-six million Canadian dollars that the company had in cash in their account. How they did it is still a good question. The police had frozen those assets because of the collapse and the resulting claims that would result from it.

"There was also building number one. No one knew that it had been sold. It was sold in complete secrecy two weeks before the collapse. The amount of the sale was $1,390,000. That money also disappeared and was never found," Robert said.

"Do you know where those two individuals are now?" Goggen asked. "No, I have never had a chance to look for them. There were boundaries regarding how far I was allowed to be involved in the case," Robert answered.

"What about the one who was called OJ?" Goggen asked.

"Nils Henrik's partner who came up here from New York with him. He was also named more than once as a possible person of interest. He disappeared two days before the collapse, and no one ever saw or heard from him again. The police searched for him, but it's as if he just disappeared off the face of the earth."

"What do you think about that?"

"I can only quote Nils Henrik on this: 'OJ had nothing whatsoever to do with this. What would he have to gain? He was a partner in a fast-growing concern.' Also, he had been with Nils Henrik all the way from the beginning in New York," Robert answered.

Goggen wrote that down.

"I read that Nils Henrik told you what he heard and told his boss at his previous job in New York. Do you think there is a possibility that these two things might be related?"

"When Nils Henrik first told me about that, I thought it seemed a little strange. After turning it over in my mind for a while, I started to wonder. It's just that both John and Jimmy were from New York. That's what made me suspicious," Robert replied.

Goggen wrote down more notes and continued. "What are your thoughts and reflections about the collapse and then the cabin fire?" "In the beginning I wasn't able to see any connection. I also didn't have any reason for making one. I was not aware of the collapse since I was never told about. It was only later when Nils Henrik told me the whole story and about some threats that he had received that I started to reflect on it. I was very angry at him for not letting me know sooner. And yes, I started to see the connections between the two cases. Despite that, I felt that the two of them should be investigated independently of each other. The Edmonton police did not agree, and it ended up with me being taken off the case completely. The Edmonton police took it over and Lieutenant McKenzie, now Captain McKenzie, became the chief investigator. Needless to say, I was not satisfied with that decision."

Goggen said, "The cabin fire. Is there anything else you could add to what we have read and what we already know? We now have a better understanding of what TJ went through, and we know that she went to several schools for only three of four months before going berserk." "Yes, as I understand it, that is true. The person you need to talk to about this part is Joan. She's the one who followed up on the details of TJ's situation. I was only given a rough description of what happened during that period of time. It's odd though, because Nils Henrik and I had become good friends by then, but still he talked very little about it. He held it very deep inside himself.

"Anyway, I think that you should talk with Joan. She has been a central figure in this case."

"Yes, we understand that." Goggen thumbed through his notes. "What about the happenings in the psychiatric hospital? I see that the case was cleared up, but what happened later? Also, the last incident, the one when you were shot. Again, it was McKenzie who investigated it," Goggen spoke.

"Yes, that's true," Robert answered.

"And there are still no suspects?" Goggen asked. "Yes, that's also true," Robert answered.

"Can you tell us anything more about it? Why was the case given to McKenzie, for example?" Goggen continued.

"What happened and why, I can only guess. Myself, I am quite aware that it wasn't me that they were after. Nils Henrik thought so too, and that was what made him decide to move back to Norway. He wanted to let things lie still for a while, he said. He got really afraid now, not so much for himself, but for TJ and Asha, plus all the others who helped him with the investigation.

"Why it again became McKenzie's investigation I cannot answer. I spoke to some of my earlier colleagues about it and one of them said it was McKenzie himself who asked to be put on the case.

"After all the facts were laid out on the table, it wasn't difficult for him to be given the case. They could see that he would be able to draw a parallel with the other investigations he had conducted." Goggen took more notes. "We left out the shooting here at the ranch." "That was one shot, one time, and after analysis I decided that it was meant as a warning. Nils Henrik didn't want to report it. Again, the case would have been given to McKenzie, and Nils Henrik didn't want that to happen," Robert answered.

Goggen shuffled through his papers for a little bit before he spoke again. "This McKenzie, what do you know about him?"

"He's a highly decorated policeman in Edmonton. He has also distinguished himself outside of the city. I know very well who he is, but I don't know him personally except for these cases," Robert answered.

"Don't you think it's unusual that such a highly decorated and successful detective hasn't gotten any results at all from these investigations? He must have done a lot of good work over the years to be so singled out." The question come from Goggen.

"Nils Henrik thought the same thing, and that was why he didn't want to report the warning gunshot. I have thought about that as well, but McKenzie is a captain now and chief of police in Edmonton. You know how that sounds.

I was no longer in a position to look into his suitability given the way the situation was, and now it is even more difficult."

"We know that," Goggen continued.

Goggen continued to thumb through his files.

"As you know, this is a totally foreign place for us. If we are going to make any headway in this case, we need to know what the police might be sitting on and the status of the case as of now. We have been informed that you were an outstanding policeman and a talented detective. Do you still have contacts in the police whom you can trust and who can help us?"

"Yes, there are several people who have indicated that they would help me when the time comes. My son also works closely with the police, and TJ is a computer freak; what she doesn't know about a PC hasn't been invented yet. She has helped the police with many investigations. Asha, or Hope, as she calls herself, is a licenced attorney. She works in a firm in Edmonton."

"Interesting," said Goggen. He didn't say anything more for a few minutes. Then he said, "Whenever I think about these cases, there is one thing that keeps coming back to me, and that is TJ and her problems with the different schools. Something tells me that there is a clue here. Maybe I'm wrong, but we have to start somewhere. Is it possible to get a list of all the schools that she was sent to? I am also interested in the names of these schools' principals at that time and the names of her teachers. Is there a way to find all that out?" "Yes," Robert answered.

"I would also like to speak with Joan. Did you tell me her last name?" "No, I didn't. It's Arnold, Joan Arnold."

"No problem. Could you please call her and let her know I would like to speak with her as soon as possible? Also, do you think TJ would be able to tell us anything?"

Robert started to look a bit worried. "I don't know about that. Maybe. I'd rather not ask her."

"OK, Henrik, I need your help. Could you please go through these three separate piles of paper and write down the names of all the witnesses who are named there? Be sure to get their full names. Then please sort all the pictures. There are a lot of pictures. All of us need to look at them all. One of us might see something that the other one might miss. Then we need to research TJ's family tree going as far back as possible. We need to know what kind of work her relatives do or did in the past. I'm sure that TJ can help us with that.

"Conrad and I will start with Joan. I want her to take us over to the fire site. Robert, I don't know if you want to come along or not," said Goggen. "I know that Joan can do it by herself. The place is probably overgrown with brush, I am sure, especially since nothing was ever done there afterwards. It might be difficult to navigate a wheelchair around there now. Maybe you could stay here and help Henrik?" "No problem."

"All right then, we all have something to do. Any questions?" Goggen looked at everyone. Nobody answered. "Then let's get going."

"Robert, can you call Joan?" "Sure. I'll do it right now."

CHAPTER 11

Goggen and Conrad were on the way to the place where the cabin had been. Goggen was reading the map. They were going to meet Joan at the cabin site, the crime scene, because that is what it still was. As long as the case was not closed, it was a crime scene. She had indicated that she was tied up with another case, but she thought she could take a few hours off and meet them out there.

Goggen concentrated on the map. "In a few minutes we're going to turn off this road. The road coming up will take us to Lake Patricia. "Here it is."

Conrad made the turn.

"OK, now take the first left, and then the first right," Goggen said. "Then we should be there." And indeed, after the last turn they came to where the driveway led down to the cabin.

There was a car already parked in the driveway. "That must be Joan Arnold's car," Goggen said. They drove down towards what used to be a cabin. It was almost impossible to tell that there had ever been a fire here.

As soon as they stopped the car, Lt. Joan Arnold came over to them with an outstretched hand. They introduced themselves.

"Well, this is actually the crime scene," she said. The case is actually still open. Unfortunately, it is gathering dust in the Edmonton Police Department's archives."

"Yes. We understand from Robert that the Edmonton Police District took over these two cases, the cabin fire and the building collapse. They believe there was a connection in some way."

"What do you mean by that?" asked Conrad.

Joan looked around a little.

"It might very well be that there is a connection, but I don't understand why they absolutely demanded to take charge of this investigation. They just came to Robert one day and said that he was released from the case and that they were taking it over. I question why we were not able to conduct the investigation together. I was just told that this was the way it was going to be.

"It was very hard on Robert, but he is a professional, so he let it pass and concentrated on other pursuits instead."

"Does he still feel that way?"

"Well, yes. He has never forgotten. And it's one of his strongest wishes to this day that the crimes be solved and the criminals be brought to justice. He called me right away the day Nils Henrik's last letter arrived. He started the conversation with, 'Joan, now we can finally solve the case.' I knew immediately what he was referring to. Then he said, 'I have made peace with several of my contacts, and they are now lined up to help us with this.' Then he hung up.

Robert was a brilliant policeman and investigator, but he had a few personality problems with some of the house detectives in Edmonton, and they hadn't forgotten that."

"They wouldn't happen to be in the department of Captain McKenzie, would they?"

"You're onto something there," she answered. "What is the reason for that?"

"It had something to do with the investigation of the collapse. Nils Henrik was the prime suspect in that. Lieutenant McKenzie was so sure he was guilty that they arrested him. That's when Robert began to involve himself in the collapse investigation. He gained possession of some materials that the police had used as evidence to arrest him, and under heavier scrutiny he determined that the evidence was faked. McKenzie lost face because of this and never forgave Robert for it."

"OK, but back to this place. Has anything changed since the fire?" "No, but the ashes were carefully gone through at the time."

"We read what you found. Can you confirm it for us?"

"Of course, but let me begin at the beginning, from when we arrived at the scene that evening."

She began to tell and show Goggen and Conrad how the fire had spread and how they had found TJ. They walked around and looked thoroughly at the ruins.

Conrad said, "This is such an idyllic place. Did Nils Henrik ever think of selling it?"

"No, he saw this place as a memorial to his wife and son."

"In the ruins you found two bodies, and the report says that they were Sisiska and Albert."

"Yes, and both of them were so burned that they couldn't be positively identified. Nils Henrik recognized a piece of jewellery that Sisiska used to wear. Albert was never officially identified. But they were the only ones purported to be in the cabin when TJ came home that night."

"In the interview, TJ said that her mother was raped and shot. Albert was never mentioned."

"She never saw him at all."

"Where was his body found? Was it near his mother's? That was never mentioned in the report."

Joan studied the ruins for a little while before saying, "The cabin's living room and kitchen were here. There was a little platform outside near the lake. From there you could go down to the dock. On the other side was the master bedroom with its own bathroom. There was also a guest bath adjacent to the entranceway. That was right here. You still can see the outline of the toilet bowl. Albert's body was found there. There were indications on his body that suggested violence. It was speculated that he might have hidden himself there, but there was never a consensus of opinion that he was alive or dead when the fire took hold.

"Why that was not in the investigative documents I cannot say. I find that rather remarkable, since I remember that there was talk about it. We made a point of it in our report.

"TJ was found under the woodshed here. She managed to get under it and way up in the corner there. It has grown over a lot since I was here last. I remember over here, there was a spot for cars to park.

The car was parked there, with the front pointing out. That way the perpetrators could run right to the car and speed away quickly, which they did. There were deep skid marks in the gravel that showed that was the way it happened."

Goggen went around with her and scrutinized all of the places that she'd pointed to. He brought out a camera and took some pictures. "What about witnesses?"

"Like it said in the report, it was observed that there was a car parked here, a station wagon, possibly dark green or black. Darkness had started to descend, so no one could for sure state what colour it was." "Which cabin was it that the witnesses lived in, the ones who called in the fire?"

Joan pointed up at one of the cabins. "It was that one right there. As you can see, there are a lot of cabins here now, but that was not the case back then. There were not more than five cabins from here to the main road at the time of the fire: that one up there, two at the crossroads where we turned in, and two right where we turned off from the main road. Everyone was interviewed and questioned about whether they'd seen anything, but the only two who saw the car were the two who lived in that cabin there. The people in the farthest cabin weren't home. TJ said that she saw them in Jasper that afternoon and they were still there when she began to bicycle home that evening." "OK, I know that you have to get back to the other job you are on, but I have just a few more questions. You have established a good relationship with TJ. Has she ever mentioned anything to you about what happened in the different schools she was sent to after the cabin fire? From what I understand, it usually went well each time for about three or four months, then suddenly she would change and become aggressive and behave so badly that she would have to be sent away." "I wasn't informed of that until much later."

"Did you ever think about that or come to any conclusions as to why?"

"We were very careful when we questioned her. She was so weak and vulnerable. And no, I didn't. As I said, I didn't know about it." "I'm sure she was. Do you think there could be a connection there? Like she was being threatened or terrorized or something?"

"I don't know, but it could be a possibility."

"This is just a thought from my point of view, especially after what I read about how she tackled the problem in the psychiatric hospital. "Thank you for showing us around here. It was very nice to meet you. I'm sure that we'll see each other again soon."

Joan smiled. "Same here. If you have any other questions, please don't hesitate to call. I do have to get back to work now."

"Of course." Goggen shook hands with her and thanked her once more. Conrad waved goodbye to her from down at the dock.

It was late when they arrived back in Drayton Valley. Conrad and Goggen had stayed at the cabin site for more than an hour after Joan had left. But they did not find anything other than what was already mentioned in the police report. Goggen had said to Conrad that they needed to come back again later. He wanted to talk with the neighbours, if they still existed, but he said that could wait until another time.

There was a note in the kitchen. "I have gone to bed, but here is a list of the different schools that TJ attended. I have also listed the different time periods and the names of the principals. I have not yet found out the teachers' names."

Goggen looked at the list. "Seven schools. We have to talk to every one of them."

"Do you want to have a beer before we go to bed?" "Why not? It's been a long day."

"How did it go out at the cabin site yesterday?" Henrik had just come downstairs and was pouring himself a coffee.

"Pretty much as I had expected. It was quite overgrown after all these years, but what a beautiful spot," Goggen answered.

"And Joan?"

"She was very nice and helpful."

"Was she able to give you any more information than what you already know?"

He pointed to all the piles of papers that had been delivered to the house.

"No, but I really didn't expect her to either. We just have to take it one step at a time. It's an old case that has stretched out over many years. We have to be patient."

"Yes, we sure do."

"I saw your note from last night. Was it difficult getting the information?"

"No. I asked Robert. It was him who got most of it. I didn't want to confront TJ with it."

"All right, but I still think I would like to have a talk with her. Shall we see if she is free to have lunch or dinner today?"

"That we can do. Let me see what time is good for her."

"TJ can meet us at Tim Horton's in Drayton Valley at 1 p.m.," said Henrik. He had gone to find the telephone and call her as soon as Goggen had suggested he wanted to talk to her.

"What kind of restaurant is that?" Goggen asked.

"It's just a hamburger joint, a Canadian fast-food place. Tim Horton was a legendary hockey player here in Canada, and he started his business down in Hamilton, Ontario. The main staples of his menu were initially coffee and doughnuts. Later on, the menu was expanded. They do pretty good hamburgers there. Conrad, do you want to come along?"

"Yes, why not."

Goggen continued, "While we are there, I am going to try to speak with her. I need to dig a little deeper with her in regard to the different schools she went to. I will try to get her to open up a little more, but

I will do it carefully. I might have to go one-on-one. I'll see how she reacts and if she is ready.

"I'm going over to Robert's now. I want to ask him about how TJ feels about this now. That way I can find out what kind of a reaction I might get when I ask her about her school experiences. His gut feeling is that there is a connection between the crimes and what happened to her at school. He might be wrong, but he thinks that we can find some answers through TJ. And I can't ignore that.

"Conrad, can you find that map where we marked down the different schools' locations? Then put it with the information that Henrik got for us yesterday. I'll be back soon."

TJ was already there when they arrived at Tim Horton's. She got up and came over to greet them.

"Have you ever eaten at Tim Horton's before?" she asked. All three shook their heads.

"Well, there's a first time for everything. This is my favourite place. I don't think much of McDonalds or Burger King. They have a fantastic salad bar here, and in addition to hamburgers you can get fish and chips. It's very good; they use fresh cod. Shall we sit down?" She pointed to the empty table that she had been sitting at when they came in. They all walked over to it and sat down.

"I brought some menus with me. After we decide, we go up there to order. Then they bring the food over."

They all looked at their menus and made their decisions. Then Henrik went over to the counter and placed the order.

Goggen said to TJ, "Robert told us that you are quite an expert with a computer. Is that true?"

TJ smiled a little and looked down at the table.

"Is it true?" Goggen continued.

"How good I am depends on the eyes that are looking. But I like to work with computers."

"Robert also told me that you might be able to assist me if I need some help. I would really appreciate it if it could be you. He said that you have been very interested in police work over the years, but that you didn't join the police force for personal reasons.

"He also told me that you have helped both him and Joan several times as well."

TJ didn't answer him.

"I am not a police officer anymore. I was for many years. Now I am a private investigator, which you know. You also know why I am in Canada. But being in Canada, I will really need someone to support me. I am unfamiliar with the Canadian system, and sometimes the language confuses me. Therefore, I am asking you if you would consider working with me in an official capacity during this investigation."

Goggen looked closely at TJ while he said this.

"You also have personal reasons to finally solve these cases."

TJ still didn't say anything. She just looked quietly down at the table. Everyone at the table was silent.

"I know what you have gone through, TJ, and I know that you have many thoughts about this."

Ashes to Strength

Still silence.

"I also know everything about your father—what happened here and why he moved back to Norway.

"We now believe that the danger no longer exists. Of course, we could be wrong, but we definitely hope that is the truth. It would be great if you could come on board with us and be my right-hand person. You would be an important part of the team. You don't need to answer me right now, but would you please give it some serious thought?"

He looked at her seriously. "Meanwhile let's have something to eat." The food was delivered and the conversation turned to anything but the investigation. Time passed.

"OK, I'll do it." TJ looked directly at Goggen. "But you must promise me that you will protect Asha. I can't bear to thought of her being hurt."

Goggen looked at her and then over to Conrad. "Conrad, can we find a sure way to protect Asha no matter what?"

"I am sure, but let's talk to Robert about it."

"Then we'll talk to Robert right away. I think you should move to the ranch as well if you want to be part of the team," Goggen said to TJ. "I can do that," she answered. "Give me the rest of the day. I'll be there tomorrow. I also have to talk about this to Asha. She is an independent woman and quite stubborn, so she will probably refuse protection. I'll invite her over to the ranch for dinner tomorrow night. We can persuade her together."

"That's a good idea. We can probably use some help from her as well."

"All right," TJ said, as she got up from the table. "I have to get busy. See you tomorrow."

Robert agreed immediately when he was told that TJ was going to join in the investigation. He also saw how it would be easier to extract information from her while she was working as part of the team. It would be less personal than asking her directly. Goggen's plan was to let her work with all the materials for a while. This would bring up memories and would also help her to remember things she might otherwise have forgotten. She might then start really opening up, or so they hoped.

Robert also thought that was a good idea. Now he rolled himself into his office to make a few telephone calls.

"I have just engaged a firm who will protect Asha. It's a previous colleague of mine. She has a little firm where she employs people for exactly what we need. They protect people who feel themselves threatened and wish for protection. She will come over tonight after she closes her office at five o'clock. It will take her a while to get out here. She works over on the other side of Edmonton, and the traffic can be pretty bad after work. Shall we agree that all three of you will come back here when she arrives? I'll call you when she's here." "OK, we'll be back then," Goggen answered.

"Perfect. Now you have to excuse me. Right now I'm setting up a contract regarding the security of a building in Calgary. My son Mark will take it with him when he leaves for there in the morning, so I'm going to be busy most of the day putting it together."

"All right then," said Goggen. "We'll see you tonight."

Kim Harrison was a petite and beautiful woman. She had arrived about 7 p.m. The traffic had not been quite as bad as she had expected. She stood up while the men introduced themselves. As she was in the process of sitting down again, she said, "So you need a bodyguard?"

"Yes, we do," Goggen answered.

"Robert has given me a rough description of what you are dealing with. I have three candidates you can choose from, Louis, Richards, and Magen. All of them are former officers of the Royal Canadian Mounted Police, but they have now left the force. All three of them have the best references. All are agreeable, but professional. They are all available to work as of right now."

"Can any of them come here as soon as tomorrow?" Robert asked. "Yes, I can make that happen."

"It's going to be a twenty-four-hour-per-day job. Are they capable of that?"

"Again, the answer is yes, but we might possibly need a rotation. Again, that shouldn't be a problem."

"Whom would you personally recommend?" Robert continued. "Maybe Louis. She is a very likeable person, easy-going and discreet. She would probably be the best one to protect … Asha, was it?" She looked over to Robert for confirmation.

"Yes, that's her name, Asha."

"The candidate who takes this job needs to stay very near to the

person he or she will be protecting twenty-four hours a day."

"What I'll do is have all three of them come over tomorrow and you all can interview them."

"No, that won't be necessary. We'll take your word for it. If Asha can't get along with the person, then we can think about choosing another one."

"OK," answered Kim. "I'll have her here tomorrow night."

"No, not tomorrow. We'll call you. It'll probably be more like two days."

"What about a place for her to sleep?"

"That's what we need to discuss with Asha and TJ. Asha lives over in Edmonton and stays there most of the time," Robert answered.

"OK then, now we come to the last part of the arrangement, the price of our services. The day rate is four hundred and fifty dollars plus expenses. If the job lasts more than fourteen days, we change over to the monthly rate, which is seventy-five hundred dollars per month plus expenses."

She looked at Goggen and Henrik.

"That is OK," Robert answered.

"Then we have a deal." She put out her hand in front of her. "Louis will have her contract with her when she arrives."

Kim was even more beautiful when she smiled.

"Then I'll just say that it was very nice to meet all of you. I have to be on my way back to Edmonton. We'll meet again soon."

She left quickly and without looking back.

The next day Goggen and Conrad went back to looking at the papers, but this time together with TJ. She was stronger and surer than they had expected her to be, and she came through a few times, especially about the cabin fire and what had happened there. After that, there wasn't much she knew, at least for now.

Goggen went over to Robert's house. He needed to speak to him right away.

"Robert, during the different investigation, several samples and material was collected. Do these still exist?"

"Yes," he answered.

"And where are they? Please don't say over in Edmonton in Captain McKenzie's office."

"Yes, that is where they are. When he took over the cases, we had to give all the materials to him."

"Is there any possibility that we can get a look at it and maybe draw some DNA profiles from it?"

Robert looked at him with a rueful smile.

"When we got the message to deliver all the materials to Lieutenant McKenzie, we made copies of everything we had. We even helped ourselves to small parts of the physical evidence."

Goggen smiled.

Robert continued, "It was not completely lawful, but it's just how it was. I have it in a safe deposit box. The only other person who knows about it is Joan. It has been there, safe, since the beginning."

"Where is it? Here in Drayton Valley?" "No, but not so far away."

"Is there any possibility of doing a DNA test of any of that material? And if so, do you know anybody who can help us with that? I think that we should keep it a complete a secret for now," Goggen said. "Yes, I agree. However, I must speak with them first," Robert answered.

"OK, see what you can find out," Goggen said. "In the meantime, let's take another trip to Jasper. There are a few people whom I would like to speak to out there. We can stay there for a few days. TJ can stay back here. I will be needing her computer knowledge at some time." "How is it going with Louis and Asha?"

"Just fine," Robert said. "TJ says that it looks like they are becoming friends."

"Great," Goggen answered.

"Kim has been a good support for me in several investigations, so I knew that this one would go OK."

The next morning, as usual, Goggen was already up when Conrad came downstairs. He had breakfast out on the table and the coffee was ready. They had decided to leave early, by 7 a.m.

Goggen had been up since five and had been busy writing a timeline. He always did this; he didn't know why. He never looked at the timeline again later; he remembered all of it anyway. It was probably a result of having written it down that made him remember.

They were going to meet up with Joan again. Robert had insisted on it. The reason for this was that she was a police officer and Goggen and Conrad were foreigners. They would have a hard time getting people to talk to them without an official representative. Joan was also the only person whom Robert trusted fully in this situation. They hoped to keep their inspection a secret and not let the police get wind of it.

Goggen and Conrad were well on the way when Goggen said, "I caught TJ in a slip last night."

"Oh? How was that?" Conrad asked.

"It started when I began to fish a little about the schools she had gone to," Goggen answered.

"But she didn't come alone. She brought a friend with her," Conrad said.

"I know, but as soon as her friend left, I tried asking her about it. TJ admitted that every time she began at another school, it went well for a few months. Then suddenly out of nowhere, and for no reason, several of the students began not just teasing her but also tormenting her."

"Yes, the words they used were, 'you rotten Indian whore'."

"I thought that she was placed anonymously into these schools so nobody would know who she was?" Conrad said.

"Yes, that's true, but it happened anyway. And what disturbs me is that the time frame for these abuses was almost the same," Goggen spoke.

"You mean that there was someone following what was happening and then finding out where she was again? And when the found her, they incited the students to do these things to her?" Conrad asked. "Something like that, yes," Goggen answered.

Goggen had begun to thumb through some of the paperwork he had brought with him. "I will check out the first school she went to after the cabin fire. Then we will proceed in the proper order, from first to last."

Conrad didn't answer right away. He sat and thought about this for a while. Then he said, "OK, which school was that?"

"West of Jasper in the area of Yellowhead out in Mount Robson." "We can pick up Joan in Jasper."

"The next school is located in Hinton."

"Hinton? Aren't we going to pass right through there in a little while?"

"Yes, but we're supposed to pick up Joan first. Then we'll go to Jasper. I'm going to close my eyes and take a quick catnap. We should arrive there in about an hour. Think you can find your way alone?"

Goggen smiled.

Goggen told Joan what TJ had said to him the evening before. "You two need to know that I am with you all the way on this. I might be in the police department as well, but I will be helping you as a private citizen. I just took a week's vacation so that I can assist you full-time. I discussed this with Robert last night. The best way

for me to help you with nobody knowing that we are driving around and questioning people is to do it like this. As a police officer I would have to document all of my movements, so it would be way too easy for them to find out what we are doing. I will also stay at whatever hotel you two want to use while you're away," Joan said.

"Of course, but we don't know where that will be yet," Goggen answered.

"That's all right. There are plenty of hotels and motels, and now that it's the off-season we shouldn't have any trouble finding a place to stay," Joan said.

Goggen continued, "I have made a list of persons that we need to try to talk with. The first is, or rather was, the first school that TJ was registered in after the fire. I would like to take them in the same order that she went to them. What do you think?"

"Sounds right to me."

"I will also try to talk to the neighbours of the cabin at that time. I was only able to locate three of them so far. When we were there, you mentioned five cabins, one just a short way from the fire, two further away, and two even further. I would like to check with all of those people to find out if they saw or heard anything that night. It might be that they are not even alive any longer or that they have moved away, but I need to find out for sure."

"We tried to talk to all of them back then too, but in two of the houses no one was home when we were there. Why we never went back to try again I can't remember. Shall I drive?" She looked at Conrad, who was holding the car keys.

He held them out to her and said, "Help yourself."

"Geikie School" said a sign on the outside of a small schoolhouse. "Here we are," said Joan. "What is the principal's name?"

"R. Danyshyn," said Goggen. "Thanks. Shall we go in?"

Joan walked directly over to the little office in the corner. "Principal Danyshyn?" she asked.

"Danyshyn, no, sorry she isn't here any longer. She left four years ago."

"Can you tell us where we can find her?" "And who are you?" asked the woman.

Joan took out her police badge and introduced herself.

"She lives just down the road. Just continue on Yellowhead until you pass the gasoline station. It's the first house on the left. I think I remember it's a red house."

"Thank you," said Joan. "I just need to ask you one more thing. Is it possible to get a copy of the school portrait of the grade five class from 1965, with names on it?"

"Which year did you say, 1965? I have to go down to the archives in the basement for that. It might take me a little time to find it." "That's all right. Could we stop by on our way back?"

"That would be fine."

"No," said Goggen. "We can wait until you find it, and then we can take it with us."

"All right, I'll try to find it. Just give me a little time."

"We'll go across the street and get a cup of coffee in the meantime," Joan said.

"A half hour should be all it takes."

Joan looked enquiringly at Goggen. He said, "I just want to take it with me to show to an elderly lady. It will help to jog her memory." "Yes, you're right," Joan agreed.

After they rang the front doorbell, they heard some sounds coming from the inside. "All right, all right, I'm coming." The locked turned, the door opened, and there stood Ruth Danyshyn.

"Yes? May I help you?"

Joan took out her badge again. This time she introduced the others as well.

"Can we come in?" Ruth stepped aside and let them pass.

Once inside, Joan continued. "We are here to ask you a few questions about something that happened at your school forty years ago." Ruth looked at them expectantly.

"Can you remember a student named Tehya Jane Ellefsrud, also known as TJ?"

Ruth thought about this for a few moments and then asked, "Can you give me a little more to go on? I've had my fair share of students over the years."

"She began at your school at the end of November 1965. After a few months she had to leave school because she became aggressive towards the other students."

"Oh yes, now I remember. I sensed a lot of sadness in her. She was quite clever at first, but then she changed radically. I didn't understand what happened until much later, when I overheard a conversation between two of my other students." "What kind of conversation?" asked Joan.

"Well, there were two students in her class who discussed how they should share some money they had received. They were paid to harass her and call her an 'Indian whore' or some other nonsense. I can't really remember; it was a long time ago."

"Can you remember anything else?"

"No, but after I heard that, I understood why the sudden change in her had come about. I also investigated a little on my own by reading some of the back issues of the *Edmonton Sun*. That's when I made the connection of who she was and what had happened to her. But by that time there was nothing I could do about it. The damage was already done and she wasn't at the school anymore."

"We went to the school before we came here. They gave us your address. We were able to get a copy of the class portrait from that year. Would you be able to remember who the two students were and possibly point them out to us?"

"I only saw one of them. The other one stood with the back towards me. But I can certainly identify the one that I saw."

Joan held the picture out to her. She looked at it and pointed unhesitatingly to one Joachim Nielsen.

Joan asked her a few more questions, but she was not able to answer them. She didn't know where Joachim Nielsen lived or what type of work he was doing.

Joan shook hands with her and said, "Thank you very much. We won't keep you any longer." Ruth asked, "Is that all?"

"Yes, but if you remember anything else, it is important that you call me." She gave Ruth her card.

"All right, now we have something to go after," said Goggen.

"How is the individual registered in Canada, and how does it work? Do you have to notify the county if you move?"

"What do you mean?" Joan asked.

"I mean that if somebody moves from one community to another, do they have to register or notify the community in any way?" "No. We just use Social Security numbers."

"Just like in the States?" "Yes, you could say that." "So how do you find people?"

"There is an office and database in Ottawa, Ontario, where the information is stored."

"Then that is a job for Robert or TJ. We should try to find that Joachim Nielsen," Goggen said. He added, "Well, folks, I don't know what you want to find, but I need to find something to eat. I'm starving."

"Me too," Conrad answered. "What about you?" He looked at Joan. "Yes, why not? There is a nice cosy little restaurant down on Point Alison. We can stop there."

"Sounds good," said Goggen. "Let's go."

It was just like Joan had said, a cosy restaurant on a charming Victorian-style street in Point Alison. The waiter was getting ready to show them to a table when Joan asked, "Can't we sit over there?"

"Of course, help yourselves." She gave them some menus. "Can I get you something to drink?"

Joan said, "I'll have a Molson." "OK, I'll have one of those too." "Conrad?"

"Just a cup of coffee and a glass of water, please." "I'll take a coffee as well," said Goggen.

The waitress wrote down their orders and walked away. They picked up their menus.

"What do you recommend?" Conrad asked Joan.

"Well, I don't know if you've tasted it before, but this is a popular buffalo—bison—area, so they serve both bison burgers and bison steaks. Otherwise, it's pretty much the same things they serve in all of the restaurants. We can ask what they have for specials."

"I'm going to try a bison burger. Conrad?" "I'll have one too. I've never tasted it before."

"I'll just have a salad bar. I'm trying to lose weight."

Weight? thought Goggen. He looked at Joan carefully. It didn't look like it was a problem for her. She was a beautiful woman despite the fact that she was past sixty. He wondered why she wasn't married and thought that maybe she was divorced like he was. He held his thoughts to himself.

"We have now spoken with the first of the seven principals and we have gotten a small lead. What school is next?" It was Goggen who spoke.

"The next school is in Hinton, which is about a one-and-a-half-hour drive from here. That means that school will be out before we can get there. What if we drive out to see the neighbours of the cabin this evening? We probably have a better chance of somebody being home in the evening."

"Yes, I agree. Who's driving? Conrad?" "No, I'll drive."

"But you just had a beer."

"That's OK. One beer is acceptable."

They drove out towards the cabin site and stopped at the neighbours' cabin. They didn't have time to get out of the car before an older man with a grey beard came out of the cabin. He asked if he could help them.

"Yes, maybe you can," said Joan. When she got out of the car, she showed her badge as she introduced herself. She also introduced the others. They were out of the car by now.

"And you are Ivan, is that correct?" Joan asked. "Yes."

"We have some questions for you regarding the evening of August 15, 1965. Do you remember that night?" Joan asked.

"I remember it just as if it happened yesterday. I also wrote everything down that very night so that I wouldn't forget anything in case you ever came back some day," Ivan answered.

"Do you still have that paper?" "Yes, I do."

Joan asked, "Can we see it?"

"Of course. Please come in with me." They followed him inside his cabin, which was kind of roomy. It was kept nice and tidy inside. "Now let me see, where did I put it? Oh yes, here it is." He lifted a pile of papers and took out a brown envelope. He gave it to Joan, who passed it over to Goggen.

"Would you like anything to drink? I have everything from whisky to Coke," Ivan said.

"Thank you for the kind offer, but we have to say no. We have other places to visit yet this evening," said Joan. "Maybe some other time." Goggen carefully read all that Ivan had written down.

Now Goggen spoke: "You wrote here that you had noticed a car, a green station wagon, the night before, but that it had just driven quickly past the driveway of the cabin. Was it the same car that you saw that night, the one that left the area at high speed? That detail is not written here."

"That I cannot answer for sure. It was beginning to get dark when the car disappeared at high speed, but what I am absolutely sure of is that the car I saw parked in front of the cabin on that night was the same one that passed by the day before."

"A green station wagon?" Goggen asked. "Yes," answered Ivan.

Goggen read further. He gave a page to Conrad.

"Is there anything else you can remember from that night?" "No. I purposely wrote down everything that I saw so I wouldn't forget any details."

"What relationship did you have with Nils Henrik Ellefsrud? You write here that you had begun to know each other quite well," Goggen said.

"I met him for the first time down at the country store. We started up a conversation. After that we met up almost every time he and his family were here. He came over or I went by over there. He was a very nice guy."

"You also knew his wife and children?" "Yes, I did."

"Did you know that they were Indians?"

"Yes."

"Did you ever talk about that?"

"No. I did see that she was an Indian, but it was never mentioned." "Did you have any prejudices about that, or did you perhaps know anyone in the area who might have felt that way?"

"Personally, absolutely none. And I don't know anyone around here who felt that way either. Not back then and not now."

"All right. We don't want to take up any more of your time, just one more question. Do you know all of your neighbours?" Goggen asked. "Yes, I do. The one in the nearest cabin is Frank Pedersen. That's a new family. They bought the cabin from the estate of John McNeal." "OK, so they are completely new people there now, which means that they weren't there when the cabin fire happened? What about that other cabin?"

"That's Fred Post. He was here. Those two others I don't know much about."

"OK, thank you again."

Fred Post answered immediately when they knocked. "Just a minute." Then the door was opened. "Yes, can I help you?"

Joan went through the same procedure, showing her badge and introducing herself and the others.

"We are here in connection with an investigation of what happened down at the Ellefsrud cabin on August 15, 1965. Do you remember that day?"

"Of course, who doesn't? It's not like something like that is a daily occurrence out here."

"Yes, that's true. What we were wondering is whether you could remember any other details in addition to what you told us at that time?" Joan asked.

His face changed and he shook his head before he answered. "No, not that I can remember."

"You can't remember seeing a car there earlier that day or maybe the day before? A strange car, maybe?" Joan enquired.

His face changed again while he was thinking. "I remember a car disappearing at high speed that evening, but it was beginning to get dark so I couldn't see what type of car it was. It was a station wagon and it was a dark colour, but that's all. There weren't so many cars around here back then, so almost any car would be noticed. But no, I can't remember any other car."

"All right then, we are just following up on some new information that has come to light. Here's my card just in case you remember something later," Joan said, handing him her card.

Fred Post took the card and read it before he put it down on the table by the entrance door.

"One last question. The house over on that side of yours, who is it that owns it or lives there? Is it the same people who were there back then? And how would I be able to get in contact with them?" Joan asked. "No, the previous owners are dead. It was their son who lived there for a long time. But he sold it not so long ago. I do not know the new owner. But he does not live here; he only comes at weekends or on holidays.

Joan continued asking about the new neighbour.

"I am not sure, but I think he lives there. But I haven't seen him there lately."

"OK, thank you again."

That information was correct. Nobody was home in the cabin next door. So, they drove on out to the farthest house on the road in to Patricia Lake. The man who opened the door might have been in his late thirties.

Again, Joan went through the same procedure, showing her badge, making introductions, and so on, before she began the questions. "Michal More," the man answered.

Joan said, "We understand that you purchased this cabin not very long ago, from Scott Johnson's family." "Yes, that is correct."

"So, you weren't here way back on August 15, 1965."

"No, I was home with my parents in Jasper. I wasn't more than, let me see … eight months old."

"Well, in that case, there can't be anything you can tell us about that day. Sorry to disturb you, but we have to investigate every avenue."

Joan turned away to leave.

"Wait a minute. I have something that might be of interest to you."

Joan turned around and looked at him.

"When I took over this cabin, there were a whole bunch of old books and magazines that belonged to the previous owner. I took a quick look through everything before I threw it out. Somewhere in the mess I found a few valuable books, and in one of them I found something else, something that caught my attention. I don't know why, but I felt I had to save it. It was just a piece of paper, but it was very interesting." Joan looked at him intently.

"Just a minute. I'll go and get it." He went into another room and came back with a paper in his hand.

"Here it is." He gave it to Joan.

She looked down at what was written on it:

August 14, green station wagon, licence plate YYZ – – 4. Drove in the road to Patricia Lake.

August 15, same car drove in, now without a licence plate.

The paper didn't say anything about the car leaving the area. "You found this in among a bunch of books and magazines?"

"Not just a bunch of junk, though. There were some valuable books, like I said. But yes, I thought it was a little remarkable. Later I heard some neighbourhood gossip that Scott's wife, the previous owner, was very nosy and was always watching everything."

"It doesn't say anything about the car leaving the neighbourhood." "Yes, I noticed that too, but that might be because right down there the road divides. You can drive out a different way than you drive in. Both roads are visible from here, but if you are looking in one direction you can't see the other."

"Is this person still alive? Is it possible to get in contact with her?" "Yes, she lives with her daughter down in Hinton."

"Do you have an address?"

"No, but the daughter's name is Laurie Simonek." "Thank you very much for the information."

They went back to the car. Joan was still holding the paper in her hand. She handed it over to Goggen.

"We have to try to find the person who owned the car. The plate number is missing two numbers, but it's something we still might be able to get," she said.

"What do we do now?" Goggen asked.

"Now we go and look for a hotel or motel. It's been a long day. "Let's try Nelson's Inn. I know the owner. It's a small motel about ten miles from here. They don't have a restaurant, but we can find something along the road."

Goggen asked, "Is there a liquor store in the area?" "Why?"

"I would like to have a little glass of whisky after a day of good work."

"We can try the local country store. They sell liquor."

Goggen got up early again as usual. It was like he had said earlier: his brain couldn't rest when he was heavily into a case. He had therefore learned to keep a notebook and pen on the table next to his bed.

That morning he awoke with a completely different thought than the one he had the night before. The last thing he had thought of before he went to sleep was Joan. He had been thinking about her a lot the day before.

Conrad and Joan came and knocked on his door at the agreed time. They were going to drive out to Hinton High School, which would take about two hours. They didn't want to get to the school too early, so they had agreed to meet at eight o'clock.

The visit to Hinton High School didn't provide them with any more information. The story was the same: TJ had integrated herself very well at first and had started out as a clever student. Then suddenly she changed and became extremely aggressive. What lay behind this behaviour the principal had no idea. They had tried to talk to her, but she had refused to answer.

The next two principals told the exact same story, and they also couldn't come up with any explanation for the problem or the sudden change for the worse.

When passing Hinton, they stopped at the home of Laurie Simonek, the daughter of Scott Johnson, whose wife was living there. But she was not able to say any more about the fire. She did remember writing the licence plate number down on the paper.

The next school was in Edson, a tiny little town. They were hoping it wasn't too late, as it was almost four o'clock.

"Looks like we are too late," Joan said, looking around.

The school was very quiet, there were no students anywhere to be seen. They parked in front of the main entrance. Goggen got out and went to try the entrance door. It was open. He waved to the others, and both of them got out of the car to follow him inside.

Joan thought it was strange, the door open and nobody to be seen. She suddenly got a strange feeling. They walked in and then went up a stairway. There was a sign that said "Principal's Office" with an arrow on it, so they followed the arrow. There over in the corner was the office. There were some shaded windows as part of the wall. It looked like a person was sitting at the desk inside. They could glimpse the person through the glass.

Joan knocked at the door. Getting no answer, she knocked again. Still there was no answer. She turned around to face Conrad and Goggen and pointed. She wanted them to crouch down. Conrad had never seen anything like this before, not in real life, only in the movies.

Goggen, of course, knew immediately what Joan meant by her signal. She didn't say anything. She took hold of the door handle and opened the door silently and carefully, while in a full crouch. It was still silent. She straightened up slowly and continued into the room while looking carefully around. There was nobody in the room. The person whom they'd glimpsed through the shaded glass was a man, but he didn't react at all to Joan's voice or to the fact that she was in the room.

"We are clear," she said.

She went forward to check the pulse of the man who sat in the chair.

"He's dead. No pulse," she said.

There was a revolver in his hand, and there was a lot of blood which had streamed down from the right side of his head.

"Suicide," said Joan.

Goggen didn't answer; he just looked around the room.

"I'm not sure about that. Usually people who do that leave some kind of letter. There's nothing here."

Joan looked around. "You're right. Don't touch anything. We have to call this in."

She took out her cell phone and punched in the number to the Edson

Police Department.

"What were you doing there?"

The question came from First Sergeant Jones, a heavyset elderly man. Joan answered, "We were here to ask him, the deceased, about an episode that happened in this school almost forty years ago. It was a happening that involved a young girl." And then Joan told Jones the story of TJ and the school.

"And who are they?"

Jones looked pointedly at Conrad and Goggen.

"They are with me. There is considerably more to this story." She began to tell about the cabin fire, the different schools, and what had happened at Edmonton Psychiatric Hospital. The police officer listened patiently. She didn't mention the building collapse.

"OK," he said, "but this appears to be a suicide. We have to get forensics here to confirm that."

"Aren't you Joan Arnold?" Jones said as he studied Joan again. "Yes I am."

"You're in charge of Department 4342 of the Royal Canadian Mounted Police?"

"Right again."

"I've heard a lot about you." "Only good things, I hope."

"You have been decorated several times for successful investigations." Joan pretended not to hear his remarks and tried to get back to the subject at hand.

"I agree, forensics needs to take a look at this first, but there is one thing that doesn't seem right. The deceased didn't leave any kind of a note or letter."

Jones looked at Joan again. "You have a point. But we will take over now. Don't leave Edson tonight. I might need to speak to you again later."

"That's fine. We were just about to look for a place to spend the night anyway. Can you recommend a good hotel?"

"We have a Holiday Inn down on Lower West River Road. It's only about five minutes from here. There are a couple of other hotels in the same area. Can you give me your cell number, or do you have a card?"

Joan took out one of her cards and gave it to him.

Goggen still had the whisky bottle he had bought the night before. The liquor store hadn't any Scotch, so he ended up buying something called Black Velvet, which was a Canadian whisky. Now they were sitting in his room talking about the principal they had found dead. Conrad was still a bit shaky from the experience. To be mixed up in something like this was something that he, as a lawyer, had never imagined happening.

Goggen just sat quietly for a while sipping his drink and listening to Joan and Conrad while they discussed and analysed what they had found. He did offer them a drink, but both said no.

"This is just too stupid," Goggen said, "that the principal we were on the way to interview should suddenly decide to kill himself. There is something behind this. Somebody that we interviewed has betrayed us. They have sent a message to whoever is responsible for these crimes, and the principal was implicated. So he was murdered, and then it was made to look like a suicide. Maybe we came a little bit early. Maybe the murderer didn't have time to compose a fictitious letter or note, a letter or note that would make it seem more like a suicide. Remember, we arrived at the school at 3.45, and that can't be long after all the students and teachers had left the area."

Joan looked at Goggen in amazement. She nodded with understanding, but was not yet totally convinced. The telephone rang.

"Hi, Robert. I was waiting for you to call back."

Goggen and Conrad could hear what Robert was saying.

"Now you aren't going to believe this," said Joan. Then she told Robert what had happened. There was total silence on the other end.

When Joan had told him everything, he said, "Nothing more on the telephone. I want you to come back to the ranch as soon as you possibly can tomorrow morning. This changes everything. We'll tackle it here in the morning. Be careful." He hung up.

CHAPTER 12

Joan turned the car into the ranch's driveway just after noon the next day. She had sent a message to Sergeant Jones informing him that they were leaving for Drayton Valley but would be available on her cell phone anytime he needed to talk to them. He had agreed.

Now they went into Robert's office. He was sitting behind his desk. He looked up at them very seriously and spoke at once. "Let me have all of the details."

He took a lot of notes as they told the story. When Joan was done, he leaned back in his chair.

"I agree with Goggen. This was more than a simple suicide. We are most definitely back into the situation that Nils Henrik warned us about. It was the reason that he went back to Norway.

"We therefore have to take some precautions. I want everyone involved to be a part of the decision. I want TJ and Henrik to be here. My sons will hear about it from me later."

He lifted the telephone receiver. "Hi, TJ, this is Robert. Can you and Henrik please come over here right away? Yes, right now." He hung up the telephone. "They're coming."

Robert quickly informed TJ and Henrik about all that had happened before he proceeded.

"The first thing that must be decided is this: do we continue with this investigation, or do we not?"

Robert looked at each of them one by one.

"I am aware that this was the last and most important wish that Nils Henrik had, but my question is, is it worth it?"

Everybody sat quietly as they carefully thought about the situation, everything that had happened earlier, and what had just happened yesterday.

Goggen was the first one to say something.

"I am a stranger here, a stranger to Canada, and I am not a family member. But what I am is an ex-policeman, and as policeman I was taught that there is always a reason to carry on with an investigation of a case even if it becomes dangerous to do so. Even if there are threats to our family and friends. This is so that people who employ these tactics will be brought to justice and not be able to continue their tyranny any longer."

"Conrad, you're a lawyer. What do you think?"

"What Goggen just said is true, but it's a little out of my league. I have only been involved in things like this within the confines of the courthouse."

"I understand. Henrik, what about you?"

"I don't know, but I do know what my father wanted."

"Joan, I know what you are going to say; you are a professional. "TJ, you are probably the one who carries the heaviest burden, because of what you have been through and because you have a daughter."

TJ was staring straight ahead silently, and it didn't look like she was going to say anything at all. But then she suddenly turned to Robert. He saw an expression on her face that he had never seen before.

Then she said in a strong clear voice, "Let's take those sons of bitches. Let's see them hang!"

Then she left the room. Joan followed after her.

"Well, that was about the clearest answer we have gotten today, and from the person with the most to lose.

"I agree with Goggen and Joan. If we don't put a stop to this and find out who the people responsible are, none of us will ever be safe again," Robert said.

He continued: "Now the question is, how do we proceed? We have a completely different situation than we had yesterday at this time, and we better remember that.

"We have to take some more precautions, for one thing. Goggen, the first thing I want to do is get you registered in the Canadian system. You need a licence to be a private detective here in Canada. I'll take care of that. Conrad, what about you? Shall I obtain papers for you too? That might prove to be a little more complicated."

"No, you don't need to do that. I can't stay here much longer anyway. I have other business waiting for me back in Norway."

"Henrik, how heavily do you want to become involved?"

"There's not much that a simple worker in the packing business can add to this investigation. That being said, I am with you all the way and will do anything to help the cause," Henrik answered.

Robert continued. "I have an idea. Goggen, you will now be hired by the company Robert Blake's Investigations, Inc. I'll make up a contract after we are finished here. That contract needs to be sent in and registered, but it will only take a few days. Then you have to take a test. I'll provide you with all the materials you will need to study before taking that test. Meanwhile, I'll need copies of your licence and other documents from Norway, including your police department documents. Also, I'll need documents of your services in the other countries you have worked in."

Goggen answered that he would take care of it at once.

Robert looked at Henrik and Conrad.

"Now, when it comes to you both, I think you need to retreat. Don't think that I say this because I wish to see you leave, but I really believe that you need to go back to Norway. There is a good chance that more violence might occur. I hope I'm wrong. But it will be much safer for you in Norway."

Conrad said, "We are aware of that."

"I don't want you to disappear totally out of the picture. It's going to happen that things will come up that we need assistance with, and then we'll call you. Then when the danger is over, we will all meet here again. We're partners, and after this is behind us, I would like to meet the rest of your family, Henrik."

Henrik smiled. "I would like that too."

"Then we are in agreement. Shall I arrange for tickets for you?" "No, that's fine, we'll do it ourselves," said Conrad.

"OK then, the next person is Asha. We need to inform Kim of the situation. I will call her and ask for a meeting tonight. That's all then. Any questions?"

No one answered.

Joan followed TJ out of Robert's office. "TJ, you don't need to do this."

She didn't answer. She just stood looking out over the field with the oil pumps. Her eyes were black. Joan almost didn't know her.

"You have a lot to think about." Again, no answer from TJ.

"I have waited and hidden long enough. Now I want those who did this to my family—my mother, Albert, and my father—which I felt all the guilt of for years, to be punished."

She spoke calmly but with a deep, quiet voice that was filled with conviction. And hate.

"No, let's get them."

She turned around and went back inside.

Conrad and Henrik had gotten seats on a flight home the next day. They had said farewell to everyone and promised to come back as soon as it was over. Henrik got an extra hug from TJ.

Goggen had obtained the necessary papers by fax. Robert had executed them and sent them on.

Robert addressed himself to Goggen. "I will call in a friend of mine, Stanley Daly, to assist you with this. It will be much easier this way. He was with me for many years, and now he is retired. I always call him for extra things when I need him. I already spoke to him. He should be here shortly.

"Joan here can only help us in a limited way. She has to go back to her post up in Grand Cache."

She nodded in agreement.

"When he arrives, I would like us all to sit down and go through the cases again. Then we can draw up an agenda for how we are going to tackle the task. TJ, I have already ordered extra security for Asha.

"I mean, and I truly believe, that she will be well protected. What does she say about it?"

"She says it's all right, but she hopes it won't be for too long."

The doorbell rang. Lori went to see who it was. It was Stanley. Lori knew him from other visits. She showed him immediately to Robert's office.

Robert introduced Stanley to Goggen. "You know Joan and TJ from before." He greeted all three of them.

"Is there anybody who would like some coffee or anything else?" Robert looked around at them.

"Coffee, please," said Goggen. Nobody else wanted anything.

Robert started, "I have given you a rough description of this case, or rather I should say what this case requires in the way of handling. We had just started our investigations when Joan and Goggen stumbled in on somebody who appeared to have committed suicide. We here in this office believe that this was not the case. There are too many coincidences for that to be true."

Robert began to fill in the case for Stanley in more detail. He sat and listened without interrupting. Once in a while he would write down some notes. When Robert was finished, Stanley said, "I think I must agree with your suspicions. Have you heard anything back from the police?"

"No, and I don't think we can expect much from that area either," said Robert.

"Who was the supervisor out there again?" "Sergeant Jones," said Joan.

"I know him. He owes me a favour from way back. I'll have a chat with him." Robert nodded.

Stanley said, "You mentioned that you had spoken to several neighbours and some of the school principals. Now I think that it is time to try to find out who tipped off the people behind this and caused Principal Svensson's death. That was his name, right? Svensson?"

"Yes," Joan answered.

"We should be able to find out who it was by checking back through your telephone calls and emails. Robert, do you know anyone who can help us with that?" Stanley continued.

"We already have that covered," Robert answered.

"The emails I can probably get a hold of myself. Cell phones too, but landline telephones I don't have a way of getting into. I'll have to contact someone, a friend, for that."

Now it was TJ who spoke. "Robert, don't worry about me. This is what I have been waiting for, for years."

Robert could not remember ever seeing TJ quite this way before. It seemed she was glowing inside like hot coal.

"I'm going to try to find the owner of the car that so many witnesses saw. Goggen and Stanley, you continue to interview the rest of the school principals. And Stanley, try to get as much out of Jones as you possibly can.

"We're going to be really busy for the next three hours," said Robert. "Three hours?" said TJ.

"It's a joke. It is our way in the Royal Canadian Mounted Police of saying we are busy for the next three days, weeks, months, or maybe years."

The meeting in Robert's home office was not finished until almost 7.30 p.m. Goggen and Stanley had agreed that they wouldn't get back out on the road until the following morning. Now they were walking together over to the main house, Goggen, Joan, Stanley, and TJ. TJ had a sudden idea. "Why don't we order a couple of Domino's pizzas?"

"Yes, why not?" Joan answered. "Are you going to stay here tonight, Stanley? You don't have anybody at home waiting for you."

"That's true, but I had pretty much decided to go home," he answered. "That has all changed. You'll stay here and eat pizza with us, have a couple of drinks, and relax a little. I need to disconnect for a little while. I'm on vacation." Joan looked at Goggen when speaking.

Goggen was wondering what pizza had to do with dominoes, but before he could voice his question, TJ was asking him what he wanted to drink. He said, "Since you asked so nicely, I would like a rye whisky with ice." He had started to like Canadian whisky.

Joan said, "I'll take a CC with 7 Up."

Stanley added, "Since you have all have decided that I'm going to spend the night here, I'll take a CC and 7 Up too."

TJ went over to the bar and started mixing the drinks.

Asha came in together with her bodyguard. She had driven out to the ranch to be informed fully by Robert and TJ personally.

"We're going to order some pizzas; do you want some too?"

"That sounds good. We were going to go out and find something to eat, but pizza sounds just right. Do you have any wine?"

"There's some in the kitchen."

Asha and her bodyguard returned from the kitchen, each with a glass in her hand. Asha had wine, and the bodyguard had club soda.

It took almost a whole hour before there was a knock on the door and the pizza arrived. TJ opened the door and asked the driver to put the pizzas down on the hall table. She went looking for some money. "Domino's Pizza." Goggen smiled to himself. "Of course."

The voices grew louder, and reached their loudest about 10.30. By then all the glasses had been filled and emptied several times. TJ stood up and was dancing alone across the floor. She really was beautiful, and she had such a beautiful rhythm in her body. Joan remained seated, but she had a gleam in her eyes. Goggen had looked at her enquiringly several times. He believed that she had answered him with her gaze, but he was not completely sure. How should he proceed? It would certainly be wonderful to have some company in his bed tonight. She would return to Jasper in the morning. He didn't think it would cause any problems with the continuing investigation. The opportunity might just present itself, he thought.

At midnight it was over. Goggen sat and waited to see when Joan would go upstairs. TJ had already gone up, and Asha and her bodyguard had left soon after they had eaten. Stanley was sleeping in his chair. Joan finally got up. Goggen could see that she was a little unsteady on her feet. He went over to help her, and they went up the stairs together.

"Your room or mine?" he asked with a smile.

"My room and only me alone," she answered with an even broader smile.

"Goggen, you are very sweet, but you probably don't know that I'm a lesbian."

Goggen smiled and laughed at himself several times when thinking about it before he finally fell asleep.

Edson police station

"Sergeant Jones?" Stanley asked the receptionist at the Edson police station.

"Who shall I say is enquiring?" "Stanley Daly."

"And him?" The receptionist pointed to Goggen. "Ole Olsen."

"OK, just one minute." He lifted the telephone and punched in a number.

"There's a Mister Stanley Daly to see you."

He listened for a moment and hung up the phone.

"He'll be right out." "Thanks."

They met up a little distance from the reception desk.

"Stanley, how are you? It's been a long time." Jones came across the floor while he was speaking, with his hand outstretched.

"I've been just fine."

"And who is this? Oh yes, it's Ole Olsen from Norway. Now I remember. You were together with Joan Arnold last time." He checked Goggen out carefully with his gaze.

"Come in, come in." He led them further into the station. They crossed through the whole main floor to an office that was located in the furthest corner. Jones's name was on the door. "What are you working with these days? I thought you were retired," Jones continued.

Stanley replied, "Yes, that's true. But I work temporary jobs once in a while just to stay active. Right now, I'm working for Robert Blake together with Ole here."

"Robert Blake. That name I've heard before."

"Yes, that's very likely. His name has been in the news quite often over the years. It is the Robert Blake who was in the Royal Canadian Mounted Police. Then he was shot and he now is in a wheelchair. He runs a detective service, and both Ole and I work for him."

"All right, so what is it that brings you out here?" Jones asked.

"We are here in connection with the death of Principal Svensson. We need more information about it. Have you reached a conclusion yet?"

Stanley answered.

"What do you mean?" Jones asked.

"Can you tell us that it really was a suicide, or was it a criminal act committed?" Stanley asked.

"As of right now it does look like a suicide, but the forensics team isn't finished yet. He had gunpowder residue on his hand though," Jones answered.

"Have you found any kind of a letter or suicide note?" Stanley asked. "No, we haven't."

"Isn't that a little suspicious?" Stanley continued. "Yes, but we don't always find one."

"No, that's true, but in about 85 per cent of suicide cases, a note of some kind is left behind," Stanley said.

"Which hand was it that had the powder residue?" Goggen asked. He had done nothing but listen so far.

"It was his right hand," Jones answered. "The same side where he had the bullet wound in his head."

Goggen continued, "I think that's a little strange. If you wish to shoot yourself, wouldn't you use the same hand that you use for practically everything else? Like writing, etc."

He looked over at Jones before continuing.

"What I am saying is that Principal Svensson was left-handed." "How do you know that?" Jones asked him.

"I know because on his desk there was a cup full of pens, and it stood on the left side of where he sat. There was also a pen placed down on the desk right in line with his left shoulder. Both of these things were placed in the natural position for a person who is left-handed. His glasses case was also on the left side," Goggen said.

Jones looked long and hard at Goggen.

"Where did you say you came from?" he finally asked. "Norway."

"And what was it that you did there?" Jones continued, "That was an interesting observation."

"Well, now we'll add a little more meat to the pot," said Stanley.

He then told Jones about the investigation Joan and Goggen had recently begun and he told him why.

Jones sat and listened with his full attention.

"So, you mean that there could be something related here?" he asked. "Yes, absolutely. There are just too many coincidences."

Jones sat still and thought for a while.

"We want to assist you with your investigation," Stanley said. "Well, first of all, we don't know if there is going to be a wider investigation here. It will first be reviewed tomorrow. You do have your licence and you don't need my permission to conduct your own investigation. You are only required to keep me posted as to what you find out. If you discover any criminal behaviour, I have to take over," Jones said.

"I know that. But please try with all your influence to keep the case within the Edson Police District."

Jones asked, "What do you mean?"

"We do not wish the Edmonton police involved in this. Not one thing has been solved in this case since they took over," Stanley answered. "Why?" Jones asked. His face looked like question mark.

"That's a very good question. I have my thoughts about it, but they will remain private for the time being. When I decide to tell these thoughts, I promise that you will be the first to know. If this crime gets linked together with any of the other cases down in Edmonton, things will get infinitely more complicated. At that point you will not be able to stop Ole and me. We can do our own investigation in any way we please as long as we don't hinder the police in any way. You will not be able to. We are therefore laying our cards out on the table for you. If the Edmonton police and Captain McKenzie get wind of this, then anything can happen."

Stanley continued, "We two have some years serving together and we know each other well. Take it for what it is worth and trust me in this respect. We are now in the process of checking the telephone records of those people Joan and Ole visited before they went to Mister Svensson. There must be a connection somewhere there, a connection between one of the people they spoke with and whoever killed Svensson. It's only those persons who know we spoke about the cabin fire and TJ's school experiences."

Jones suddenly got up from his chair. "I need a cup of coffee. What about you?"

"Yes, please, that would be nice." Goggen felt a little queasy. Last night was a little bit over his usual limit of two whiskies.

Jones came back with three cups of coffee on a tray. There were some sugar packets and half-and-half containers next to them. He gave Ole and Stanley each a cup. "Sugar or cream?"

"No thanks, just coffee," said Goggen. Jones and Stanley each took both.

"Well, I have to admit that you have gotten me to see this death in a different light. I'm going back to the crime scene later on today because I have some more questions I need to ask the people at the school. If I find the answers I'm looking for, don't worry. Then I'll call you, Stanley."

"That sounds good. Meanwhile we have several other schools we need to visit."

Stanley and Goggen got up and thanked the officer for his time and the coffee. Then they went out.

Their next stop was White Court.

They found Principal Pantee at Hillsborough High School down on the school's athletic field. He was running. They immediately recognized the fact that he couldn't possibly have been a principal

during TJ's time, as he was barely thirty-five. They flagged him down anyway and asked him who had been the principal about thirty-five to forty years ago. He looked at them before answering. "Well, the previous principal died. But the main teacher is still alive. And most likely she would have been the teacher then."

"Is she still around?"

"Yes, she is. She had moved to a small town outside Edmonton called Camrose. That was where she was born and raised." He gave them her name, but he had no address for her. He didn't think they would have that information up at the school office either, but they were welcome to ask.

Goggen and Daly went up to the office, but it was like the principal had said: they didn't have any address on file for the previous principal. What they did have was a class picture with TJ in it.

It was nearly six o'clock when Stanley's telephone rang. "Yes?" He listened to what was being said on the other end. "OK, we'll see you tomorrow." He hung up.

"You were right, Svensson was left-handed. Jones wants to talk to us again tomorrow. He offered us lunch. OK, let's do lunch. We can touch base with him tomorrow morning to name the time and place." Goggen nodded.

"What do you say we find a hotel? I'm not a kid anymore, and evenings like we had yesterday wear me out." Stanley looked at Goggen when saying this.

Goggen looked at him and smiled. "Yeah, why not?"

The hotel, a Ramada Inn, had a bar right inside off the main lobby. "Shall we meet there in half an hour?" Goggen asked Stanley.

"I think I'm just going to turn in if you don't mind."

Goggen just smiled again, and said, "OK, see you in the morning." "See you then. Good night."

It was a typical suburban bar. It had all the things you would expect to find, a pool table, a dartboard, a jukebox, and some tall tables and chairs, as well as a long bar counter. There were several TVs hung up in strategic places, and right now it was baseball that dominated the screens. Goggen thought to himself, *Grown-up people hitting a little ball. I don't get it.* He sipped on a Black Velvet again. The selection of Scotch around this part of the world was pretty limited. In this bar the only Scotch was Johnnie Walker Red, and that was not going to happen. He never touched the stuff.

He had a burger and fries off the bar menu, and it was surprisingly good. Now he sat alone with his thoughts and occasionally looked at the baseball game.

"Is this seat taken?"

He jumped, since he hadn't noticed anybody come in. He turned towards the voice and said, "No, please help yourself."

He didn't need to say it, as she was already seated. "Jennifer," she said, extending her hand.

"Ole Olsen," he answered.

"Do you want to buy me a drink, Ole?" she asked. "Sure," he said. He waved at the bartender.

Goggen looked at Jennifer as she lay there naked in his bed sleeping. He had moved over to the chair next to the table. She was pretty. He wondered who she was. He was sipping one more Black Velvet.

Goggen was awoken when the telephone rang.

"Yes?"

He looked at his watch and saw the time was 8.30.

"Good morning. I just talked with Jones. He'll meet us at a little tavern at Shining Back Lake at 12.30. It's about a forty-minute drive out there. Do you have any preferences on what we should do in the meantime? Maybe we could get some breakfast?"

Goggen looked over at Jennifer, who was still sleeping.

"No, I'll pass on that. Why don't we just take our time this morning? If we don't need more than forty minutes to get there, we don't need to leave until 11.30."

"That sounds fine for me," said Stanley. "I'll see you at 11.30." Goggen had other plans for how to use the next few hours.

Stanley had already checked out and was standing by the car when Goggen got there.

"Did you sleep OK?" he asked. "Can't complain," Goggen answered.

"I slept until about 6 a.m., but that was it. I went to bed too early. It was only like eight o'clock. I didn't look at the time, but it was around there. I talked to Robert for about half an hour first."

"Did he have anything new to tell us?"

"No, not at the moment, but I told him what we did yesterday. I didn't get a chance to let him know what Jones came back to us with, as he had already hung up."

"He hung up?" Goggen looked at Stanley questioningly.

"Yes, but then I got a message from an unknown telephone number."

He gave his telephone to Goggen.

He looked at the display, which read, "I'll call you in ten minutes from this number. Robert."

Goggen looked at Stanley. "Did he call back?"

"Yes, ten minutes later. He told me that he was concerned. He's afraid that someone might hack into his telephone. He went and got another telephone that can't be traced back to him, a telephone registered to a totally different name. He made the call from the balcony. He's also afraid that someone might have placed bugs in his house. It really seems like it."

Goggen nodded his head in agreement.

"He wants us to send him a message as soon as we have spoken with

Jones," Stanley said. "Then he'll call us back."

Stanley told Jones what Robert had said. Jones sat and listened with interest. Then he said, "There is also something I would like to take up with you. There's a good reason why I suggested that we meet out here. There are things happening at the station that lead me to believe that we are being watched. At the moment I don't have any concrete proof. I was called in to the chief's office early this morning. Then I was questioned about things that I can definitely say I was the only one who knew about pertaining to this case."

"What do you mean?" Stanley asked.

"There were several things, but one of them was that he knew I called you two last night. The other was that I had found a note in Svensson's pocket where he had written a farewell before he shot himself. That note was neither shown to nor talked about with anyone."

"But Erik knew about it."

"Right. He did. I know Erik, the chief, very well. I would have no problem discussing everything with him. We grew up in the same neighbourhood, went to the police academy together, and have been partners, but then he moved on and became a lawyer. That's why he's in that office and I'm sitting out here. It was also him who asked for me to be transferred to the Edson Police District.

After I filled Erik in on everything we had found so far, like your noticing Svensson was left-handed and that the powder residue was on the wrong hand, he could only share his suspicions with me. We then discussed the different possibilities, such as bribery or an internal leak. "He told me that he stands behind me 100 per cent, but he said I should be very careful. Everyone knows that we must investigate a suspicious death. And we are doing it this time, but our hands are tied when it comes to certain procedures. It's in this area that Erik and, I believe, that you and your independent investigation can shed more light on what happened. We, or mostly me, will keep you informed about anything we find out or don't find out. But you both have to help me too."

He looked at Stanley and Goggen and continued. "We have to do it outside of the police station."

"That's right," said Stanley. "So where do we do it?"

"In my pocket I have a list with some addresses on it. They are marked with some words and names. When we want to talk to each other, we will send a text message including a sentence that uses the word or name connected to the addresses on the list. Then we write the time by putting the two middle numbers on the outside. For example, 12.30 becomes 21.03." He wrote it down on a napkin. "OK?" He looked again at Goggen and Stanley. They nodded, indicating that they had learned the system.

He passed the note to Stanley. "Take good care of it."

"Goggen, I understand that's what you like to be called. You can call me Patrick." He smiled and asked, "Do either of you have anything to add or any questions?"

They both shook their heads.

"OK then, I should get back to headquarters." He reached into his pocket to get some money to pay the bill.

"No, that's OK, we'll get the check," Goggen said. "I'll get the money back."

Jones shook hands with both of them and went out of the restaurant.

Goggen and Stanley continued to look up the earlier principals and teachers who'd had something to do with TJ. They were not able to find out anything else from any of them. They all told the same story, that she began as a good and conscientious student and then suddenly changed and became aggressive and impossible to deal with.

It was when they had just arrived at the very last school that TJ had gone to, the one that resulted in her being committed to the Edmonton Psychiatric

Hospital, that they got their first lead. Principal Ruth Wilson, an elderly lady with white hair, said that she was TJ's teacher back at that time. She remembered her well. It was a school up in Rocky Mountain House.

She couldn't remember exactly when the development happened. She remembered it almost eighteen months afterwards, when she got to thinking about the dark green station wagon that had come to the school several days in a row. It always parked out by the football field.

It arrived very shortly before the lunch recess in the middle of the day and left very shortly after it was done. She had noticed that two students, a Miss Suzy Perkins and a Miss Lori Parker, had always loitered around the car. She had thought that perhaps the people in the car were boyfriends of the two girls, who were of an age when boys started coming around them.

She really didn't think anything about it until about a year and a half later. She thought it was at least that long, or maybe longer, when she had come across an article in the *Edmonton Sun* that made her think more carefully about that.

It was an article about a psychiatric hospital. It was written about what could happen to patients or employees who worked there. The article detailed a case that had happened there, but of course without the names, but something about it made her think. It kept coming back to her over and over. Finally, she had gotten into her car and driven out to the hospital, because she needed to settle her suspicions. It was TJ Ellefsrud. She had tried to visit her but was informed that she was no longer there. No one was able to tell anything about what had happened to her. They might have known, but they weren't going to tell her.

That's what made her think about the car that parked down by the football field every day for about two weeks.

"Can you remember what the two guys in the car looked like? Have you ever seen them before?" asked Goggen. She said no, she had never seen them before, but she did remember that one of them had very dark hair like a Native American and the other one was light blond. She couldn't remember anything else. She had only glimpsed them a few times at a distance.

Goggen asked, "What about Miss Perkins and Miss Harper? Is there anything you can tell us about them? Do you know where they live now?"

"Yes, they both live right here in Rocky Mountain House. Miss Harper is now Missus Robinson and lives over in McNutt Estates. Miss Perkins, I am not sure about. The last I heard was that she was living on the street. She hasn't done very well—too many drugs and too much alcohol."

This time it was Stanley who asked, "What made you connect seeing that green station wagon with TJ Ellefsrud's change of personality?" "Because I remember hearing a conversation concerning some remorse. I can't remember who repeated these rumours, but the truth hit me when I read the article."

"You have been an enormous help to us," said Stanley. "Just one more question. Is it possible to get a copy of the class picture from the class that TJ was in when she was here?"

"Of course. I have all the class pictures here in my office. I don't have every single picture, but I've kept all of the ones that I was responsible for while I was the head teacher." After rooting around for a moment, she said, "Here it is. You can take it with you, but I would like it back later."

"Of course, we'll bring it back to you. Can you point out Miss Perkins and Miss Harper?"

She pointed to two girls on the left side of the picture. "There they are. I remember that those two girls stayed together through thick and thin."

"We'd like to thank you again for all your help. You have really aided the investigation."

They went back to their car and drove away.

As soon as Stanley had started the car and began to drive, Goggen said, "That green station wagon again. Do you know your way around Rocky Mountain House?"

"No, but it certainly isn't a very big town. We'll find our way around." "Shall we stop for lunch? We can text TJ. Maybe she can find the address for Missus Robinson/Miss Harper. I think we should visit her first. If it's like Ruth Wilson said, she and Miss Perkins were always together. They might still have contact with each other."

Goggen nodded. "I agree with you there."

"Shall we stop at that tavern over there?" Stanley pointed to a building coming up on the right.

"Why not?" said Goggen. "It looks as good as any other place."

"OK, can you give me the address again? It's 2254 Southwest 24 Court, Hillside."

Goggen read from the display on his cell phone. TJ had found Lori Robinson's address rather quickly. She texted them the address and telephone number. They had agreed with Robert to make no telephone calls to known numbers. Text messages were more difficult to hack into—difficult, but not impossible.

Stanley had called the number first to check that Lori was home. They had first gotten the answering machine, but while Stanley was in the process of leaving a message, Lori had picked up the telephone. She had said that she was willing to speak with them, but not until her husband was at home. Stanley had gone along with that.

They had arrived. It was almost 6 p.m. They walked up to the house and rang the bell. A plain-looking man opened up the door. "Yes?"

Stanley took out his badge and introduced himself and Goggen. The man looked at the badge.

"OK, come in. Lori told me that you two were coming."

He stepped aside, and they went past him into the house. Mrs

Robinson was waiting for them in the kitchen. Stanley greeted her and then introduced himself and Goggen.

"Sit down," she said. "Can I get you anything, coffee or tea?"

"No thank you. Nothing for me. Do you want anything, Goggen?" "No thank you."

"We don't want to take up a lot of your time, but like I told you on the telephone, we are trying to solve an old case. In the process of doing that, something has come up that you might be able to help us with." Stanley looked at Lori Robinson.

"Can you remember a girl who started new at your school in the midwinter of 1970? Her name was TJ Ellefsrud."

Lori answered immediately. "Yes, I remember her." "What can you tell us about her?"

"Well, she was a very nice girl when she first came, but then something happened."

"What do you mean when you say something happened?"

"She became very aggressive and she threatened some of the students with a knife."

"Can you think of any reason why she would do that?"

Lori looked for a few moments at Stanley before she answered.

"What do you mean?"

"I mean, can you remember if there was anything that happened to her, or was she tormented in any way during that time period? The reason we ask is that this occurred several times at some other schools that TJ was a student at. The students began to harass her, and it had something to do with a green station wagon."

Stanley carefully studied Lori's face as he said this. He continued, "We have confirmed that you and a friend of yours were seen hanging around a car that answers that description, a dark green station wagon."

Lori's gaze sank down to the table. She sat tensely for a few moments, and then tears began to run down her face.

"That has kept me awake many nights and I have shed a lot of tears over my involvement in it, but Suzy convinced me, or rather she more or less forced me, to take part in it. I was young and stupid."

"What was it that Suzy wanted you to do? Can you tell us the whole story?"

Lori looked over at her husband.

"Let me first explain to you, Nils, that this happened a long time ago. I have never told you anything about it. I wanted to many times, but I didn't have the courage to. I wasn't sure how you would react.

"I have also had nightmares about what I heard later and how it set off a chain of events.

"The way that Suzy got me to go along with it was she threatened me that she would tell the whole school that we had lesbian sex. Suzy is a lesbian, and one night after we had smoked a joint, she lured me into her bed. So, when the green station wagon came, she had a way to force me to go along with what they wanted us to do. They offered us money to spread some rumours." Tears were running down her face now.

"They told us to spread it around that TJ was an Indian whore, that she had had sex with everybody.

"We got three hundred dollars for doing that. Suzy took two hundred and fifty of it. I didn't know about Suzy's drug problem then."

Lori still had tears in her eyes while she continued. "We began very carefully to spread these rumours, but it didn't take long before the whole class believed them. That's when TJ changed completely." Stanley and Goggen looked at each other in disbelief.

"What can you tell us about the car? Can you remember the make, model, licence plate number?"

"I remember that it was dark green with red interior." "What about the make or type?"

"I think it was an Oldsmobile, but I'm not sure." "Registration?"

"No, but I think it was a licence plate from British Columbia." Goggen jotted down, "BC."

"Do you remember anything about the two men?"

"One of them was an Indian with very black hair, and his name was Jim. I think the other one's name was Scott, and he was white with light blond hair."

"Can you tell us where they were from? Or where they lived?"

"No, and I don't know their last names either. But they had a lot of money and they waved it around. We were asked to go out with them several times, but I always said no."

"Your friend Suzy, do you have any contact with her now?"

"Not much. Once in a while I stop by and give her a few dollars. She has it pretty bad."

"Why is that?"

"She has a drug problem and she lives on the street." "Do you know how we can find her?"

"She usually is down around the railroad station. I think she sleeps in one of the empty cars now and then. That's where I usually find her."

Stanley looked at Goggen and asked, "Do you have any questions to add?"

"Yes. The two guys in the station wagon, about how old were they when you met?"

"I don't really know, but they were definitely older than us." "Can you give us an approximate age?"

"Maybe about twenty-five."

"OK, I think we have all the information we need right now." Stanley took out his card.

"If you think of anything else that might help, please call me." He gave the card to Lori. She took the card but didn't answer.

"Now we won't bother you any longer. Thank you for your help."

As they were heading for the door, Lori, following them, said quietly, "I am sorry again for what I have done. You can pass that on for what it's worth.

I don't expect to be forgiven, but it would mean a lot to me if you told it to TJ if you see her again."

The railroad station was located right in the middle of Rocky Mountain House, and it was like Lori said, a lot of empty railroad cars sitting unused on a side track. Goggen counted twenty-two cars. "Where do we begin?" he asked.

"Let's begin there," answered Stanley, as he looked over at the steps to the platform. Goggen followed his gaze. There was a man sitting there. Maybe he would tell them where they could find Suzy.

"Do you know Suzy Perkins?" asked Stanley. The man looked up at him. They could easily see that he wasn't going to tell them anything. Stanley took out a ten-dollar bill. There was still no reaction from him. Stanley took out another ten-dollar bill.

The man took them both and said, "She's in wagon number 374."

Goggen and Stanley set out down the side track.

"Here it is," said Goggen.

The side gate was locked, but they walked around to the other side and that door was cracked open.

"Is there anybody here?" Stanley called out.

No answer was forthcoming, so he called out once more. Then he slowly opened the door. He looked in, and over in the corner he saw a pile of clothes. Maybe there was something in them.

"Come on," he said to Goggen, and hopped in. Goggen followed. "Is she alive?"

"Yes, I can feel a pulse." Suddenly she opened her eyes. She was startled and looked very afraid.

"Don't be scared," said Stanley. We're just here to ask you a couple of questions."

She didn't answer, just shrunk further into the corner.

"We're investigating an old case." He waited for some kind of response from her.

"We just got done talking with your friend Lori. She told us where you were."

Still not a sign of her understanding or answering. Stanley took out his badge.

"My name is Stanley Daly, and this is Goggen. He came here all the way from Norway. Do you know where Norway is?"

He might have seen a small glimmer of understanding in her eyes. He waited for a few moments before proceeding with his questions.

"Can you remember a girl who was put into your class back in junior high school named TJ Ellefsrud, the one who got so aggressive? We know what happened to her and that you and Lori were involved in it. What we're wondering now is if you can tell us anything about the two guys who contacted you and paid you to spread rumours about TJ in the school."

Suddenly she answered, "What's it worth to you?"

Stanley took a roll of cash out of his pocket. He peeled off a ten-dollar bill, and then another. She just looked at him. When he had thirty dollars in his hand, she said, "His name is Jim McCoy."

"Where can we find him?" She just stared silently at him again.

Stanley offered thirty dollars more.

"He has a cabin up at Abraham Lake."

Stanley said to Goggen, "I know where that is. What else can you tell us about him?" "Nothing."

"What about the guy called Scott?"

Again, no answer. Thirty more dollars came out into the light. "I think his last name was McKenzy."

"What else can you tell us?" No answer. Jimmy began to thumb out more money, but she didn't try to take any of it. She wouldn't say any more, and possibly she didn't know any more.

Stanley put the money back in his pocket and turned to Goggen.

"Let's go. There's nothing more to learn here."

"You better be careful. They raped me a bunch of times."

Stanley and Goggen turned back to her.

"I don't like cocks, but it was the only way that they would give me any crack."

"Tell us more," said Stanley.

"Not much more to tell. They gave me money and drugs to start rumours. It was how they got me to rat out TJ. I liked TJ." "How did you meet them?" asked Stanley.

"It was downtown. I was down there one afternoon all alone. They came over to me and offered me a Coca-Cola. First, I said no, but then after a while I thought it could be fun to go into the corner café and get a Coke with two cute guys. They came back again the next day and the next. After a while we became friends. One day they offered me a smoke, and I didn't know it was a joint. To make a long story short, I found out I liked to get high. But I didn't know the joint was laced with cocaine. So here you see the results."

Stanley took out his roll of cash again. He took out fifty this time and put it into her pocket. She made no sign of noticing it. "Is there anything more we can do for you?"

She just stared at him. The conversation was over.

Stanley and Goggen drove back to the ranch that night. Rocky Mountain House was not very far from there. Robert straightened up quickly when they came into the room.

"Good, you're here. I didn't expect you until tomorrow. Sit down, both of you." He wrote something on a notepad while he talked. "How did it go?" At the same time as he asked the question, he passed them the note. "Don't say anything. The room is probably bugged."

"Well, we still have a lot of unsolved questions." "What about the principal you found dead?"

"It looks like suicide. They are still looking into a note that was found, and we are waiting to hear. Other than that, we haven't found out anything more."

"It's getting late, so how about a nightcap?" Robert asked.

"I would if I could spend the night here, but I have to go home. I have something to take of there. I'll come back tomorrow, but don't look for me before late afternoon, OK?"

"No problem, but on your way back would you drop by Kim's for me? She has a package for me. I was going to have it sent here by courier, but since you're going by, you can take care of it instead."

"Of course."

TJ was sitting watching TV when Goggen came into the main house. "Hi. You're still up."

"I couldn't sleep." "Why not?"

"Good question. I should know why myself. Too many thoughts running around in my head. I'm also worried about Asha. Now I understand much better what my father went through."

Goggen sat down in the chair next to hers. "What are you watching?"

"Oh, I don't know exactly. I was just channel surfing, nothing special."

"I was thinking of taking a little walk. Want to come?" Goggen asked. "Where?"

"Just around the property."

Goggen had gotten up again as he spoke.

"Sure, why not. I'll come."

She got up and went to fetch a jacket. Goggen hadn't taken his jacket off yet.

While they were outside walking, TJ asked, "How did your trip go?" "Good. We think we have begun to find some answers to several things. The principal who was found dead and was mistaken for a suicide was murdered. It's not official yet, but Inspector Jones informed us about it. It is only he and his chief who know about it. They want to keep it that way for the time being. They know for sure that someone is leaking information out of the police department, but they don't know who. Stanley and I have been asked to assist them. It's going well.

"There's another reason why I invited you out for a walk with me tonight. It's something I have to ask you about. Can you remember two girls who were in your class at Rocky Mountain House, a Miss Perkins and a Miss Harper? That was the last school you went to before you were sent to Edmonton." Goggen could see that she was thinking hard.

"I have a class picture out in the car that was taken at that school. I was hoping that it might jog your memory. When we finish our walk, I'll get it for you."

"That might help me. I can't picture them in my mind right now." "Anyway, they have given us information that it was two men who came to the school and paid them to spread rumours about you in your class, which spread to the whole school."

Goggen was carefully watching TJ's reaction when he said this, wondering if she could handle it.

She said that she could handle things, and it seemed to go all right, but her face looked tense and Goggen was a little concerned for her. "The girls said the men came in a dark green station wagon. They said that one was white and one looked like he was an Indian. Miss Harper was not sure, but she thought they were about twenty-five years old. The last piece of information was that their car licence plate was from British Columbia; she was quite sure about that."

"BC. So that is the reason I was never able to find out who owned the car that drove away from the cabin." TJ nodded to herself with understanding.

"We also got two names," Goggen continued, "and one address. Jim McCoy and Scott McKenzy. Do you know either of those names?" "No, I don't."

He took out his notebook to read off the address they had gotten. "Jim McCoy had, or has, a cabin on Abraham Lake."

"I know where that is. Can you be a little more specific?" Goggen looked into his notebook again. "No."

"But it does look like we've finally found something to work with." "Tomorrow I'm going to do some research at the BC auto registration office."

Goggen went to his car, got the school picture, and locked the car up. TJ looked at the picture for a long time.

"Miss Harper and Miss Perkins are standing way out on the left of the picture, right?"

Goggen nodded. He was standing holding a flashlight on the picture so she could see it.

"So now I know who they are." She looked at the picture for a little longer, then gave it back to Goggen. She was very quiet. It was easy for Goggen to see that she was struggling with her thoughts.

"They weren't the two whom I threatened." Her voice was very low now. "They didn't harass me very much. It was him with the light curly hair in the middle of the picture that I held down on the floor with a knife at his throat."

Goggen turned the flashlight back on again and looked at the picture. "His name was Joe. He said that Mama was an Indian whore and that she had liked it. That was what pushed me too far. I almost cut his throat." She looked distant, and he could see some tears fall. It was too late now.

CHAPTER 13

Vancouver, British Columbia

8 October

TJ landed at Vancouver International Airport at three in the afternoon. During the breakfast meeting it was decided that TJ should fly out to Vancouver to research the automobile registration department personally. It was decided that this would be the best way, not just because they suspected they were being watched, but also because they wanted to have it done as soon as possible. The decision was made that immediately after breakfast TJ would get into her car and drive away. She was instructed not to drive directly to Edmonton International Airport, but to take a roundabout way before ultimately going there. She agreed with Robert about using this technique. Now she had finally arrived in Vancouver. The airplane trip went smoothly, and she was sure that no one suspected what her final destination was. Stanley had just arrived back at the ranch. With him he had the package Robert had asked him to pick up from Kim.

"There you are, and I see you brought the package." Robert pointed to what Stanley had in his hand.

"Set it down there on the desk," Robert said. Stanley put it down as instructed.

"Did you finish what you had to do at home?" asked Robert. "Yes, it went fine."

"Good. Goggen is over at the main house. Would you please go and get him?"

"Of course," Stanley answered.

Ten minutes later all three were sitting in Robert's office. Robert had opened up the package from Kim. Both of them saw immediately what it was, both having had experience with the type of device. It was a little rectangular black box with a couple of buttons and dials plus a display. Kim had sent a machine that would detect any bugging devices that might be hidden on the premises. Robert gave Stanley and Goggen a sign to keep on talking. He pointed to Goggen and signalled that he should take the device and start using it. Robert was not mobile enough to do that job. Goggen picked up the detector and checked it before he got up and started moving it around the room. They continued to speak normally while Goggen was doing the search. He had set the detector to vibrate if it detected something. Goggen continued to move slowly and methodically over the entire office, but the machine didn't pick up anything. Could they have made a mistake?

Goggen checked the device again, along with all the connections. It seemed to be functioning properly. Still no indication of any bugs. Robert took out the instruction book and made a sign to Goggen to give the detector back to him. He looked at it while they continued to talk. Then he turned the detector off. He took out the batteries, waited thirty seconds, put them back in, and turned it back on. Then he gave it back to Goggen, who continued to search with it.

Suddenly a red light came on and he felt the vibration. It zeroed in on a shelf behind Robert. As he went nearer, the signal became stronger. There it was, an extremely tiny microphone camouflaged in the centre of a Phillips screw. Robert gave the signal to Goggen to just let it stay there. Then he signalled to continue looking.

They found one more microphone. Again, Robert signalled to let it stay there. Robert and Stanley continued to talk about the case, but without giving away any important information.

Goggen came back to Robert and signalled that there was nothing more to find. Robert gave him the thumbs-up sign.

"Robert, what do you say we go get something to eat? I'm hungry." It was Goggen who spoke.

"Yes, let's go to the kitchen and see what we can find. Lori is out this morning."

Once they were well into the kitchen, Robert turned his wheelchair around and looked at Goggen. He spoke in a low voice and said, "Let those two microphones stay there." He continued to look at Goggen. "If we take them away, then whoever placed them will know that we are on to them. If we let them stay, they won't suspect anything. Agreed? We know that there aren't any bugs here in the kitchen, and we can always check, but meanwhile let's eat." He smiled.

"Well, Stanley, Goggen has informed me what you found out at the different schools. TJ is in Vancouver right now at the automobile registration office. What about the address out on Abraham Lake? Are you going to visit that tomorrow?"

"That was my plan," Goggen answered.

"OK, while you two do that, I'm going to pay a visit to Sergeant Jones."

TJ used the whole next day in the registration office in Vancouver. She was already at the door when the first person came in to work. They allowed her to accompany them in.

The receptionist's name was Judith. "Can I help you?" she asked.

"Yes," TJ answered. "I would like to talk with Daniel McDonald." Robert had told her to ask for him. He was one of his good friends. "Daniel. Please wait one minute. I'll see if he has arrived yet."

Ten minutes later a man came in the door.

"Can I help you?"

"Yes, I'm looking for Mister McDonald," TJ said again. "That is me."

"TJ Ellefsrud. I should say hello from Robert Blake." "Oh, yes. How is he?"

"He's fine."

"What was your name again?" "TJ Ellefsrud."

"OK, what can I help you with?"

"Robert was hoping that you could help us find an automobile plate number and eventually the name of the owner. It was a number that was used in a crime more than forty years ago."

McDonald looked at TJ in a way that told her that he was checking her out.

"I owe Robert a favour, so sign in here." He pointed to a list that was on the receptionist's desk.

"Do you have any identification with your picture on it? Like a driver's licence?"

"Yes, I do."

"OK, give that to her. You'll get it back when you are finished in here." He nodded to Judith and said, "She's with me."

She followed him into a door to the right of the lobby. "When did you say that the crime took place?" "About forty years ago."

"Hmm, that's a very long time ago. Do you have anything to go on?" "Yes, we do. It was a licence plate from British Columbia with the following numbers and letters: YYZ, blank, blank, 4. We are missing two of the numbers But we know that the car was a dark green station wagon, possibly an Oldsmobile."

"It looks like it's going to be a long day for you. There were lots of cars in BC even in that time, but it's not impossible to find the one you're seeking. The fact that you are missing two of the characters on the plate will present you with about one hundred possibilities. All previous licence plates are now on microfilm, so it will be easier. But it's still a lot of material to go through."

McDonald was talking while going through a number of shelves. He went over to a cabinet and took out three large boxes.

"In these boxes you will find all the licence plates with the letters YYZ on them. It just requires you to begin at the beginning. You can use the screen over there to read the magnetic strips. If you have any questions, I'll be right over there." He pointed to a desk over against the wall.

TJ looked over at the desk.

"Sorry, but I'm not allowed to help you go through them." "That's all right," she said. "I'll manage."

"Here's a coffee. I thought you could use one right about now." McDonald was standing right in front of her with a coffee cup in his hand.

"Thanks. I absolutely do." She smiled back at McDonald. "Are you finding your way?"

"Yes, it's better now. It took me a while before I picked up the threads of it."

"You need to be very organized."

TJ looked into the screen again. "I have now looked at sixty-eight possibilities."

"Then you only have thirty-two left. Is there anything else I can get for you?"

"No, this coffee hits the spot." "OK then, I'll leave you to it."

TJ concentrated again on the screen.

Two hours later she had checked out all the auto plates with the combination YYZ – – 4, but none of them were ever used on a green station wagon. McDonald looked over at her. It was very plain to see the disappointment in her face.

"I see you didn't find anything." "That's right. Not a thing."

"And you're sure that it was a BC plate?"

"Sure? Only as sure as the testimony of one witness. She said she was quite sure it was from BC."

"Well then, in that case we'll look in another place."

TJ looked at McDonald.

"Since you didn't find any match here, let's see if the plate was moved to another car. What you were checking here is when the plate was used for the first time."

TJ looked at him questioningly.

"Once in a while it happens that the number and letter combination becomes available again. Then the plate is remade and assigned to another car."

TJ felt herself fill with new hope.

McDonald walked over to the other side of the shelves. He came back with another box.

"Here are the plates that have been used again."

TJ took it from him and then asked, "Before I begin, is there anywhere to eat around here?"

"Not really anything good in-house, but there's a Burger King right behind this building. I'll go with you if you want."

"Yes, please. I need to look at something else besides magnetic strips for a while."

"Bingo!" TJ said out loud.

McDonald looked over at her. She was still reading the screen. "Oh no," she said. "That can't be true." "What is it?" asked McDonald.

"The car with the tag YYZ 449 was a green Oldsmobile station wagon. But it was reported missing, stolen on June 21, 1965, by the owner. It was never found again. It was registered to a Jerry Smith, address Gamozzi Road, BC. No telephone number."

McDonald had gotten up from his desk and gone to stand behind TJ, who was still looking at the screen. She read out loud what was on the magnetic strip.

"That's an address out in Revelstoke. It's not very far from the border of Alberta, is it?"

"I have to check on that."

"That's OK. Can I have a copy of the strip?"

"Yes, I'll do that for you. Our copy machine is a little tricky."

TJ looked at the copy that McDonald gave her.

"That looks good, but can I have one more copy just in case?"

McDonald printed one more.

TJ took both of them and put them together.

"I guess I'm finished now. I put everything back the way I found it. Can I help you put the boxes back?"

"No, that's no problem. And you won't be able to reach anyway. I'll get one of the others if I need help."

TJ looked at McDonald. "Now I just want to thank you for your help." "Help? It was you who did all the work, I just got the boxes for you." "Thanks anyway." She shook his hand and went out to the reception desk to sign herself out. Judith gave her driver's licence back.

Goggen and Stanley had just turned off David Thompson Highway. They were expecting the cabin belonging to Jim McCoy to be at the end of the road, just ahead.

Stanley said, "It looks very desolate out here. The road had started to become overgrown."

Goggen didn't answer him; he just kept on driving. There! They caught a glimpse of some kind of house or cabin, just visible through the trees. There it was again. They came to a clearing and there it was, a house, a building that had been most likely a barn, and a building that could be a garage. They searched the area with their eyes, scanning back and forth. There was no sign of life.

They got out of the car, still looking around. The grass hadn't been cut for weeks, maybe months. Around the house the weeds were even higher than the grass. Stanley loosened the gun from his holster.

His training had taught him that you never know what to expect in situations like these.

Goggen didn't have a weapon. Robert had managed to get him a licence to carry one, but he didn't feel the need.

They walked cautiously towards the front door of the house. Stanley carefully tried the door. It was locked. He looked around and stuck his hand in a little opening in the wall. He took out a key and smiled broadly before he inserted the key into the lock and turned it. The door was open. He signalled to Goggen to stay put. Then he went in, his gun pulled. It was perfectly quiet. He moved further in. Nothing happened. There wasn't anyone there.

"All clear," he called, loud enough for Goggen to hear.

The house consisted of a bedroom, a kitchen, and combination living room and dining area. There was no second floor. Goggen thought there must be some kind of loft, though, because there was a trapdoor in the corner of the kitchen. Goggen had noticed a window up there when he was outside.

They didn't find anything of interest in the house, just some very dusty furniture. Neither was there anything of note in what was left of the barn.

It seemed like nobody had been here for a very, very long time. They tried the garage doors; there were two of them. They were bolted together with a lock. The grass had grown quite high in front of the doors. Goggen walked around to find something he could use to break the lock with. He went back to what was left of the barn, where he found a crowbar. *I could use this,* he thought, and took it back to the garage door. He tried to pry the bolt from the door with all his strength, but he was unable to budge it.

He went back to see if there was anything else he could use. He found a pipe about three feet long and inserted it into the crowbar to use for extra leverage. This time the lock gave way with a loud crack. They both rocked the door back and forth until they got it open far enough to get inside.

There it stood, an Oldsmobile station wagon, green, with the licence number YYZ 449.

Robert had arranged to meet with Sergeant Jones out in Nojack, a cosy little village on the Yellowhead Highway. Robert had grown up there, so he knew almost everybody in town. His family still owned property there. Jones was not able to get there until four o'clock, but that was all right. Robert would use the extra time to visit his sister. "What are you doing here?" Rose was more than surprised to see him. "I'm meeting somebody here later."

"Who?"

"You ask too many questions."

"Have you found a new woman?" Rose looked at him.

Robert just looked back at her. "Can I borrow your telephone for a minute?"

"Why? You have your own telephone in your hand." "I know that. It's a long story.

"I only need it for a minute—just a quick call. I promise to keep it short."

After dialling, he said, "Hey, Jones, this is Robert. Can you come over to Rose's Diner instead of Kim's? OK, see you there."

"Thanks, Sis. Now you have two more guests for dinner. You should be glad I got you more business."

"Why should I? You never pay for yourself." "Never mind, you get great PR from me."

"Forget about PR. What I need is money in the cash register."

Jones was very late. There were things in the station that required his attention. But when they had spoken on the phone, Jones had warned Robert that such a thing might happen. He promised that he would get there as soon as he could.

"Hi. Sorry I'm so late. I just couldn't get away any sooner."

"That's OK."

"Rose's Diner. I've never come here before."

"It's my sister Rose who owns it, and it was her telephone that I used when I called you before."

Jones looked enquiringly at Robert. He told Jones about finding the two microphones in his office out at the ranch. Goggen had also found two microphones in the main house.

He also explained that he had left them alone and mentioned the reason he had done this. Jones agreed that to leave them in place was probably best.

Robert and Jones placed themselves at the end of the dining room. He had asked his sister that she, if it was possible, not put any guests too near them. He had explained that he needed to speak to this man unheard by anyone. She had asked, "Is that why you needed to use my telephone?" He told her yes, and she hadn't made any further comment. Rose knew what Robert worked with.

"There were several reasons why I needed to meet with you," Robert started to talk to Jones. "We've never met before, but now we have a common goal to work towards. Therefore, I thought I should come out to where you are and we should meet face-to-face. I've always felt strongly that that is the best way to communicate. What do you think? "Yes, I feel the same way."

"OK, so here I am. As you can see I am a little hampered in my movements."

"I already knew that. I read up on you a little after my first meeting with Joan and Goggen."

"Then you must also know how I got to be this way?"

"Yes, I do. A long and tedious story that still hasn't been resolved." "And that's exactly why I requested this meeting. There is something very twisted going on here. I don't know what yet, but this time I'm going to put all the pieces together and find out," Robert said. "I am also surprised that this has something to do with the dead school principal, Mister Svensson, the one Joan and Goggen found," he continued.

Jones just sat and listened. Robert told him the whole story involving

Nils Henrik Ellefsrud, including the building collapse, the cabin fire, TJ's school experiences, TJ's stabbing of the nurse Mary and Doctor Irvine Jr., her pregnancy, the shooting where both Robert and Joan had been wounded, and now the dead principal, the principal who had been in charge of the school when TJ was there.

Jones himself had heard almost all of this story already from Joan, but he listened intently to the whole thing.

When Robert was finished, he asked, "What do you think, shall we order some food? I'm hungry."

"Sorry, I guess I was getting carried away with my story."

They had a long conversation together during the meal which consisted of everything but police work. It wasn't until Rose came with the coffee that Jones returned to the subject of the case.

While they were eating, he had used small talk to draw Robert out and get to know his character. It was a technique that he often used. Robert was fully aware of this technique.

"As I said before to Stanley and Goggen, I also see the possibility of a connection here. There are too many coincidences that point in that direction. But I still can't say definitely. We won't know for absolute sure until the case is solved. The dead principal is a current matter. The rest of the case is more than thirty years old," Jones said.

"Yes, but it is unsolved," Robert answered. He continued, "Then suddenly a witness dies. Maybe he took his own life immediately after some private investigators started asking about the case again. There is something that makes me a little uneasy about that. I have been informed by Goggen that you and your superiors suspect that someone is leaking information from your station. That is another reason for me to say that I think there is a connection."

"That's correct, we suspect that," Jones answered.

"You have also grasped why we believe that," Robert said. "Yes. Stanley told me," Jones answered.

Robert said, "Stanley also told me that you were interested in working together with us towards the possibility of solving this case. I am very thankful for that."

"What do you think of Goggen? He has a very strong reputation in his homeland."

"I've only met him a few times, so it's difficult for me to form a judgement, but I have noticed that he is extremely alert and he notices things that nobody else does," Jones answered.

"You're right. I've noticed that too. It was my good friend and partner Nils Henrik Ellefsrud who wanted him on the case."

Then Robert told Jones the rest of the story of Nils Henrik Ellefsrud. Sergeant Jones sat still again and listened carefully to what Robert had to say. When he was finished, Jones said, "If I understand this right, then you are saying that the whole investigation of the happenings over thirty years ago was handled incompetently. "What do you base that on?" Jones asked.

"I have nothing concrete to base that on. If I did, things would have been so much easier. What I question is why the Edmonton police stepped in every time the investigation started to connect with the rest of the cases. What was the reason? Did it have anything to do with the fact that the cases involved First Nations people, who were very poorly treated in our country back at that time? Or did it have something to do with Nils Henrik marrying one of them? A white person who married an Indian was often shunned back then. There are so many unanswered questions.

"It was only when Joan and I got involved in the case that it got publicity, but even then, it was never resolved."

Jones said, "It's correct what you say about the Indians and people who got involved with them. There's been many tragic examples of that. Luckily, it's gotten much better today, but there is still a long way to go."

Robert studied Jones again. "We, first Stanley and Goggen, and now me, have given you a lot of information and theories concerning these earlier cases. You will need more time to think this through, but there's one thing that I ask of you: keep it to yourself. It could be quite dangerous for you if you don't. Obviously, you can discuss the case with your chief, as I understand you both feel the same about the school principal case. But I have a suggestion for you. How about if you make a trip down to Drayton Valley, where you will be able to look at all the materials concerning these cases? Then you can really familiarize yourself with all the information we are in possession of.

I'm sure that would help you a lot." "Sounds like a good idea," Jones answered. "Anytime it suits you."

"How about Friday night?" Jones answered.

"Perfect. We'll get a room ready for you. Let me know if there are any changes. Call me on this number: 515-221-5820. That's a secure telephone that I have established."

Robert shook Jones's hand and thanked him.

Goggen and Stanley were in the process of investigating the green station wagon that they had just found on Jim McCoy's property. Goggen opened the glove compartment and took out all the contents. He studied them carefully.

"The car was registered to Jerry Smith, address Gamozzi Road, Revelstoke," Goggen read out loud.

"The insurance company: Allstate."

He kept sorting the contents of the glove compartment, old receipts from fast-food restaurants, gas station receipts, etc., all the way back to 21 June 1965. There were some empty cigarette packets and lighters. Goggen opened the ashtray. It was full of cigarette butts. The floor had been used as a garbage can; it was filled with empty coffee cups and soda and beer cans.

"Here we might be able to find a DNA profile or two," he said. "Whoever left the car here didn't think it would ever be discovered. We need to find some professionals to go over this evidence more thoroughly."

Stanley nodded his agreement.

"Let's take some photographs while we're here." He went to his car to get the camera.

An hour and a half later they were back in their car, driving on the highway.

Thursday, 18 October

Robert, Stanley, Goggen, and TJ sat at the kitchen table. The men had just had breakfast and were lingering over their coffee. TJ had made herself a cup of tea. Goggen had made a quick check with the bug detector, so he knew that the room was free from microphones.

Robert spoke as he looked at each one of them, one after the other. "What have we found out in the last few days? TJ, what did you come up with in Vancouver?"

"Well, first I would like to say hello to you from McDonald. He said that he hopes you two would meet again soon. Without his help I think I would still be out there. Yes, I found what I'd travelled out to Vancouver for. The full licence plate number is—"

"Wait!" said Goggen. "Could it be YYZ 449?" Goggen smiled a little. TJ's eyes widened as she looked with surprise at Goggen. "How did you know that?"

"We found the car at an address out on Abraham Lake yesterday. It was hidden in a garage where it has stood for a very long time. On the way back, we stopped and spoke to some people who lived in the two houses along the same road. We asked if there had been any activity there anytime lately, and they both said that they had never seen anybody drive by in years. We were the first ones in years. We also asked if there had been a lot of activity there earlier, like thirty years ago or more. The ones who lived in one of the houses said that there were a lot of things going on back around then." Goggen continued, saying, "The registration said that the car was registered to one Jerry Smith."

"That's right," said TJ, "but according to the report, the car was stolen in June of 1963. That was when the owner reported the car stolen. "His address at the time was Gamozzi Road out in Revelstoke, BC. I have not had a chance to check whether he still lives at that address. I was hoping to find that out today.

"Revelstoke, BC, is only 155 miles from the border of Alberta," TJ said.

"Find out whatever you can about Jerry Smith," said Robert to TJ. "Goggen and Stanley, what did you find in the car?"

Goggen answered, "Well, besides the automobile registration, we found out that the car was insured by Allstate." "TJ, check on Jerry Smith with them too." "What else did you find?"

"There were some old receipts for gasoline, McDonalds and Burger King, nothing newer than twenty-five years ago. We also found some cigarette butts, empty drink cups, beer cans, and soda cans."

"That sounds like a good possibility to get some DNA profiles and fingerprints."

Robert said, "That sounds good. Maybe that will give us some answers as to whether that car was involved in this or not. Remember, I also am in possession of some material from the cabin that can give us a DNA profile."

He looked quickly over at TJ. She was sitting there with that hard, scary gaze that she got sometimes.

Robert continued, "We have to get some forensics technicians out to the car as soon as possible.

"As you know, I had a meeting with Sergeant Jones last night. I told him Nils Henrik's whole history. He's going to come over here tomorrow night and go through all the materials we have pertaining to this case. He was not totally convinced that the dead principal is connected to this case, but nevertheless he still wants to examine everything. I am totally convinced that by Sunday morning he will come to the same conclusion as we have, that there is a connection." Goggen asked, "Until Jones gets here, maybe we can take the time to find out what we can about Scott McKenzy and Jim McCoy."

"That is also on my agenda for today," TJ answered.

"Great. It looks like you have everything under control. Is there anything else we need to discuss this morning?" Robert looked at everyone. Nobody spoke up.

Friday, 19 October

Sergeant Jones drove up to the ranch right on time. He parked his car next to the others and got out. The passenger door opened too, and out came Jones's superior officer, Captain Nielsen. Jones had not informed Robert that Nielsen would be coming along. When Jones had told Erik where he was going and for what reason, the latter had insisted on going along with him. All police officers are required to let their station know all their movements, where they are going and what they are doing at all times when they are not on watch. This especially applied if a police officer was going out of his or her own police district.

Now they were approaching the main house at the ranch. "Jones, Jones, I'm over here!" It was Robert who called from the doorway of his house.

Jones and Erik turned quickly and walked over to Robert.

Jones put out his hand to greet Robert, who was looking at Erik. "This is Captain Erik Nielsen, our station leader out in Edson. He insisted on coming along, but he'll go back home tonight." Robert greeted him, saying, "Robert Blake."

"Don't you recognize me? Or maybe I should ask if you recognize my name."

Robert thought for a moment. "No, I'm sorry, but I don't," he said carefully.

"I was the first on the scene when you and the woman were shot in the car."

"Now I remember the name," Robert answered.

"I arrived together with my partner. We were out on patrol. I had only been on the police force for about eleven months at that time. I was still a rookie.

"When Jones here mentioned your name, I wanted to come with him and see you again.

Jones and I have worked together for many years. We were also partners for some time before I took my law degree. Jones told me about the meeting you had and about your theories. We are not able to see that there is a connection between Svensson's death and these other cases. Therefore, I am giving Jones all the time he needs here with you.

"Would you allow me to look again into the shooting of you and—" "Joan Arnold," said Robert. "That would make me very happy." "Well, maybe we can solve the case this time, but I don't want to take up any more of your time. I'm leaving. Jones, please keep me informed."

He shook hands with Robert again, thanked him, and left.

"I didn't know anything about that," Jones said, looking at Robert.

They both looked equally surprised.

"I believe that," said Robert. "The positive part is that he knows the case from earlier."

Jones agreed.

"Come on in and make yourself at home. Are you hungry? Lori made some pasta for tonight. Tomorrow night everybody involved is coming over for dinner. I'm pretty sure that you're going to be here until at least Sunday. I'm also waiting for Goggen and Stanley to get back tonight, but I don't know what time. It might be late. But they'll be here tomorrow." "Yes, thank you, I'll take some pasta."

"Want a beer with it?" "Yes, why not?

"I have to ask you to go and get it from the kitchen yourself. We don't have any left here in the bar fridge."

"No problem. What about you?"

Yes, I'll have one too. Actually, why don't you just get a six-pack from the kitchen and we'll put it out here in the bar fridge."

"Since we probably are going to work together, I'd like to know your first name. Your last name seems a little formal."

"Sorry, I meant to tell you earlier. It's Patrick Thomas. I really only use the first name."

"OK. I have set aside a room for you over in the main house. There's a note on the door with your name in case nobody is there to show you where it is. But there should be people there. TJ's daughter and her bodyguard should have arrived, but they might have gone out somewhere. Here's a key.

"All of the material is over there. Make yourself at home and go through those items at your leisure. There's club soda, beer, and wine if you want any. You'll probably have to make your own coffee.

"So, we'll meet again at breakfast. Don't forget that there are two microphones placed in the living room—in case you need to use the telephone."

Saturday, 20 October

The next morning everybody was arranged around Robert and Lori's breakfast table. Robert said, "TJ, you're the only person who hasn't met Sergeant Patrick Jones from the Edson Police District. He's here to discuss the cases we are now investigating. Patrick has been quite well informed already, and he knows that you, TJ, are a very central person in this."

Robert asked Patrick, "Did you look at any of the material last night?"

"I just read some of the newspaper clippings and looked at some of the photographs that were there. I think it would be best to have somebody with me when I begin on the maps, right from the beginning."

Robert asked Goggen, "Can you assist Patrick?"

Goggen nodded yes.

Robert continued, "We have been very wary of what might happen when we continued with this investigation again. Therefore, we all wished to hold as low a profile as possible. We learned the hard way that this was not going to be possible. I refer to the school principal whom Joan and Goggen found dead. After that we had a meeting where we discussed whether or not we would continue. That was when TJ exhibited the strength that she inherited from her father and mother. Now she is ready to take on those who stand behind these crimes, or as she said in her own words, 'Let's take those sons of bitches.'

"You all know why Patrick is here this weekend. I want all of you to help him as much as you possibly can."

He looked around. Nobody had any comments about what he had just said. Robert got back to the current status of the case.

"TJ, do we have anything more to go after? What more have you found out about Scott McKenzy and Jim McCoy?"

"So far nothing more." "What about Jerry Smith?"

"Same, nothing yet, but possibly I have found a lead. I'm checking it out now."

"OK."

"Patrick, after you examine the material, you will see that there was a car involved, a green station wagon. We actually found that car two days ago. It was registered to a Jerry Smith. Mister Smith reported the car stolen on July 21, 1965. We are now trying to locate Jerry Smith. The address on the registration was over in the Revelstoke area. "The car was found at an address up on Abraham Lake. A man named Jim McCoy had previously used the property. According to Goggen and Stanley, the place didn't look like it had been used for a very long time.

"These are the leads and clues that we are working on right now." Robert looked at Patrick.

"In connection with that, we have to have some forensic workers to go through the car. Goggen says that we can find both DNA and fingerprints there. We need to get those as soon as possible. I know

that it's a little way out of your district"—he looked at Jones—"so I have spoken with some friends of mine, two retired forensic scientists from Calgary. They are coming here today to talk to us. Any objections?"

Patrick replied, "Not off the top of my head. It's like you say, a little way out of my district. But I want to know whatever you find out. Do you have any DNA profiles to compare these ones with?"

"We have them from the cabin fire. When the Edmonton police told us to have the files from the case sent over to them, I copied them all. Then I did one other thing: I took a little bit of the collected samples before sending it all off. All of that is in a safe place. What was found after the collapse I have no idea. I'll send Stanley and Goggen down to the Edmonton police to go through the materials they have regarding it.

"But that can wait. Right now, the priority is to get a hold of the evidence in the car and get it tested as soon as possible."

Goggen walked with Patrick Jones over to the main house. They sat and talked together for a while. Patrick wanted to hear more about Norway. His parents on his mother's side were from Norway. He wasn't completely sure, but he thought they were from Kristiansand, or maybe it was Kristiansund. He would have to look at some old papers of theirs he had saved to be sure. He knew he had them someplace, but that was another story.

Patrick looked at the piles of files on the table. "Do you want to start? It looks like it's going to be a long day."

"Yes, we might as well begin. We have organized it so that each of the piles represents a case, and they are placed in order of when the crimes happened. We have also written a short list of the cases for convenience's sake."

"Let me see that."

Patrick and Goggen went through one file after another. It went faster than they thought it would. Goggen was familiar with the material from before, and he also knew what was in each of the different files. When they laid the last file down on the table, it was 5.33. Goggen looked at the clock.

Patrick looked at him for a moment before he said, "I better see the connection you mentioned now. I also feel absolute sympathy for what Nils Henrik and especially TJ went through. It sure wasn't easy to be them. For TJ to have to go through all of this again now must be very tough."

"We have tried to let her come into this carefully and get focused on the work, but I have noticed that her eyes and her face really change and become very grim under certain circumstances.

"What do you say we have a drink?"

Goggen had gotten up and gone over to the bar.

"OK, maybe I will. Do you have any Canadian Club?"

Goggen started to look at the different bottles in the bar cabinet.

"I don't see any CC, but I have Seagram's 7." "That's fine. Can I have some with ice?"

He took a Cutty Sark for himself, also with ice. That was his favourite Scotch.

They went and sat down out in the living room. They had to be careful what they talked about.

The telephone rang. It was Robert. "Can you two come over?" "Yes. We'll be there in fifteen minutes," Goggen answered.

Patrick looked at him with a question in his eyes.

"Better drink up," he said. "I don't like to drink too fast."

"Hi, come in." Robert waved them into the salon immediately when they came through the door. TJ was there together with two unknown people, sitting in the salon already.

"Here are the two forensic technicians I told you about this morning. They just drove up right now. This is Bob Pratt, and this is Steve Olsen." Patrick and Goggen introduced themselves.

"Bob and Steve are going out to Abraham Lake tomorrow. Can you take them out there?" Robert looked at Goggen when asking. "Stanley is busy in Edmonton."

"Of course. Just let me know what time you want to leave." Steve looked at Bob and then said, "How about eight o'clock?" "OK for me," Goggen answered.

Patrick asked, "Can I come with you?"

"OK," said Goggen. "Is there anybody else who wants to go?"

"Yes, I do." This time it was TJ who answered. "I want to take a look at that car. Maybe I'll remember something when I see it."

Robert stole a quick glance at Goggen. He said to TJ, "All right then, you go too."

Robert asked his two new guests, "Can we provide you with a room here? Or do you prefer to book in at a hotel? We have plenty of space and we're all having dinner together here tonight, so you're more than welcome to eat with us. There is plenty of food for everybody, I think. Right, Lori?" He called to her in the kitchen.

"No problem," she answered. Steve and Bob looked at each other and said they would be glad to.

"Then that's what we'll do. Goggen, will you take Bob over to the main house and show him where the microphones are? He just got rid of the ones in here. Now whoever placed them will be aware that we know about them. In the meantime, it's just about happy hour." He smiled at them.

Sunday, 21 October

The evening didn't go exactly as they had thought; therefore it was 9.20 before the two cars finally drove out from the front yard the next morning. Now, two and a half hours later, they took the turn off David Thompson Highway and onto the 2.8-mile-long road up to Jim

McCoy's place. On the way they passed a black bear with two cubs. The cubs had grown up to be pretty big now.

That was a new experience for Goggen. The only real live bears he had ever seen were at the zoo. Here was a mother with two babies right in the middle of the road. The mother bear didn't try to urge them to run away; she just turned to the car and gave the men a threatening look that seemed to say, *Just try to catch us!* Then after a few minutes the trio disappeared into the woods.

"Are there many bears out here?" asked Goggen.

"Yes," said Patrick, "but only black bears. You have to go farther up north and out closer to the coast to find the grizzlies. The ones you just saw were pretty big black bears."

"What does a person do if he meets one of them out in the forest?" "If you make a lot of noise when you're out there, you'll never see them. But if the bear has any cubs with her, you should be very careful."

Goggen sat and thought about the bears he had just seen. Then suddenly he was ripped away from these thoughts. It was right before they turned into the space in front of Jim McCoy's place. His gaze went immediately to the garage. The doors were open. When they were here last, they made sure to close them before they'd left. "Someone has been here," he said.

Everyone in the car went silent. Patrick signalled to Steve and Bob to sit still.

"Do you have a weapon?" Patrick asked Goggen.

"There's a pistol in the glove compartment," Goggen answered. Patrick opened the glove compartment and took out the pistol. He checked to see if it was loaded. Everyone was sitting quietly while their eyes roamed around the property.

"TJ, you stay here. Goggen, I'll cover you. Start going up to the house."

Goggen got out of the car and ran the fifty feet up to the house. Nothing.

Patrick followed after him. Still nothing.

Goggen opened the door to the house very carefully while keeping himself behind the wall. Patrick raised the pistol and ran in. One minute, two minutes … "All clear," Patrick called. He came out.

He pointed to what most likely had been a barn before. Goggen got himself ready to run again. The distance was about seventy-five feet. Goggen ran to the woodpile first.

Patrick followed once Goggen was there. Goggen looked at what was left of the door. He kicked as hard as he could while Patrick ran in with the pistol raised.

"All clear here too," Patrick said.

He came back out again and signalled the others that they could come out of the car. Goggen was already on his way over to the garage.

There was a strong smell of bleach.

"Somebody has been cleaning up in here," said Patrick.

He opened the car door and looked in the ashtray. Empty. And there was nothing under the seat. The car had been thoroughly washed.

Anything that could possibly yield up a DNA profile was gone. Steve and Bob had come over to the garage too now.

"Looks like there was a massive clean-up here," said Bob.

"It sure looks like it, and they did a good job at it. It's going to be difficult to find any usable material here." Steve was looking around as he said this. "But we'll do a thorough going-over of the car anyway and see what we find."

Goggen went over to what was left of the barn. Five minutes later he came back with a black plastic bag that he handed to Steve.

"I had a feeling that this could happen," he said.

Steve and Bob looked questioningly at him before they looked into the bag. In it were empty drink cups, soda and beer cans, cigarette butts, and fast-food receipts.

"Luckily I had a plastic bag available last time we were here. We stopped at the liquor store and bought a bottle of Cutty Sark when we came this way. I got the plastic bag with the bottle."

Steve and Bob smiled. Patrick shook his head and smiled too. Goggen said, "I also have some pictures of where these items were found and a list of all of them."

Bob went over to their car and put the bag in the trunk before they began to work on the station wagon.

"Even if all the trash were gone and the car had been carefully washed, there would still be a very good possibility to find clues. There is always some tiny little place that they forget to clean," Bob said.

Patrick and Goggen went through the house and the falling-down barn again.

TJ was following what Steve and Bob were doing. She was very impressed.

She had no memory at all of the car from earlier.

"Here's some blood," said Steve to Bob. "Yes, I see that."

"Here too." Steve pointed under the back seat.

"Cut out a piece of the carpet in both of those places." Bob didn't answer. He got some numbers and placed them on the carpet where the blood was found, and then he got the camera and took a picture of those areas. Then he clipped out the pieces of carpet and put them in their numbered bags.

Steve was holding up a strong light to see whether there was any more blood. That was a negative.

They had now gone through the car's interior thoroughly.

Steve opened the hood of the car. He hoped that whomever had stolen the car had left some fingerprints there. The ones who washed the car might have forgotten to wash there.

He checked with his light again, concentrating on the parts where they would have most likely touched.

"Take a look at this. Here we have some fine examples."

TJ hurried over to see what he was talking about. There it was right in front of her, three fine examples of perfect fingerprints. They were right on top of the air filter.

Steve marked the spot and shined the light further around the engine compartment.

"OK, here's another pair. These are on the fuses, and one of them is a thumbprint." He marked the area again. He continued for about fifteen minutes more.

"It looks like that's all. Bob, do you have the camera?"

Bob gave the camera to Steve, and Steve took some more pictures.

Then he took impressions of all the fingerprints and put each of them in their separate envelopes.

The last thing the men did was take a picture of two broken lights on the front of the car. One was a parking light and one was a turn signal. They had gone through the car thoroughly, and now the time was almost 6.30. Bob said, "I believe that we have everything that is possible to find on this car. Do we want to begin on the house or the falling-down thing over there?"

"No, it's getting late. We can do that later, if necessary. Hopefully what we have already gotten will give us all the answers we need." "How soon can we expect to get any results?" Goggen asked. "Give us three days," Bob answered.

"OK, then the next thing we need to do is get the other materials to you, the ones that Robert has in a safe place. Then we will make the decision whether or not we need to come back here and gather more evidence."

Steve and Bob said their farewells to the others. They had a four- or five-hour drive back. If all were to go well, they would be back in Calgary around midnight.

Tuesday, 23 October

The telephone rang in Robert's office. He looked at his watch: 9.05 p.m.

Robert had been sitting dozing in front of the TV. "Robert Blake," he answered. He had his phone right next to him. "Hi, this is Steve."

Steve? He thought for a second. He must have been sleeping a deeper than he'd thought. "Oh yes, Steve. How is it going?"

"We have now finished the DNA and fingerprint profiles. We have to sort them through the database we have here. There is a secure source in the Calgary Police Department who is helping us with that. What we now need to do is to compare it with the material that you have." "Of course. I discussed that with Goggen just this afternoon. He says that we have to get it down to you as soon as possible."

"Yes, that's right. You need to get it down here."

"All right, I'll arrange it tomorrow. I'll call you as soon as it's ready to go."

The conversation was over.

Robert called Goggen. "Hi, can you get over here? I just got done talking with Steve."

"I'll be right there."

Goggen looked at Robert, who had moved himself back to his office again. "OK, what did Steve say?" Goggen asked.

"That they were finished compiling all the analyses. Now they need the materials that I have in store in order to make a comparison. I said that you and TJ are on your way to Jasper again tomorrow, but I said that I will get the materials to them tomorrow anyway. I think we'll change the plans that you and TJ have. I want you two to drive out of here just as though you were going to Jasper as planned. When you're sure that nobody is following you, then drive to the place where I have secured the materials. I'll give you the directions while you're on the road. Then you drive to Calgary. A couple of hours later Stanley will drive out from here. He'll take the direct route down to Calgary. He'll also have some materials with him, but those will just be copies. I'll find somebody else to go along with him."

Goggen listened to Robert's plan.

"Do you agree? We are being watched in one way or another. I can't put my finger on it yet, but because of that we have to be extremely careful. You noticed it yourself how they managed to find out that you and Stanley had located the car. I hope that this decoy tactic will work. I want it to be kept only between the two of us." Robert looked closely at Goggen, whose expression told him that he agreed and would be careful. Robert said, "I have to call Stanley now. What time do you and TJ plan to leave?"

"She has a dentist appointment at eight o'clock, so we had planned to leave around ten."

"Good, that helps us. Drive her to the dentist, then head towards

Jasper. How long do you think you'll be out there?"

"We plan to be back by Sunday, but it might be Monday. We thought we might stop by Revelstoke, BC, and check up on Jerry Smith, the one whom the car was registered to."

"OK, that sounds good. After the dentist, do as planned, head towards to Jasper. Then you keep on driving until you feel completely free of any followers. When you are 100 per cent sure, turn around and call me. I will then tell you where to go to get the material I have."

Back at the house Goggen knocked on TJ's bedroom door. "Yes?" she said.

"It's me."

"Just a minute."

He heard her moving around the room a little before she opened the door. Goggen gave her the short version of what Robert had told him. "I'll eat breakfast with him and be ready to pick you up at 7.40. Is that enough time for us to get to the dentist?"

"Yes, he is only about a mile away." "OK."

"Now I'm going to try to get some sleep. Good night."

He closed the door and went back downstairs. He sat and thought for a long time about what Robert had said. Someone had managed to warn the ones who had cleaned the car before they'd gotten out there again. He thought that he would probably think even better with a Cutty Sark in his hand.

TJ was finished at the dentist after only twenty-five minutes. "That was fast."

"Yes, it was only a loose filling that needed a minor adjustment. Next time I'll only need a cleaning."

"All right then, let's drive to Jasper."

TJ looked at him. Goggen just smiled and began to explain the plan to her. They would drive towards Jasper. If they were followed, they would just keep on driving. But if they were absolutely sure that they were alone, they would meet Kim in Carrot Creek. There they would switch cars with her. From there they would drive down to the Wabamun reservation and to the bank there. "It was your father,

Nils Henrik, who wanted to have the material placed there. Within the reservation it would be as safe as almost anywhere on earth. Even the police have to get special permission to open a safe deposit box on an Indian reservation. They had their own separate laws that were in effect there, and the Canadian government couldn't come in even with a search warrant. They would have to go through several other channels before they would be allowed to do so."

They passed through Nojack around 10 a.m. So far it appeared that they were alone. "It looks like nobody is following us," said TJ, after looking in the mirror again.

"Yes, it does look that way, but let's make sure."

TJ looked at Goggen.

"Do you see that gas station just ahead? Let's stop there." Goggen pointed to a Chevron sign.

"OK." TJ put on her turn signal and turned off the highway.

"Now you go inside while I pump some gas." Goggen nodded towards the building.

TJ looked at Goggen and asked, "And what then?"

"Then we'll take a peek at whatever cars come behind us and see if any of them are interested."

Goggen walked around the car and took off the gas cap before he picked up the pump nozzle. He watched the road carefully. A few cars drove by, but nobody in them looked over at the car parked in the gas station.

He was finished pumping the gas and was on his way in to pay when the car came, a silver-grey Dodge. Goggen noticed that both of the people sitting in the car were very interested in what was going on in the gas station. They slowed down the car as they went by.

That's them, he thought to himself, and continued on into the station. They continued to drive towards Jasper, with Goggen in the driver's seat this time. They had not driven very far when they saw the car again. It was parked at a rest area by the side of a lake that was located at Wildwood Junction. It didn't look like anyone was there. "Now I'm going to stop and look for a place to pee. Meanwhile,

you write down the car make, model, and licence plate number. Be discreet; they're looking at us."

He took out the pistol from the glove compartment and put it under his jacket. If they were really paying attention, they would notice that his jacket was bulged out on one side. He hoped that they would notice that he was armed.

He came back after a few minutes. "Did you get it?" "Yes."

"Text Robert and inform him that we won't be stopping in Carrot Creek. Send a copy to Kim and tell her to follow up with Edson. We'll contact her later."

Goggen was watching in his rear-view mirror again. "Here comes the car.

"Now please call Sergeant Jones for me and put it on speaker."

TJ did what Goggen asked. He could hear the telephone on the other end ringing.

"Jones here."

"Hi, this is Goggen."

"Hi, what can I do for you?"

"We have a car that is following us. It's a silver-grey Dodge, plate number LLK 035. We need to get away from it. Can you help us? We are near Edson and will be passing through there in about fifteen minutes. Can you get a patrol car to stop me for speeding?"

He continued, "When I see the patrol car, I'll speed up. Then the patrol car can stop me. Hopefully those who are following us will continue on after they see us get stopped. I need to get rid of them. I'll explain later."

"I'll try. What kind of car are you driving?"

"It's me and TJ, and we are driving in her car, a red BMW. At the same time, can you check out the other car?"

"I remember TJ's car. Got that. I'll check out the Dodge. We'll talk later."

Goggen drove on with a speed of ten to fifteen miles per hour over the limit. That was normal out here. He knew that the ones following him wouldn't be alarmed by it.

Then he saw the patrol car. He raised his speed to 130 miles per hour, about 40 miles per hour over the speed limit. The patrol car swung in behind him. No blue lights yet. Goggen stomped a little heavier on the gas. There came the flashers. Goggen saw them in his mirror, but he continued on as though nothing was happening, until the patrol car came even with him and the cop pointed to the side of the road. This was an unmistakable message to stop. Goggen therefore immediately slowed down and pulled over. The patrol car pulled up behind him.

The police officer walked up to TJ's car and ordered Goggen and TJ out.

The Dodge went past. The people in it showed a strong interest in TJ and Goggen. The policeman escorted them over to the patrol car and told them to get into the back seat. He sat himself behind the wheel and drove out in the direction of Edson. "Where are we going?" he asked.

"We don't know yet," said Goggen. "Can you find us a place where we can meet with a colleague?"

The policeman thought for a moment before answering. "There's a little place right down here called Beaver Creek. We can stop there." "Sounds good. TJ, send a message to Kim."

Kim arrived in Beaver Creek about ten minutes after they did. They had been sitting in the car and talking together. The weather outside was not at its best; it was raining.

Kim signalled the policeman quickly. He drove right out behind her. Goggen told Kim what had happened. Goggen and TJ were sitting in Kim's car now, and she was following the police car. They were on the way back to TJ's car. The plan was that Kim would take TJ's car back to Edmonton. Goggen and TJ would continue on to the bank in the Wabamun reservation in Kim's car. After that they would go to Calgary to deliver the materials they would get from the bank to Steve and Bob.

Goggen had gotten the key to the safe deposit box from Robert during breakfast that morning, along with a list of what they should take out this time.

That part was easy. Everything was organized inside the box, numbered and lettered.

This time they didn't have to worry about somebody following them. It wasn't happening.

Goggen and TJ didn't get down to Calgary until almost midnight.

They had communicated with Steve so that he was informed about the time and place of their arrival. He had therefore arranged for two rooms next to each other at the Holiday Inn Downtown. They agreed to meet there.

Steve and Bob were both sitting in the lobby when Goggen and TJ arrived. The two men stood up when Goggen and TJ came in. Goggen went over to the reception desk and checked them in. Then everybody went up to Goggen's room.

"So, you had a few problems this morning," Steve said. "Yes, we did, but it was pretty much expected."

"We are a little worried about Stanley. We haven't heard a single peep from him since this afternoon. It was just before 4 p.m. when he called and said he had a flat tyre. They had stopped for something to eat, and when they came out again he noticed that one of the tyres was flat.

"He wanted to find a service station to patch it up before they continued on. He thought it was too far to drive on a spare tyre. I understand that he had a former colleague with him."

"Want a beer?" Goggen had stuck his head into the minibar fridge

and was holding up a cold one.

"No thanks. It's late and we were hoping to start on the materials as early as possible in the morning. But thanks anyway."

"TJ? What about you?"

"Is there any wine in there?" "Yes, red wine."

"I'll take it."

Steve asked, "Are you two leaving in the morning?"

"Yes, we're headed up to Revelstoke. We're going to try to locate Jerry Smith. He's the one the green Oldsmobile station wagon was registered to."

"Good luck. We have to leave. You'll be hearing from us in a few days."

TJ and Goggen were still sitting together in his room, TJ with her glass of red wine and Goggen with a beer. The conversation turned to Stanley. Goggen had an uneasy feeling.

TJ suddenly realized that she was sitting and staring at Goggen. He was a nice-looking man. She forced herself to think about something else. So, she said goodnight and went to her own room, which was right next to Goggen's.

She lay there and thought about him and couldn't sleep. She hadn't had many positive experiences with men, but there had been times when she wished she had someone to be with. Her body began to become warm thinking about it, so she put on the TV in order to concentrate on something else.

Wednesday, 24 October

Goggen awoke suddenly. The telephone was ringing.

"Yes?" He looked at the clock: 6.15.

"They have found Stanley's car. They found it up at Red Deer River, Innisfail, at Gleniffer Lake. It was completely burned out."

It was Steve who was calling.

"As of yet there's no sign of Stanley or his friend. The car was found by a pair of young lovers who had driven out there late last night. The area is known as a popular place for young couples to go.

"The police are out there now, but I also want to take a look. Do you want to come with me?"

"Yes, of course. How and when shall we meet?"

"As soon as possible. I can be at your hotel in forty minutes." "OK. I'll wait for you here."

Goggen called TJ.

"Hi. They found Stanley's car. Steve's coming to pick me up. Do you want to come along?"

"Yes, I do."

"OK, then. Meet me as quickly as you can. I'm going down to get a cup of coffee while I wait."

It wasn't long before TJ came in through the door of the dining room.

She had her purse with her.

Goggen said, "Everything is in order. I have already spoken with the front desk and told them that we will keep the rooms for one more night. You better plan on it being a long day." He told her everything that Steve had said. "I think we can leave the car here. Then we'll continue on up to Revelstoke tomorrow."

"That's fine with me."

Goggen thought that he could hear a little uneasiness in her voice. *Can she handle seeing that burned-out car?* he asked himself. Well, he was just going to have to watch over her carefully. She had done very well so far.

The police had already set up a blockade around the area. Goggen counted six policemen so far. Steve introduced himself and asked to speak to the supervisor. The policeman picked up the radio microphone that was hanging on his chest.

"Chief, can you come here? There is somebody that wants to talk to you."

"I'll be right there." They could hear through the radio.

Ten minutes later a very young dark-haired woman came over to them.

"Captain Ross, Juliette," she said. "What can I do for you?" Steve introduced himself again, and this time he also introduced Goggen and TJ.

"Can we go somewhere where we can talk in private?" Steve asked. Captain Ross pointed to a table and bench several metres away. They walked over to them but remained standing.

Steve asked, "Do you have anything more on Stanley Daly?" "No, the only thing we know is that the car is registered to him.

We don't know if he has been here. The technicians are doing their investigations right now. We have also started to search in and around the lake." They stood silently listening to what Captain Ross said. "As you know, I run a private investigations bureau where we also do technical investigations."

"Yes, you said that," said Captain Ross.

"This is how it is. Stanley Daly was on the way from Edmonton to me with evidence connected to an old murder case. He had a friend with him, an earlier colleague, and the last time I heard from them was yesterday afternoon at 3.50," Steve said.

Then he told Captain Ross a short version of the story. She just stood and listened, often looking at either TJ or Goggen.

When he was finished, she said, "Thank you for the information. That puts everything in a different light. Now we know that there could have been two people in the car. If they have been here, I can't say yet, but it gives us more to work with."

"Now I probably know the answer before I ask it, but I'll ask anyway. Can we be of any help to you?" Steve looked directly into Captain Ross's eyes when he asked this.

"No, we will manage on our own. But if it should be necessary, I'll contact you."

"Yes, I knew that. Is it all right if we look around a little outside of the area you have cordoned off?"

"I can't deny you that," she said. But if you find anything, you have to let us know right away. Otherwise, we will keep you updated." She walked back to the scene.

Steve, Goggen, and TJ watched everything the technicians did from a distance. It seemed to Steve and Goggen that they did their work very thoroughly. TJ didn't really have any experience in this field, so she didn't have an opinion on what they were doing. But still, Goggen was quite surprised about how detail-oriented she could be sometimes.

She could see things in nature that the most trained investigator would have overlooked.

Goggen and TJ found themselves way down in the woods, near the lake, and on the southwest side of the parking lot and cars. They were about half a mile from the car. This was also the northernmost point of Gleniffer Lake. From here the lake flared out again, with a long sand beach full of different kinds of birds, but mostly Canada geese. The beach turned here and went south. At the farthest point was a little spit of land. It was a beautiful area. TJ could name every different bird that they could see.

"This is a national park," she said. "There are a lot of them here in Canada." They had sat down, each on their own stone. The day before it had rained. Now the sun was shining, but it was cold. It wouldn't be long before winter set in.

Suddenly TJ said, "National park, research. I wonder if this is an area where they do research on birds. This would be a perfect place for that. There are enough bird species here."

Goggen looked at her. She had begun to look up into the trees. She looked carefully, back and forth. Then she pointed. "Do you see that box up there?" Goggen looked in the direction she pointed.

"Yes."

"That is a surveillance camera. It records the wildlife around the lake twenty-four hours per day. They use the recordings to keep track of the different birds and wildlife around a national park. Let's see how many cameras they have and where they are placed."

Goggen immediately followed what she was thinking.

"Let's go out on that spit of land there. The parking lot is on the other side."

Goggen followed after her without saying anything, but he took a paper and pen out of his pocket.

"Wait a minute," he said. "Let me make a sketch of the area." He began to look around, getting it all down on the paper. TJ watched him while he did that.

"OK, let's go. I'm done now."

They looked up into the trees, and TJ pointed again. There was another camouflaged box containing a camera. Goggen would have never seen it. He notated its location on his sketch with an arrow pointing in the direction in which the camera pointed.

They continued on. It was Goggen who found the next one. He had learned quickly what to look for. Again, he notated the location of the camera and the direction on his sketch.

They walked even further, right out to the end of the spit of land. There, one more camera. Goggen looked up at the camera and then over across the water to the parking area. There was a very good possibility that this camera had recorded whatever had happened on the other side. The camera lens was pointing in the direction of the parking area.

Goggen looked over and saw that the police were still examining the burned car and the area around it.

He again marked the spot where the camera was placed.

"Who would it be that placed these cameras?" asked Goggen.

"That would be the Provincial Office of Wildlife, the department that monitors animal life. There are the different provinces that supervise them. The provinces are run by the Canadian government, which has a department like that. They get a good part of the taxpayers' money for doing it."

"We have to get a hold of the recordings that were taken last night,"

Goggen said, without ever taking his eyes off the last camera. "We can do that. It's often Indians who are put in charge of these things. I'll find out who does the job out here. Shall we inform Captain Ross?"

"Let's talk to Steve first. But at some point, we have to inform her."

Steve was standing and talking with Captain Ross when TJ and Goggen came back to the parking area. She went back to the others as they walked up.

"Did she have anything new to tell us?" asked TJ. "No."

"But we do. The Canadian Department of Wildlife has cameras placed on the other side."

Steve looked at both of them. "Surveillance cameras, out here?" "Yes, and one of them is pointed right at this parking area." TJ had a small triumphant smile as she said that.

"What do you think? Do we inform Captain Ross about that?" Goggen asked.

"At one time or another we are required to do that, but let's get a copy of the disc recordings first before we do so."

"Can we find out who it is that is in charge of these cameras?"

"I'll do that," said TJ. She took out her cell phone and punched in a number. She spoke the Native American language into the phone and then hung up.

"The one in charge of this immediate area is Joe, who is a Blackfoot Indian. He goes by the name of Little Joe. His telephone number is"— she looked at the display on her phone—"516- – – – -2424."

"Call him," said Steve.

TJ punched the number on her display. They could hear it ring on the other end before the other party picked up the phone.

"Hi, is this Little Joe? This is TJ. Tehya Jane Ellefsrud." She was speaking her own language again. "That's right, you don't know me. I got your telephone number from the reservation office. I was told that you operate the cameras for the Department of Wildlife out on Gleniffer Lake. When will you be changing the discs in the cameras out there? Tomorrow? Would it be possible to get copies of the discs? Oh, you're not allowed to do that? What if I told you it would be a favour from one Blackfoot to another? Yes, I am a Blackfoot. I'll explain everything to you tomorrow. What do we need to bring in order to make copies? OK, we'll bring that along with us. We'll see you tomorrow at ten o'clock."

She hung up.

Goggen looked at her, speechless.

She said, "We'll meet him out here at ten o'clock tomorrow morning. We need to bring some DVD recording equipment."

"Is that all?"

"Yep." She smiled when she said that.

Goggen got his voice back. "We'll be here. Do you want to come too, Steve?"

"No, you two can take care of that alone. I want to continue on with Bob. There's a lot we need to go through at the lab. Unless you need me, then I'll be there."

"No, that's fine. We'll do it alone. It's better if you and Bob go on with the research."

They got in the car and drove back to Calgary.

CHAPTER 14

It was 10 a.m. Goggen and TJ walked around the burned-out car. The police must have finished with it the night before. There was no guard at the scene, and the police tape was gone. Goggen tried to open the trunk. It was stuck. Then he tried to open the hood. There was a click. He felt under the edge for the hood release, and after a little exploration he found it. As he was trying to get it loose, he heard a vehicle coming in to the parking lot. He let the hood stay down and turned around.

It was a red Land Rover, and it came in at a high speed. Goggen read the emblem on the door: Department of Wildlife, Alberta. He walked up to the SUV. TJ was there already.

The man in the Land Rover got out, and TJ approached him to shake hands. "Little Joe?" she asked.

"Yes."

"TJ here, and this is Ole G. Olsen from Norway."

Little Joe shook hands with him too.

TJ changed over to the Blackfoot language. "Like we talked about yesterday, I hoped we could get a copy of the DVD from the camera over there on the other side. We need to know what took place between noon on the twenty-third and noon the next day."

Little Joe replied in their same native language, "Did you bring the DVD recorder?"

"Yes, we have it. We also have an external hard drive. We are hoping to copy it directly over to that. It would be much easier that way." "We can try. I've never done it that way. I usually just use the DVD recorder."

TJ said, "How do we do it? Do we take the hard drive out with us, or do we wait until we come back here?"

Little Joe said, "We take it with us. We'll copy it directly from the camera. I can't copy it myself. What I do is copy onto these DVDs. Then I mark each of them and put them into an envelope. Then I reset the camera so it's ready to go again."

"OK, I'll go get the DVD recorder and the hard drive from the car."

Goggen had heard the whole conversation between these two without understanding one single word of it. TJ was nice enough to explain what they had said while they were walking over to the spit of land.

Three hours later TJ had copied all five of the camera's recordings of the times they wished to study. Now they were back at the parking area.

TJ reverted to the Blackfoot language: "First, I would like to thank you for your help. Here is a little extra for you." She held out her hand. Little Joe shook hands with her at the same time as he took what she had offered. He looked at it in amazement: $300. He looked up at her. "We appreciate it a lot. Don't spend it all in one place." She smiled at him when she said that.

"Now I have one more question," said TJ. "When will you be looking at these DVDs?"

"I can't say for sure. It is not me who looks at them, so when the others will look at them I don't know."

"That's OK."

"We're only using these copies to give the police tips about them. This is in connection with this burned-up car right here." She pointed to what was left of the car.

"We are investigators, private investigators, and we are fully licenced." She took out her wallet and handed him her ID card so he could read it. He did and gave it back to her.

"Please don't worry about what we have copied. We'll take care of the rest. I want to thank you one more time for the favour, and I hope that sometime in the future we can return it to you." She put out her hand one more time to shake, and this time it had a business card in it with Robert Blake Investigations' information on it. Little Joe looked at it briefly and then put it in his pocket. Goggen nodded to him, and then Little Joe got in his Land Rover and drove away.

Goggen went back to the car hood, and this time he opened it.

Even though the car was badly burned on the outside, the engine compartment and what was in it was still in relatively good condition.

He found several places where there were clear fingerprints. He pointed to two very clear ones. TJ looked at them with interest. "There might not be anything important about them," said Goggen. "Most likely they are just Stanley's fingerprints." He continued to inspect the engine compartment while putting on a pair of latex gloves.

He stuck his fingers up under the firewall just below the windshield.

He pulled out a big brown envelope.

"Look at that." Even though TJ was standing right next to him, he spoke mostly to himself.

He opened the envelope. It was the material that Stanley believed was the evidence he was taking to Calgary.

"Why do you think he put that up there?" asked TJ.

"I don't know for sure, but he probably thought he might get stopped, so he hid it."

Goggen put the contents back into the envelope.

"What do we know about the person who was with Stanley? Does Robert know him?"

"I don't know, but I can text him."

Goggen continued to inspect the car. He had manoeuvred himself into what was left of the car now. He opened the glove compartment. This was not very badly damaged on the inside either. He took a look through the contents. Only official papers.

Whoever had started the fire was not very proficient at doing something like that. The fire was fast and hot, and not nearly as destructive as it could have been.

The seats had burned completely, and so had the centre console. There were only ashes left of what had been there.

Goggen now concentrated on the dashboard, the steering wheel, and the sun visors.

TJ came over to him again.

She said that no, Robert didn't know the person who'd gone with Stanley, but he commented that Stanley knew what he was doing. Goggen heard what she said, but he didn't answer. He was too busy checking out the car.

TJ felt a little disappointed.

"Bingo!" said Goggen.

He had taken down the sun visor on the passenger side. On there was a pocket to store CDs. He had taken out one of the CDs and pointed to it so that TJ could see it. There were some nice fingerprints on it. "See how one of the pockets is empty? Let's hope the mystery man put the CD into the player. I think I want Steve and Bob to go through the car. Can you call Steve for me?"

"Of course."

"Since the police are finished, we can probably move the car now. Ask Steve to contact the police and ask them if we can tow away the wreckage."

TJ took out her phone and called.

Fifteen minutes later TJ's phone rang. It was Steve calling her back. "We can take the car. The police are finished with their investigation of it and are just glad that they don't have to do anything with what is left of it. I have called a tow truck to come out there. It should arrive in about an hour. Can you two wait there?"

"Yes. We'll stay here until they get here," TJ answered.

Goggen and TJ watched them haul the car up onto the flatbed truck. After that they followed it back to Calgary. Goggen wanted to ensure that the car would arrive at the lab in exactly the condition he had found it, and that no one would be able to tamper with it along the way.

They arrived in Calgary just before 8 p.m. Both Steve and Bob were waiting for them.

The car was lifted up and put onto a big trolley, then hauled into the lab garage with the help of a winch.

"We'll begin on it first thing in the morning," said Steve, looking at Goggen. "How did it go with the copying?"

"Very well," said TJ. We got copies from all five cameras. Little Joe was nervous, but I explained to him that under no circumstances would we divulge that we had gotten the copies from him. I also told him that we might tip off the police that those cameras exist in case there are things on the DVDs that are of interest to their investigation."

"Has there been any word from Stanley?"

"No, absolutely nothing; I have a very uneasy feeling about it," said Bob.

 Steve nodded in agreement.

"Well, hopefully we'll know more tomorrow. I'm planning on looking through these DVD copies tonight."

Goggen hadn't said anything about doing that until now.

"So, if you don't need anything else from us, we're going to leave." "OK, but call me tomorrow," Steve said as they went out.

Once they got back to the hotel, they went directly to Goggen's room. TJ began to boot up her computer, while Goggen ordered room service.

TJ began to open up some files. She had connected her PC so that what was on the monitor could be seen on the TV.

"Shall we look at the file from the camera that was pointing to the parking area first? That's the one most likely to show something." "Yes," Goggen answered.

TJ concentrated on her PC. "Here it is." There was a knock on the door. Goggen went to open up. The room service had come. He opened the door and let the server in. She set down the tray with the two meals on it and gave him a receipt to sign. He gave it back to her with some cash for a tip.

Five Cutty Sarks and two hours and twenty minutes later, they were just about finished reviewing the recordings. Each recording was seventy-two hours in length, but TJ had fast-forwarded through them as much as she could without missing any of the contents. There were a lot of cars that had come into the parking area and then left. Then came one more car. TJ slowed down the recording to normal speed. It was a grey Chevrolet. A white man came out of the driver's side, but the distance was too far to be able to see his face. He paced a little back and forth and looked around. Then he got back into the car and moved it over to the side. He got out of the car again and lit a cigarette. He was alone. TJ fast-forwarded again. There. Stanley's car. It was about one hour and fifteen minutes since the Chevy had come. The driver had mostly sat in his car during that time, and it looked like he had dozed a little.

TJ reversed to about five minutes before Stanley's car pulled in. Then she and Goggen watched the recording again, Stanley's car pulling into the parking area. It was so clear that they both leaned forward in their seats. His car drove right by the parked Chevy. It turned around and parked about three spaces away from it. A man got out of the driver's seat.

Both TJ and Goggen could see that it wasn't Stanley. They didn't recognize who it was. He walked over to the other car and knocked on the driver's-side window.

The driver must have opened his window, because the newcomer was standing looking down at it. He moved to the side and the other man came out. They walked over to Stanley's car together. The second man opened the back door of Stanley's car, bent down, reached in, and pulled someone bodily out of the back seat. It was Stanley.

Goggen and TJ both recognized him. It appeared that he was groggy. They pushed and pulled him over to the other car. The driver went back to Stanley's car and opened all the doors and the trunk. It was apparent that he was looking for something.

The other man punched Stanley in the stomach, and he doubled over. Then the man punched him in the head. Stanley sank down to his knees. Then he was kicked, hard. Stanley now lay motionless on the ground. The guy lifted his head and let it drop limply back on the ground. He turned around and called over to the other man, who was still searching the car. He came over to Stanley and bent over him.

He straightened up and spoke to the other man, and at the same time he raised a revolver and pointed it at Stanley. One flash, then another. Two times he shot Stanley at point-blank range.

It happened so fast. TJ jumped in her seat. Goggen got a sip of his Cutty stuck in his throat. He couldn't believe his own eyes. They both had just witnessed a brutal murder— the murder of a friend.

Goggen caught TJ just as she was about to fall down on the floor. She had jumped out of her chair and screamed. He held her tight against him. He was absolutely speechless. What could he possibly say?

She clung to him. The screaming changed to crying.

"It's all right, TJ, I'm here. Just cry. It helps a little." Goggen tried to calm her down, but he didn't think he succeeded very well. All the bad things that had happened to her came flooding back. He felt enormous sympathy for her right at that moment.

They sat that way for a while. He wasn't sure exactly how long, but it seemed like an eternity. He had gotten her to lie down on the bed. She was a little calmer now. He could see that the tears were still running down her face. Her eyes were closed.

"Do you want to sleep here tonight?" he asked her. She carefully nodded a yes.

"OK, you should get under the blanket. I can leave the room while you get undressed. Do you want me to get anything from your room?" "No, don't go. Don't leave me alone," she begged him.

She reached out her hand to hold his.

"I think you should try to sleep a little now. I have something here that can help you." He took out his toiletries bag and found some Unisom sleeping pills.

"Here, take one of these. It will help you to sleep. Don't be afraid, I'll sleep in the chair. I won't leave this room, but don't think any more about me."

She took the pill and swallowed it.

It was two in the morning. TJ had been sleeping for an hour. What a horrible burden that had been laid on her. But finally, she was able to lie there and sleep. It had taken a while from when she took the pill to finally go to sleep. Goggen had held her hand the whole time. Now he had moved over to the chair again. He had started to reverse the DVD. He wanted to see the murder one more time and also review what had happened after that. He went back to the time when Stanley's car had first pulled in. He looked at his whisky glass. It was still half full. He added some more ice and then filled it to the top.

The driver of the Chevy went to the back of the car and opened up the trunk. He came back with two red cans that looked to be made of plastic and went over to Stanley's car. He poured the contents over the car before he struck a match and threw it on the car. An enormous flame shot up. The car was completely covered in flames within seconds.

They took Stanley between them and dumped him into the trunk of the Chevy before they drove away at a high rate of speed.

Thirty-seven minutes later, the young couple drove into the parking area and called the police.

Goggen pushed the stop button and leaned back in the chair to try to get some sleep.

It wasn't until he took one-half a Unisom that he finally went under.

Saturday, 27 October

It was almost lunchtime when the telephone rang. TJ and Goggen were still sleeping. The room was dark because Goggen had dragged the heavy drapes across the window before they'd begun to watch the DVDs the night before. It was very unusual for Goggen to sleep this late, but he hadn't turned off the DVD until almost five in the morning. He fumbled for the light switch before turning on the lamp and finding his phone.

"Yes? This is Goggen."

TJ had also awakened.

"This is Robert" came from the other end. "I've just had a call from a Little Joe, who asked after TJ."

"What did he have to say?"

"He wouldn't tell me, but he asked for her number. I told him that I couldn't give that out but that I could ask her to call him. He said it was very important. Is she there with you now?"

"Yes. I'll tell her to call him right away. Before I do that, I have something important to tell you."

For the next few minutes it was only Goggen who spoke. He told Robert everything that they had seen on the DVDs.

Robert listened without interrupting. Even after Goggen had finished, there was complete silence on the other side.

"How is TJ holding up?"

"I don't know exactly, but she's been here with me during the night. I gave her a sleeping pill. We were both sleeping until you just called." "You haven't been in contact with Steve or Bob?"

"No. It was too late. I'll call them now."

"We also have to notify the police. They need to have access to the DVDs."

"We need to get them on board with this."

"Yes, I know. I'm coming to Calgary. I'll get one of my sons to drive me.

I'll try to leave within the next hour. I'll call you again when I'm nearby."

"OK, sounds good."

TJ came back from the lobby, where she had gone to call Little Joe. She couldn't get reception on her cell phone in Goggen's room. "Little Joe wants to meet with us right away. He says he found something that he wants to show us."

"What is it?"

"I don't know, and he won't tell me over the telephone. He's waiting for us up in Bowden at the Pelican Hotel. He sounds awfully nervous." "OK, let's go. We can drive through Tim Horton's and get something to eat on the way. How are you feeling about things this morning?" "Better now."

"Are you sure?"

"Yes. That is one thing that I am absolutely sure of. I have decided that this is going to end one day. And that day is coming soon. I'm not going to run any longer."

Goggen looked at her and saw that she had gotten her dark gaze back.

It was a little after two in the afternoon when they drove into the parking lot of the Pelican Hotel.

Little Joe was sitting and waiting for them in the restaurant. He was paler than TJ remembered him from their last meeting.

"Hi, Joe," she said. "What can we help you with?"

Little Joe looked around the restaurant carefully before he answered.

"I think I found the owner of the car."

TJ looked quickly at Goggen.

"Where?"

"Over on Range Road 23." Little Joe said, "I was on my way to Bowden Lake when I noticed a flock of brown eagles circling. That's an unusual sign. I thought there might be a carcass out there, like an elk or a deer. Anyway, I drove off the road and up to where the eagles were gathered. At first, I didn't see anything special, but there were so many eagles everywhere. Then I noticed what looked like a pile of blankets lying under a tree. When I looked under it, I saw a man. A dead white man. My first thought was to call the police immediately, but then I remembered what you said to me up at Gleniffer Lake." He looked at TJ when he said that.

"Can you show us the way?" Goggen asked. "Yes, follow me."

Goggen nodded.

Thirty-five minutes later Goggen had identified Stanley Daly. Now he was talking to Little Joe.

"Thank you for calling us first. Now I don't want you to think any more about it. We'll take over from here, and we'll call the police. But first we're going to do a little of our own investigating. When we call the police, we won't mention your name at all. We'll say that it was we who saw the brown eagles and decided to find out what they were doing. Then we'll mention the cameras. Is that a deal?"

"Yes."

"OK." He put out his hand, and Little Joe took it.

Then Little Joe went back to his Land Rover and drove away. "Let's call Steve," Goggen said to TJ.

TJ took out her cell phone and scrolled up his number.

"Steve here."

"This is TJ." She proceeded to tell him where they were and why. "Don't leave that spot. I'll be there as quick as I can."

A good two hours later, he finally turned up. Bob was with him this time. They both quickly got out of the car and looked around with experienced gazes.

Steve came over to TJ and Goggen, who were sitting several metres from Stanley's body, but near enough to keep the eagles away. The eagles were waiting for a possible mealtime.

Steve greeted them quickly. "We have to work really fast. It's beginning to be very late to report this to the police."

"Yes, we know that."

"Let's see what we can find first."

"There are some very good tyre tracks right over there. They're not from our car or Little Joe's either. I took a picture of his tyre treads before we sent him away."

Steve followed where Goggen was pointing with his eyes. "Otherwise, there's not much else here. The only other thing is the blanket. We could take it away with us before the police arrive. We might be able to get a DNA profile of the person or persons who committed this crime."

Steve looked at Goggen. "What about Little Joe?"

"He won't say anything. I've already instructed him about what we are going to do. As soon as we are finished, we'll call Captain Ross. Then I'll tell her that TJ and I were driving down Range Road 23 and noticed all the eagles circling. We had been up to Gleniffer Lake looking around. We noticed that there were cameras placed out there to photograph the birdlife. That way we'll be informing them of an important clue at the same time."

Steve smiled and said, "I hope we never have to work against each other in competition anytime."

He turned around and went back to his car. Bob had already put on coveralls and plastic shoe covers. They began to mark the places that they thought might be of interest, before taking pictures of them.

They finished about an hour later.

"OK, we're finished. We're leaving. Now it's up to you." Steve looked at Goggen.

"Call me when you get back to Calgary. I'm interested in seeing the DVD surveillance."

"That won't be until tomorrow, at least. I'm going back to Gleniffer Lake. Now that I've seen the DVD, I have a better picture of exactly what happened. And, after seeing how the cars were placed, I might be able to find a few more clues."

"OK, we'll see you when you get back then."

TJ called the police in Innisfail. "Is it possible to speak with Captain Ross?"

Goggen couldn't hear what was going on at the other end, but he thought that TJ was put on hold.

"This is TJ Ellefsrud. We met up at Gleniffer Lake by the burned- out car."

TJ listened again.

"Well, we have found the owner of the car dead. Where? About five miles up Range Road 23, from Township Road 340. There's a little road in to the left. Follow that road for about two hundred metres." She listened again.

"Yes, we'll wait here for you."

She hung up and turned to Goggen. "They'll get here as soon as possible, about forty minutes. She said not to touch anything." "No, we won't do that," said Goggen drily.

TJ was surprised again about how much she kept looking at him. She

had never looked at men like that before, well, except in Acapulco. She generally hated men for what they stood for. She again had to force herself to think about something else.

She jumped when she heard Goggen's voice. "Are you OK?" "Yeah, I was just thinking about something special."

Captain Ross had been precise about the time they would arrive at the scene, missing it by only two minutes. Now she was standing speaking with TJ and Goggen, while two other police officers put up the barrier.

"How did you find him? And what were you doing up here?" she asked them.

Goggen let TJ explain exactly what they had decided to say. Captain Ross listened with great interest.

"So, you saw those cameras when you were up there today?" Captain Ross asked.

"Yes, we were on the way to the main office of the region's wildlife association down in Bowden. We went too far south. We should have turned off further up," TJ informed Captain Ross.

"I need to know how to reach you."

TJ gave her one of her cards. "Here is the address of the firm we work for. I have written down my name and my direct number. Please don't hesitate to call us if there is anything we can do.

"I have a question. Which police district will you send the body to for autopsy?"

"We are under the jurisdiction of Calgary."

"OK. We're going now. It's been a long and difficult day."

Captain Ross shook hands with them both before she started to issue orders.

"Shall we look for a hotel or motel? I'm hungry too."

"Yes. Why don't we go back to the Pelican Hotel in Bowden?" "Yes, why not? It looked like a cosy place. Or should we drive up to Innisfail?"

"It's all the same to me. Just one thing, though. Which place would be easier to find a metal detector? I just thought of it now."

"That would be Innisfail."

"Then let's go there and see what we can find."

TJ awoke suddenly. It was dark in the room, but there was a sliver of light coming in from the street light outside. Her whole body felt very warm, in a way that she had almost never felt before. Well, maybe once. She thought again of Acapulco.

She had the exact same feeling now.

She had gone to bed naked, and now she'd also kicked off the blankets. That must have been because she'd felt so warm. She could glimpse herself in the mirror on the wall.

Now she lay there and thought of him. She thought about how it would feel to hold his body close to hers. She thought about the scent of him, his breath breathing next to hers. Her body became even warmer.

She began to carefully touch her breasts. They were very sensitive. They were not really big, but they were nice and firm. She looked in the mirror again. She imagined that she saw him there together with her. She didn't know what was going on. She hadn't fantasized or had feelings like this since Neal.

She moved one of her hands slowly down her body. There she felt the edge of her pubic hair, and further down she was very wet. She enjoyed the feeling, and she knew she was wanting him inside her.

She imagined him near her again, while gently massaging her nipples with one hand and massaging her lower area with the other. Her hand slid down towards her mons pubis. She stroked herself between her thighs. Her fingers went near her clitoris, but she didn't touch it yet.

Not yet, she thought. The whole time she was doing this, she was imagining that he was doing it to her.

Then her fingers were on her clitoris. She couldn't wait any longer to twist it gently and massage it, first with her middle finger and then the others. She used the moisture from her vagina. It was heavenly.

Her orgasm was like nothing she had ever experienced before. Her body arched while she threw her head from side to side. Her whole body shuddered with the force of it. She groaned loudly, and then finally her body went completely limp. She felt a sense of well-being like she had never felt before. She just lay there and enjoyed the wonderful feelings that were flowing through her whole body. Then everything faded and she went back to sleep.

Sunday, 28 October

He sat and waited for her in the restaurant. They had agreed upon breakfast at eight o'clock, but he had gone downstairs almost an hour early. This was his third cup of coffee.

"Hi. Did you sleep well?" He smiled at her while he said it.

She wondered if he could have heard her, as there was a connecting door between the rooms.

She thought about the night before, the experience she had, and the dream she had about him after that. She had awakened very unsatisfied, and the first thing she had thought of was him. Was it possible that for the first time in her life she was in love?

"Not bad," she answered. "And you?"

"As usual. I was up at 4 a.m. the first time. But that's just how I sleep."

Oh my God, he did hear me! she thought to herself. She looked closely at him to see if there was a sign that he might have heard, but she couldn't pinpoint anything. How was she going to get through spending a whole day with him now?

She jumped a little when he said, "Shall we eat?" He asked, "Did I scare you?"

"No, my thoughts were just in another place. I was thinking about Asha. I haven't spoken to her in a few days, and that's not normal for me."

"Oh, well, let's order some food."

It was very quiet out on Gleniffer Lake when they arrived. The sun was shining through, but it was obvious that winter was well on its way. The temperature had been down below freezing during the night.

They had stopped at Canadian Tire in Innisfail and bought a metal detector.

Now Goggen was standing and checking over the area where Stanley had been shot. TJ wondered if he was talking to her or to himself. He was talking pretty loudly.

"Stanley's car stood here." He pointed to the place. "The other car was parked over there." He pointed to a place a little farther away and to the left. "The man in that car came out several times and smoked." Goggen had now moved over to the place where they had seen the Chevy waiting. He walked forward carefully while holding the metal detector in front of him. He walked systematically back and forth, checking only small areas one at a time. Then he went the other way in a grid system. He stopped and took out a plastic bag. Then he picked up a cigarette butt and put it in the bag. He continued to search. TJ just watched him. He bent down again. This time he picked up a wad of chewing gum.

One hour and twenty-seven minutes, three gold rings, one watch, and one bracelet later, he finally found what he had come out here to find. The metal detector began to peep, first weakly and then more intensely. He bent down and began to dig a little in the sand. *Bingo!*

TJ looked at him. He pointed at a shell casing from a revolver or a pistol. Again, he took out a plastic bag.

"Let's see if we can find the other one too. In the DVD Stanley was shot two times." He continued with the metal detector and moved it all over the area, but he couldn't find anything more than some small change and a key.

Finally, he clicked off the metal detector and turned towards TJ. "I think that's all we're going to find. What do you think?"

TJ looked at him. "Well, you know much more about this work than I do. If you are satisfied, then I don't have anything more to say."

She had sat and followed every movement he made all day, and thought about what had happened during the night several times. She was afraid that he could read it in her eyes.

"I think we should go down to Calgary now. Do you want to drive?" He was busy stowing the metal detector in the trunk while he asked. "Yes, that's no problem."

"I'll be right back. I have to go into the woods for a moment on an important errand." She smiled

They drove directly to Bob and Steve's office. "Did you find anything?"

Goggen handed them the case with everything in it. "I think that the only things of interest are the bags with the shell casing, the cigarette butt, and the chewing gum. The others are probably things that other people lost earlier."

Steve looked through the contents. "That's probably correct. Would you two like some coffee?"

Goggen looked at TJ and asked, "What do you say? Shall we have a coffee before we go back to the hotel? Robert is waiting for us back there. We're going to play the DVD for him."

Steve said, "Then we'll go with you too. There's nothing here that can't wait for an hour."

He gathered all the evidence he had in front of him, put each item in its marked envelope, and locked it all into the safe.

Everyone sat in silence with their thoughts. They had just seen the DVD where their friend had been brutally murdered. TJ had decided not to look at it again; she was back in her own room.

It was Goggen who finally broke the silence. "Steve, can you get more definition out of that DVD? Is it possible to enlarge the picture or anything?"

"Yes, it can be done, but I have to pass. It's outside my area of expertise. TJ would be able to do it if she feels she can take it. Otherwise I can call a friend I have used many times to do it. The quality of those kind of enlargements can be really good. It depends on the number of pixels the recording was taken with and also the quality of the equipment used on the original job. The chance of identifying the people as well as the car is good."

Goggen said, "Then you take a copy with you and give it to your friend. I don't want TJ to be unnecessarily burdened with that. How is it going with the other materials?"

"I have an appointment at the lab for tomorrow morning. We're going to go through the DNA analyses and the fingerprints we already have," Steve answered.

"What time?" "Nine o'clock."

"Can I come with you?" Goggen asked.

"I want to come too if possible," said Robert. He had held his silence up until this point.

"Yes. I assume that should be no problem. I'll come and pick you up around eight."

"OK, we'll be ready when you get here."

TJ came in.

"Are you finished?"

"Yes, but we're going to make some copies of the DVD," Goggen answered.

"OK, how many?"

"Since you're making them, do five," he continued. "OK, give me at least an hour."

"One hour gives us time for a drink. I think I need one," said Robert. The scene on the DVD was engraved on his brain, or at least it felt that way. "Let's go down to the bar."

Everybody got up except for TJ, who sat down and began to work on her computer.

"Are you finished?" Robert asked. TJ had just come into the bar. "Yes."

"Do you want something to drink?" Now it was Goggen who spoke. "I'll take a diet Coke."

Goggen waved the bartender over.

"What about the rest of you? Shall we have another round?" "Not me," said Bob. "What about you, Steve?"

"No, that's enough for me too. If I know Robin, the first thing he'll want is to have a beer with us."

"You mean you want to drop him off a copy of the DVD tonight—already?" Bob asked Steve.

"Yes, I thought we might as well. He likes to work all night. If he's home, we'll drop off the copy tonight."

"Who is Robin, and what is it that he'll be doing?" TJ asked. "He's going to try to enlarge some pictures from the DVD," said Goggen.

"I can do that," TJ answered.

Goggen looked at Robert while he answered. "We know you can, but we didn't want to burden you with it."

"Burden me! What the hell do you mean?! Didn't I say that I want to take those motherfuckers?!" Her eyes were totally dark again.

I hope I never get on her bad side, Goggen thought. Her gaze alone was almost enough to kill someone.

"Steve, do you think TJ can work with Robin on this? She can be a great help to him since she knows exactly what we are looking for."

"I don't know, but I'll ask him. He's a little sensitive about that kind of thing." He got out his cell phone and punched in a number.

"Hi, this is Steve. I have a job for you."

He listened.

"I had hoped to come over right now. I can't? What about tomorrow, midmorning? OK then, let's say twelve noon. I'm tied up at the lab before that. I know that you like to work alone, but I'm bringing someone along whom I want you to work with. She goes by the name TJ. She is a computer expert, and she know the case from A to Z. She also knows exactly what part of the DVD we want to enlarge."

He listened for a while.

"I know that, but it's just this one time. You owe me, OK?"

This time when Steve listened, he smiled.

"OK, it's a date. See you tomorrow."

"Well, that is that. He's a pain in the ass, but I overrode him. It's going to cost me a lot of favours in the future. Yes, TJ can go and work with him."

He looked directly at her now.

Monday, 29 October

Goggen drove together with Robert over to Steve and Bob's office. Robert ended up driving his own car down to Calgary. Both his sons had gotten busy and couldn't drive him. TJ drove alone in Kim's car. They still had her car because they hadn't been back to Drayton Valley yet.

Now they had arrived at the police laboratory down in Calgary as scheduled. They usually used a private laboratory to get DNA profiles. The technical work they did themselves. But this time they needed to use the police laboratory in order to do comparisons of the fingerprints and the DNA samples.

They were well-known there, and they had many friends within the organization. Both Steve and Bob used to work there before their retirement.

They were met with friendly words and nods. Of course, that didn't exempt them from having to sign in to the official visitors' book that lay on the reception desk.

Steve signed all of them in before he took out his driver's licence and put it down on the desk. He turned to them, and they all in turn took out their licences.

Bob had not come with them after all. He had stayed back to work on the materials that Goggen had brought in the day before.

"Is Mrs Taylor upstairs?" Steve asked the receptionist. "Yes. She's waiting for you in the office."

"Thanks. We'll see you in a while."

The receptionist smiled and waved.

They all walked over to the elevator and took it up to the third floor. Mrs Taylor's office was down at the end of the hall.

She got up and went around her desk to come out to meet them.

"I see you have brought your entourage today, Steve." She put out her hand to greet him.

"Yes. These are some of the lead investigators in this case."

Mrs Taylor put out her hand again and greeted each of them as Steve introduced them.

Then she went back behind her desk and sat down. Steve sat down in a chair in front of her desk. TJ and Goggen remained standing, since there weren't any more chairs. Robert had his own wheelchair to sit in.

"So, what is it you have for me this time?" she asked Steve, looking at him enquiringly.

He picked up a document file and opened it up. "Well, so far we have several different DNA profiles, seven sets of fingerprints, four shell casings, and two bullets." He set down everything he had brought with him on her desk. She looked through the materials quickly. "OK." She got up again. "Let's go over to the DNA department first. They take the most time. The fingerprint department is one floor up, so we'll go there next."

They all followed her out of the office.

"This is Kathy. She will be doing the tests for you." They all greeted

Kathy politely without introducing themselves.

"Steve, you know Kathy from before, don't you?"

She gave Kathy the DNA profiles Steve had brought with him. "Yes, you could say that," he answered.

He waved at Kathy and smiled at her.

"So, you are interested in how a DNA test is conducted?"

"Yes, but first, my name is Ole George Olsen and I am from Norway. You can call me Goggen."

OK, first of all, how much do you know about DNA?"

"I have a rough understanding of what it is. I have learned that all people have in every cell of their bodies forty-six chromosomes that control the life of the cell and decide what characteristics they have." "Not bad. Then maybe you also know that those forty-six chromosomes lay together in twenty-three pairs. Twenty-two of the pairs are autonomous, and one pair are sex chromosomes, XX for women and XY for men."

"I have heard that, but I have to warn you that I don't have it fixed very well in my mind. At least not very technically. That's what we have people like you for."

She smiled again. "Do you want me to go on?" "It sure wouldn't hurt to hear it again."

"OK," Kathy said. "DNA, otherwise known as deoxyribonucleic acid, is at the core of all the cells. It is a molecule that carries the genetic instructions used in the growth, development, functioning, and reproduction of all known living organisms and many viruses. DNA and RNA are nucleic acids. They have a form like a double spiral staircase. The sides of the stairs consist of sugar and phosphate, and the steps are the actual DNA molecules.

"The two DNA strands are termed polynucleotides since they are composed of simpler, monomer units called nucleotides. Each nucleotide is composed of one of four nitrogen-containing nucleobases—either cytosine (C), guanine (G), adenine (A), or thymine (T)—and a sugar called deoxyribose and a phosphate group. "Do you follow? Shall I continue?"

"Yes, I think I got it."

"OK, there will always be certain bases that belong together. For example, A will always connect with T, and C with G. These nitrogen bases make up the base pairs. The pairing of these is important. For example, A+T is not the same as T+A. If there is an A on one string, it can only connect to a T on the other string. That's the key.

"Three of these bases on one step makes up a codon, or triplet. A series of these codons makes up the gene that holds information on how the amino acids make up the proteins."

Goggen rolled his eyes and kept listening.

"As you know, human DNA consists of forty-six chromosomes or, correctly, twenty-three chromosome-pairs, which again we have two varieties of. That means that we have two types of chromosomes.

From each chromosome pair we inherit one from Dad and one from Mom. The twenty-third chromosome pair is the sex chromosome that determines if we will be a male or female. The female has two copies of the X chromosome, but the male has one X and one Y chromosome. So how does this DNA transfer from one generation to another? It's like this! When two people enjoy a private moment with each other, a new life is created. The new life will receive twenty- three chromosomes from Dad and twenty-three chromosomes from

Mom, and these melt together randomly. However, the Y chromosome is only transferred from father to son. At the beginning of time, mitochondria were independent organisms. They still have their independent DNA, mitochondria DNA. This DNA is present in both male sperm cells and female eggs. In the sperm cell it's located in the tail, and this tail is discarded when the egg gets fertilized. And that's why the mitochondria DNA comes from the mother, and again only the female can pass it on to both genders. It is therefore the

Y-DNA and the mitochondria DNA that makes up the family string. It does not blend but follows a clean line backwards for generations. In principle this means that father and son will have identical Y-DNA; however, over hundreds of years it may have minute mutations. That means that it may not be 100 per cent the same. The mitochondria DNA, on the other hand, mutates much slower that the Y-DNA. It may take thousands of years to mutate. This is why it is the most reliable tool to determine family relationships.

"Do you still follow?"

"Yes, but it's way too technical for me. What happens with DNA profiles that are used by the police?"

"What we do is we compare these new profiles with the DNA profiles already in our database."

"How is a person's DNA profile established in your database?" "Well, it starts with any materials and clues we find at a crime scene, items such as this cigarette butt or this drinking cup. Another is a strand of hair or skin particles, anything with saliva on it, et cetera.

These are all potential carriers of DNA. As you know, these items need to be handled in very special ways. Each is collected and placed in a sealed tamperproof container or bag. They are tagged and labelled with all the information about where and when at the specific crime scene they were collected. And as much detail as is available is included in the notes. It is then sent to an official approved laboratory. The material will undergo the process to establish a DNA profile. The process involves heating and cooling. This produces millions of the original DNA. This process is called polymerase chain reaction, or PCR. The result is then sent through a laser detector, where it is copied and inspected. The various DNA fragments will be determined by their size.

"Now we shall compare what we found with what we have in our database here in Alberta. Unfortunately, we do not have access to a national database yet."

Kathy looked at Goggen and asked, "Did this help you? Do you understand the DNA process better now?"

Goggen smiled back at her but did not say anything.

Kathy had already placed the data card from the first profile under the scanner.

"This is Tommy Nelson. He will help you with the fingerprints you have brought. Steve, I think you already know him as well."

"Yes." Steve shook hands with him too.

Mrs Taylor gave Tommy the fingerprints she had gotten from Steve earlier.

"Now let's just hope that we find a match or two."

I'll take the shell casings and the bullets down to the cellar and give them to George. He's not here today, but he'll be back tomorrow. As soon as he gets here, I'll ask him to take a look as soon as possible. He's a very busy person, so that can take a little time, but you know that already, Steve. I have to go down again, but please stop in to my office before you leave."

"Of course. See you later."

Tommy looked at TJ. "These two others know all about fingerprints, but how much do you know about them?"

"Not much more than I've seen in the movies," she answered. "Well, fingerprints have been used for more than one hundred years for identification purposes. Sir Francis Galton has the credit for discovering the process, even though he was not the first person to identify fingerprints.

"Already in 1686 fingerprints were written about by Marcello Malpighi, but he didn't realize that they could be used for something practical. Neither did John Evangelist Purkinjean in 1823. The first person who ever used fingerprints for something practical was Sir William Herschel, in 1858. He used fingerprints as signatures.

"In the 1870s, Doctor Henry Faulds invented a classification system for fingerprints, and in 1880 he published an article where he discussed finger-prints and their unusual characteristics.

"The first time fingerprints were used in police work was in 1892. That was the bloody fingerprints of a mother on the door frame used to establish the fact that she had murdered her son.

"Today, fingerprints are the most widely used method of identifying of criminals. Even where DNA is completely alike, like in the case of identical twins, their fingerprints are different. But we have modernized the way in which we collect and catalogue fingerprints.

We have giant databases that store millions upon millions of fingerprints. In the future they will take over for PIN codes and other things."

Tommy took a look in the microscope. "These are some very good prints," he added, chatting with TJ.

He put one of the fingerprints on the glass plate in front of his computer and adjusted the light and picture quality. Then he put the arrow on Search and pressed the button. The computer began to search the database.

"How many fingerprints do you have in your database?" asked TJ. "That's a good question. I can't say exactly, because there are always more coming in, but the last time I checked it was a little over eight million."

The counter on the screen was moving at lightning speed. There was a counter on the left side that changed every 1,000 prints. So far it had gone through 2,365,000 prints. Suddenly it stopped, and the word MATCH came up on the screen and began to blink. Tommy went to the side and brought out the information.

Name: George Nokoot Race: First Nation People Born: 1941

Social Security number: 5353473

Address: Edmonton Correctional Institution Charges: Armed robbery and murder

Earlier address: Wabamun Lake Reservation

TJ watched, interested, over Tommy's shoulder. She didn't say anything.

Tommy took a copy of the information and then brought out the next set of fingerprints and did the same procedure. The search began again. TJ watched the screen in suspense while it counted down. It didn't stop until 8,042,571: NO MATCH.

Tommy came back. The search had taken about fifteen minutes. He looked at TJ.

"Sorry, but we don't find one every time."

He copied the print onto the database and found the next one. Whenever they didn't get a match, they still copied the print into the database, in case they came up with something later. They might possibly find a match for it in the future. They notated which case it was from so that it would be easier to match up later.

Tommy continued with the next fingerprint, but it wasn't until the fifth one that he got another match. He brought up the information.

Name: Scott Leroy McKenzy Race: White

Born: September 20, 1941

Address: 1254 Avenue 34 NW, Greenfield, Edmonton Ex–police officer

Tommy looked at Steve and TJ. "Anyone you know, Steve?" "No, but an interesting match."

Tommy continued, "He was brought in, in connection with an armed robbery. But they had to let him go. He was still in the police department at that point."

Tommy continued to read.

"He was also brought in, in connection with a shooting episode in which his partner was killed. The bullet that killed his partner was from McKenzy's service revolver. An eyewitness backed up his explanation. He said that he had lost his service revolver while he was running after one of the two men who had robbed a couple of Native Americans. The man whom Scott had run after turned with a knife in his hand and attacked him. When Scott's partner saw that, he shot at the suspect, who fell down on the ground. Meanwhile the other man got a hold of Scott's service revolver and shot Scott's partner.

The shots were fired simultaneously, but only Scott survived. The eyewitness who saw the whole thing and testified for Scott was one George Nokoot."

Tommy read on.

"The case was investigated, just as all cases like this are, but the charges were dropped very quickly."

Steve looked at Tommy. "Can we have a copy of that?" "Of course." Tommy clicked the copy button.

There were no more matches to any of the fingerprints they had brought in that day.

"At least we now have entered all the fingerprints in Alberta's database. If any come in the future that match them, we'll identify them then. They continually update these things, and there are a large number of fingerprints that have not yet been registered. I'll check them again in about a week."

Steve understood what Tommy was saying. The process took time and there were many factors involved.

"It's going to turn out fine," Steve said to Tommy. "At least now we have something to work with. You have my number, so please give me a call right away if anything else turns up."

"Of course. By the way, when are we going to get together and have a beer? It's been a long time since we did that."

"Anytime, but at the moment I am a little tied up with this case. What do you say to coming with me to a Dinos game? I have three season tickets."

"Give me a call and I'll be there in a heartbeat."

Steve smiled. "I'll do that." He turned to TJ and Robert. "Shall we go find Goggen and see what he's up to?" Robert and TJ also thanked Tommy for his help before they left.

"How is it going here?"

"It's been interesting to see how one DNA profile is matched up with another, but so far we haven't found a match," said Goggen. "Kathy has also tried to teach me all about human DNA, but I don't think she succeeded. What about you?"

"Two matches."

Goggen's eyes brightened. "And who are they?"

Steve gave Goggen a quick rundown of what they had found. Goggen listened interestedly.

"Did it say anything about who investigated the case of the shooting?" Steve took out the envelope of copied information that they had taken with them.

"It was one Lieutenant McKenzie. Does that tell you anything?" "Maybe, maybe not. We'll tackle that later."

"Well, there are no matches here. Kathy had been away for a moment and had just gotten back and looked at the screen where the results of the search were posted.

"No match."

"There's nothing much we can do about that," said Steve. "But you have our thanks for taking so much of your time to try to help us. We'll be back pretty soon. There are more profiles in the works." "OK, you are always welcome here, you know that. But before you go, is there any possibility of getting any DNA profiles from the cabin fire? I know it was a very long time ago, but I would really like to have them in the database. You never know. Only by eliminating some people can others be identified.

"One of the profiles you gave me was from a Native American Indian.

We are in the process of going through that material now, and we will bring it over when we have it finished."

"What about me?" TJ spoke now. "I was on the scene. I was one of the victims there."

"Then I'll take a DNA sample from you if you'll allow me to," Kathy spoke directly to TJ.

"Of course."

"Let me go and get the equipment."

She was back in a matter of minutes.

"OK, open up your mouth. I'll take two different samples from you, one from your mouth and the other being one of your hair strands. Is that OK?"

TJ nodded and opened her mouth. Kathy took a cotton swab, put it into TJ's mouth, and moistened it well. Then she pulled three hairs one by one from her head.

"I think that should give us what we need. I'll take it over to the lab and start on it immediately. That way we can have the profile done by tomorrow." She looked at Steve while she said this.

"That sounds good. Is Mrs Taylor back yet?"

"No, but she asked me to tell you she'll call you later today."

"Say hello to her from me. And to you, I thank you again for giving us so much help."

Everyone else thanked her too before they headed to the elevator. Steve looked at Robert. "I haven't heard any comments from you. What do you think about all these things we have found out?" Instead of answering him, Robert suddenly grabbed his chest and gasped.

"Robert!" Steve was the first one to react.

Goggen called out to the personnel, "Call an ambulance!"

Kathy ran directly to the telephone, and the others in the lab came running over. One of the older men who worked there stepped forward. "I'm a doctor. Can I help?"

Goggen immediately stepped aside and urged him forward. The first thing he said was, "We have to lay him down."

Steve and Goggen took hold of Robert, one on each side, and gently lifted him out of the wheelchair. Then they laid him down on the floor. The man who'd said he was a doctor immediately took over, loosening Robert's collar and beginning to administer CPR.

"Get the defibrillator!" he shouted to one of the others who had come over. Someone was already on the way to fetch it long before he called out. It was less than two minutes before he had it there.

The doctor instructed Steve to continue with the CPR while he got the defibrillator ready. When he was finished, he told Steve to stand clear while he administered the first shock. Then Steve began the CPR again. There was another shock; Steve paused and stood clear. After the third shock, the doctor was able to detect a weak pulse. He asked Steve to continue. The pulse became a little stronger.

The ambulance had arrived. The paramedics came running up the stairs and took over immediately. Steve and the doctor stood back. One paramedic asked, "What happened?" The doctor quickly told him what had happened and what they had done. The paramedic listened to him while he worked on Robert.

They placed a stretcher on the floor next to him and prepared to lift Robert onto to it. Two paramedics stood, one at each shoulder, and Steve and Goggen each took one of Robert's legs. One, two, three, and he was on the stretcher. One of the paramedics had already started preparing portable monitors to attach. The other prepared to connect an intravenous apparatus.

Robert was awake. One of the paramedics said to him, "Now you're coming with us."

Robert didn't answer; he just stared out into space. They lifted him up and went into the elevator which would take them downstairs and out to the ambulance.

"Where are you taking him?" asked Steve. "Foothills."

TJ rode in the ambulance to the hospital. Steve drove Goggen directly there after they had left the laboratory. From there, Steve drove on to his office.

When he came in, Bob looked up at him. "How did it go?" Steve proceeded to tell Bob what had happened.

"How is he doing now?"

"I don't know. I'll drive over to Foothills Hospital again as soon as I deliver the DVD to Robin. Can you come and pick me up afterwards? I'm going to drive the car that TJ and Goggen are using over there. I'll leave Robert's car here for the time being."

"Of course. Just call me when you're ready to be picked up."

Steve went out again.

He had to ring the front doorbell several times before he heard someone coming to answer it.

"OK, OK," he heard someone saying from the inside. "I'm coming."

The door lock slid open and the door opened.

"Oh yeah, it's you. I forgot. It was pretty late last night." "Last night?" asked Steve.

"Well, this morning then."

Steve smiled. He knew Robin. They had been friends for more than thirty years, and many times he had sat up all night with him. "Weren't you going to bring a student with you?"

"Not a student, but a very intelligent woman. She can do most of the things with a computer that you do, but she doesn't have the necessary equipment."

He told Robin about Robert's heart attack. "Maybe she'll come over later."

"OK, tell me now what you want me to do for you. I know you told me last night, but I'd like you to repeat it. You know how I am." "Yes, I sure do know how you are.

"On this DVD you will witness a violent murder. If you are able to do it, we need as many still photos of it as possible, and we also hope to enlarge them enough for us to be able to identify the perpetrators. The same goes for the car make, model, and licence plate. The important happenings occur at seven hours and twenty-three minutes into the DVD. The scenario takes about one hour and thirty-eight minutes to unfold."

Robin poured himself a coffee and asked Steve if he would like one. "No thanks, I have to go back to the hospital to see what's happening. I'll call you or come back here later."

"OK, you do that. I'll start on this right away."

Steve went out again.

Forty-five minutes later he was back at the hospital. "Robert Blake," he said to the receptionist.

She began to read her computer screen. "Surgery ward 9H."

He thanked her and went on.

"How is it going with him?" Goggen had seen Steve come in and had gone down the corridor to meet him. "He's still in surgery," Goggen answered. "What did the doctor say?"

"So far nothing. But there's been a lot of activity." "How did it go at Robin's?" Goggen asked.

"He's working on the DVD right now. I said I'd stop by later." "Maybe I'll go with you. I have to see how it's going here first." "Of course. How is TJ taking it?"

"She's worried, but otherwise OK."

"Well, I'm just going to let her stay here in peace. We have a lot to go through in the meantime. I drove over the car that you and TJ have been using. I'll call Bob to come and pick me up. In the meantime, I need to have a word with TJ. Give me a call as soon as you find out anything."

He went over to TJ.

It was 6 p.m. before the doctor came out to talk to TJ and Goggen.

Both of them looked at him before Goggen said, "Tell us."

"Robert is resting right now. He is out of danger, but we came close to losing him. His heart stopped three times while he was on the operating table. We have done an angioplasty and removed a blockage on the right side of his heart, so he will be able to get well. It's going to take some time, though. What he needs most right now is rest, and then he will have to build himself up again."

"Can we see him?"

"Yes, that's no problem. But don't say anything that would make him upset."

TJ said, "No, no, of course not." She was already on her way in to the room where Robert was.

"Hi, how do you feel?" She was anxiously holding his hand.

Robert looked twenty years older, but he was awake. Now he was trying to look at them.

"What are you two doing here?" he asked. "Don't you have an investigation to conduct?"

"That can wait," said TJ.

"TJ, I am thankful that you care, but I have it as good as I can in here. Go out there and take those sons of bitches. I think that's how you phrased it."

TJ looked at him with tears in her eyes. She didn't know what to say. "TJ, I'm not going anywhere. Go and do what you have to do. Then come back and give me the good news tomorrow. I have to rest now, you know."

Goggen hadn't said a word up until now. "We'll come back tomorrow."

TJ didn't say anything more. She just let go of Robert's hand, turned, and walked out of the hospital room. Goggen almost had to run to keep up with her.

"He really does mean well," he said, as he overtook her.

She didn't answer him, and she had the black look in her eyes again.

"How is Robert?" was the first thing that Steve asked when they arrived at his office.

"He's out of danger now, but it was touch-and-go. The doctor said that his heart stopped three times. It was a main artery that was blocked. They went in and unblocked it. He's still in intensive care, but tomorrow morning he'll be moved to a private room if nothing else happens," Goggen replied.

TJ didn't say anything.

"The doctors are very good at Foothills. I'm sure he's going to be all right."

"TJ, do you want to go over to Robin's?" asked Steve. "I thought we'd both go over there," said Goggen.

He gave a very careful sign to Steve. Steve saw it but didn't understand what it meant. However, he said, "OK, I'll go with you. I don't know how he's going to take me bringing two people along."

Robin opened the door almost immediately when Steve rang the bell. "Hi. Here I am again. I brought TJ, the one I told you about yesterday."

Robin was inspecting TJ while Steve was talking.

"And this is Goggen. He's from Norway. He's come all the way over here in connection with this case."

"This case?" asked Robin. He looked very questioningly at Steve. "Well, not directly, but the case that this is a part of."

Robin nodded. "OK. From Norway, you say?" "Yes."

Robin smiled. "What part of Norway?"

All three of them were startled by the question, especially Goggen. "Oslo," he said.

"I'm from Arendal," said Robin with a smile. "But I've been over here for more than thirty years. It was my parents who emigrated, and you know I had to go with them."

"Do you still speak Norwegian?"

Now Robin switched to Norwegian. "Yes, we always spoke Norwegian at home, even though we were here. It was mostly for my grandmother's sake. She stayed back in Norway with her daughter when we moved over here."

He changed to English again and quickly filled in TJ and Steve, repeating what he had just said to Goggen.

"Can I offer you anything?"

"What do you have?" asked Goggen.

"I don't have any Arendal's Pilsner, but I have just about everything else."

"Well then, I'll have a Scotch. What kind do you have?"

Robin went to his kitchen cabinet and said, "Let me see. I have Ballantine's, Johnnie Walker, and Cutty Sark."

"I'll take a Cutty with ice and club soda on the side if you have it." "Coming right up. What about the rest of you?"

"I'll have a Molson. I have to go back to the office." TJ said, "Coke, if you have it."

"No, but I have ginger ale." "That's fine."

Himself, he took a Molson.

Robin's apartment wasn't very big. He only had a kitchenette, a small table, a sofa, and a small TV. But in the corner was equipment of first class and high technology. Goggen counted no fewer than six computer screens.

Robin saw what he was looking at. "Yes, it's my life," he said. Steve broke in. "Have you looked at all at the DVD?"

"Yes, I looked through it. I'm planning how to capture the still photos and how to blow them up for identification purposes."

TJ said, "I think I changed my mind. I need something stronger to drink. I forgot what we're going to look at." "What would you like?"

"Just dump some Canadian Club right into this ginger ale." She reached out her hand with the glass in it.

Robin found the bottle and did what she'd asked. Steve got up and said, "I have to go. I'll call you later."

Goggen looked at TJ. "TJ, since I'm here, can I assist Robin? Then you can see what you can find out about George Nokoot and Scott McKenzy."

She always had her laptop with her wherever she went. "OK. Can I connect to the Internet somewhere, Robin?"

"You can plug in over there." He pointed to a corner of the kitchen. The password is Arendal, small letters."

He looked at Goggen and smiled when he said this.

Robin sat down in the big black command centre chair. It looked like something an airline pilot would sit in. "You can take that chair over there." Robin pointed to another office chair over to the side.

"Shall we see? Where was I? Oh, here we are. I thought we would begin to take stills from the moment when the first car comes into the parking area."

"Sounds good."

"Let's see, how about it?"

The car was on the way in to the parking area and was coming straight at the camera.

"Very good," said Goggen. "Can we zoom in on it?"

Robin was concentrating on the screen. The car came nearer. One more time and the car was even nearer, but the image was very distorted. "Wait, I'm not finished yet." Slowly the picture became clearer by degrees, and the car kept coming closer.

"Here we have a Ford LTD," said Robin. "But the licence plate number isn't readable yet."

"Can you get it?"

Robin didn't answer; he just concentrated on his computer.

Again, the car appeared closer. He tried to focus it in more clearly.

They both waited in suspense.

Robin shook his head and said, "I don't think we're going to be lucky with this picture at the moment."

"At the moment?" Goggen asked. He looked at Robin expectantly. "I have another method to use, but it takes time and it's very expensive. Let's see what other possibilities we have here first." They moved on to the next scene that was of interest.

At 5.30 a.m. Robin shut off his computer. They had worked eleven hours and had taken forty-four pictures. And Goggen had finished the bottle of Cutty Sark. Some of the pictures were better than others, but they had just not been able to identify the car plate. Robin still claimed that there was a way to focus the car licence plates even clearer, but he wouldn't say how. That was a secret, he said.

"What did you find out yesterday?" Robert was still in intensive care, but he was already feeling much better. He was raised up a little higher in his bed today.

Goggen set his briefcase on a table and took out some papers.

"We got a lot of good pictures of the happening with Stanley, but so far we have not been able to identify either the car or the persons.

Robin is still working with a portion of the pictures, and he said he believes he can focus in on it until the license plate is readable.

He said it will take time and cost a lot of money. I told him to buy whatever he needs and to do whatever he can, saying that money is no object."

"Can I have a look at the pictures?"

Goggen gave them to Robert. "Are you sure they won't upset you?" "No, I can handle it."

He began to study the pictures.

TJ's telephone rang. It was Robin.

"Hi. I have the licence plate number. Do you have something to write with?"

"Just a minute." "OK, give it to me."

"AOX 442 Alberta. Ford Impala, grey, 1998 model." "But wasn't the car a Ford LTD?"

"That's what I thought last night, but I must have been mistaken."

TJ thanked him and hung up. Goggen looked at her.

"The tag number is AOX 442, but the car is a Ford Impala." Robert was still thumbing through the pictures of the car. "That's incorrect. It is an LTD."

"How can that be when Robin says it's an Impala?"

"The licence plates must have been stolen," said Goggen. "Everything else matches up, the colour grey and the year." Robert was lying there looking at one of the pictures. He went back through all of them. He stopped and studied one of the pictures at length. "The man on the left is the one Stanley had with him."

Goggen took the picture from Robert.

"You mean the one who's standing right next to Stanley?" "Yes. That's the one who went along with him."

"And you don't know who he is?"

"No, he was completely unknown to me. Stanley said that for sure he was OK."

"So, Stanley must have known him quite well." "Seems like it."

"Do you know the other man?"

"No, but we might be able to find out if we ask around." TJ's phone rang again.

"Yes? TJ here."

"This is Steve. I just got a telephone call from Kathy at the DNA department."

"OK, what did she say?"

"One of the DNA profiles is a relative of yours. The only difference is that it's a man."

TJ stood very still.

"Are you there? Hello? Are you still there?" Goggen could hear the voice on the other end.

"Yes, I'm here. Could you please repeat what you just said?"

"I said that one of the DNA profiles from the car up at Abraham Lake matches yours."

TJ was still again. She thanked Steve, hung up, and turned to Robert and Goggen.

They both looked at her curiously.

"One of the DNA profiles from the cabin up at Abraham Lake shows a relative of mine."

Robert looked at Goggen, and Goggen looked back at Robert. It was very clear what they were both thinking.

CHAPTER 15

Wednesday, 31 October

Edmonton Correctional Institution

It was 1 p.m. when Goggen and TJ drove through the gate. "Parking for visitors," they read, and followed the sign. There weren't very many cars there. They walked into the reception area.

"Visitors for George Nokoot," said Goggen, who showed his identification badge which read, "Private Investigator, Robert Blake, Inc."

The receptionist went through several lists she had in front of her. She talked to herself while she read through them. "Robert Blake, Inc. George Nokoot. OK, here it is."

"Go over there and wait. I'll send a message to him." They went over and sat where she'd told them to.

Ten minutes later she called them over.

"George Nokoot was transferred to the prison hospital. He's been very sick for the last few days."

Goggen asked, "Would it still be possible to talk to him?"

"I can't answer that," she said. "But you can certainly go over there and ask. The hospital is in H Block. Just turn right as you leave this area, and then H Block is on the right side. It's about three hundred metres down that way. I'll call them and let them know you're coming."

They thanked her and left.

The reception of the prison hospital was quite larger than the one at the prison block. There was also a small counter where there was coffee. Besides that, it was like going back in time. They went straight over to the receptionist. TJ introduced herself before she introduced Goggen.

"We wish to speak with George Nokoot. Is that possible?" "One moment." The receptionist picked up a book.

TJ whispered to Goggen, "Two thousand and five." Goggen thought the same.

The receptionist began to read down the page.

"He's in department C, which is the cardiac department. I have to speak with the doctor in charge first."

"OK, we'll wait."

The receptionist dialled a number and waited. She spoke for a few moments before she turned back to TJ.

"It's all right for you to go in and see him, but you must not upset him. There will also be a guard in the room with you." She looked at them. "That's all right," TJ answered automatically.

"Sign yourselves in here." She pointed to a logbook that lay open on the counter. Now she dialled another number.

"A guard will be here in just a minute, and he'll take you up to Nokoot. You can wait for him over there." She pointed to some folding chairs in the corner next to the coffee maker.

Ten minutes later they introduced themselves to the female guard who had come to fetch them.

"Mister Nokoot is very unwell, but he gave his permission for you both to come in and see him. I was also given strict orders that you may not do or say anything that might upset him. I will stay in the room during your visit." She looked seriously at TJ and Goggen while giving these instructions.

Neither of them made any comment.

"Fourth floor. Here's the department where he is. Do we have a deal that you won't upset him?"

"Yes, we promise not to upset him," said TJ. She looked up at Goggen.

"Of course we won't," he said.

So, with that they went through the double doors.

George Nokoot was lying in a single room far down at the end of the corridor. They went in. It was very obvious that there was no luxury at this hospital. Besides the normal equipment you find by a hospital bed, there was one wooden stool.

"Are you awake, George? It's Rachael."

He opened one eye.

"I have some people with me who want to ask you a few questions."

Now both eyes opened up. He exerted himself in order to see who it was that the guard was talking about.

"This is TJ Ellefsrud, and this is Ole G. Olsen."

The guard kept her eyes on George.

"TJ is from here in Canada, but Ole G. Olsen came all the way from Norway. Do you know where that is?"

George made no attempt to answer. Rachael left the question alone. "Can you manage it?"

George nodded heavily.

TJ moved closer to him. She changed over and spoke to him in the First Nations language. He looked up at her with his eyes open wide. She continued.

He answered her in the same language.

"Can I call you George?"

George nodded.

"Well, we came here today because we have gotten a positive match of some fingerprints from a car that was used in the commission of a crime. These fingerprints match yours perfectly."

She looked closely to see if he had any reaction. There was none. She continued to look at him.

"That means that you have been at the place where we found these fingerprints."

Still no reaction from George Nokoot.

TJ looked at Goggen, but she didn't say anything. She didn't need to. Her face told Goggen plainly and clearly what she wanted to do now. He nodded almost imperceptibly. That was the signal she was waiting for. Goggen knew her. After all these years of frustration they finally had someone in front of them who could answer some of her questions.

TJ looked again at George Nokoot.

"You are an old man now, and you have been through a lot. I don't know if you have any children, but if you do and one of them was killed, wouldn't you wish for the murderer to be found?"

Still no reaction.

"You are really sick. Do you want to go to your grave with the explanation that could solve a situation like that?" She was still speaking in First Nations. Goggen couldn't understand a word of what she said.

George still didn't exhibit a sign of wanting to answer.

"Well, we came here to ask you if you had any information regarding a fire in a cabin out on Jasper and some other crimes. But it's obvious that you're not interested in answering us at all."

TJ gave him time to answer once more.

"Do you really mean that those who are involved in that will never find out what happened? You're doing a life sentence and nobody can touch you. And you really wish that? I am one of the sisters of our tribe. We should fight together, not be enemies of each other."

No reaction.

TJ looked at Goggen silently, but the question was right there in her eyes: *What do we do now?*

"Let's go. We're not going to get anything out of him."

"OK." But before she left, she put one of her cards into Nokoot's hand.

TJ and Goggen didn't say a word to each other until they got back inside the car.

Then, TJ's first question was, "What is your input on this?" "He's a proud man."

"You can say that again."

"He knows that he doesn't have very much longer to live." "Then why doesn't he say anything?"

"It must have something to do with his pride." "I tried to ally with him by using our language."

"I know that, and I think on some level you succeeded." "How can you say that? He didn't say one single word to me." "No, but you hit a nerve."

TJ looked wonderingly at Goggen. "What do you mean?"

"I studied his eyes while you were talking. He tried very hard to be strong and not show his feelings. But I saw subtle changes in his eyes while you spoke. I didn't understand what you were saying, but I could clearly see the changes.

I am almost sure that we'll be hearing from him again."

"So, what do we do in the meantime?" asked TJ.

"Now I think it's time to contact Kim and get her car back to her. Then we'll drive back to the ranch. I need to get out of these clothes before they walk away by themselves."

"Oh yes, the car. I almost forgot."

Goggen was sitting in the chair downstairs when TJ came down. Her hair was still wet. He just sat and looked at her, but he tried to do it as discreetly as possible. She was a really beautiful woman. She had all the Scandinavian features and the Indian skin and hair colour. He smiled to himself. *So, you're starting to get a crush on her, are you?* he thought to himself.

"Do you want another drink?" she asked, pointing to his glass, which was almost empty.

"Yes, why not? I'm not going anywhere tonight." "What are you drinking? Silly question."

She went over to the bar cabinet and poured a rather large portion of Cutty into a clean glass, then added ice. She took a Molson for herself.

She gave Goggen the new glass before sitting herself down on the sofa. Goggen dumped what was left in the glass he had into the new one she had just set down in front of him.

Then they both sat there silently with their thoughts, Goggen with his and TJ with hers.

"TJ, what is it that we have overlooked? What did Nils Henrik overlook? How is it that your DNA profile matches with what we found in the green station wagon? There is something here that we are missing. I think we need to find George Nokoot's associates. You know a little about reservation life, so how do we do that?"

"We can begin with my grandfather. He is very old but still perfectly clear in his mind. If he can't answer our questions, he'll know somebody who can. Let's drive over and see him tomorrow."

"How far away is it?"

"That's hard to say. If he's on the reservation it's only about a forty-five-minute drive. If he's still on the summer reservation it's about three hours from here. But I don't think he's still out on the summer reservation. It's getting pretty late in the year, and he doesn't like to stay away from home too long."

"Can you find out?"

"Yes, but I think I have to wait until tomorrow morning." She looked at the clock on the wall. "It's already after nine, so they've gone to bed. He lives on a very strict schedule like most older people." Goggen smiled. "Then we just get to relax tonight."

TJ looked at him and thought to herself, *What a man.*

Thursday, 1 November

TJ smelled coffee when she woke up at 6.30. Goggen had already been up for a few hours.

"Good morning," she said.

"Good afternoon," he replied with a smile. "I didn't know if you were going to get up today."

TJ, not yet in the mood for jokes, just looked at him. "Coffee?" He got a cup and filled it for her. "I can see that you slept well."

She didn't answer him, just took the coffee and sat in the corner to drink it.

Goggen understood the situation and backed off a little.

"Sorry. It wasn't a good night for me. I had nightmares the whole night. Well, anyway, it felt like the whole night."

"Do you want to talk about them?"

"No, there's really nothing to talk about. I'll call my grandfather at seven o'clock. Will you be ready to go?"

"I've been ready for hours."

"I'll have a little breakfast first. Maybe it will put me in a better mood. Have you eaten?"

"No."

"OK then, what do you want?" She got out a frying pan and a box of eggs. "I'm going to make an omelette for myself."

"Why not?" he answered.

She said no more but busied herself making two omelettes. Goggen just watched her from the table.

It took a good hour before TJ began to be agreeable enough to talk to, but she was still not herself. They were in the car and had already been driving for half an hour.

She called her grandfather—who was at his home and fairly close. Goggen kept quiet until she said, looking at him, "I don't mean to be impolite. There are a lot of things I should have told you. I wish that I could talk to you about them.

"There are things that come back again and again. Earlier when that happened, it would make me nervous, but not anymore. Now I just get very angry."

She was now staring straight ahead. Goggen could sense that she was not seeing the road ahead, but was focused deep into her thoughts.

He didn't say anything, but he listened to every word that she said. He had wondered about when she would talk to him about all the bad things she had just alluded to.

All of a sudden, she said, "We should get there in about twenty minutes."

Nothing else was said before they turned in and parked in the front of TJ's grandparents' house.

Her grandfather had been sitting and waiting for them, so when he saw them pull in, he came outside. He took TJ into his arms and gave her a long warm hug. Then he came over to Goggen with an outstretched hand.

"This is Ole G. Olsen from Norway," TJ, formally introduced Goggen while Jimmy greeted him. "He's the one who came over to help with the investigation for Papa." Goggen could sense that he was being scrutinized by the peaceful old man standing in front of him. Anyone who came in contact with Jimmy immediately recognized how proud and dignified he was.

"Shall we go in?" He pointed towards the door.

TJ went in first and was greeted by her grandmother Peta. She also took TJ into her arms for a big hug before being introduced to Goggen.

They walked over to the living room, where Goggen was invited to sit down. He looked around the room. The décor was very different from what he was used to. Some of it was what you probably would find in a house of a First Nations couple. The décor was therefore compatible with their culture. It was very interesting. "Can we offer you anything?" asked Jimmy. TJ asked, "Do you have some coffee?" Jimmy looked over at Peta, who nodded.

"Then we would like a cup of coffee." TJ looked over at Goggen. Jimmy addressed himself to Peta again. It was clear that he was directing her about what to do. He then turned to Goggen and said, "TJ tells me that you both have some questions that I might be able to answer."

"Yes, and it concerns a George Nokoot. Do you know him at all?" "George Nokoot. Is he the one who is sitting in jail for life?" Jimmy looked over at TJ when he asked.

"Yes, he's serving a life sentence. We wondered if you could tell us anything about him."

"I don't know him personally, but I know who he is. He comes from the Buck Lake Reservation."

"Do you know any of his friends or relatives?"

"No, but his wife still lives down in the Buck Lake Reservation. I think I remember hearing that they got divorced. I met him one time. It was during a tribal meeting and rodeo down here at

Wabamun Lake. He came along with your cousin Iniwa [which means "buffalo"]. Other than that, I don't know anything else about him." "Do you know his wife's name?"

"No, but that should be easy enough to find out. You just have to contact the reservation office."

"Yes, I know that."

"What about this Iniwa? Where can we find him?"

"That I don't know. I haven't heard from him in more than fifteen years. He does have a sister, Koko. Maybe she can help you. She lives right down here."

TJ continued, "We have one more question. We have managed to find a DNA profile, and in connection with that I gave a sample of my own DNA to the lab. I gave it so that the laboratory would have a sample of mine so that we could eliminate any findings later that might be mine. Because of that they have now found a match to mine, except that it's a man. We found that DNA sample out at Abraham Lake inside a stolen car.

"Can you think of who it could be?

"Any DNA sample that matches with another has to come from a direct line, so it would have to be a brother or an uncle. I only had one brother, and he died in the fire. What about an uncle?"

Jimmy looked away from her and stared stiffly at the opposite wall. It was plain to see that he was having some kind of an inner struggle. "I have three children. Your mother, Sisiska, was the oldest. Then came your aunt Sinope, whom you know, and then the last, called Jim.

You never met him, and we don't know what ever happened to him. He and I have not had any contact in forty years or more. He is about ten years younger than your mother.

"He started getting into trouble at a very young age, and your mother tried to help him, but the more she tried the more difficult he became. He had a very bad alcohol problem."

"So, you have no idea where he is?"

"No. I don't even know if he is still alive. But we have never been contacted about his death."

"Was he married? Did he have any children?"

"I don't know." Goggen wrote something down in his notebook. "I don't remember so well anymore."

Goggen noticed that both TJ and Jimmy were watching him while he wrote.

Now Goggen said, "You mentioned a sister of Iniwa. Where does she live?"

"She lives down next to the parking area of the athletic centre. It's a yellow house. You can't miss it."

They must have rung the bell at least five times before Koko finally opened the door. Jimmy had warned them that she couldn't walk very well, but he'd said that she was home. She was always home; she didn't have any family, or at least not any except Iniwa. And nobody knew how much, if any, contact they kept with each other.

She looked at them questioningly.

TJ took the lead and introduced herself first. Then she introduced Goggen. She spoke the First Nations language again.

Koko invited them to come in.

It was a very poorly lit house and had just a table and two chairs by the side of an ancient TV set.

TJ asked, "I have never met you, have I?" "No, but I have heard of you," said Koko. "OK."

"It was your grandfather who told me about you. You have had it very tough."

TJ didn't answer that remark, but instead countered with a question. "We are in the process of investigating these cases, and while doing so Iniwa was named. Do you know where we can find him?"

"What has he done this time?"

"We don't know if he was involved in anything wrong. We only know that he had a person with him whom we are looking for. They were together down at the rodeo at Wabamun Lake twenty-five years ago. Jimmy remembered that.

"All we want to do is talk to him regarding some of the people he might have been involved with."

"You will find Iniwa at Drumheller prison." "What is he in there for?"

"This time I don't know, but I suspect it has something to do with being drunk and disorderly again. He can't handle alcohol. He's in for three years this time."

"That must be very difficult for you. The only one you have, and then he gives you nothing but problems."

She didn't answer.

"Can you tell me anyone he might keep contact with? A friend or maybe a girlfriend?"

"There were a few times that he would bring someone here to visit.

But that was a pretty long time ago."

"Can you remember who they were, or maybe even their names?" "No, I can't remember that, but what I do remember is that one of them is an ex-policeman. I also remember somebody named Jim. He came over two times, and both times they got so drunk that they couldn't stand up. One of those times the ex-policeman came with them. I don't think he came the other time."

TJ looked for a long time at Goggen before she framed the next question in her mind.

"That Jim, was he one of us?" "Yes, he was."

"Do you know where I can find him?"

"No, but I seem to remember that he had some kind of cabin at a place south of here."

"Do you know anything else about that ex-policeman?"

"Nothing. I just met him that one time. I do remember that he was polite. But that was the only time I ever had contact with him." "You can't remember a name?"

"No."

"Scott, maybe?"

Koko thought carefully. "Maybe, but it was a long time ago." "Did he have light or dark hair?"

"Light."

"Can you remember what kind of car he had?"

"It was green, and I think it was a station wagon. But I'm not very good with cars; I never owned one."

"How do you live now, Koko?"

She looked at TJ without answering.

"Come on now, Koko. You are my cousin. I'm only asking because you're family and you might need a little help."

Koko still wouldn't answer her.

"OK, I have a suggestion for you. I'll give you a little extra cash so you can buy yourself something special once in a while. In return I would like you to call me if you remember something or have any other information about Iniwa's friends. Do we have a deal?

"I would also like it if we two could have a little more contact. I also don't have very many friends. Do you think we could try to be friends?"

Koko looked at TJ silently for a long moment, and then the tears came. They were proud tears, TJ could see immediately, so she took Koko into her arms.

"Just cry. It'll do you good. Believe me, I know what I'm talking about. I have also been very alone."

Koko clung to her while she cried. TJ responded by holding her even tighter.

Goggen just looked at them.

"Have you been out to lunch lately?" TJ asked Koko.

Koko just looked at her. "Out to lunch? I haven't had enough to be able to afford food for lunch for the last month."

"Well, we're going out to have some lunch right now, and you're coming with us. I won't take no for an answer. After that we'll discuss what else we can do for you."

Koko asked TJ, "Why are you doing this?" "It doesn't matter why. I have my reasons."

Koko gave TJ one more look and then went to fetch her jacket. It was beginning to be quite cold in Alberta, and it was only the first of November.

"What do you want to get for lunch?"

Koko smiled weakly. "How about a burger?"

"A burger? Good idea. Have you ever been to Sizzlers?" "Not for the last thirty-five years."

"Then we'll go over to Sizzlers on Lakeside. You'll find the hamburger you want there."

Koko had a look of utter anticipation in her eyes.

It was only 11.30 in the morning, so not a lot of people had come to the Sizzlers yet. They found a table near the window. TJ said, "We have to go over there to order."

She looked at Goggen at the same time and signalled to him that she wanted to talk to him in private. It took a couple of moments for him to realize what she meant. When he did, he excused himself to go to the men's room. Three minutes later TJ came and met him where he was waiting for her, right outside the ladies' room.

"Can you go over to the shopping centre across the street and buy a proper jacket for her? She's a little smaller than me, and I take a medium."

Goggen understood immediately what she was referring to. Koko's jacket looked like something that should have been thrown in the trash years ago.

"Of course I will."

He smiled before saying, "I never thought I would be spending my investigative salary to buy a jacket."

Back at the table TJ said, "I passed by Goggen on the way back here. He got a phone call about the investigation and had to leave. He said he would be back as soon as he straightened it out."

Koko seemed satisfied with the explanation. They started up a conversation in their Native American language. Goggen returned after about forty-five minutes. He had a shopping bag with him.

TJ gave him a sign to wait before giving it to her. "Koko, is there anything else you want before we go?" "No, I'm satisfied."

"OK then, let's leave." They went outside and got into the car. Goggen took the wheel. "Where shall we go now?"

"Back to Koko's house," said TJ.

While they drove back, TJ sat silently in thought. Goggen knew what she was thinking, but he didn't ask her anything. If she wanted to say anything, she certainly would. He stayed in the car and waited for her when they got back to Koko's house.

Now they were on the way down to the police station in Edmonton. "I gave her five hundred dollars," TJ said, staring straight ahead.

Goggen heard what she'd said without comment.

"And she was very happy with the jacket. It fit perfectly. You have good taste."

He smiled.

TJ changed the subject. "Do you think we'll get to see the necessary papers on that Scott McKenzy?"

"That's a good question. We'll just have to keep our fingers crossed."

"Can I help you?" The receptionist at the Edmonton police station was an older policeman. TJ had already presented both of their cards. "We would like to see whatever information you have on Scott McKenzy."

The receptionist looked at them for a moment before he picked up the two cards and read them carefully. He didn't say anything, but picked up his telephone and punched in a number.

"I have two people here who want to see Scott McKenzy's file." He sat and listened to what the person on the other end was saying. "OK. Want to go to Hooter's after work?" Obviously, the receptionist was friendly with the person on the line. "OK see you there." He hung up.

"You two can go over there and wait." He pointed to some chairs and a table up against a wall. "David will come and get you in about ten minutes."

TJ thanked him politely and then went and sat down.

David came out in about twelve minutes.

"Sorry, but today we are changing over some systems, I have a lot to do."

David was about the same age as the receptionist, but that's where the resemblance ended. The receptionist was tall, dark haired, and muscular, while David was short and wiry and had very red hair. He also had a very big belly.

"What can I do for you?" he asked.

"We wish to see what you have for information in your files on Scott McKenzy."

David looked at TJ, then at Goggen.

"That's information that I am not authorized to show you."

"We are certified private investigators and his name has come up in a case that we are working on."

Goggen held out his official badge that showed he had a Canadian government licence to investigate. TJ did the same. David looked at both of them. Then he took their badges over to the receptionist and asked him to check the numbers on them. He came back.

"I apologize, but we are required to check all badges for authenticity before releasing any information. It's standard procedure." "We understand."

David didn't answer that. He just walked in front of them down the stairs to the archives.

"We're in the process of entering all this into the computer, but we have a lot more to do. OK, let me see, Scott McKenzy." He began to thumb through an alphabetic file. Then he wrote something down on a notepad. He turned to Goggen.

"We have three Scott McKenzys. Do you have any other information

I can use—middle name or address?" "No, but he is an ex-policeman." David began to thumb through again.

"Ex-policeman, hmm, let me see." He thumbed back and forth. Then he took out another list.

"That's odd. We don't have an ex-policeman by that name in this file." "OK, what can you give us on the three Scott McKenzys you do have here? Their ages, maybe?"

"The one is thirty-four years old. And there's one who's sixty-three. He's been on the Most Wanted list for several crimes, but we've never found a trace of him. The last one is also sixty-three, but he's in prison serving a life sentence. He's been in prison for almost thirty years." David looked up.

"Then it has to be the one who isn't in prison," said Goggen.

David wrote again on the notepad before he took it with him into the storage room. He came back with a box under his arm and put it down on the table in front of them.

"Here it is." He looked down into the box. "Everything is notated and marked. You are permitted to look through it as much as you like and to take notes. But you can't remove anything from here, all right?" "Yep. We'll just look through and see if there is any connection with our case. As I already told you, his name has come up several times in connection with our case.

"Can we use that table over in the corner?" Goggen pointed to a nice big table near the back of the room.

"No, you have to use this one here. Rules."

There were three folding chairs around the table. Goggen and TJ each sat on one of them and put the box down between them. Goggen soon stood up again. It was difficult to get the things out of the box while he was sitting down. He decided to dump out the whole box and start sorting the paperwork from there. There were six envelopes. They were each marked with an identification number and a chronological number. There was also a list of the contents of the box. TJ picked that up and began to read it. Then she checked the envelopes and counted them.

"David, here's something that's not right. The contents list says there are seven envelopes, but here there only six."

David came over and picked up the contents list. Then he counted the envelopes.

"That's funny. Nobody's been here to look in these boxes for a very long time."

He went back to his paperwork and began to thumb through it again. "Nobody has asked to see this information for more than seven years. At that point it was all here, or at least that's what it says on this. We always have to physically check all the contents and make sure they jive with the list after someone comes in."

David continued to thumb through his notes while TJ and Goggen started reading through the materials that were in the box. "Which of the files is it that's missing?" asked David.

"File number one," said TJ.

David continued to read through his papers.

TJ and Goggen had divided the envelopes between them and were each reading their own.

Goggen found two of the cases interesting and one he just couldn't get into. But he wrote it down nevertheless. Scott McKenzy had been involved in several doubtful happenings in which nothing could be physically proven. The happenings stretched a long way back. The shooting episode where the armed robber and shooter was killed was special. Here it was George Nokoot who had been the witness and given the alibi. There was no connection established between the two of them; it was only Goggen's research which had brought that to light. But there was also another shooting episode that caught Goggen's interest, an episode up at Hastings Lake. The witness there was Jim McCoy.

According to the report, there had been a shooting where McKenzy had been shot at first. There was a black man who had tried to avoid being accused of killing a woman. She was killed with a knife and was lying at the edge of the lake. She was only partially clad. The report said that the perpetrator had attempted to rape the young woman but that he had been interrupted by Scott McKenzy. Jim McCoy had been a witness from his canoe out on the lake.

The man's name was Johnny Walker, and the young woman's name was Judith Roberts. Both were from Edmonton.

Scott McKenzy had testified that he was only passing by and had decided to take a walk around the lake. He thought he might try his luck at fishing. Goggen felt that there was more to the story, just as he had felt about the story involving McKenzy's partner.

The case that Goggen couldn't identify anything special about was the one where Scott McKenzy had been first on the scene after a crime was called in. When they got there, nobody was around. They didn't think it meant anything, and they checked out the house. The owner was never heard from again.

Goggen asked David if he could give him a copy of those documents. "I'm not officially allowed to give you copies, but here's the deal. The copy machine is right over there, and it's turned on. I'm going to go to the men's room, and then I'm going to stop by and talk a little with Richard."

Goggen smiled but didn't say anything. He just winked.

TJ and Goggen were very busy during the fifteen minutes that David was away. When he came back, he asked, "How did it go?"

"Just fine. I think we have all the information we need, at least so far. Everything is put back in its place. You can check."

"OK, I will."

"When it comes to the last file, were you able to find out anything? I noticed that you went through a lot of trouble and materials after we found out that it was missing."

"How did you see that?"

Goggen smiled. "I have my methods."

"Well, I didn't find out anything much. It's either lost or misfiled. But the interesting thing is that the case was investigated by that day's police chief."

"What do you mean? McKenzie was the investigator of the case that has been lost?"

Goggen turned an amazed look at David. "Are you saying that McKenzie was the investigator of the case?"

"Yes, but he was also the investigator of the other two cases you were interested in."

"How long has McKenzie been the police chief here in Edmonton?" David thought about it. "I think about seven years now."

Goggen continued to look at David, without saying anything more. Finally, he spoke. "David, you have been a big help to us. Is there anything we can do for you?"

"No, I have just done my job, no more, no less." TJ asked, "Do you like hockey?"

"Of course I do."

"Do you ever go to any Oilers games?" "I wish. Way too expensive for me." "So, you watch them on TV?"

"Of course."

"I do too. David, it might happen that we'll come back, but if we don't, I hope you'll have a merry Christmas. Christmas isn't very far away from now."

David answered, "Merry Christmas to you too. If there's anything else I can do, you know where to find me."

Once they were back in the car, TJ picked up her phone and punched in a number.

"Hi, this is TJ Ellefsrud from Robert Blake, Inc. I would like to buy two season passes for the Oilers' home games. Do you have any available?" She waited. "Nothing?

"Oh, so you have some on the west side, row twenty-two? That's too far away. I know you have some better places than that." She listened politely.

"Sir, I hear what you are saying and I know what you have been told, but just please put me through to Ricard and we'll see what he has to say."

"You know Ricard Olson?" Goggen could hear the voice on the other end now.

"Yes, just check that out."

"We have some tickets left on the east side, row six." "That sounds much better. How much?"

"Twelve hundred dollars per ticket."

"OK, I'll take two. The name is David Hall. Send the bill directly to me." She gave him her address.

Goggen looked at TJ and smiled.

"It doesn't cost that much for some good cooperation." Goggen couldn't have agreed more, but he didn't reply.

"Can I get you anything to drink?" TJ asked Goggen. They were back at the ranch and in the main house.

"Yes, please. I'll have a Cutty. I'm worn out tonight." "What do you mean?"

"I don't know, I feel a little out of it."

TJ thought, *I could have maybe given you some strength.* She had looked at Goggen all day, and yes, she was in love with him. But she didn't know how to proceed. She had never felt this way before. And she knew even less about what to do.

It was true that she had gone to her bed feeling very warm several times. It was also true that he had been present in her fantasies while she had played with herself. Her orgasms had been a little different, but strong. Her thoughts about the tall, strong Norwegian had been very intense. She had no idea whether or not he looked at her as a woman. But she knew that he made her feel hot.

She put the glass of Cutty with ice on the table next to him. For herself she took a Coca-Cola. Just by looking at him she could see that he wasn't the same Goggen tonight.

He sat there with his own thoughts.

"Is there anything I can do for you?" She sat there hoping that he would say yes. She wanted so much to do something for him.

He just sat there and looked at her. Then he said, "I'm going to have one more of these and then call it a night."

She got up and reached for his glass.

"No, no, that's all right. I can do it myself."

"I know that, but I'm going to get it anyway. I'm just happy to do it."

She was suddenly afraid that he might discover what she felt for him.

She looked at him a little fearfully, but no, it didn't appear that he noticed her feelings. She was relieved. She went and got him another Cutty with ice, and this time she filled it up almost to the top.

"I thought you might like to take an extra-big one to bed with you."

Goggen looked at her and smiled.

"You read me better than I do myself. I'll see you at breakfast." He got up from his chair and went upstairs to bed.

TJ stayed where she was and turned on the TV. But no matter what she tried to watch, she didn't see it at all. She simply couldn't concentrate. He was inside her thoughts, and she wasn't able to get him out again. It had been over an hour since they had said goodnight. He was asleep for sure by now. Her thoughts wandered to thinking about what it would be like to lie next to him and sleep in his bed.

She would be naked and move closer to him. Suddenly her thoughts were interrupted by Barbara Mandrell coming on the TV screen and singing, of all things "Sleeping Single in a Double Bed."

Then it came again, that special feeling down low in her body. She wanted him badly. She thought that she must go and take a cold shower as soon as possible. She couldn't stand it any longer. Her body cried out for love and sex.

She tried to pry her thoughts loose from the song and her imaginings, but she couldn't do it. Instead she began to touch herself, first her breasts and then her stomach, before her hand went down into her belt and she found the most wonderful place. She thought to herself, *My daughter is in Edmonton, and he's sleeping, so why not right here, right now?* Then Goggen came into the picture in her mind. He had a big, stiff erection right down below his stomach. Now he bent down and began to lick her. She had read about such things but had never experienced them. It wasn't right. One afternoon at Joan's house, Joan's girlfriend had come into her room and began to fondle her. She had suckled her breasts, took off her clothes, and licked her where she was so wet right now. TJ didn't know what homosexuality was at that time in her life. Joan's lover had come up with a whole lot of explanations of what it was, but TJ didn't understand them. What she did remember was how good it felt, especially the licking. She had never told Joan about it.

But now, oh, having a man, particularly that man, do it to her was something she desperately craved. She had only read about it, but now she dreamed about how wonderful it would be.

Suddenly her thoughts came back to where she was and what she was doing right now. She began to work on her clit. Should she go to his room? Just the thought of it made it so very much more intense. Maybe she wanted Goggen to come out of his room and see what he was responsible for. Then the orgasm came, intense and powerful, very powerful.

It was so powerful that TJ was totally worn out and fell asleep. She awoke about a half hour later. She felt so very peaceful in her whole body. The suspense was over. She turned on the TV again.

Friday, 2 November

"Good morning. How was your night?" Goggen was standing in front of her with a smile.

"I can do nothing but complain."

"Complain? It's a new day with new possibilities. The world has not burned up, and we have a roof over our heads and food on the table. How can we possibly complain?" He looked at her with the same smile.

TJ just looked at him for a moment and then walked over to the coffeepot.

"What made you so positive today? Last night you almost didn't even say goodnight."

Goggen continued to smile.

"That was before I solved the case," he answered. "Solved the case?" TJ looked at him questioningly.

"Last night I didn't feel very well. That happens to me every once a while. But I didn't disconnect my thoughts because of that."

"OK, so what do you mean by solving the case?" TJ asked.

"I didn't solve any case. I was just trying to be funny. But I have thought through all of the answers that we have gotten in the last few days.

"I think the best when I am sleeping, or maybe I shouldn't say when I am actually sleeping, but I have the clearest brainpower between four and five in the morning. And this morning was no different." "What do you mean?" TJ asked.

"TJ, you are a fantastic girl—woman. I understand better than most what you have been through. But life must and will go on. You have shown me that you can handle situations that maybe most people wouldn't be able to, even without all the traumatic things that happened to you. That shows that you are an extremely strong woman.

"Now, since Robert is still in the hospital, have you called to check up on him yet today?"

"I called and talked to Mike about a half an hour ago. He's improving, but it's going a little slower than the doctors first thought. He's out of intensive care, but they want to hold him for observation for at least one more day."

Goggen heard her out and then said, "Like I was just saying, without Robert here it's just you and me left on this investigation. That makes it extra difficult. Robert is the one who knows how to open doors.

Now that we have to fend for ourselves, it's going to cause difficulties. Therefore, I think I'll have a talk with Patrick Jones today. I'm going to the little boys' room for a minute. Would you mind giving him a call and seeing if he can meet with us? Maybe we can get lunch together in the same place as last time. Do you remember where that was?"

"Yes, I do."

"He says he'll try to get there around 1 p.m., but he'll probably be a little late."

She didn't use the agreed upon code when she said this.

"What time is it now, 9.30? He looked at the clock on the wall in the kitchen and read the time out loudly. "That gives us some time. Let's look at the information we obtained yesterday."

"I see a thread here." "A thread?"

"A thread is a normal term used to express yourself in the investigative world. A thread is something like a connection."

TJ watched Goggen as he continued to speak. "We have now analysed the fingerprints and the DNA profiles. We have gone to see George Nokoot. He wouldn't say anything, but my feeling is that he knows something about the case. We can connect him to Koko's brother Iniwa, who's sitting in jail at Drumheller."

"Where is Drumheller?"

"It's located southeast from here, and northeast from Calgary. I don't know how long it would take to drive there, maybe four or five hours." "OK, let's concentrate our attentions on Scott McKenzy and Jim McCoy and see what else we can find out about the two of them." "We have a little time, so let's get on the computer and see if anything comes up on them."

They went into the other room where TJ had her computer set up. "Let's google them first. It's amazing how much information people put in these days."

TJ found Google's search engine and typed in "Scott Leroy McKenzy", then pushed Search.

The computer began to work. It took less than a minute for the results to come up. Up in the corner of the screen it indicated that 5,870 results corresponded with the search. TJ began to read from the top. Goggen had brought over a chair. He sat down behind her and read over her shoulder.

"Open up number seven."

TJ did what Goggen asked. Nothing came of it. There was a Scott Leroy McKenzy down in Texas who had died in 1998.

"Let's modify the search to focus only on Canada."

TJ found the search engine again and this time she put in "Scott Leroy McKenzy, Canada". She pushed the search button again, and this time there were 1,766 results.

They scanned over the pages again, and TJ punched in link number six. She read out loud: "Scott McKenzy, arrested for a bar fight down in Leduc." She continued to scan through, and then read out loud again "The former police officer got into a fight with two oil workers over a woman. The woman was an Indian, and the fistfight started after McKenzy had shouted racial slurs at the woman. One of the oil workers had told him to calm down and to apologize. That's when

McKenzy suddenly threw a punch at him that landed squarely in the face of the oil worker who had spoken to him. He fell backwards over a table. McKenzy drew out a knife and proceeded to attack the oil worker with it. The other oil worker came up behind him and prevented him from stabbing his friend. The other man got back up and helped hold McKenzy until the police arrived. Then he was handcuffed and taken away."

She read on.

"I'll be damned," said Goggen when he saw it.

"Scott Leroy McKenzy received a fine of fifteen hundred dollars, which was paid by his older brother, Mister McKenzie."

TJ looked at Goggen.

"McKenzy, McKenzie. Did he change the spelling of his name?" TJ became extremely curious now. She pulled up another search engine, one that Goggen had never heard of before.

"This is the official site of the Canadian government."

She typed in "Scott Leroy McKenzy". It took a little more time on this site, but then the search was over.

There were 671 Scott Leroy McKenzys in Canada. "Let me do that again."

This time she typed in "Scott Leroy McKenzie, Alberta". Results: sixty-seven people.

Both of them read over the list. When they got to the second page, they opened up number 37.

"Scott Leroy McKenzy, born McKenzie."

TJ wrote down his address.

"We have to get out of here or else we're going to be late meeting Patrick." Goggen was looking at his watch.

"Oh, you're right. I'll go grab my jacket. Do you want to drive?" "Sure," he said.

The conversation in the car was mostly about what they had just discovered online. But there was also time for some other things. "What is it like in Norway?" asked TJ.

Goggen looked at her before he answered. "How much did your father tell you about it?"

"Not very much. Most of what I know, I learned online."

"Have you looked at the area where your father and half-siblings live?"

"Yes, I looked at Kongsberg and at my father's address. I also read about the Norwegian political system. I know that four and a half million people live there and that it's one of the world's biggest oil producers."

"Well then, I'd say you know quite a lot. As you know, the temperature and climate are just about the same as here. But the air up here in Alberta is drier.

"Yes," TJ answered. "It's quite a bit colder here in the winter as well, and that is because of the great prairie."

For the most part TJ just sat and enjoyed listening to him. It was she who asked the questions, but it was the man sitting next to her who occupied her thoughts. It was almost physically painful to sit so close to him, the only man she had ever had feelings for, and yet he seemed so far away.

They had arrived at Shining Bank Lake and were now driving into the restaurant's parking lot.

The tavern lay in a very idyllic place right down on the edge of the lake. In summer it was absolutely beautiful, but now at the beginning of November it was mostly only locals who patronized it. There were only two cars in the parking lot, and TJ and Goggen didn't recognize either of them. Patrick had obviously not arrived yet.

They went in quickly, since winter was already showing its arrival. The first thing they saw when they entered was a sign that said, "Please seat yourself." In the summer months, no doubt there would be a host waiting to seat them. They walked in and found a table next to the window and far from the other two guests in the room.

The bartender saw them come in and approached with two menus in his hand, which he gave to them. He asked, "Can I get you something to drink?"

Goggen looked at TJ and said, "What would you like?"

"I'll just have a coffee, but I might decide to order something else in a little while."

"What about you?"

"You know, I think I'll have a Black Velvet with ice and a glass of club soda on the side, also with ice."

The bartender turned around and went back to get their order.

When he returned, he put a cup of coffee in front of TJ first, and then he set the whisky and club soda down for Goggen. The waitress came over and asked, "Have you decided what you would like to have?" "No, not yet, we're expecting one more person to join us."

"Oh, OK. I'll come back in a while."

"May I have a glass of Chablis?" TJ asked the bartender. "Sure. I'll be right back with it."

"Ugh, that is terrible coffee," TJ said with a grimace. "They must have made it about five hours ago."

The bartender came back with the wine.

"I'm sorry, but this coffee is undrinkable. When did you make it?" "I apologize. I'll make a new pot right away."

He left again.

"That was the worst coffee I have ever tasted."

"They probably don't sell much of it at this time of the year." "That's for sure. It's probably a little better if you put a lot of sugar and milk in it."

"Not me. My father taught me to drink my coffee black. He said that's the way they drink it in Norway."

"That's right."

That was the last bit of conversation they were able to have before Patrick suddenly appeared at their table.

"Wow. How did you get in here? We didn't see you coming at all."

He just smiled.

"Well, here I am. I'm sorry for being late, but that's just how it is sometimes. Have you ordered?"

"No, we've just been having a drink. Would you like one?"

"Yes, thanks. I told Erik I'm going to take the rest of the day off. He asked why, but I didn't answer him. It's been a lot lately."

"What will you have?"

"I'll take the same as you're having."

"You're absolutely right. I have a glass of club soda on the side."

"Forget about the soda. I like my whisky just the way it is." He smiled.

"What do you want to eat? I'm hungry." "I haven't looked at the menu yet."

"I have," said TJ.

"So, what are you having?"

"You both know that I'm a First Nations girl, so I'm going to have a buffalo burger."

"That sounds good. I'll have the same," Goggen said. "Patrick, what about you?"

"Why not the same? It's been a long time since I had a buffalo burger."

The bartender had already written everything down. "Do you want another?" He looked at Goggen's glass. "Yes, please."

He wrote it down and went away.

"So, how is it going out in Edson? Have you found out anything more about Mister Svensson's death?" Goggen asked.

"Not really. However, we have come as far as to know with certainty that he was murdered."

"Have you been able to find anyone who saw or heard anything?"

Goggen enquired.

"No. Nobody was seen arriving at or leaving the school. Neither did anyone see an unfamiliar car. It's frustrating. That's especially the case because we have determined that he was shot by someone unfamiliar," Patrick said.

"How did you deduce that?"

"What do you mean?" Patrick asked.

"So far you have said that he was murdered, but no one saw a stranger or a strange car. Nevertheless, you say that he was shot by an outsider."

Patrick just looked at Goggen before he answered. "Yes."

"And you believe that he was killed by someone outside of the local population. But you can't rule out the local population, right?" Goggen asked.

"No, but the way that the case is unfolding is what we are going by. The population out there is very small and investigating such a dramatic crime is difficult," Patrick answered.

"That's the point there. But it can also work the other way. The possibility of people noticing a stranger or a strange car is bigger with a small population."

"That is also true," Patrick replied.

Goggen noticed that Patrick wasn't comfortable with the present conversation, so he steered the subject over to their own investigation. "Did you hear that Robert had a heart attack?"

"No."

"We were down in Calgary in connection with the evidence we found at the cabin on Abraham Lake and from the cabin fire site. When we were on our way out of the police lab, he experienced a heart attack." "How is it going with him now?" Patrick asked.

"It looks like it's going well so far, but he's still in the hospital,"

Goggen answered.

"Let's hope it keeps on going well. What about your own investigation? Have you come any further with that?" Patrick said. "Actually, that's why we're here now," Goggen answered. He picked up the envelope he had placed on the chair beside him when they'd first gotten there. He took out all the pictures they had gotten from the DVD.

Patrick gazed for a long time at the pictures of Stanley's murder. Goggen spoke to him while he was looking at them and filled him in on what other discoveries they had made.

When Goggen was finished, Patrick asked, "You said you had found some empty bullet casings out where the car was parked. What kind of weapon did they come from?"

Goggen answered, "I don't know, but the size is nine millimetre. They are being investigated now, but we haven't gotten possession of the bullets yet. The police have them. That was one of the things I wanted to talk to you about. Do you think you can find out anything about them? I was hoping that you would be able to get us more information if you asked to see them in connection with the case you're already working on."

Goggen continued, "The other thing is, how do we go about investigating Captain McKenzie?"

Patrick took a long, hard look at Goggen. "Do you know what you are asking? This is a high-profile, decorated police captain," Patrick answered.

"Yes, I know that. But no matter what, he has to abide by the rules and laws that he has sworn to enforce. And I'm quite sure that there's been a few times he hasn't." Goggen had a very determined look on his face.

"You yourself must have noticed how time after time his name comes up in relation to these cases. Especially where Scott L. McKenzy and Jim McCoy have been named. That stretches way back in time." Patrick sat and nodded while he listened to what Goggen had to say. Then he said, "I see that. The question remains, how do we go about checking on him?"

Goggen was looking at him. "We can begin by taking a look at all the cases that he has been involved in. Now that I've been in Canada for a while, I understand that the Canadian police document all cases and crimes."

"Yes, you are correct."

"So that would also pertain to Captain McKenzie. I can't get access to that information, but maybe you can."

Patrick made no comment. He sat and thought for some time before he said, "If I find out where we can get this information, and I pass on the information you need to look at these cases, can you and TJ do the investigating? It probably is a special link and code needed."

"If I get the link and code, then we would be all set," said TJ.

Patrick said, "I am assuming that there's a giant amount of material to go through, and to be honest, it's too big of a job for me to tackle."

"I realize that," said Goggen. "If you can give us what we need to get in, we'll do the work."

He continued, "Now let's get back to the dead principal. I am, without any particular reason, convinced that the murderer or murderers are to be found among the people we are now investigating. As I said, I don't have anything concrete, just my gut feeling. I have learned to pay special attention to it over the last many years. The weapon that was found in his hand, was it registered?"

"No, we didn't find any papers on it. But it is the type of weapon commonly used by police."

Just like Goggen thought, an unregistered weapon.

"Did you get a hold of the bullet? And would it be possible to compare it to the others?"

"No, it was totally destroyed. It was most likely scored with a cross at the tip so it would tear apart."

Goggen asked, "What about the casing?" "We have that, of course."

"Good. I'd like to check it out and compare it with the casings from the cabin fire and the site of Stanley's murder."

"Do you believe there could be a connection?"

"I don't know for sure, but I need to rule out all possibilities."

"OK then, I'll send it up to you, or have someone bring it just as soon as possible."

Goggen asked TJ, "Can you think of anything else that we might have forgotten?"

"No, I don't think so."

"Then it's time to eat. I'm absolutely starving now. Do we want to have one more round?" He looked at everybody's empty glasses. "Yes, why not? Like I said, I'm going to take the rest of the day off." "TJ, should we take the rest of the day off too?"

"What do you mean?"

"Shall we let investigating work be investigating work and take the afternoon off?"

She smiled at him and said, "I didn't know you were able to do that. I thought you needed to work 24/7."

"Well, I'm sure that my brain won't take the afternoon off, but I can. Let's go book into the local bed and breakfast, and then take a companionable night together out here in Shining Bank Lake." Patrick looked at Goggen and said, "Why not? I haven't had a night out on the town in several years." He laughed at himself when he said it. The town consisted of four small houses along the water, one country store, and a gas pump.

CHAPTER 16

Robert came home five days after TJ and Goggen had met with Patrick. He had the shell casings from the cabin fire with him. Goggen had told Steve that there was no need to specially transport them. At the time he'd said that, Robert was supposed to come home two days later, but as it turned out he didn't come home until five days later. So Mike took them and drove them to Edson.

The telephone rang in the main house.

"Hello, this is TJ."

"Are you coming over or what?" asked Robert.

"Yes, but I'm right in the middle of something at the moment. We'll come over in about an hour. How do you feel?"

"Pretty well. You'll see for yourself in not very long."

The telephone conversation was over.

"He's waiting for us." "He just arrived home."

"You only know one side of Robert."

"I told him that we are busy right now with something that's going to take at least an hour."

"I heard you say that. What are we busy with right now?" "Investigating Captain McKenzie."

"OK, I'm going to go and take a shower."

TJ immediately began to wonder what it would be like to wash

Goggen's back for him.

Did he know how she felt? No, she didn't think so. He couldn't possibly be so controlled if he knew.

"Come in, come in." It was Robert himself who opened the door. "Are you alone?"

"Yes, Lori is out shopping. So, come in and tell me, what have you found out?"

"Wait just a minute. Didn't you receive orders to take it easy?" "This is taking it easy. I can't understand how anyone can get better while they're in the hospital. People come and go, personnel as well as visitors. There's always noise."

"I guess that's true. Well, since we've talked to you last, there have been several interesting things discovered."

TJ began to inform Robert, with Goggen occasionally breaking in. Robert sat still and listened. When she was finished, Robert said, "OK, so what have you found out about Captain McKenzie?"

"So far we have barely begun to investigate him."

"Very well. TJ, tomorrow you come over to my house and work so that I can be involved in the investigation."

"But Robert, you're supposed to rest."

"I'm resting now. Come over right after breakfast." TJ looked at Goggen, "Do you agree with that?"

Robert looked menacingly at Goggen. He didn't say anything at first, but then he came out with, "Let's take those sons of bitches," and smiled.

Goggen couldn't do anything else but smile back. TJ did the same. They said goodnight to Robert and walked back to the main house. Once they went inside, Goggen asked TJ if he should make some coffee or if he could get anything else for her.

"No thanks, it's getting late and I need my beauty sleep." "Believe me," said Goggen, "you don't need any beauty sleep."

She looked at him and smiled. She said goodnight and went upstairs to her room. She lay there on her bed and thought about what he had just said. Had he begun to notice how she felt about him?

Goggen sat downstairs in front of the TV and began flipping channels. When he couldn't find anything of interest, he took out his notes instead.

Shall I have a Cutty or not? he asked himself. He went to look in the bar cabinet. He went and got some ice from the freezer. The TV was still on and it was tuned to a local station. He had the sound turned down.

He sat and went over his notes. He thought that his first priority must be to try to find both Scott McKenzy and Jim McCoy. He was going discuss it with Robert tomorrow morning, to find the best way to go about it.

He wanted TJ to concentrate on Captain McKenzie.

He picked up the remote control to turn off the TV and go to bed. A strip across the bottom of the screen caught his eye: "Breaking News. A man's dismembered head was found up in a loft in the Hamptons on Hope Road. Stay tuned for the eleven o'clock news."

Goggen read the trailer. Then it came up on the screen again. He read it again. He got up, turned off the TV, and went up the stairs. Halfway up the stairs it suddenly hit him. The Hamptons? Hope Road? Wasn't that where OJ had a house?

He hurried back downstairs and turned the TV on again. While he was waiting, he thumbed through his notes one more time, but there was nothing in them that said anything about OJ.

Should he call Robert?

Before the thought was fully formed in his mind, the telephone rang. "Goggen here."

"Do you have the TV on?" "Yes."

"Did you read the trailer about breaking news?" "Yes."

"Come over here. The news doesn't start for another nine minutes." "I'm on my way."

Goggen ran out, grabbing his jacket on the fly.

Robert was sitting glued to the TV screen when he came in.

"OJ's address was Hope Road 11." Robert already had some papers in front of him. "The house was sold by his family over thirty years ago."

"Let's hear what the police have to say."

The commercials were over and the eleven o'clock news came up on the screen.

The news announcer appeared.

"Today's top stories: A disembodied head, appears to be a male, was found in the attic of a house in the Hamptons.

"The mayor denies taking bribery money to help build his new house. "Prostitution is not as profitable in Edmonton now that some new laws are in place.

"The weather: Well, winter is on its way. There's going to be some snow in the Jasper area, maybe as much as twenty centimetres. "Edmonton will only get about two centimetres of the white stuff, but it's a start. Better get out your winter jackets."

After a few commercials, the newscaster returned on the screen. "Tonight, a head, which appears to be a male, was found in the attic in a house that is under refurbishing at the Hamptons. The police are on the scene."

The picture came up from the scene. "What can you tell us about this?" asked the reporter, as he stood and interviewed Captain McKenzie.

"It's too early to say anything about it yet. We got a call regarding a find of a human's head at this address."

Robert said, "What the hell is he doing there? He's the police chief!" Goggen said, "He is the police chief. He has a lust for publicity, and he knows more about this case than he wants anyone to know. He's going to take full control of this investigation."

Robert looked at Goggen.

"Do you mean what I think you mean?"

"Well, if you think that I mean this man knows more about this than he wants you to know, the answer is yes."

"I think so too," said Robert. "Let me make a couple of phone calls. "Goggen, if you want anything to drink, please help yourself. I'll be back shortly." He went into his office.

Goggen could see from where he stood that Robert was browsing through some documents. Then he picked up the telephone.

He couldn't hear what Robert said, so while he waited, he went and got himself a Coke.

"Robert came back into the living room and said, "The house where the head was discovered is Hope Road 11. Captain McKenzie has named himself as the investigator."

Goggen looked at Robert and asked, "What do we do now?"

"What we do now is go and get my car. I'll be ready in ten minutes." "Wait a minute, Robert. You're supposed to take it easy."

"That's what I'm doing."

"That's what you're doing? It's the exact opposite."

"Well, if that's true, then there's something wrong with Webster's dictionary, because that word is incorrect. See you in ten minutes. The car key is hanging in the hallway."

Goggen went and got the car.

"Don't bother with all the extra equipment. Just use the regular controls on the car. The hand controls are for me." He smiled when he said that.

The trip took about a half hour. There was no traffic that late in the evening. There was a police barricade on both ends of the street. Robert presented his badge to the police officer at one of the barricades. Lt. Robert Blake, Royal Canadian Mounted Police, Private Investigator. The officer looked at the badge and gave it back. "What can I do for you?"

"We have been engaged by the present owners of this house, in addition to the previous owners. We are representing their interests in this case."

"This is a police matter."

"We know, but we do have the right to follow the investigation." The policeman looked one more time at Robert and then said, "I suppose you do." He let them in.

"Was it the family you called before we left?"

"Yes, I called the current owners. I don't know where OJ's family lives at this time. The current owners have called me a few times previously in connection with some other issues. They have never lived here themselves; they have always rented it out."

Another police officer showed up, and Robert gave him the same ID. He asked him who the lead investigator would be. "Captain McKenzie," he said.

"The chief of police?" Robert asked.

"Yes. He felt that he needed to be involved in this case again, primarily because he didn't want to lose touch with his grassroots investigations skills, he said."

Robert looked at Goggen but said nothing. "Where can we find him?" Robert asked.

"He's inside the house." "OK, thanks."

"Hey, Goggen, do you think you can get me up those steps?" Robert

pointed at the steps at the entrance of the house. "I suppose so. Maybe he can give us a hand." Naturally he said yes.

Captain McKenzie was standing inside the living room, looking up to the ceiling.

"Hey, do you remember me?" Robert said.

McKenzie turned around to see who was speaking. "What are you doing here?" he said.

Robert produced the same credentials that he had shown before. McKenzie looked at them and said, "Robert Blake. Should I remember you?"

"Maybe. We have investigated the same cases several times now. It was you who investigated the case when I was shot and got injured." "Oh yes, now I remember. What are you doing here?"

"We are engaged by the owner of this property." "Well, this is a police matter," said McKenzie.

"We know that, but we will just follow the investigation as the law allows us to do."

Goggen could see that McKenzie did not like this answer. "OK, you gave me your card, so I'll call you when we're done." "No, I don't think so. We'll hang around if you don't mind."

McKenzie was obviously irritated, but he didn't answer. He just turned around and looked up at the ceiling again.

Robert looked at Goggen and smiled triumphantly before he asked, "What have you found so far?"

"We found an old skull upstairs in the attic." "How old is it?" asked Robert.

"Hard to say, but it's been there a long time." "Found anything else?"

"No, and there's no indication that there is anything else, either. We have now gone through everything and nothing else was found. We are now about to conclude our investigation. Where the skull came from is impossible to say. It could be a skull that the previous owners had found somewhere somehow and had just forgotten to take with them when they left. It's old." "Do you have it here?"

"Yes, we have it in a box." "Can I see it?"

McKenzie was again annoyed.

"It's not much to look at."

"Well, we'd like to see it anyway."

McKenzie nodded at the policeman guarding the door and said, "Let them see the evidence." And then he turned away.

Robert told the policeman to take the object out of the box and put it on the chair next to him. Goggen and Robert began to study it.

Goggen took his camera out of his pocket and began to take pictures. He looked at Robert and then pointed to the skull, but he didn't say anything. Robert followed the pointing finger with his eyes. The skull had a clear mark, and the mark was a crack, most likely a crack from a heavy blow. Goggen took several pictures of it from different angles. He turned the skull upside down and pointed again, this time at some marks at the base on what had been the neck. He took some pictures of that too.

"What do you think you're doing?"

Captain McKenzie had just come into the kitchen.

"We are inspecting the skull and taking some pictures," Robert answered.

"No pictures. We won't allow any pictures to be released to the public."

"Then we won't be able to determine the cause of death," Captain

McKenzie said.

"That's nothing for you to think about. We couldn't care less about who you are."

"Have you seen this?" Goggen pointed to the crack mark in the skull. "Yes, of course. Somebody must have dropped the skull on the floor or something."

Goggen and Robert just looked at each other.

"Or, maybe someone used a very hard object to hit the person on the head while he or she was still alive."

McKenzie looked at the mark again.

"No, that's a mark from hitting the floor. I have seen marks like this many times."

At that point Goggen and Robert realized that there was no point in discussing it with the captain any longer. "What are your plans for both the house and the head?"

"Well, I can't see where there is anything else to be found in here. We'll take the skull with us. We'll see if we can identify it."

"So, the police believe themselves to be finished here and the owners can freely use the house again?"

"Yes, I don't see any reason why not."

"Well then, in that case you won't have anything against us looking around a little ourselves. We promised the owners who engaged us that we would do so. They would like to rent out the house again as soon as possible."

"I don't mind at all." "OK, thanks a lot."

McKenzie and his policemen immediately left the scene.

"How did that man become the person he is?" Goggen asked in amazement.

"He can't possibly be aware of what we know and that we've begun to investigate him."

Robert didn't answer; he just put his finger up to his lips, the common signal to say nothing. Goggen understood at once. The police might have placed some kind of listening device somewhere.

"I think we should drive home now. It's late and I'm feeling tired. Let's come back again tomorrow morning."

"OK."

"Let me see if I can find a key so we can lock the house up." Goggen came back almost at once. "We can go now; I found the key. Now the next question is, how do we manage to get you down the steps?"

"It'll be easier than getting me up the steps. Tomorrow morning we'll take the portable ramp that I have at home."

It was almost 3.15 when they turned into the driveway at the ranch. "Are you still feeling OK?" Goggen was a little worried about Robert; he had been through a lot in the last week.

"Sure, I'm all right. Bring TJ with you to breakfast around ten o'clock."

"Ten sounds good. See you then."

Goggen had a lot of scattered thoughts in his head as he entered the main house. He went directly to the room where TJ had the computer equipment set up and found the cable he needed to transfer the pictures from his camera to the computer in order to print them out. As they came through, he pressed the "copy to disc" button. It only took a few moments until the computer asked, "Do you want to save the images, or do you want to run them?" He punched "save", then printed all of them out. Then he took all the pictures out to the comfortable chair in the TV area. There was a good lamp in there. As Goggen sat and inspected the pictures, he found it almost impossible to believe that a police officer, a highly qualified and decorated one, could not see that the crack in the skull had been caused by anything other than a fall to the floor. He now understood more clearly why Robert had so many unanswered questions about the investigations of all that had happened to Nils Henrik Ellefsrud and his family.

Saturday, 7 November

Goggen had no idea how long he'd sat there and thought about all this.

He suddenly woke up. TJ was standing in front of him.

"Did you sleep here the whole night?" "What time is it?"

"Eight thirty."

Goggen then proceeded to tell her everything that had happened the night before.

TJ sat still in wonderment and just listened.

"We're invited to eat breakfast at Robert's. He asked us to come around ten o'clock."

TJ didn't say anything; she just went back upstairs. She came down again in about fifteen minutes.

"OJ didn't have any children, but I remember meeting his brother and his children once. They gave me their address at that time, but we haven't kept in touch. At this point I don't even know if they are alive or dead. I do not know if we can find them or not in order to match up their DNA to see if it is OJ."

"Good morning, TJ. Did Goggen tell you what happened last night?" "Yes."

"Did he tell you who the lead investigator is?" She nodded. "Well then, are you hungry? Lori has made pancakes. If you don't want them, there is also bacon and eggs."

"Robert, I didn't tell you earlier, but I'm trying to watch my weight. You never know if a prince might come along and offer me half of his kingdom. If that happens, I can't be fat."

"TJ, my friend, the prince will come. You just have to allow him to come. Now as to the subject of fatness, I don't see where you have to think about that at all. You look absolutely fantastic. What do you say, Goggen?"

"She is a sight for the gods."

TJ thought to herself, *If only you knew who I want the prince to be.* Robert looked at Goggen and asked, "Have you given any thought to how we should inspect the house today?"

"Well, first I think we should hire a cadaver dog." "A cadaver dog?"

"Yes, don't you have that here in Canada? It's a dog that's specially trained to seek out dead bodies. We should get one to check out the whole house and garden."

Robert didn't comment. He was busy writing in a notebook. Now he answered: "Yes, we do, but if the cadaver dog can't find anything, what do we do then?"

"We are totally convinced that there is more to find either in that house or on the property. McKenzie doesn't think so."

"McKenzie isn't interested in finding anything. I thought you agreed with me about that."

Robert answered, "I am just trying to focus, focusing in from several angles." Goggen spoke again. "Do you know how to get a hold of a cadaver dog?"

"I have a friend up in Jasper. But I don't know if he still has Tilla. If he does, she's pretty old now."

"Could you give him a call?" "Of course."

All of a sudden TJ asked, "Where did they find the head?"

"They found it when the owners were renovating. They pulled back the insulation and got themselves a severe shock," Goggen answered. He continued, "Robert, have you spoken with the owners of the house yet?"

"No, I was just getting ready to call them."

"Ask them if there have been any renovations lately. If there has, then we'll most likely know which walls are going to be stripped and so on. Just in case we don't find a cadaver dog."

"Where do we begin?" Goggen had looked around before he spoke. Robert's friend who owned Tilla the cadaver dog had told him that she was too old to work anymore. He apologized. And he didn't know anyone else who could help them. He was sure that the police had connections with those who could. But he didn't know any more about it.

Robert got a message from the house's owner saying that the house was going to be totally renovated, so it didn't matter which walls they wished to break into.

Now Goggen was standing with a sledgehammer in his hand. TJ had also found one. They were both dressed in coveralls and wearing gloves.

"Where do we begin?"

Robert just shrugged his shoulders. "It's all the same to me. It's like a lottery."

Goggen walked over to the outer wall nearest to the kitchen wall. The wall was made up of plasterboard, so it wasn't difficult to knock a hole in it.

After only three hits, Goggen was able to tear a piece out of the wall and look in behind it. He used a crowbar that he had brought with him. There was nothing to see.

TJ started on the other side, doing exactly the same as Goggen. There was nothing to see there either. They continued like this for most of the day without finding anything of interest. It was almost three o'clock and they were starting to get frustrated.

Robert had been watching them all day without saying anything. "What do you think, Goggen, did we make a mistake?"

"No. It's here somewhere."

He pounded down another wall. Still nothing. He gave two more tremendous blows with the sledgehammer, and a large piece of the wall fell down. He was extremely startled. There was no need to look any further. Along with the big piece of wall, the remains of a person fell down.

"Bingo!" called Robert.

TJ just stood there, riveted.

Goggen set down the sledgehammer and carefully looked behind what was left of the wall. He used his crowbar to pry out the rest of the skeleton that had not fallen out when the wall came down. He put the pieces back together like a puzzle in the order that they would normally be in.

Everything was there, the upper body, hips, and legs. Only the hands and the head were missing.

Robert now began to study the skeleton as it was laid out on the floor. "One of the ribs is broken." He studied it in detail, rolling his wheelchair around the floor and checking out every centimetre of it. "Goggen, will you give me those two brown objects that are lying there in the sheetrock pieces?"

Goggen tried to see what Robert was pointing to. Then he saw them too. He looked at them for a long time before he handed them to Robert. They were two slugs, one very damaged and one almost like new.

"I'm going to knock down those two parts of the wall too. Do you see how this part of the wall is thicker than the part we have torn down? Since it's extra thick, there's more room behind it."

"Yes, we might as well tear them down too. It's only those two that are left."

Goggen went back for his sledgehammer and knocked down most of the wall. Then he addressed the last one. The same happened again: a big piece of the wall fell out. It was obvious that that part of the wall had been modified. He looked behind what was left of the wall, and way down in the corner he saw a backpack pressed between the two wall sections. Goggen turned his whole body around so that he could reach in as far as possible, but he still couldn't reach it. He grabbed the sledgehammer and gave a third tremendous hit. Then he was able to take hold of the backpack.

He took it out and opened it before he had turned it right side up. The contents fell out on the floor.

The contents consisted of clothes and shoes. There were also some papers. Goggen immediately gave the papers to Robert so he could inspect them.

He lifted the sledgehammer again and knocked a hole in the last part of the outer wall in the kitchen. This time it was only one good hit, and about 80 per cent of the wall came down. Dust flew everywhere. When Goggen looked into this last part of the wall, he saw two laundry bags in there. He emptied one of them, and out came what looked like a towel. Wrapped inside it were the two hands.

He emptied the second bag, and its contents appeared to be only laundry of some kind. Goggen looked at it a little closer and it appeared to be a bed sheet. It was full of dark brown streaks. "Blood," he said. "A lot of blood."

TJ stood at his side and was also looking at the sheet.

Robert heard what Goggen had said and looked up. He reached out his hand and gave Goggen a pair of official documents.

Goggen took them and turned them around to read them. They were two official Canadian government documents.

One of them was OJ's official immigration document to Canada, and the other was his registration paper for the ownership of a 9-millimetre pistol. It was a 9 millimetre that was used at the cabin fire.

Goggen looked at TJ. She appeared to be totally calm.

"Let's see if we can find any fingerprints on these papers." "I'll ask Mike to drive all of this down to Steve."

They had already taken the two slugs and put each in its own small bag, which he marked. Now Goggen put the sheet back in the laundry bag. "Let's take this with us too." He looked at the skeleton and took out his pocketknife and scraped a little off the leg bone. It was very porous. He scraped a little more and then put it into its own little plastic bag.

Goggen said, "Now that we've found what we need, let's put everything in the car. Is Mike at home, Robert?"

"I don't know, but I will call him."

"Do that, and tell him that he can meet TJ on the way. I want to get this down to Steve as soon as possible, before anyone knows that we found it. Wait a minute, let me cut out a little piece of the bloody sheet." He got the bag, took out the sheet again, and said, "Steve will only need a couple of centimetres. That way no one will be able to see that we have taken any of it away from here. Just in case anyone is watching the house.

"I know that we didn't find any bugs earlier today when we searched the place, but that doesn't mean that they aren't watching us.

"TJ, I want you to take the car and drive to where you can meet Mike. I want you to take Robert with you. This is enough for him now; he is not fully recovered yet.

"I am going to stay here and wait for the police. We have to call them. This has now become a police matter. So now we'll see how interested they are in investigating it."

As soon as Robert and TJ left, Goggen called the Edmonton police. "This is Ole George Olsen. I am a private investigator. I am now in the house at Hope Road 11 in the Hamptons, the same place where you found the skull yesterday. I have now found a skeleton."

The dispatcher on the other line asked, "Can you please repeat that?" "You will find me at the Hamptons, Hope Road 11, where you found the skull yesterday. I have now found a skeleton. Do you have that?" "Stay where you are. We'll be right there."

Goggen used his time wisely while waiting for the police to arrive by taking a lot of pictures. It took the police exactly twenty-four minutes to arrive. Captain McKenzie got there about ten minutes after that. He came directly over to Goggen.

"What is it that you all have found?" "Not us, only me."

"What do you mean?"

"You know who Robert Blake is. You also know who TJ Ellefsrud is, but you don't know me."

McKenzie looked at Goggen for a long moment before he said, "That's true. I don't know you. But I have a feeling that you're going to tell me who you are."

"Yes, I want to do that, and I'll begin right now." McKenzie looked directly into Goggen's eyes. "We can begin with this investigation."

"What do you mean by that?"

"What I mean is that I had the pleasure of studying you last night and of seeing just how you conduct an investigation. I have never, and I mean never, seen a sloppier investigation in my entire life.

"A construction worker finds a skull that was supposedly hidden up in the attic. Instead of launching a complete investigation, you sweep the whole thing under the rug and say that the previous owner must have found it or bought it somewhere, then hidden it up there and forgotten it. Then you proceed to look at clear and distinct marks of blunt trauma on the skull and try to explain them away by saying that somebody must have dropped it on the floor. Then you closed the investigation.

"I'd just like to tell you, Mister McKenzie, Captain, that now is the time to investigate as it should be done. I have looked at your résumé, and it's very impressive. So why is it that every single case that involves Nils Henrik Ellefsrud and his family has never been solved?" McKenzie didn't answer these charges. He stared back at Goggen, but his gaze began to waver a little. "Are you threatening me?" "Absolutely not."

"So why did you come up with these statements?"

"Because enough is enough. You have protected your youngest brother long enough."

It was very obvious that Captain McKenzie didn't like this. "What do you base these allegations on?"

"Come on, any investigator with normal intelligence can see that there is something big going on here.

"You have always striven to be the investigator in all cases that involve Nils Henrik Ellefsrud or his family." "Who is Nils Henrik Ellefsrud?"

"You know very well who I am talking about. One of his family members is TJ, whom you have met many times." "Have I met her before?"

"You know very well that you have met her before."

"Robert Blake, whom you met last night, was a personal friend of Nils Henrik Ellefsrud. You also know him very well."

Captain McKenzie stood very still. He didn't try to interrupt Goggen. "Who is it that has such a hold over such a highly decorated officer as yourself? Is it Scott Leroy McKenzy? I was shocked after observing your work last night, but I didn't yet know why. You don't realize that people notice things. Believe me, people notice more things than you would want them to sometimes.

So, here you have a corpse, and a few other things. I am now waiting to see them handled in a professional manner." Goggen held McKenzie's gaze while he explained what he should and shouldn't do in regard to the evidence in front of them.

Then he waited for a reply, but McKenzie remained completely silent. "I know that I can't prove what I have told you as of yet, but I will find the necessary answers. And, oh yes, I will use every resource available to me to get them. I forgot to tell you, my résumé is pretty impressive too. And it lists all of the cases I have worked on, with none of them left out. You can take that statement for what it's worth. "I've seen what I need to see here today. I'm turning it over to you.

But before I go, can you tell me where I can find your brother Scott Leroy McKenzy?"

He received no answer, just a tired look.

Goggen walked out and away from the house. He didn't have a car, so he just walked down the street in the direction from which he had come. It was a windy and cool evening. It felt good to be out in the fresh air. He was still considerably stirred up from his conversation with McKenzie.

CHAPTER 17

"Did you send the materials out to Steve last night?" Goggen asked. They were eating breakfast with Robert again.

"Yes, Mike drove down with them as soon as we gave them to him at Crow Hill."

"That's great. We should be getting some answers before too long." "TJ, can you continue checking out Captain McKenzie? I had a long conversation with him last night out at the house in the Hamptons." "How did you end up getting home?"

"I took a taxi. After my talk with McKenzie, I walked down to the mall. I needed to get some air. I was planning to call you from there, TJ, but on the way down I walked into a TGI Friday's and got something to eat. I was sitting and chatting with the bartender afterwards, and it got to be late, so he ordered a taxi for me." "What did you say to McKenzie?"

"I told it to him like it is." "What do you mean?"

"I told him that the police work I had seen him do the day before was some of the worst I had ever seen in my life." Robert looked at him questioningly.

"I told him that we know why, and I wondered what hold his younger brother McKenzy had on him since he was always protecting him.

I also told him that we couldn't prove it yet but that we would use every resource available to us to get the answers we need. So, at least now they know where we stand."

Robert asked Goggen, "What is your agenda for today?"

"I want to go back to the cabin on Abraham Lake. I want to see if I can find anything else out there."

"I don't think you should go out there alone." "I'll go with you," said TJ.

"What about McKenzie?" asked Robert.

TJ said to Robert, "You can do that investigating as well as I can. If I give you the code and the link, you'll get right in."

"What do you say, Goggen?"

"That's fine with me."

"OK, TJ goes with you, but I want you to take a pistol along with you too."

"Why should I take a pistol? I've never needed one before." "And let's hope that you don't need one now. But after McKenzie tells Scott or Jim what we know, and you can be sure that he will, then they'll also think to go back to the cabin and check to make sure that there's nothing there for you to find. We know what they are capable of."

Goggen didn't argue with Robert's logic. He just promised to take the pistol with them.

"It's also going to be very cold out there, so be sure you dress warmly enough. TJ, you know how it gets."

"Yes, I do. We'll be sure to do that."

The drive out to Abraham Lake normally took two hours. They had about fifteen minutes left before they would arrive. "It looks like we're going to have to walk the last part of the way. I think the snow is too deep for the car to get through," TJ said.

"Yes, it looks like we have to."

The area had just gotten about ten to twelve centimetres of snow. They got out of the car and brought along the backpacks they had with them. Goggen was carrying the metal detector he had bought earlier.

It was cold, with a north wind blowing. They walked at a good pace, but not so fast that they would sweat; otherwise later they would freeze.

After about forty-five minutes, they were near the cabin. Everything seemed very still. The only tracks they had seen belonged to several kinds of deer. TJ explained which tracks belonged to which type of deer. Goggen wasn't totally unfamiliar with deer tracks either. Now they had finally gotten through. They stopped right at the edge of the woods and had a good look at the cabin before going any further. There didn't appear to be any people there.

The cabin was dark and no smoke came out of the chimney. They walked the last few metres up to the entrance door. Goggen tried the doorknob. It was locked. The last time they had been here it had been open. He looked for the key again, but it wasn't there this time.

He took out a dirk. TJ saw him and said, "Are you the type that uses one of those?"

"I don't know. I've never used one, but I'm going to try." "I've never seen anything like that except in the movies."

Click. Goggen had successfully picked the lock. He slowly opened the door. He waited for a moment and listened before he proceeded. Everything was totally still.

TJ followed right behind him. They closed the door, because it was windy and freezing outside. Goggen tried a light switch. Nothing happened. Maybe the power was turned off. He tried another one, and this time a light came on. It was a light bulb over what might have been a dining area.

"Do you think there is any kind of heating system in here?" Goggen asked.

TJ smiled. "That would surprise me."

Goggen understood what she meant. He set down the metal detector and took off his backpack. He opened one of the side pockets and took out a flashlight.

"TJ, I want us to do this together." "How do you mean?"

"I want us to go through the house together, and whatever happens, we are together."

"All right. Any special reason?"

"Several reasons. First, four eyes see much better than two. And as you know, I'm a former policeman. We were always trained to do things two by two."

TJ asked him where they should begin.

"I've gone through this cabin before, but the first thing I want to check again is the fireplace and the chimney. After that, we'll look behind the bookshelves over there. Then I'm going to look for a false hiding place or room, and then eventually the floors and walls." "OK."

"All right. So, as I just said, I have checked everything in this cabin before, but that was then. I think we have to start over as though we have never been here. There have been people here since last time." The cabin was old and not very well maintained.

They had come to the kitchen without finding anything of interest. They had taken out and checked behind all the books in the bookshelf, then taken out the bookshelves themselves. This wasn't so difficult, because there weren't very many books. They looked through a cabinet that stood along the wall. Goggen tried to pull it out, but it was screwed to the wall.

After that they had moved the chairs, sofa, and table without finding anything, so now it was the kitchen's turn.

They didn't find anything interesting in there either. It began to get dark outside. They had been working more than four hours. Now there only remained the bedroom on the inner side and the crawl space. Goggen walked into the bedroom.

"Here's something that isn't right. Do you see that cabinet? Look at the depth of it. Now look on the outside and you can see a big difference." TJ looked at both the inside and the outside of the cabinet and saw immediately what Goggen meant.

"Yes, there's a big difference. What do you think it means?"

"I don't know for sure, but I think there's a false room in the back. See? It's like that on this side too."

"I need to get my tools out of the bag." He turned around and left the bedroom to get his backpack.

How long he had been unconscious before he awoke he had no idea. It must have been quite a while. Now he was sitting in a chair almost naked, with his hands tied behind him. TJ was lying on the floor, also tied up and with even fewer clothes on than he had. Even under such terrible conditions as this, he couldn't help but notice how beautiful she was.

Two men were standing in front of her. Goggen recognized one of them from the DVD that was taken out at Gleniffer Lake. He was the one who had shot Stanley. The other man was unknown to him.

It was cold in the room, very cold. But Goggen didn't feel it at all. It was unmistakable that the man from the DVD was the leader.

"You people just couldn't let the case alone?" "What do you mean?" asked Goggen.

The man shifted his gaze away from TJ to Goggen.

"Who are you?"

"My name is Ole George Olsen."

The man looked at him for a long time.

"And what are you doing here?"

"I am fulfilling a request from a friend." "And who is that?"

"Nils Henrik Ellefsrud."

"So, he hasn't understood any of our messages so far. We have sent him numerous warnings about what would happen if he didn't stop snooping into our business. We clearly let him know that more of his family and friends would have bad things happen to them.

"How is he doing these days?"

"He is very well, thank you. Especially now that we are starting to find answers to the different happenings."

"Answers to what? You don't know shit."

"You can believe whatever you like, but there is a good reason why we are here. Why would we come back here to this cabin a second time to do a more thorough investigation if there was nothing to find?"

"What you say doesn't mean anything at all because you both won't live long enough to tell anyone."

"We're not the only ones who know about it. We have already put together a pile of evidence that all points to you, and there are people working on it as we speak. We are just the errand boys. If you kill us, it will only make it that much worse for you. They know where we are and what we are doing."

"So that's why you brought the 9-millimetres with you?"

"You might just say that. We brought it in case we met up with somebody like you."

"Then you don't have a very good use for it now." "The day isn't over yet."

Goggen had a sense that the man's self-confidence was still very strong.

"But now that you are going to kill us anyway, can't you tell us why you have run such a campaign of terror against Nils Henrik, as well as his family and friends?"

"Oh, wouldn't you like to know."

"Yes, we have used a great deal of time and resources on that." "Money, money, money, my friend."

"I'm not your friend. I would die before I would be friends with someone who could kill and injure women and children. It's way beneath my dignity."

"What does it matter? They're only half-breeds." "What are you talking about?"

"Half-breeds like your girlfriend here." "Half-breeds? What about your friend Jim?"

"Jim, he has passed the test even though he is a First Nations." "What test?"

Goggen didn't get an answer to that. "Who is it that is giving you money?" "Now you're asking too much."

"Well, like I already mentioned, it would be nice to know before a man dies. And it can't matter much to you whether we know it or not. You've already planned how the evening is going to end."

"You're right. The money came from across the border." "The States?"

"Yes, but through straw men in Edmonton."

"Interesting. Did it have something to do with the building collapse?" "Not us, but those same people did."

"What about OJ? What ever happened to him?"

"What happened to him? Bloody hell, that's the reason you're here. If those workers hadn't found his head, and then you the rest of him, everything would have just stayed like it was."

"How do you mean?"

"My brother told me everything. He even told me that after the conversation that you had, he was not going to be able to protect me anymore. I got really pissed off at him, and told him what I was going to do. But now I have the problem solved tonight."

"Shooting us doesn't solve the problem. I already told you that a lot of people know about this. When I say this, I mean the murder of Stanley and the killing of the school principal in Edson. We have pictures of you shooting Stanley. And, to top it all off, we know who you are and what your real name is. Goggen could see the anger building up inside Scott. "You know, everything has its price."

Scott didn't answer.

"Jim, why don't you cover your niece? She's freezing. Haven't you already done enough damage to your family?" Goggen said.

Jim's eyes began to waver.

"You should be ashamed of yourself. I have spoken personally with your father, a proud chief, and for him to have such a son …"

It was very clear that Jim didn't know how to answer or what to believe.

"I still hate that man Nils Henrik."

"Why? He took you in, gave you a job, and guaranteed you a percentage of what you would find at the gold mine. But it wasn't enough. You had to have more, so you stole from those who had shown a willingness to give you a chance at a better future.

"It was your sister who asked Nils Henrik to fire you. She was a proud woman, and she couldn't live with the fact that the man whom she loved and who gave you a job should be fooled by you. She was already wildly in love with him, and she would later marry him." Goggen stopped there.

"We were three and should have split it three ways. But that's not the way he wanted to do it."

"But did you take part in running the business? Did you invest any of your money in it?"

Jim didn't answer.

"Jim, give TJ some clothes. She's freezing. If you're going to shoot us anyway, you don't have to kill us with the cold. Have you ever been cold, Jim?"

Jim grabbed the bedspread and threw it over TJ where she still lay on the floor. While Goggen had talked to them, he had met her eyes many times. She had looked scared, of course, but he sent her as many positive signals with his eyes as he could. He believed from the looks she gave back to him that she understood and believed him.

"Which one of you raped your sister? Was it you, Scott, or was it Jim? Jim, did you rape your own sister?

"So, it was you who raped your own niece, a nine-year-old little girl." Goggen knew that he had scored a direct hit now. He also knew that the cold was beginning to take its toll on him. He had to find a way to get a hold of the pistol that lay next to Scott.

At least they hadn't turned on any more lights than the one he had turned on when he and TJ first entered the cabin. This had enabled him to work in secret with the knot they had tied around his hands. It was beginning to loosen. He could move his hands more and more. TJ was holding very still, but Goggen could see that her eyes were very dark, like they had gotten the last time they talked about the cabin fire.

Then her voice came forth in the First Nations language: "May you rot in hell for all eternity, you sick disgrace to your people!"

That's all she said, but Goggen could see in her eyes that she hadn't given up.

A door suddenly squeaked, and both Scott and Jim jumped up, startled, to their feet. They stood silently and listened while looking at each other. Everything remained quiet. They were just about to sit down again when the sound came again, maybe a little louder this time.

Scott and Jim were now on high alert. They sneaked quietly into the bedroom from where the sound had come. Scott had taken out his revolver, while Jim pulled out a knife. They didn't look back at Goggen or TJ. The pistol that Goggen had taken with him was still lying on the table.

Scott was already through the bedroom door, and Jim followed behind him. Scott pushed the door carefully closed so that he wouldn't show his silhouette from the light in the other room. He pushed the door with Jim right behind it.

There came that sound again, but this time maybe from the roof or the loft. Scott must have also decided that the sound came from up in the loft. Then came a tremendous crash as Scott shot the revolver. Then he fired it again and again. He continued shooting until the revolver was empty. Goggen counted six shots. Scott had emptied the chamber before he was even sure where the sound had come from.

But that was exactly what Goggen needed. He ripped his hands free from the rope and took the distance from the chair to the table in two steps. He had the pistol in his hand.

Scott and Jim were still in the bedroom. It was quiet again. They were standing and looking up while they listened. The sound came again, and again several shots rang out.

That was the moment when Goggen decided that if he and TJ were to come out of this with their lives, he would never complain about the cold north wind again. He had realized right away that it was the strong wind from outside that had caused the creaking, probably from a window that wasn't closed properly.

And Scott had extra shots with him. Good to know. Himself, he only had the one magazine. Ten shots. Goggen threw a leatherman's tool over to TJ. She saw it coming, and stuck her hands out from under the bedspread Jim had given her. They had tied her hands in front of her. She held the tool and was able to get the pliers out, but she couldn't cut the rope with them. She had to pull out the knife.

Scott and Jim continued to listen, but now it was totally quiet. They started to move towards the living room again, but their full attention was still focused on the loft. Now they were back in the room. TJ had taken out the knife. Her hands were loose under the bedspread.

Scott shifted his gaze from the loft and back to them again as if to reassure himself that they were there where he had left them. His gaze brushed past the table, but it didn't seem that he noticed that the pistol was gone. But as he readied himself to sit down again, the realization slowly penetrated his brain.

He lifted the revolver again as he turned towards Goggen. Some new shots thundered through the room, but this time they came from the hand of Goggen.

Scott's rotation became even more pronounced as the bullets hit him. Goggen shot again, this time lower. He hadn't had any time to place the first one, but now he tried not to hit a vital part of Scott's body.

Jim realized the situation when Scott roared, "Goddamn! He's got the pistol!"

He threw himself on to TJ, with his knife in the attack position. TJ rolled over quickly and Jim hit the floor instead. That gave TJ time to come up into a crouch and get ready for him.

She pointed the leatherman's tool with the knife out and for a brief second was glad that she hadn't folded it up again. Now she lifted it and stabbed at Jim. She hit him in the shoulder, and could feel the knife go into his muscle, right up to the hilt. He screamed. She drew the weapon out and stabbed one more time. This time she hit an area nearer to his back. Then she accidentally dropped the knife. Her eyes were totally coal-black. She saw Dr Irvine Jr.'s face in her mind and she tried one last time to stab, but Jim was on his feet and running out of the room as fast as he could go.

TJ let him run. Scott was lying on the floor, trying to turn around and get the revolver that he had dropped. Goggen went over and kicked the revolver out of Scott's hand just as he grasped it. He saw that Scott still would have intended to kill them both.

"Are you, all right?" He addressed himself to TJ. "Yes, I'm all right."

Goggen bent down to check Scott. He could see that he had been shot in the thigh. He began to turn him around. He had a big bloodstain high above his stomach region, a bloodstain that was growing larger every minute. Goggen looked for the bullet hole. The first shot had hit Scott there, a little high up. He'd probably been shot in the lung. He was still alive, but if he didn't get medical help soon, it would be too late. There was nothing Goggen could do for him.

"Where did Jim disappear to?" "I don't know, he just ran out." "TJ, keep your eyes on the door." "OK."

Goggen moved Scott into a better position and saw that the sore on his thigh was much less serious. But the one in his abdomen was still bleeding badly. He ran into the bedroom and grabbed a sheet that was lying on the bed. It had most certainly been there for many years, but he didn't have much of a choice, so he took it out into the living room. He ripped it into strips and found something hard to hold them in place. He packed some of the strips into the wound first. Then he wound the strips around Scott as tightly as possible to try to stop the bleeding.

He checked Scott's pulse, which had already begun to weaken.

Deep inside himself he knew that he probably wasn't going to be able to save Scott's life. Should he go looking for Jim? No, he didn't want to leave TJ alone. He looked down at her and saw that she was staring straight ahead.

"What did they do with our clothes?" Goggen began to look around. They had to be here somewhere. There they were, thrown into a corner. He went and got them and first put on his own before coming over to TJ with hers. Then he saw that she had begun to cry. He sat down on the floor next to her, took her in his arms, and held her tightly. She answered him silently by putting her arms around him, returning his embrace. Neither of them said anything; there wasn't anything to say.

Goggen didn't know how long they sat like that. It didn't feel like very long, but it must have been a while. Suddenly TJ pulled back and looked him directly in the eyes, and then she pressed her mouth to his. One of her hands moved up to the back of his head and pressed him tightly to her. He answered her fully and completely with his own kiss. She let go of him for just a moment, and said "sorry" in a deep low voice, but he immediately pulled her back to him and continued the kiss. She felt a deep sense of well-being, stronger than she had ever felt in her life, while the kiss was happening.

Scott was trying to talk.

"Is there something you want to say?" asked Goggen.

It was obvious that he was trying to get something out. Then a very weak voice asked, "Where is Jim?" "I don't know. He just ran out."

Scott was thinking. It was clear that he was in a lot of pain.

"There is a cabin up on Pigeon Lake that you might want to inves—" Goggen felt for a pulse, but there was none. Scott Leroy McKenzy was history.

Goggen looked up at TJ with a look that she understood at once. He took the blanket that TJ had covered Scott with and drew it up over his face.

They just looked at each other.

"What do we do now?" He looked at his watch and saw that it was 1.23 a.m.

"Let's try to get some sleep. We've got a long day ahead of us."

"We can't do anything for him here, and we don't know where Jim is, so let's go into the bedroom and lock the door. If anyone comes in, I'll hear them."

"What about the loft?" TJ looked up.

"I'll tell you right now that I'll never complain about the north wind again."

"What?"

"The sounds up in the loft were caused by a cold front that passed through, by the north wind."

TJ just nodded.

Monday, 9 November

As soon as they got back to David Thompson Highway, they got cell phone coverage. "Robert here." "This is TJ."

"Where have you been? You were supposed to contact me last night." "A lot has happened."

"Tell me."

TJ told him everything that happened the night before, and Robert just listened.

"Do you two have any idea what happened to Jim?"

"No, but we followed a trail of blood all the way back to where we had put our car. There were tracks of another car right there." "OK, call the police. You will have to remain there until they arrive. You have to give them the weapon that Goggen had. Do you understand?"

"Yes, we know that. We're waiting on the road where we parked."

It took almost an hour for the police to come. It was a Lt. Louise

Armstrong and three constables. TJ began to relate the happenings of the night before. They listened attentively.

"Here are the weapon and the knife that were used." She gave them both the guns and the leatherman's tool.

"What were you doing out there?"

"Well, as you saw on our badges, we are private investigators, and it was an investigation we are currently working on that brought us there. Scott Leroy McKenzy was one of our prime suspects, together with Jim McCoy. He was the other one who was here, and also the one I stabbed two times with the knife that you now have. He got away, but we don't know how far he got. We followed a trail of blood all the way down here to the road over there."

"OK. Shall we go up to the cabin now?" asked Lt. Armstrong. "How far is it?"

"About three and a half miles right up in that direction." "Where is the road?"

"I think it should be all right for us to drive up there with your all-wheel-drive vehicles. Our cars are also a lot higher than yours."

It took about ten minutes to get back up to the cabin. It looked just as deserted as it had when TJ and Goggen had arrived the day before.

This time they walked right in. There was no reason to believe that anyone would be waiting for them this time.

When they came in, everything was exactly as they had left it. They immediately began to explain to Lt. Armstrong how everything had happened.

One of the constables took pictures. She periodically asked questions, which were answered factually by TJ or Goggen.

They showed her all the bullet holes in the bedroom ceiling where Scott had emptied his revolver almost two times. She asked them if they had gone up there to see what made the noise. They answered no, adding that there was too much going on downstairs and they would have lost control of the situation had they done so.

"How do we get up there?" "There's a trapdoor in the kitchen."

There was a string hanging down from the trapdoor. Goggen reached up as far as he could and got a hold of the string. Then he pulled the trapdoor down. There was a folding ladder. One of the constables helped Goggen get it down.

"Will you go first?" Goggen asked Lt. Armstrong.

"No." She pointed to one of the constables. "You can go."

He took out the flashlight that was attached to his belt and climbed up. It was a completely open room with a window at each end. After a brief look around, he climbed the rest of the way up and into the room. Goggen followed behind him. There was nothing up there but some old empty trunks, some old cardboard boxes, and a cabinet that stood right in the middle of the room with its doors open. He had already seen what was in the cabinet—absolutely nothing. He closed the doors and commented: "These are the doors that saved our lives." He studied them a little closer and opened and shut them a couple of times. His assessment was absolutely correct. The same noise came again. He wondered where the draft had come from, since both of the windows were closed. It didn't really matter.

He went down again.

"There is nothing up there but a couple of old trunks and an empty cabinet with the doors open. You can go up there and see for yourself."

"No, that's all right."

"Do you need us to stay here any longer? You know where to find us if you have any questions."

"No, you can both leave. Will you drive them down to where they have their car?" she asked the constable who had helped Goggen with the trapdoor.

"Of course."

"Do you have cell phone service yet?" TJ looked at her phone. "No, not yet."

"OK, as soon as you get coverage, call your grandfather and let him know that Jim is alive. But you must also warn him. Let him know that he is wounded and you don't know where he is. I don't know how many friends he has, but we do know that one of his friends, maybe his only friend, is dead. He is hurt and probably needs help. So, it's possible that the next thing he'll do is seek out family.

"We're only talking possibilities now, but I want your grandfather to know right away. To be forewarned is to be forearmed."

TJ understood immediately what Goggen meant.

She had coverage now and called her grandfather. The conversation was in their own language, so Goggen had no idea what she said or how she said it. He could only assume that it was what he'd advised her to say. He interrupted her for a moment: "Say that he is wounded and could be dangerous and that they should call us right away if he shows up."

She talked to her grandfather for a few more minutes before hanging up.

"My grandfather was very saddened by this news. But he did promise to be on the lookout and to call us at once if Jim shows up."

"Good."

"Now I think we'll try another conversation with Captain McKenzie. Can you please call and see if we can get through to him?"

She punched in the number of the Edmonton Police Department. After finishing her phone conversation, she said to Goggen, "He is at work, but he doesn't want us to meet with him there. Instead he wants us to come to his house tonight after six o'clock."

"Do you have his address?"

"No, but he's going to text it to me."

"OK. That gives us enough time to swing by the ranch and change our clothes. Shall we call Robert and ask him to have some food ready for us? We could stop somewhere on the road, but we need to talk to him anyway."

"Let me call him and see what he says."

After hanging up, TJ said to Goggen, "He's asking Lori to make us some lunch."

"That sounds good."

Robert sat and listened to Goggen tell him everything that Scott McKenzy had told him. He didn't say anything; he just listened. But when Goggen was finished, he turned to TJ and asked her, "How do you feel now?"

"I don't know yet. I haven't taken those sons of bitches who raped and killed Mama yet."

He caught a glimpse of those black eyes, which were back for a moment.

"And what about Albert? We haven't gotten any answers regarding him either."

Neither Goggen nor Robert commented on what she'd said, as her assessment was completely correct. They hadn't found out anything about him yet.

"I'll go over with you to Captain McKenzie's if you don't mind." Robert looked enquiringly at Goggen.

"Of course. I guess you'd like to use your own car?" "Yes. Just give me ten minutes and I'll be ready to go." "OK, I'll go get your car in the meantime." He went out. TJ was left sitting alone with her thoughts.

"Ready to go?" She jumped when Robert spoke. "Yes, yes, of course."

She jumped up quickly and rushed out of the door, grabbing her jacket as she went.

Cameron Heights was one of the best areas of Edmonton. Captain McKenzie had sent a text to TJ indicating that his address was Chahley Court NW #4. He lived very comfortably in a big house with a double garage. Lights were lit up in every part of the house, both inside and outside.

It was probably Captain McKenzie's car that was parked outside. There were four steps up to the front door, but this time Goggen was able to back the car up to the steps and use the portable ramp that they had with them. This enabled Robert to get easily to the front door.

They rang the bell and waited. Nothing happened. Goggen rang the bell again. There was still no reaction. Goggen suddenly got a very strange feeling.

He tried the doorknob. The door was open. He signalled to Robert to stay put. Then he started to enter the house. "No, Goggen, wait a minute. There's a Beretta in the glove compartment of my car. Take that."

Goggen went back to the car and got the Beretta before carefully entering the house. TJ followed behind him. The house was totally quiet. Goggen moved forward very slowly, checking every millimetre of the room with his eyes: first the entryway, then the kitchen, the dining room, and the living room. Everything was still perfectly quiet, but quite suddenly the smell of a newly fired gun met his nose.

He looked past the door marked "Office". He slowly went towards it after silently signalling TJ to stay where she was. He pushed the door in order to go into the office, but it wouldn't move. He pulled it outward instead. The smell of gunpowder was even stronger here. He crept silently into the office and saw a large desk made out of mahogany with Captain McKenzie lying face down on it. He was holding a pistol in his right hand. His head lay in a pool of blood on the desk. Nobody else was in the room.

"He has shot himself," said Goggen to TJ, who had just joined him at the office door. "You can go and get Robert now."

TJ turned around a little too fast and lost her balance for a moment. Goggen thought, *It's getting to be a little too much for her now.*

She came back a short time later with Robert.

"TJ, don't look at this. You can go into the kitchen and sit down. There's nothing you can do here anyway." Goggen held her in his arms for a moment while he said this.

"Yes, I think I'll do that. I don't feel very well." Robert could also see the change in her.

"What have we here?" he asked after she had gone out to the kitchen. "Suicide. He knew that he was going to be implicated, and he couldn't bear to think about how he would be hung out to dry by the media." "He brought it upon himself."

Goggen gave the letter that was on the desk to Robert. It was formally addressed to him, Lt. Robert Blake, Royal Canadian Mounted Police. Robert studied McKenzie where he lay.

"It looks like he put on his best uniform before he did it."

Goggen also examined the corpse. "It looks like you're right. What did he write in the letter?"

Robert took his glasses out of his shirt pocket, opened the letter, and began to read out loud.

I address you today with your official title from the Royal Canadian Mounted Police Force, a title you earned in honour, in contrast to the one that I earned and am ashamed of. I have been ashamed for a long time, but there's a long distance between being ashamed and actually doing anything about it. And every day that passes makes it more and more difficult.

Now is the time for me to come clean, once and for all. I just don't want to be around when everybody hears the truth about Captain McKenzie.

The problem began when I was a very young cadet in the police academy. It was at the cadets' ball that it happened. These balls were part of the cadets' learning experience. To make a long story short, I met a fellow classmate and he and I fell in love. Yes, I am a homosexual, and that was not accepted in the police ranks at that time. We managed to keep our relationship a secret for almost two years, or until I discovered my partner had stolen from me. I was angry and disappointed, and I ordered him to disappear out of my life forever.

That's when he turned on me and said these words: "If you throw me out, I'll go to the school officials and report that you are a homosexual, and then I'll go to the newspapers." I went absolutely crazy with anger. My baseball bat was standing nearby in the kitchen. I grabbed it and hit him on the head so hard that he sank to the floor. I didn't stop there. I kept hitting him until I couldn't hit him anymore. Then I began to cry. I knew that he was dead.

I sat there for many hours crying with my lover lying dead on the floor in front of me. I didn't wake up out of the nightmare until I was startled by someone ringing the doorbell. I didn't know what to do. It was my younger brother Scott standing out there innocently ringing the bell.

I let him in, which is something that I lived to regret many times afterwards. He helped me get rid of the body. We rolled it up into a carpet and carried it outside, but first we went to Eaton and bought a new carpet, which we brought inside. In this way we hoped to fool the neighbours who might have seen us, making it look like a simple new carpet purchase. We dumped the corpse into an incinerator, still wrapped in the carpet.

We never talked about it again, Scott and I, until one day much later when he called me and asked me to meet him at the Horseshoe Saloon. There he told me that he needed my help to cover for him so that nobody would suspect him in a missing person case out on Hope Road. If I didn't help him, then he would report me to the police in connection with the murder of my lover Frank.

By this time, I was a police inspector, so I used my influence to take charge of the case, and the missing person was never found. You probably know the rest of the story now.

About two months later Scott came to me again. This time it was about a cabin fire out in Jasper.

That was more difficult, but after the building collapse in Jackson

Heights, I was able to link the two cases together and bring the cabin fire case over to the Edmonton Police District. That included the cabin fire and the episode when you were shot,

Robert. Every time the name Nils Henrik Ellefsrud came up, it was turned over to me. This suited me very well. But the shooting episode caused me a lot of problems. It was nothing less than a highly respected Royal Canadian mounted police officer who was shot. And now I was so deeply embedded in the deceptions that there was no way out for me, or at least not if I wanted to keep my highly respected status.

The earlier case was easier for me to cover up, just a guy who had an Indian squaw and two half-breeds. That was the last time that Scott asked me for help until about six weeks ago, when the school principal was killed out in Edson. The problem was that this wasn't yet linked with any of the other crimes I had taken into my jurisdiction, so I couldn't do anything about it.

Scott was furious that I couldn't help him, but there was just no way to help him this time. The murder of Stanley out at Gleniffer Lake was something different. I have known Stanley for over twenty years, and we worked together many times. He was a great man, but unfortunately for him I discovered him stealing money from the evidence room. It was wrong of Scott to shoot him. He told me that there was no way to get through to him. And there's one more thing that you don't know. The man who went with Stanley to Gleniffer Lake was Scott's son, who, by the way, has also gone wrong. He lives at the following address: Apt. 4C, 46th Street, Fifty-second Avenue, Leduc.

When you contacted me again today and wanted to talk with me, I knew that the day had come, the day when I would be exposed, lose my job, and be degraded in the news media. I didn't think that I could handle it, so I made my decision to end it here. But before I did it, I needed to explain these things to you, Lt. Robert Blake, and also to say with all sincerity that I truly am sorry and I apologize for all the terrible things that my brother did to you and to your friends.

That also includes the little girl. I can't remember her name any longer. I am, to put it mildly, totally worn out and defeated, and my head is no longer working the way it should. I would ask you to forgive me, even though I don't deserve it and you probably won't be able to do it.

I have one favour to ask, and it's totally up to you whether you want to do it or not. When you call the police to report my suicide, would you just give the last page of this letter to them? And please, if you can find it in your heart, keep the rest just between us.

Robert read the last page, meant for his eyes only.

It is with deep frustration that I do this. I have battled with these feelings for many years, and was never able to come to terms and accept them.

I don't wish to live any longer.

I am a homosexual.

Signed,

Captain McKenzie, Police Chief, Edmonton Police District

Robert looked at Goggen. They sat looking at each other without saying anything.

It was Robert who finally broke the silence. "What do we do with this?"

"I don't know, but we have to call the police."

"I know that's what we must do, but what about this?" "Who do you know in the Edmonton police?"

"Right now, I don't know anyone whom I'm sure I can trust."

Goggen knew what he was thinking.

"There's the police master, a politician as well as a policeman." "If we call the police station and ask for the next in command, we won't get any answer."

"Do you know the mayor?"

"No, but I do know where I can get a hold of him." "OK, get busy."

Goggen went into the kitchen to TJ. She was sitting on a chair and staring straight ahead. He got down on his knees and took her into his arms. She let her head fall down on his shoulder. He could hear her crying quietly. He let her cry without saying anything at all.

Forty-five minutes later the deputy police chief drove up to Captain McKenzie's house. His vehicle was escorted by two other police cars. Then came the mayor of Edmonton. They all went directly in. "Which one of you is Robert Blake?"

"I am."

The mayor went over and greeted him. So did the assistant police chief.

"And who is this here?"

Robert introduced TJ and Goggen to everyone.

The assistant police chief had already gone into McKenzie's office. The mayor also went to the office door, but when he got a glimpse of what was in there, he turned around. His complexion had turned a shade that was almost grey.

The deputy chief came out again.

"OK, I have to ask you what you are doing here tonight."

Robert explained to her the reason they were there. She listened to him, as did the mayor.

"Was there any note or letter here?"

Robert brought out the letter that was addressed to him. The assistant chief of police began to read the part that was addressed to Robert only. Every time she finished a page, she handed it to the mayor for him to read. When she was finished, she waited for the mayor to be finished. She didn't say anything; she just looked at the mayor. He thought for a long moment before saying, "What a scandal."

"Yes, what do we do? Do we give it to the press?"

The mayor was still thinking.

"I believe we should do what McKenzie asked and just make public the last page."

"I agree," the deputy police chief said.

"Like hell you will!" TJ's eyes were coal-black again. She had read the letter after Robert and Goggen.

"That motherfucker has ruined my life and the life of my whole family and some of my friends. He put Robert in that wheelchair! Plus, the case isn't solved yet. We don't even know for sure if my twin brother was killed! That man is going to be hung out to dry so everyone can see what kind of man he really was! If you don't do it, then I will!"

Her eyes were snapping with righteous indignation while she stood there and told the mayor of Edmonton what he was going to do.

He looked at her uncertainly, and then he looked at the deputy chief of police.

"She is right. Scandal or not, this has to come out to the people."

He took TJ by the hand. "Thank you," he said. "And I, as well as the government of Alberta and Canada, can never apologize enough for what you and yours have gone through."

Tears began to flow for TJ again. The mayor gave her a warm and earnest hug.

Then she turned around and walked out of the room.

The mayor gave his order to the deputy police chief: "Start the investigation, and don't tell the press more than necessary."

Goggen, TJ, and Robert had seated themselves in front of the TV and were waiting for the eleven o'clock news.

All three of them had visited Robert's bar cabinet several times, and the conversation began to be very relaxed. Goggen had his Cutty and ice, and TJ was drinking her father's favourite, Canadian Club mixed with 7 Up. Robert was sipping a beer very moderately because he was still taking a few medications for his heart trouble. But he wasn't thinking at all about his heart trouble right now. The trial which was the current breaking news had been up on the screen every ten minutes.

"This is the eleven o'clock news."

The newscaster said, "Edmonton's popular chief of police has today brought about his own death. He was found in his house with a pistol in his hand, and the police say that it appears so far to be suicide. "Mayor Thompson has just held a press conference, so let's hear what he has to say."

"It is with a heavy heart that I must give the news that Police Chief McKenzie has found it necessary to end his own life. He was found tonight at six o'clock by some acquaintances whom he had arranged to meet with at that time."

"Who were these acquaintances?"

"No questions at this time. It looks like Captain McKenzie chose this way out due to some earlier crimes committed. They are now being fully investigated, so we cannot comment at all at the moment. We will come back to this as soon as we are finished with this investigation. Deputy Chief Sampson will take over as police chief until a later date. Thank you.'

"Well, there you have it, Edmonton's police chief, Captain McKenzie, has taken his own life, and Deputy Chief Sampson will take over for an undetermined time."

Robert found the remote control and turned the TV off.

"You two can sit here for as long as you like, but I need to get to bed right now. See you both in the morning."

He turned his wheelchair around and rolled himself into his bedroom.

"So, what do you say, Goggen, shall we go too?"

"Yes, let's go. We have a lot of things to do tomorrow too. We'd be wise to call it a night."

Once they got back to the main house, Goggen asked her, "How are you doing? Are you, all right?" "Yes, I'm all right now."

"Are you sure? You've been through an awful lot over the past few weeks."

"Yes."

Goggen watched her out of the corner of his eye. He wasn't sure she was telling the truth.

She said goodnight to him and went upstairs.

Goggen did the same. He needed to get some rest. The last few days had been hard on him as well.

How long he had been asleep he didn't know, but suddenly he awoke feeling a naked body right up against him. He acted as though he were still sleeping, but he was aware of every millimetre of her body. She was lying so that she was partly on top of his upper body and her head was on his shoulder. She was stroking her hand very lightly over his hairy chest. He let her know that he was awake.

"What are you doing?"

She answered him silently with the tip of her finger over his lips, a clear message that said "don't speak."

He did as she wished. He felt her hand on his chest again. This couldn't be happening. He felt himself reacting to her nearness. She smelled wonderful.

She must have noticed his excitement. Her hand carefully moved down, nearer and nearer. She pressed herself harder against his thigh. He thought he felt a crop of hair, but he wasn't sure. Now she turned her face towards him and her lips sought his. She kissed him for a long time. Then she laid her head on his shoulder again and moved her hand slowly and deliberately down over his stomach, up and down, each time farther and farther downwards. Then suddenly she had her hand on his manhood. He still had his underwear on. She rubbed her hand gently over the hardness she found there.

Her hand moved to the side and began to tug at his underwear, pulling it down. He helped her by lifting his hips until she was able to take it right off. Then the hand was back, holding right around him, and this time it was Goggen who sought out her lips. Her hand continued to massage his rock-hard manhood.

Her head began to move itself downwards over his chest, kissing it as she went down over his stomach. And then she was there. She let her lips moisten him while she moved over the tip of it. She licked it carefully before taking it deeply into her mouth. She began to move her head up and down.

He lay totally still and just marvelled in the wonderful feel of it. He was glad that he had five Cuttys inside him.

They changed into the sixty-nine position. It was just as he thought he had felt: she had a tight and trimmed covering of hair down there. He began to part it with his fingers. She was extremely sexy. Goggen preferred women who kept their pubic hair as it was meant to be. He didn't have any wish to go to bed with little girls. He placed a pillow under his head and began to move his tongue in a circle round and round over the hard knot that was her clit. He also put his tongue up inside her a little. It was heavenly. He noticed the way she was working together with him, and it made him extremely hot.

He noticed that she was pressing her thighs together a little. It made him wonder, *Is she shy?*

He encouraged her to press right up against his mouth, and he held his head at an angle so he could breathe. He stopped for a moment and let her regain her rhythm before he began to slowly lick her again. Now she was moving even faster and was handling his cock with even more intensity. Five Cuttys or not, if she continued like that he was going to spray out right in her mouth. He tried to make her pause, but she responded with even more intensive treatment. Her body began to rock while she pressed even harder against his mouth. That was all he needed to let go. He felt himself coming right into her mouth. He had waited for her to pull away when that happened, but instead she just moved her mouth up and down some more, but slower. She was lying completely still. He still had her right in front of his face, so he kissed her inner lips and the inside of her thighs. She pulled away a little, but he kissed her gently again. She pulled away and then pushed his head away from her.

They lay that way for some moments before she turned around and went back into the same position they'd been in when he awoke. She didn't say a single thing.

So came sleep.

Goggen awoke suddenly again, but this time it was a violent awakening. TJ stood in the bedroom door with her telephone in her hand.

"It's a phone call from Grandfather, but he won't speak. I can just hear a lot of noise."

Goggen took the telephone from her and listened.

He said, "Get your clothes on," while he quickly searched out his own clothes.

In the course of a few moments, they were on the road. The clock in the car said 4.33 a.m. Neither of them said anything. It was Goggen who was driving, and they went quickly.

Jimmy and Peta's whole house was lit up. Goggen drove past the house a little.

TJ looked at him, but he didn't say anything until they had gotten out of the car. There were no street lights, and it was very dark. Goggen signalled to TJ that they should keep quiet. He walked up onto the frozen grass, from where they could approach the house almost silently. Goggen stretched up and looked into a window at the back of the house.

He didn't see anything at first, but then in the kitchen he could see Jimmy sitting on a chair with his hands tied behind his back. He was sitting with his back to the window that Goggen was looking into.

He let TJ take a quick look in after giving her the hush signal. They silently walked back to the north side of the house. Here there was a door with a glass panel in it. They passed a woodpile with branches for kindling. Goggen found two suitable hefty sticks that could be used as clubs. He gave one of them to TJ. He looked through the window in the door, peeking carefully so he wouldn't be seen. The window had a thin curtain over it, but he could still see right through it with the lights on inside.

There sat Jim on a bench with Peta bandaging him. His voice sounded weak.

He was holding a large butcher knife in his hand, and it was obvious that she was being forced to help him. It must have been very painful for him. Goggen could see him grinding his teeth together.

Goggen gave a silent message to TJ to stay where she was. He demonstrated with a kind of sign language that when Jim came out the door, she should hit him with the branch. She nodded to him in return that she understood.

He went around the back of the house again, looking for a possible way to get inside the house without being seen. He tried the door to the garage, and it went up. He went in and discovered no door leading into the house, so he went out again.

What about the window over there? he thought to himself. It was at the back of the house. The room inside was in complete darkness. Goggen tried to open it. It was a very different kind of window than the ones they had at home in Norway. Here in Canada the lower part of the pane was pushed up, or half of the window was pushed over to one side or the other. The window locks were often shoddy or defective. If that was the case here, Goggen couldn't tell. He tried with all his strength to push the window up, but it was very tight. He took the stick he had gotten from the woodpile and used it as a lever to exert greater force. The window began to open slowly. He opened it enough to get his arm in, and then he was able to raise it enough to crawl through. He found a bench in the yard that he could stand on. He was in. He took off his shoes and walked over to the door. He bent down to see through the keyhole. It was dark on the other side too. That was good, because it meant that this room was not directly connected to the kitchen. He carefully and silently turned the knob and opened the door. Then he snuck in to the next room.

Now he could hear voices. He tried to hear what they were saying, but they were speaking in their language. There was a shaft of light over on the other side of the hallway he now found himself in. He moved carefully towards it.

Though he couldn't understand their language, it was very plain to hear that the conversation was anything but friendly.

He had to get over to that doorway over there. He had the advantage that the kitchen was brightly lit and he was still in the dark. It took him quite a while to get over there. Now he was there. Peta was finished bandaging Jim now, but she was still standing at his side.

And what was that? Goggen suddenly saw a rope tied around Peta's foot. It went from her right leg to the leg of the chair on which her husband Jimmy was sitting, then to the trigger of a shotgun pointing directly at him. If Peta didn't stay completely motionless, the weapon would go off. Her other foot was tied to the bench that Jim was sitting on. He was still sitting where Peta had bandaged him.

The first thing Goggen had to do was get Jimmy out of the line of fire. It was a lucky accident that Jim had not tied his father's feet together. Goggen thought long and hard about whether he should take the chance. He stealthily showed himself to Jimmy, who saw him at once but remained still and quiet. Goggen signalled to him that he would attack Jim and that Jimmy must throw himself out of the range of the shotgun. Jimmy nodded at him almost imperceptibly. He understood. Goggen took the car keys out of his pocket and threw them over to the other side of the kitchen. Jim jumped with surprise when they hit the floor. That was all that Goggen needed. He moved swiftly forward.

The moment Jim saw him coming, he hit him over the head with the improvised club he had taken with him into the house. The shotgun went off, but Goggen concentrated solely on Jim. He did see out of the corner of his eye that Jimmy had escaped being shot.

Now Jim was lying on the floor only half-conscious. He tried to get a hold of the butcher knife, but it was clear that he couldn't see very

well. Goggen kicked the knife away, then hit Jim again with the club. Jim screamed in pain. Goggen took hold of the rest of the rope that Jim had used to tie up his mother and father. He was able to get it around one of Jim's wrists and was trying to get it around the other, but Jim was thrashing wildly. He ended up getting it around his ankle instead. Now Jim had one wrist and one ankle tied up behind him. He couldn't move.

Goggen went over to the front door and unlocked it. Then he opened it out to where TJ stood. He had heard her try to get in earlier, but the door had been locked.

TJ grabbed the knife and cut Peta loose first, then Jimmy. Then they were standing together hugging each other. The tears of both TJ and Peta began to freely flow. Jimmy let go of them and walked over to Jim. Then he said something to him that Goggen couldn't understand and spit on him.

Then he called the police.

Henrik and Conrad had not interrupted the conference call one single time when Goggen had contacted them home in Norway on the following evening.

Now Goggen and TJ were on their way back to the ranch after two weeks at Robert's cabin up in Jasper. TJ had asked Robert if they could borrow the cabin right after the conference call that night. He had agreed at once, but with the warning that it was going to be very cold, and also that the cabin was very isolated.

She had just looked at him and smiled.

"Well, I guess we can find ways to keep warm," she answered. They parked the car and walked directly over to Robert's house. TJ was glowing with health and well-being.

"Hi, Robert."

Robert lifted his gaze from the newspaper. He had been reading the last article about Captain McKenzie. After it became known what he'd been involved in all those years, the investigation went much faster and a lot of other things had come to light.

"Well, just look at that. You're back already. And you're both looking so well!"

TJ smiled.

"A letter came for you."

He picked it up from his desk and gave it to her. She opened it and began to read.

Goggen immediately noticed that something was terribly wrong. He caught her just before she fell. The letter slipped out of her hand and onto Robert's desk.

It was written on letterhead from the Edmonton Correctional

Institution, and it began immediately with no salutation at the top.

Just wanted to let you know that Albert is not dead.

The child who was found in the ruins of the cabin was a boy whom Scott run down and killed when he was drunk.

They switched the bodies before you came home.